# MURDER
## *in*
# MYSTIC COVE

# MURDER

*in*

# MYSTIC COVE

## DARYL ANDERSON

**WORLDWIDE**®

TORONTO • NEW YORK • LONDON
AMSTERDAM • PARIS • SYDNEY • HAMBURG
STOCKHOLM • ATHENS • TOKYO • MILAN
MADRID • WARSAW • BUDAPEST • AUCKLAND

To my husband, Steve

Recycling programs
for this product may
not exist in your area.

**Murder in Mystic Cove**

A Worldwide Mystery/December 2015

First published by Carina Press.

ISBN-13: 978-0-373-26973-0

**Printed in U.S.A.**

## Acknowledgments

I would like to thank Patricia and Shannon, my first readers. Special thanks to Beth for her friendship and support. Thanks to my editor, Deb Nemeth, for her help in shaping the manuscript. Finally, thanks to Fera and Sally, who made the lonely business of writing less lonely.

# ONE

*The Dead Man in the Woods*

THE GOLF CART whined as it lumbered up the incline. I pulled my jacket tight. Although the eastern sky blushed with the promise of warmth and light, it was cold and dark in Birnam Wood. But after the endless Florida summer I welcomed the cold, and the shadows were no matter. I knew the twisted paths and byways of Mystic Cove well enough to make my way blindfolded. I tapped the brake in anticipation of the impending curve, but as I turned, something flashed in the woods just outside my peripheral vision. It was probably nothing, and one of my security guards was waiting for me to relieve him, but I double-backed to investigate.

My headlights picked out a trace of crushed centipede grass headed in the general direction of the flash. I turned on the cart's hazard light and grabbed a flashlight. Walking the path would only take a few minutes. Birnam Wood was no true forest, just an assortment of shrubs and trees landscaped to resemble woods, and no path went too deep. And, sure enough, several hundred yards in, the trail opened into a small clearing. I paused, not liking the place.

Despite its proximity to the paved road, the clearing was strangely isolated, surrounded by a thicket of saw palmettos and hovering palms. A solitary place made for mischief, but I relaxed when my flashlight danced off the red metal of Mel Dick's red golf cart, which was sitting in the middle of the clearing. In the breaking dawn I could make out the old devil's silhouette sitting in the driver's seat. I jogged toward the cart.

"Everything okay? Mr. Dick?" I stopped, taking it all in at once.

Mel Dick looked as if he were on his way to a luau. On the coldest morning of the year he wore an ill-fitting blue Hawaiian shirt and green shorts. He looked straight ahead, as if contemplating the blooming oleander, but the eyes were strangely vacant. I touched his shoulder—icy cold through the thin fabric. My fingers fumbled for the old man's carotid, but when I pressed, there was no answering throb.

I was much too late. From the feel of that cold, unyielding flesh, the old man had been dead for hours. It had been a lonely death in this solitary place, but at least it had been quick and painless. In death Mel's face looked as it had in life, with its habitual expression of mild irritation and self-satisfaction.

I opened my cell to make the call I'd made so many times before. As security chief of Mystic Cove—an upscale retirement community in the manicured wilds of north Florida—I often facilitated in the eviction of the newly dead.

"Grubber County Sheriff's Office."

"It's Addie Gorsky, Chief of Security out at the Cove."

"Who bought the farm this time?"

I was about to answer when I saw the hole in Mel Dick's right temple, staring at me in the red dawn like a malignant third eye. I bent close, sniffed the metallic tang of gunpowder and saw the gray dust around the cylindrical wound. Mel's death might have been quick, but it was hardly painless.

"There's been a murder in the Cove," I said. "Somebody shot Mel Dick."

As I gave my report, the officer was mostly silent, probably a little in shock. Murder was rare in sleepy Grubber County and unheard of in the Cove. Next I called Jesse Potts at the Admiral Street guardhouse.

"Chief, I thought you was coming to relieve me." Jesse yawned through the words.

"Change of plan, Jesse. The police are on their way. When they get there I need you to bring them to me." I described my location. "You know the place?"

"Yeah," Jesse said, and then, "Who died?"

I hesitated. Jesse's imagination was always in gear and mention of murder would put it into overdrive. "There has been a death, but right now I need you to do what I asked. We'll talk later. Okay?"

"Was it Mr. Dick?"

Now that was a surprise. "We'll talk later," I told Jesse, only this time I meant it.

The day grew brighter with each passing second. Although the temperature lingered in the forties, as the day progressed the mercury would inch upward until it reached a perfect seventy degrees before beginning its unhurried descent. Another day in paradise. But all I saw was the awful wound in the old man's head. When I'd been on the job I'd seen similar wounds in suicides by gunshot, the stippling and cylindrical shape hallmarks of a close-range shot.

I heard the squeal of sirens and automatically glanced again at the body sitting in that ridiculous cart as if it were waiting for the light to change. But the tramp of heavy feet and excited shouts told me my time was over.

Jesse Potts appeared first, bolting into the clearing like a rabbit on the run. On his heels were two paramedics and a couple of uniforms. A flurry of activity as the paramedics descended on the body, but the frenzy was short-lived. I pulled away from the crime scene, taking Jesse with me. Security guards were either former cops like me or cop wannabes like Jesse. I feared that if left to his own devices, he would trail his heroes like a lovesick puppy. Besides, I had a question or two for my young guard.

"Shouldn't we be helping?" Jesse asked.

"No, our part is done. Well, almost done. The deputies will want to take our statements." Jesse looked beat. Sure, nobody looked fresh at the end of a graveyard shift, but he looked worse than most, his face all sharp angles and dark hollows. "Are you all right?"

I was about to repeat the question when Jesse sighed and said, "Oh, I seen dead people before. There was Grandpa at the funeral parlor and Mrs. Whitson who dropped dead on Long Pier three summers ago. Remember her?"

"No, that was before my time."

"Oscar gave her CPR but it didn't help." Jesse met my gaze. "But this is different, isn't it?"

"Yes, this is different. This is murder." And murder changed everything it touched, even bit players like Jesse and me who watched from the sidelines.

"Somebody murdered Mr. Dick," he said.

Jesse had an impressive grasp of the obvious. Too bad everything else eluded him. The small clearing was quickly filling with uniforms, so I pulled Jesse farther from the action. "Earlier when I told you that someone had died, why did you assume it was Mel Dick?"

Jesse chewed that over. "Because he looked like a dead man walking. I figured it was just a matter of time."

Before I could respond to this remarkable statement, a tall lanky figure crashed into the clearing.

"Where is he?" A deep voice rumbled. "Where's Mel Dick?" Grubber County Sheriff Bubba Spooner had arrived and was loaded for bear.

Spooner gathered his team around him. The sheriff towered over everyone—a dark oak, with his sable brown hair and face tanned by years in the Florida sun, surrounded by a bunch of saplings. I only caught snatches of conversation, but their body language told me plenty. To a person, the deputies and CSU techs were jacked, excited at the prospect of a murder investigation, but Spooner was royally pissed. He hid it pretty well beneath the cop façade, but I knew the signs well enough. When Spooner dismissed his people, two deputies trotted over to Jesse and me. It was time to give our statements.

Jesse paired off with his date and I got stuck with Deputy Berry. Before we got down to business, I tried to tell Berry about Anita. Mel and Anita Dick lived on nearby Admiral Street and by now Mrs. Dick would have heard the commotion. Someone, preferably the primary investigator, had to talk to her before she found out about Mel. But Berry wouldn't let me talk.

"We'll take care of Mrs. Dick soon enough," Berry said with a smug smile, "just describe how you found the body."

Maybe Berry thought he was being efficient, but it was a mistake. When I worked Homicide, I always let people talk, at least to a point. People revealed themselves when they spoke, even murderers. Especially murderers. But if Berry wanted the quick and dirty version, I'd let him have it.

When I'd finished my brief account, Berry looked like he'd had one too many turns on the Tilt-A-Whirl.

"Anything else I can help you with?"

"Why were you so all-fired sure it was Dick's golf cart before you even seen the body?"

Grinning, I gestured for Berry to take a gander at the death cart. The vehicle was a miniature facsimile of a Humvee, covered with American flags, liberty bells, and even a grinning Miss Liberty. One of a kind, thank God.

"Why were you in the woods so early?" Berry asked.

I struggled to keep a straight face. Berry invested each word with a laughable degree of suspicion. "I was on my way to relieve my guard Jesse Potts at the Admiral Street guardhouse."

Now it was Berry's turn to grin. "You mean Empty Potts? That boy is one pancake short of a stack."

I glared at Berry. I'd seen and heard it all before, from those who underestimated Jesse. "Boy, you is dumb as a stump!" they'd say, or "Your antenna just don't pick up all the channels." They packed their cruelty in colorful language, as if that made it less cruel. Maybe Jesse wasn't smart, but his emotions ran true. "Are we finished here?"

Berry grunted, closed his notebook and sauntered over to Spooner, who was extracting his head from the murder cart. By now the clearing was a picture of chaos—cops and techs teemed over the area like termites over rotting wood. But it was a controlled chaos. Yellow crime tape protected the scene, CSU techs searched the adjacent woods, and deputies had begun the neighborhood canvas. Spooner might not be much on charm, but he could secure a crime scene. Since Berry was still chattering away, I called my deputy chief. When Tyler Andrews didn't answer his cell—no surprise—I left a detailed voice mail. I had just ended the call when I felt a hand on my arm.

"Good job on screwing up my crime scene, Gorsey."

"The name is Gorsky, Sheriff, and I didn't screw up your crime scene." I folded my arms and glared. Spooner had a reputation as a bully and I didn't intend to be his latest victim.

"Your footprints are all over the place." Spooner's face betrayed no emotion, but his voice was intense.

"It was unavoidable. When I saw Mel, I…"

"Yeah, I went over your statement with my deputy. I've got some questions."

"Ask away."

"Did Mel Dick have any enemies?"

"You're kidding, right?"

Spooner knew as well as I that Mel Dick collected enemies like a Māori warrior collected heads.

"Just answer the question. You know anybody might have wanted Dick dead?"

Now, there were lots of people who wouldn't cry over Mel's death, but I fed him some bullcrap about Mel having a forceful personality that many people found grating. It went on like that for a bit—the sheriff asking questions about Mel and me spinning crap. I felt his growing impatience, but I didn't have his answers. Since my promotion to chief six months earlier, I'd had little direct contact with the residents. What information I had was as stale as old beer.

"Tell me about the 415 at the Grog and Grub last night."

I looked sharply at Spooner. "A disturbance at the G and G?"

The day was warming up, but Spooner's smile was cold. "You don't know about it, do you?"

I'd taken yesterday off to take Pop to his doctor's appointment and missed all the fun. But Spooner was more than happy to fill me in.

"At around six-thirty last night Okpulo County Sheriff's Office responded to a 911 call reporting a disturbance between Mel Dick and José Barracas."

"Big deal," I said, waving off the sheriff's concern. There was no love lost between Mel Dick and the owner of Mystic Cove's favorite watering hole. "Dick and Barracas probably got into a shouting match. Customers misinterpreted their dislike for aggression—an easy thing to do—and some busybody called the cops."

"Barracas wasn't the only one Dick had in his sights last night." Spooner pulled on dark sunglasses. "According to witnesses he threatened several customers." He went on, painting a picture that made no sense. None of this sounded like Mel Dick, who took care of nasty business in private, and since when did José start arguing with paying customers? But I couldn't sort it out with Spooner talking at me.

"For God's sake, Sheriff, this is the first I've heard of any of this. I'm just as confused as you."

"What good are you then? You don't know jack!" He turned to go, but I grabbed his arm.

"All I know is that some joker shot Mel Dick at extremely close range and Mel just sat there and let him do it!" I let go of Spooner's arm. He was glaring at me, and I guess I was doing the same.

"How you figure that?" he asked at last.

"Because of the stippling around the wound, of course. The murder weapon couldn't have been more than a foot away from Mel's head when it was fired." I shut my mouth, but too late.

"That's right, you were a real police once."

I flinched, whether from surprise that the sheriff knew of my past or from hurt, I couldn't tell. But Spooner was right. I was a real police once.

"Sheriff Spooner!" A female voice called. A short, round woman in jeans and a black bubble jacket jogged toward us. It was Dr. Dolores Rio, the deputy coroner.

Spooner led Rio to the body. Once the death was ruled a homicide, the forensics crew would begin its work, taking photos and gathering and bagging evidence. But that had nothing to do with me. Spooner wasn't through with Jesse, so I asked him to stop by security headquarters before heading home. We needed to finish our conversation. I left by way of Admiral Street, having had enough of Birnam Wood for one day.

Up and down Admiral Street, the circus was in full throat. Flashing lights throbbed over staid McMansions, booted feet tramped pristine St. Augustine lawns, voices pierced the morning air, demanding and incessant. Curious residents gathered on sidewalks and tidy lawns, taking in the show. In not so long a time the ambulances and cop cars and EMS vehicles would be gone, and the spectators would return to their everyday lives only to find that things weren't quite the same.

You see, murder changed everything.

As I approached the Dick residence I slowed my cart to a funereal crawl. A GCSO cruiser crouched in the driveway, a solitary uniform inside.

A disquiet overtook me, as if the earth had shifted just a little and all that was once familiar was rendered strange. The giant American flag on Mel's front lawn hung dejected in the still air, and the house was dark and silent, locked unto itself. I realized I hadn't spotted Anita Dick's face among the spectators, though I had looked long and hard. Anita was a hardcore homebody; if she wasn't home, where could she be? My uneasiness grew. I tried to shake it off, but it was like trying to shake off one of those biting horseflies endemic to Florida. Once it got your scent, it'd pursue you to the death.

I made my slow way to my office, one question running through my mind. Where was Anita Dick?

# TWO

*A Woman with a Past*

I DROVE SLOWLY through the belly of the beast, through the winding streets of Mystic Cove.

Most of the Cove consisted of residential areas, gated enclaves with vaguely nautical names like Whipstaff Hamlet or Windbound Harbor, where Mel Dick had lived and died. Each community was filled with retirees from somewhere else, seeking shelter from taxes and the cold. Miles and miles of McMansions with lawns as thick as shag carpet and twisting roads and dead ends that drive the EMS guys nuts. But I should be thankful. I only had a job because each residential area required a gate, and gates required guards to work the locks. As my boss Jud Richt was fond of saying, he sold security, which as far I could tell was just fear by another name.

But the plastic heart of Mystic Cove was Founder's Centre. A poor man's Disney World, the Centre was a cheap imitation of a nineteenth-century New England fishing village as imagined by a five-year-old girl. Richt's visioning team contrived a complicated pseudo-history for the place. There was a fake old jail, fake courthouse, fake oyster house, and so on. Some fabrications were more ludicrous than others, with one of the worst offenders being the Grub and Grog Pub, which occupied the former site of the Olde Salmon Shack, circa 1869, or so the fake plaque on the frontispiece proclaimed. Salmon fishing in Florida!

Security headquarters was located in the Financial Building. It consisted of two rooms—a small reception area and my smaller office—situated on the first floor, squeezed between the employee bathroom and the janitor's storage closet. The financial planners resided on the upper floors of the building that bore their name, and though there was little interaction between the suits and those of us in khaki, on quiet afternoons I often heard their movements from above, like rats in the attic.

Once inside I headed straight for the coffee. My hand was on the pot when I saw a sliver of light peeping from my open office door, which I was certain I had locked.

"Who's there?" I said, kicking the door open.

A dark figure coiled behind the desk. It stirred and said, "Good morning, Chief." It was Jud Richt, CEO of Mystic Cove Development.

"I was just about to have some coffee. Want a cup?"

Richt eased up in the chair, flashed his pearly whites. "We need to talk."

With Richt ensconced behind my desk, I had no choice but to take the wooden chair facing him. It was a captain's chair of odd proportions that I'd intentionally chosen for its discomfort—visitors didn't linger in such a chair. But now it was my ass that squirmed.

"This unfortunate episode is a potential catastrophe for the Cove," Richt said.

"Are you talking about Mel Dick's murder?"

Richt nodded. I wasn't surprised Richt knew about the murder, but his choice of words pissed me off. Unfortunate episode? Was he for real? Getting pepperoni on your pizza when you ordered sausage was an unfortunate episode. Mel Dick was a royal pain in the ass, but his murder couldn't be so easily dismissed. Oh, there was more than a whiff of brimstone about Jud Richt.

"Mel's murder doesn't threaten Mystic Cove."

"Of course it does! How many times have I told you that I don't sell houses at Mystic Cove—I sell security, privacy, freedom from fear."

I braced for another lecture. Richt had never been an amiable sort, but lately he'd been riding my ass hard. "I realize that, Mr. Richt, but…"

"This murder and the subsequent investigation threaten all of those. Understand?"

"Yes, but the best outcome is for Mel's killer to be found ASAP. Our best option—our only option, really—is to aid the investigation. The sooner it's over, the sooner things will return to normal."

Richt's face hardened. "No, I don't want Sheriff Spooner or his goons on my property."

"You can't prevent that."

Richt smiled, the preternaturally white teeth gleaming in the soft light. "Perhaps not entirely, but Mystic Cove Security doesn't have to make it easy for them."

"You're talking about obstructing a homicide investigation."

Richt leaned across the desk. "Not at all. I just want to ensure that our privacy is not violated. I know you, Addie—don't let your curiosity get the better of you. Mr. Dick's death is none of your concern."

"I don't…"

"There was quite a bit of grumbling when I promoted you to chief. There were other qualified candidates, candidates with more seniority and without your…irregular employment history. For once, consider your best interests."

"This is a *murder* investigation." I spoke calmly and kept my face impassive, but Richt wasn't fooled. His wolfish grin told me that he knew his arrow had struck its mark. Jud Richt might know the facts, the bare bones of

my life, but he didn't know the truth. One thing for sure—
I would not impede Spooner's investigation. I was about
to inform Richt of this when the outer door scraped open.

"Chief," Jesse Potts said, striding into my office, "I got
doughnuts—oh, I didn't know you was busy."

Richt waved off Jesse's discomfort. "That's fine. The
chief and I were finished, and I'm late for my nine-thirty."
Richt eased into his charcoal Brioni suit jacket.

"Oh, Chief." Richt paused at the door. "How is your father doing these days? Did he make it through the chemo
okay?"

I stared at Richt, a chill traveling down my spine. He
wasn't much for small talk and he could care less about
my father's health, so why ask? "He's fine."

"Good, I know how overwhelming a serious illness
can be. The bills certainly start piling up."

"My father and I are fine."

"Glad to hear it."

"Bastard," I muttered, pretty sure I'd just been threatened. If I didn't tow Richt's line, I might find myself out
of this lousy job. I wouldn't mind if it was just me, but
there was Pop to think about. But threat or no threat, I
needed answers.

"Jesse, make us some fresh coffee to go with the
doughnuts, and then we'll talk."

"Sure thing," Jesse mumbled, mouth working on a jelly
doughnut.

While the coffee brewed, I rifled through my inbox. If
there really had been a free-for-all at the pub last night,
then Tyler should have written an incident report. But
there wasn't one. Maybe the fight angle was overblown,
after all. When Jesse came back with our coffees, he was
almost bright-eyed. Good, just so his sugar high lasted
long enough for me to get what I needed from him. To

that end I edged the box toward him. He scooped up the last jelly doughnut.

"How'd the interview with Spooner go?" I hoped my question wasn't too open-ended. Jesse could be terribly literal, and getting information from him was like walking a minefield.

"The sheriff was awful fired up about the dust-up at the Grub and Grog last night."

"You know about that?" I tore off a piece of cinnamon doughnut and dunked it in my coffee.

"Sure. Last night when I relieved Oscar he told me all about it."

That would have been at eleven. I made a mental note to talk to Oscar Wall, who'd been manning the Admiral Street gate at the time of the incident.

"Did you see Mr. Dick last night?"

"Nope, Admiral Street was quiet for a change."

For a change? Now what in God's name did that mean? I rubbed my temple, feeling the beginning of a headache. If only I'd been on duty last night. The one time when something happened, I was nowhere to be found.

"Don't feel bad."

I looked at my young guard, who always seemed to sense my feelings. "You read me like a book."

Jesse solemnly shook his head. "I don't read books much."

"I just wish I had been here last night, that's all."

"Nothing or nobody could have saved Mr. Dick."

"Is that why you called him a dead man walking earlier?"

Jesse yawned and knuckled his eyes, the sugar high rapidly dissipating. His hand hovered over the box of doughnuts, fingers wiggling like worms, but for once discretion ruled and the hand returned to his lap. "The last time I seen Mr. Dick he was a dead man walking, only he was sitting in his Humvee, and he…"

"Just a sec," I said, grabbing a pen and notepad. I needed to keep track or I'd never find my way out of the rabbit hole. "When was the last time you saw Mel?"

"Saturday night Mr. Dick drove by the guardhouse."

"Was he alone?"

"No, ma'am, Mr. Jinks was sitting next to him."

"Mr. Jinks?" I'd thought I knew everyone in Mel's entourage.

Jesse's eyes bugged. "You know Mr. Jinks—that's Mr. Dick's dog!"

"The fat pug." I laughed.

Jesse grinned. "Yeah, he's a cute little fellow."

I wasn't sure about that. I recalled an old pug with lethal breath and glassy eyes. "Let's get back to the last time you saw Mel."

"It was after midnight. I waved Mr. Dick through the gate like always but he made like he wanted to tell me something, only he won't talk through the window. So I got out of the guardhouse. Mr. Dick made me lean in close, like he's afraid somebody's listening. He's grinning, but it wasn't a good grin. He told me I was looking at a real important man."

"Meaning himself of course." Mel Dick had always had a healthy ego, but this sounded a bit extreme, even for a narcissist like Mel.

"Yes, ma'am, and then Mr. Dick said, 'This time next week everybody will know who Mel Dick is. Next week I'll be more famous than Woody or Bernie.'"

"He said what?"

"He said he's gonna be bigger than Woody or Bernie. It don't make no sense, but I told him, 'Sure thing, Mr.

Dick.' I guess he didn't like that 'cause he gave me the finger and drove off real fast."

"Who are Woody and Bernie?"

"Heck if I know."

I circled the names in my notes. "Makes two of us but what…"

Jesse's knobby chin rested in a cupped hand and his eyes were at half-mast. I'd gotten all I was going to get out of him—at least for now.

With Jesse gone, I pulled out the Mystic Cove calendar and counted the days from Jesse's encounter with Mel, trying to see if some event had been in the works that would fit the timeline. Since it was an election year, Mystic Cove had been a cauldron of political activity in recent months, but nothing of import fell on or around the target date. Except for Halloween. Founder's Centre hosted an annual Harvest Fest every October 31, but Mel Dick didn't get off on pirate costumes and haunted houses. I was pondering this when my cell buzzed. My missing deputy chief at last.

"It's about time, Tyler."

"Good morning to you too, sunshine." Tyler had the kind of voice that was always on the verge of laughter. I guess it was an attractive trait, but one I'd always found grating and more than a little suspicious—Christ, nobody was that happy all the time.

"What happened at the G and G last night?"

"Just another round in the Dick-Barracas war," Tyler said.

"War?" The two men didn't like one another but Mel Dick was a loyal if fractious customer of the G and G, and José—needing all the customers he could get—always accommodated the elderly curmudgeon.

"It was no big deal. I mean, nobody got hurt."

"Mel Dick might disagree with that conclusion, but just give me the blow-by-blow."

A long pause, and Tyler said, "Meet me at Maude's Café for lunch and I'll tell you all about it."

Even though I am not a patient woman, I agreed. I had heard something beneath Tyler's words, something that warned me not to push. Information came from people and people moved best at their own speed. We agreed to meet at twelve.

But I didn't like the idea of going to lunch blind. I didn't mistrust Tyler, but I feared his narrative would be overly colored by his easygoing nature. When we had been together, his habit of choosing the path of least resistance had bugged the heck out of me. That relationship had been doomed from the start. He was a carefree Southerner who took the easy road and I was a melancholy Pole from Baltimore who never did anything easy. He used to tell me I made things too hard on myself and maybe he was right. Maybe that was why my life so far had been like a game of Chutes and Ladders, minus the ladders.

A rush of sadness and regret washed over me. The past—just when you thought it was done and gone, it turned up to slap you in the face.

Once more I heard Joey Spoletto's scratchy voice: "You gotta be careful, Addie. You're an intuitive detective. You like to walk the tightrope. Just remember it's a long way down."

"But you're on the tightrope with me, aren't you, partner?" I'd laughed, not hearing the warning.

"No way. My feet are on the ground. I'm a plodder, moving from point A to point B like a drunken donkey. I'm slow, but I get the job done and I don't gotta worry about falling."

But in the end, we both fell—Joey to a bullet on a south

Baltimore street and me to Florida. But this morning I found the body in the woods, and that changed things. So I pushed back the past. There was work to do.

I could be at the Grub and Grog in five minutes. That would give me plenty of time to talk with Barracas, and maybe chat with other staff who had worked last night. Then I'd have a sense of what had gone down before meeting Tyler. A good plan, as long as my extracurricular activities didn't get back to Richt.

I wasn't sure where this road would take me, but I'd follow it a bit longer.

THE GRUB AND Grog was less than half a mile from my office, with Maude's Café spitting distance of the G and G. My father, an old-school cop who walked a beat in Baltimore for years, used to say that the only way you got to know a place was by walking its streets. So I would walk.

The sun blazed white in the blue sky, with the piercing clarity peculiar to the South. Just enough of the early morning chill remained to make it perfect walking weather. I felt a brief exhilaration—most of my working day was spent in my dark office, poring over schedules and payrolls. I looked up at the neat brick buildings on either side of the landscaped street. Baskets of spicy-smelling lantana hung from posts. Not many cars, but golf carts hummed along their designated lanes. Not a piece of trash in sight. How could anyone have a problem on such a beautiful day? But yesterday had been just as lovely, and yesterday someone had blasted a hole in Mel Dick's head.

"I can't believe this." A voice squealed from below. "I just can't believe it!"

A young man in a dark blue suit smiled up at me, crouching over a rectangular plot of earth that brimmed with yellow chrysanthemums. It was the new financial guy, Jeremy Louis, who I'd met at last month's orientation when I gave my usual spiel to the new recruits.

"What can't you believe?"

Jeremy Louis stood, brushed imaginary dirt from his pants. He was a well-built man on the short side who would be almost handsome if not for the perpetual grin. Only idiots grinned all the time.

"Yesterday afternoon I notified maintenance that the mums in this plot were brown and droopy. Today I come in to find the old flowers ripped out and replaced. I knew Mr. Richt ran a tight ship, but this is beyond the pale. The man simply doesn't allow any imperfections."

"And you approve."

"Of course I approve." Jeremy Louis beamed at the chrysanthemums and turned to me. "I heard about Mr. Dick."

"What have you heard, Mr. Louis?" My icy voice and stony expression didn't deter Jeremy Louis.

"That Mel Dick is dead." He tittered, eyes glittering like ice. "And that his death wasn't exactly natural, if you get my drift."

"I can't speak on the matter." Tyler was right about this one—the new financial planner had all the marks of an inveterate gossip.

"Can't or won't? Yes, well, I see you're busy and I've got a morning of appointments myself."

I watched him scurry inside the Financial Building, all traces of my earlier exhilaration gone, squashed like a lovebug on the windshield of a speeding car.

# THREE

*The Jabber of Parrots*

JOSÉ BARRACAS STOOD behind the bar, arms knotted over his broad chest. His body retained traces of the muscular lineman he'd been in college, but give it another year or two, and it'd all be fat.

"Tell me what happened last night in your restaurant," I said.

José snorted, gave me a sly smile. "I don't have to talk to you. It's not like Mystic Cove Security is investigating Dick's murder." José's smile was gruesome, his breath worse. I detected something beneath the heavy Aramis cologne, and I was pretty sure that wasn't coffee in his cup. "Murder? Who said anything about murder? I'm here as Mystic Cove Security Chief. Mr. Richt wants to know about the disturbance at your restaurant, that's all. But if don't want to talk to me, I'll let Mr. Richt know."

José placed a sweaty palm on my arm. "Why didn't you say so? We'll talk in my office. Want a drink?"

I put away my cell and pretended not to notice when José topped off his mug with scotch.

"I'm gonna level with you," José said, settling behind his desk.

"I appreciate that," I said, on full alert. Whenever people tell you they're going to level with you, expect a lie.

"Last night was no big deal. Mel got ticked when I handed him his check. He must have thought I was giving him the bum's rush or something, which I guess I was, but lately Mel's been off the chain. Is that my fault?" José opened his hands in a gesture of innocence. "Nowadays Mel Dick is either tearing somebody a new one or crowing about that stupid newspaper."

"Newspaper?"

"The *Commentator!*"

The *Cove Commentator* was the official organ of the Cove Homeowners' Association, the larger of the Mystic Cove's two homeowners' associations. "I'd forgotten Mel worked for the *Commentator.*"

José smirked. "Dick didn't work for the *Commentator.* He was the *Commentator.* If Gigi wasn't the jealous sort, Mel Dick would have screwed that paper instead of her."

"You mean Anita."

"No, I mean Gigi. Everybody in Mystic Cove knows that Gigi is Mel's main squeeze."

I wondered if Anita was one of those everybodies.

"You remember the *monstruo*, don't you?"

"God, yes." Gigi Tajani was a masterpiece of modern pharmacology and surgery. Though several times a grandmother, her skin was pale as ivory, smooth as silk, and tight as a drum. A true *monstruo*. "How long have Mel and Gigi been at it?"

"I don't know and I don't care, but there's trouble in paradise." José shook the ice cubes in his scotch and drank. He tilted his torso toward me, as if about to impart a secret. "Last night Mel was just as hard on Gigi as he was on the others."

"Others?"

José smiled, well lubricated now. "Yeah, all of Dick's buddies—Alan and Tally Rand, Fairley Sable, Gigi— were here last night, watching the old fart's every move." He leaned across the desk. I managed not to flinch when

I caught the sour, acrid smell. "I saw everything. I was at the bar."

"Of course you were," I said, but I got his meaning. A large picture window separated the Grub and Grog's bar and patio. From his barstool perch Barracas had a front-row seat of the action on the patio. "Seems to me you were keeping a pretty close eye on Mel Dick yourself."

José fidgeted, eyes shifting. He polished off his scotch in one gulp. "A…a good businessman keeps an eye on his business. I got a right to watch my business. Geez, it's boiling in here!" He lurched from his seat like a jack-in-the box and stumbled to the thermostat. There was a thump, followed by a burst of cold air from above. He slumped into his chair, closed his eyes. "That's better— some dumb prick must have turned it off." He put his chin in one hand, and the eyes fluttered shut.

"Mr. Barracas? Mr. Barracas!"

A slight start and the fried-egg eyes sprang open. "Is this going to be much longer? I… I got a business to run. I don't…"

"Let's get to the altercation with Mel." I wasn't sure if José's distress was caused by his empty cup or the subject. Probably both.

"It was like this. The Dicks came in at four for happy hour, sitting at my big table on the patio even though there's only the two of 'em. By six o'clock I had a line at the door—customers who don't mind paying full price for drinks. I told Sheila to give Mel his check, hoping he'll take the hint and leave. But she wouldn't."

"Why not?" It seemed an innocuous action.

"Sheila was afraid how Mel would react. For Christ's sake, we're all afraid of that bastard! I was tired of it. It was time to take the bull by the horns. Sheila tried to talk me out of it, but I didn't listen." José rubbed his temple, deflating like a punctured tire.

"What'd you do?"

"I went to the table, check in hand. Right off the bat I had second thoughts, but…but I had to finish what I started. I mean—" his eyes met mine, "—Sheila was watching and all. So at the table I made a little small talk, asked Mel if everything was okay, though I could tell things were as far from okay as they could be."

"What do you mean?"

"It's hard to explain. When I talked to Dick, I had the feeling he wasn't listening. Like he was a million miles away. And Anita wasn't much better, just staring out at the bay. Like a couple of waxworks, you know what I mean?"

I didn't, but I nodded anyway.

"I put down the check and started to edge away. At first I thought Mel hadn't noticed my move, but he noticed. He always noticed."

"What did Mel do?"

"He looked me in the eye. Right off the bat, I knew I'd made a real bad mistake. His face was awful, like boiled tomatoes, and his eyes howled. He crushed the check into a ball and threw it at my head! I must have yelled 'cause everything got quiet. Everybody was watching me and Dick." José licked his dry lips. "I was apologizing like crazy—all I wanted was to get back to the bar, but Mel wouldn't let me go. He was screaming at me—called me a prick—said if I didn't fight him, I was a filthy coward." José wiped his damp face with the back of his hand. "It was like being stuck in a dream."

"And then?"

"I heard Gigi yelling, 'Mel, Mel!' and Mel heard it too. He stared at Gigi like he's seeing her for the first time.

That was my chance to bail. As I ran for the bar, I heard Mel screaming a bunch of paranoid crap."

"At you?"

"No, he was screaming at the people who used to be his friends—Gigi and Fairley, Alan and Tally Rand, and Anita too—Mel yelled at 'em all!"

"What did he say?"

"Paranoid crap, like I said. Stuff like 'Everybody's against me,' stuff like that. When he's said his piece, he grabbed the mutt and beat it."

"And Anita?"

"He left her sitting at the table. I tell you, Mel could care less about his wife. Even his last words were for Gigi."

"What did he say to Gigi?"

"I dunno. It was crazy talk." José waved his hands, like he was swatting no-see-ums.

"Come on, José."

"All right, he said, 'Tutu, Gigi.' Isn't a tutu for a ballerina? Hey, I told you it was crazy."

Maybe not so crazy. "Might Mel have said, '*Et tu, Gigi*'? Might it have been that?"

José stared at me. At last he said, "Yeah, it might have. It sounded like what you said."

Before leaving I spoke to the bartender, who backed up José's account. Marco the busboy was there but didn't speak English, and the person I most wanted to talk to— the waitress Sheila Green—was off today. After I got her contact information from José, I hustled over to Maude's.

Maybe they didn't teach Shakespeare at the University of Newnansville, but then José Barracas had only been there to play football. Still he should have recognized the quote.

"*Et tu,* Brute"—ultimate words of betrayal, spoken

by the dying Caesar to his murderer, his friend, the beloved Brutus.

"*Et tu,* Gigi"—words spoken by a dying Dick to his mistress.

His murderess as well?

"SORRY I'M LATE, Tyler." I waved off the menu the waitress had shoved in my face and ordered coffee.

"Sure you won't have some lunch?—the fettuccine Alfredo special was great."

"No thanks," I said, eyeballing the knot of gummy noodles on Tyler's plate. Once I'd made the mistake of ordering a cannoli at Maude's and received a sodden pastry stuffed with cardboard-tasting cheese. I grieved for all I lost when I left Baltimore, which somehow translated into a sudden craving for an almond-filled bear claw from Hoehn's Bakery in Highlandtown.

Tyler smiled at the server. "I'll have coffee as well and a big hunk of red velvet cake."

I must have made a face, for Tyler asked to be let in on the joke.

"I'd just forgotten how much you liked a hearty lunch."

"That's not it, Addie." Tyler's Southern drawl stretched my name like a rubber band—Aaaahdeeeee. I always got a kick out of the way he talked. Southerners added syllables while Baltimoreans chopped them off. In a nut, that was the difference between North and South.

"Since you asked, I'll tell you."

Tyler's face already showed regret, but it was too late.

"I don't get red velvet cake. Why put a whole bottle of food coloring in a cake? It doesn't add flavor, just a disgusting color."

"But if it ain't red, it ain't red velvet cake."

"It's just not right."

"You always did have a peculiar idea of right and wrong," Tyler said with an easy smile.

What could I say? It was true.

"Word on the street is that Mel's murder was a robbery gone south," Tyler said. "That how you see it?"

I shook my head. "Didn't appear to be a struggle, no obvious defensive wounds on the body. I sensed rage in this killing and that means it's personal." The server appeared with our coffees and a huge slice of cake the color of radioactive blood. When she'd gone, I said nonchalantly, "I just had an interesting chat with José Barracas."

"Smart move catching him early, gives you a fifty-fifty chance of finding him sober."

"He was pouring the Cutty down."

Tyler laughed. "When did José upgrade to Cutty? He used to be a rum-and-coke man." Then he looked at me, the smile gone from his eyes. "Seriously, why did you talk with Barracas? Richt ain't gonna like it."

"A spur-of-the-moment decision," I lied, "and it was just a casual conversation."

Tyler sliced off a bit of cake with his fork. "You don't have casual conversations. I'll bet you cajoled and wheedled and pressed José Barracas until you got what you wanted. You may have the face of a Polish saint, but your heart is all pit bull."

"You don't know my heart," I said, anger flashing like a grease fire.

"Sorry, I forgot you were part porcupine."

The server returned with the check and while Tyler pulled out his Discover card, I gazed in the distance. Mystic Bay was calm, a tarnished mirror. From behind the Grub and Grog, Long Pier, which was actually quite short, jutted into the water. At its terminus a young woman huddled over a little child, pointing at the miniature light-house to their right.

"You okay, Addie?"

"Yes," I said, all anger gone. "I'm sorry I lost my temper. It's…it's been a strange day."

"I'll tell you what I know about what went down at the G and G, but it's not much," Tyler said. "Sheila Green called headquarters at around six-fifteen. She said Mel Dick had gone nuts, and somebody needed to get over right away. She was trying to hold it together, but I could tell she was scared to death."

"Did you call the police?"

"Well, no."

"Even though Sheila was scared to death, as you said."

"You know Mr. Richt wants us to handle these kinds of problems in-house. He'd have a fit if…"

"What happened next?"

Tyler speared another forkful of cake and sipped his coffee. "I took my car instead of a cart, which turned out to be a mistake. I was going west on Cove Road when I spotted Dick's Humvee coming my way and hauling ass! I chased, even though I had no notion what I was going to do with him when I caught him. I was right on his tail when he turned into Birnam Wood, where I couldn't follow.

"So when I got to the Grub and Grog, Okpulo County Sheriff's Office cruisers lined the street and people were buzzing around like they'd just seen fireworks. I told OCSO about my aborted chase of Mel Dick. They said they'd send a cruiser out to Dick's house for a safety check. There wasn't much else to do. Barracas didn't want to press charges. No harm, no foul."

*Not for Mel Dick.*

"But now we're getting to the interesting part of the

evening." Tyler stabbed the last bit of cake. "OCSO was about to take off when Bubba Spooner joins the party."

I nearly snorted my coffee. "But Founder's Centre is in Okpulo County."

"Exactly."

That morning I had been puzzled by Spooner's intensity. It appeared the sheriff had more than a professional interest in Mel's murder, or else why would he show at a call outside his jurisdiction. "Did you ask Spooner why he was there?"

Tyler pushed away the plate of neon-red crumbs and wiped his mouth with the napkin. "Not on your life—I worked for that man, and the less I have to do with him, the better. Spooner is a—"

"Can we refocus?" I didn't need to hear a litany of Sheriff Spooner's shortcomings. I knew that gospel by heart.

Tyler grinned sheepishly. "After Spooner talked to OCSO, he cornered me, but I didn't tell him jack, only pointed out that he was out of his jurisdiction. He tried talking to the witnesses, but I made sure everybody knew that they didn't have to talk to him."

"Bubba Spooner is a law enforcement officer." Tyler's dislike of his former boss could get tiresome.

"Spooner is not worthy of the uniform and he had no business being here last night. If you ask me, Spooner popping up like that is mighty suspicious."

I had to laugh. "Are you seriously suggesting that Spooner is a suspect?"

"I know for a fact Dick supported Spooner's opponent in the last election."

I let Tyler rant. I'd gotten what I'd wanted. The chronology of last night's events at the G and G was clearer, but it was like looking at the bleached bones of a skeleton.

Helpful, but only to a point. I needed details to bring flesh to the skeleton, but how and where to find them? Surprisingly Tyler supplied me with the answer.

"You should stop by Eddie's Dive tonight. The guys might have some answers for you. That is, if you're sure you want to go down this road. It might get a little rocky."

Not a bad idea. I could talk with my guards, get a feel for what was up with Mel and his friends, maybe get a handle on whatever was going on in Mystic Cove.

And something was going on, of that I was certain.

I took my time walking back to my office. Paradise looked the same as it had before—people walked the sidewalks, golf carts buzzed and the sunlight dazzled. But appearances deceived. There was a serpent in paradise and last night it had slithered from its hidden place and struck, bringing death to Mel Dick.

Back at the Financial Building, I entered through the basement garage, where Mystic Cove Security stored its fleet of golf carts. It was a lot quicker than the elevator—just one short flight of stairs to the first floor. But when I got there, I found a petite woman with cropped silver hair in the hallway, just outside the door to security headquarters.

Hearing my approach, she spun round. Silvery blue eyes fixed on me and quickly filled with tears. She pulled her brick-red pashmina tight and grasped my arm. The flowery scent of L'air du Temps was almost overpowering.

"Chief Gorsky, thank God." The high-pitched voice trembled, a rolling vibrato. "I'm Fairley Sable and I need your help."

# FOUR

*The Lady in Red*

"THANK YOU," FAIRLEY SABLE said as she accepted the mug of coffee. "Do you remember me?"

I nodded. We had only met once, but it was a memorable meeting, on the day of her husband's death. Harry Sable had surprised all of Mystic Cove when he returned from his brother's funeral with a new wife on his arm. But the fairy-tale ending didn't pan out. At a backyard barbeque at the Sable house Harry had a fatal heart attack, only six weeks into the marriage. I remembered the smell of grilled chicken and Fairley Sable's pale, tearstained face.

"How can I help?"

Fairley took a deep breath. "I wasn't sure where to go and so I came here. I hope I'm doing the right thing. Sometimes it's hard to know what the right thing is." She looked at me, as if for an answer. When none came, she sighed and continued. "I'm friends to both Dicks, but I'm particularly close to Anita. When she called last night, I had to help her."

I put down my coffee cup and reached for my cell. "This sounds like a police matter, Mrs. Sable."

Fairley Sable touched my arm. "Please let me tell my story first—it won't take long—and then if you think I should call the police, I will."

"Mrs. Sable…"

"I'm not like the other people in this place. I don't betray my friends so easily. Please!" Fairley's voice cracked and her eyes filled with tears. I handed her a box of tissues. She tore off several sheets, dabbed her eyes, blew her nose.

"Go on then." No harm in giving the old woman a few minutes.

"Last night Anita phoned me. It was late and so I knew it was bad news. No one calls in the middle of the night with good news."

"What time was the call?"

"A little past midnight, I believe," Fairley said. "Anita was hysterical. All she would say was that she and Mel had just had a terrible argument, and she didn't want to be alone."

"Where was Mel?"

"After the argument he'd driven away in his golf cart—his usual way of dealing with unpleasantness."

"For the second time that night," I murmured.

Fairley smiled with relief. "You know about the incident at the G and G then?"

"What did you do then?" I asked, ignoring the question.

"I went straight to my friend of course. Ten minutes later I was at Anita's."

"That was quick."

"Don't you remember? I live on Azimuth Circle." Of course, the Sables and Dicks had been neighbors—Azimuth Circle was a stubby cul-de-sac that jutted off of Admiral Street.

"Anita was in a state—her hair a bird's nest, clothes mussed, even her shoes caked with dirt. My heart sank when she told me that she and Mel had argued over Gigi." Fairley shot a pointed look my way.

"I've…heard the rumors."

"Sadly, the rumors are true." Fairley picked up her coffee mug, peered at the liquid, then set it down without drinking. "Why is it that the wife is always the last to know? My first thought was that it might be a good thing for Anita to know the truth about Mel and Gigi. If I were in her place, I would prefer the truth to a lie. Wouldn't you?" Fairley wiped her eyes and folded the tissue into a perfect square.

"The truth is always better."

"That's just what I told Anita last night, but she wouldn't have it. In a strange way, ignorance suits Anita." Fairley took another swipe at her eyes with the tissue, then looked around for a place to dump it.

I pushed a wastepaper basket toward her. "Anita's no different from anyone else. We all see the things we want to see."

"I suppose so." Fairley held the neatly folded tissue over the container and let it fall. "Well, once I saw the state Anita was in, I knew I had to get her out of that house. I packed a few of her things and brought her home with me. I gave her a nice cup of chamomile tea and put her to bed."

I put down my mug. "Is that where Mrs. Dick is now?"

Something flashed in those ice-blue eyes. Fear? Regret? Or just a trick of the light? "I'm... I'm not sure. When I left the house Anita was still snoring away in the guest room."

"You left her alone?"

"Well, yes," Fairley cried, hands twisting in her lap. "I feel awful about it now, but I didn't know about Mel! I had an appointment with my financial advisor, you see. I left a note for Anita and went to my meeting with Jeremy. If I'd known about Mel, I would have never left my friend."

"Calm down, Mrs. Sable, it's not your fault."

"When Jeremy told me that Mel had been murdered,

I broke off the meeting at once. I called my house, but no one answered. So you see, I don't know if Anita is still there or not. I didn't know what to do, and then I remembered security headquarters was in this very building. I came here straightaway."

"And exactly what do you want me to do?"

"Come back with me to my house. It's possible Anita is still there. She might be still asleep for all I know or perhaps she felt odd answering my phone—she can be silly that way. But come back to my house with me. I'm afraid to go home alone."

Against my better judgment I agreed. "But when we get to your house, I'm calling the police, regardless of Mrs. Dick's whereabouts. I'll follow you in my cart."

"But I walked here."

I managed to hide my surprise. "No problem. It'll take me a minute to sign out a golf cart."

Fairley balked again. "I've never felt safe in those kiddie cars."

Really? A Mystic Cove resident who didn't like golf carts? So we wound up taking my current ride, my father's vintage Crown Vic.

When I pulled into Fairley Sable's driveway, she bolted from the Vic like a Baptist out of a bar. I wasn't sure how many years beyond fifty-five—the minimum age for Mystic Covians—the woman was, but she could move. At the front door, she rummaged in her purse for several seconds, then threw it to the ground. "Come with me. I keep an extra key beneath a flowerpot."

"Not a safe practice," I said, following Fairley to the backyard. "That's the first place a burglar would look."

"You sound like Harry." She stopped at a faux-terracotta pot of pink impatiens. I picked up the pot while

Fairley scooped the key. I had just replaced the flowerpot when Fairley's face drained of color.

Anita Dick, a blocky shadow, sat on a stone bench that overlooked the small pond in Mrs. Sable's backyard. She stared at the water as if it were a crystal ball, staring at the fat koi just beneath the surface. I started to call GCSO. My mind knew it was the right thing to do, but my heart was elsewhere. And the heart always won, didn't it? Why not have a few words with Anita before calling Spooner? I turned to speak to Fairley, but she was gone.

"Mrs. Dick?" My voice was barely a whisper, but even so, Anita Dick started. She was a large woman, which somehow made her more vulnerable. She wore navy polyester pants and a shapeless beige tunic that fluttered slightly in the breeze. Her short chestnut-brown hair was teased and sprayed into an immoveable helmet.

I touched her arm. "Are you all right?"

She looked at me, her eyes clouded. She supported her large body on the bench with her arms, but even so, she trembled.

"It's me, Addie Gorsky."

The lidded eyes struggled to focus. Slowly recognition dawned and she said, "Addie? Isn't it a nice day?"

I took her hand in mine and was shocked as its coldness. True, Anita sat in the shadows of Fairley's lush vegetation, but the day was warm.

"You're freezing, Mrs. Dick. Let's go inside. Fairley will fix you some tea." Something was terribly wrong with this woman. Was it shock?

Anita pulled her hand from mine. "Octobers were nice in Ohio. Pumpkins and burning leaves. Not like this jungle." She blinked at the tiny yard that Fairley had packed with foliage. A rapacious flowering vine climbed the arbor behind the koi pond, thyme crept between the brickwork at our feet, and mounds of nose-itching herbs rose from moss-covered pots. "Why do we leave our homes and come to places like Mystic Cove?"

"I don't know, but you need to get inside."

"I'm here because Mel wanted to be here, but I miss my little girl. Julie. Mel was my husband and I obeyed."

"Mrs. Dick, please!" I had to get her inside now and call GCSO—usually wives with living husbands didn't refer to them in the past tense. I tugged her arm, but she pulled away.

"I made a mistake, and now I have to tell Julie that her father is gone."

There was no doubt. Anita Dick knew her husband was dead.

"Let's go, Mrs. Dick." This time she did not resist. Once I had Anita safely inside Fairley's house, I'd call Sheriff Spooner, confess all, and step away from this pile of crap I didn't know I'd already stepped in it.

We had taken a few steps when Anita stopped cold, her eyes bulging with fear. Across the lawn Sheriff Spooner and Deputy Berry ran toward us like hounds with a nose-ful. Anita slipped my grasp and stumbled backward.

"I didn't kill my husband but God help me, I wanted to. I wanted to!"

"Anita!" I cried out.

The poor woman whimpered as Spooner grabbed one arm and Deputy Berry the other. As they led her away she spoke the awful words that could not be taken back.

"No one can blame me, Addie. No one! What wife hasn't wanted to shoot her husband?"

BACK AT THE OFFICE, I splashed water on my face and ran a comb through my cropped black hair. It helped, but not much. I still looked like I'd been ridden hard and put up wet, which wasn't far from the truth. My mind swam and my stomach ached. Too much coffee and too little food. I put a prepackaged cup of tomato soup in the microwave and scrounged a packet of saltine crackers. The soup was paste and the crackers stale, but I didn't care. I ate mindlessly, not tasting anything, which was probably a good thing.

With Mrs. Dick safely tucked in a GCSO cruiser, Spooner had cornered me on Fairley's front yard, dark and threatening as a storm cloud. "I can't believe you would interview a person of interest in a murder investigation."

I tried to explain, but Spooner was beyond listening. In fact, Bubba Spooner looked like a man about to commit murder himself, with yours truly as the victim.

"I don't think Anita Dick is well," I said when he'd stopped to take in oxygen. "I think she might be in shock or something."

"You a doctor now?"

"Sarcasm doesn't suit you." I turned my back on him, but before I reached the Vic a hand gripped my wrist. "Jesus Christ," I yelped, jerking free and facing Spooner.

"You just calm down, lady."

"Don't call me lady." I let these Florida good old boys call me *ma'am,* but drew the line at *lady.*

"Sheriff, we're ready to go here," Deputy Berry, all grins, called from the cruiser. Spooner and I both gave him a dirty look. The sheriff's dark brown eyes bore into mine. "It's awfully lucky for you Mrs. Dick is willing to talk to us, Gorsky. But you and I need to get some things straight before this day is done. I'll be in touch."

Spooner was right of course. I'd been a first-class ass. In my defense all I could say was that the whole thing had been bad timing, like so many of life's tragedies. If the sheriff had arrived five minutes later, everything would have been fine. An unfortunate coincidence, that was all. But then I wondered.

What if someone tipped off the sheriff? A nosey neighbor—plenty of those in Mystic Cove—had spotted Anita in Fairley's backyard and called GCSO. It was a small thing, but in a murder investigation the small things were important. I made a mental note to ask Spooner—once he'd calmed down of course—how it turned out he and Berry showed up when they did.

The door sprang open and Tyler stuck his head inside. "Come on in," I said, relieved to see a friendly face for a change.

"How's the murder investigation going?"

"Don't joke."

"Wanna talk?"

I did. I told Tyler about Fairley's visit and the subsequent debacle. "The last thing the sheriff said to me was that we 'needed to get some things straight,'" I said, giving it my best Southern drawl, which was awful.

"My advice is that you blow Spooner off. If he wants to talk, let him come to you. Whatever you decide, just be careful. Spooner's ambitious and ambitious men are dangerous."

"He's investigating Dick's murder, and I'll help him, if I can."

Tyler cocked his head and smiled. "You're already in this up to your neck, aren't you, Addie?"

I put a hand above my head.

"You better think this through before you get in any deeper."

There was an uncharacteristic seriousness in his voice. Tyler was right; I hadn't thought that far ahead. Since stumbling over the body in Birnam Wood I had let the day's events carry me along, like a raft in white water.

So far the ride had gotten a little bumpy, but the real danger lay around the bend—logjams, undercut rocks, souse holes. Did I really need this headache? Maybe I should let it go. Step slowly away from the body. I needed to talk this over with Pop. "Tyler, would you mind holding down the fort while I cut out early? I've had enough fun for one day."

"Uh sure, but what about the meeting with Busy Rhodes?"

"Is that today?" I'd asked Tyler to sit in on the meeting; when dealing with Busy it was always smart to have a witness.

"Yup, that's why I'm here. Busy wants to discuss the golf cart situation." Tyler shoved a folded newspaper at me, a dog-eared copy of the *Cove Commentator*. The front page displayed a color picture of a butter-yellow golf cart, a stunning facsimile of a 1969 Mustang. Above the photo a headline shouted They Will Take Our Carts from Our Cold Dead Hands!!!

I scanned the screed. Most of the writer's venom was directed at Busy Rhodes, the "enemy of the people" who wanted to limit golf carts to golf courses. Sometimes Mystic Cove was like high school, with its bullies, toadies and countless victims. Disgusted, I crumpled the paper and tossed it.

Mystic Cove was represented by two opposing homeowners' associations that got along like the Montagues and Capulets, only without the love story. The Cove Homeowners' Association, of which Mel Dick was president, purported a laissez-faire toward most things, especially golf carts. But if a resident painted his McMansion an unauthorized shade of pink, he would soon feel the full and righteous wrath of the CHA. The Homeowners' Association of the Cove advocated what its newly elected president Busy Rhodes called common-sense regulations. Almost single-handedly Busy had breathed new life into the moribund organization, but with her latest campaign to limit golf carts in Mystic Cove, she might have inadvertently grabbed a tiger by the tail and now didn't dare let go.

"This meeting with Busy won't be so bad, Addie. Just close your eyes and it'll be over before you know it."

"Sounds like bad sex."

"Is there such a thing?" Tyler laughed. "Just be prepared. Busy is gonna pump you for information about the murder."

"No way, the meeting was arranged last week and Busy might not even know about Dick's death." Busy lived in Blustery Winds, miles from Admiral Street.

Tyler shook his head. "Busy knows all right. Gossip goes through this place like crap through a goose, and this is big. Mel Dick was a player in the Cove. His death creates a power vacuum, which Busy will be happy to fill. The more info she has, the better she can spin things to her advantage."

"You make Mystic Cove sound like a banana republic."

Tyler laughed but then his face turned somber. "I feel most sorry for Jesse Potts. Once the good folks of Mystic Cove find out that Jesse was at the murder scene, they'll pick that boy dry." I hadn't thought of that angle, but Tyler was right. "In her own way she's as vicious at getting what she wants as Mel Dick. Have you ever checked out her blog?"

"Where's that newspaper? I need to check something."

Tyler plucked the crumpled *Commentator* from the trash and handed it over. With Tyler peering over my shoulder, I pointed to the byline.

"Mel Dick," Tyler read.

The door groaned open and Busy Rhodes stood in the doorway.

# FIVE

*The Woman in White*

SHE WAS TALL and toned and glowed with a neon tan from a can. As always she was swathed in white—wide, flowing pants and gauzy peasant blouse. Unlike many older women Busy wore her champagne blond hair long. Today it formed a thick braid that she could almost sit on.

"Good to see you again," I lied.

Tyler put on a dazzling smile.

"Can I get you something, Ms. Rhodes?" Tyler asked.

Busy Rhodes arranged her braid to one side and produced an aluminum bottle. "A refill of water. On cooler days like today the danger of dehydration is much greater."

A quick look between Tyler and me—Busy never missed a chance to lecture.

While Tyler played water boy, I hustled Busy to the captain's chair. I had just settled behind my desk when Tyler returned with Busy's water. When Tyler slid into the chair next to Busy's, one of Ms. Rhodes's penciled eyebrows arched.

"I knew you wouldn't mind if Deputy Chief Andrews sat in on our discussion," I said.

Her lips formed a moue, followed by an abbreviated shrug of one shoulder. "I nearly canceled this meeting because of the tragedy."

Tyler shot an I-told-you-so glance my way and turned to Busy. "It was a terrible tragedy, ma'am."

Busy frowned. Like most Northern women she didn't like being called *ma'am,* a fact of which Tyler was well aware. But Busy threw off her irritation and tried on a sad smile. "I've heard so many stories about Mr. Dick's passing, some quite outrageous. The only constant in all the stories is that Mr. Dick was murdered." Busy looked at me, then at Tyler. When nobody jumped in, she continued. "A person doesn't know what to believe. Driving over, I had an interesting thought. It might be helpful if security set up a rumor control task force."

Tyler made a strangled sound and passed a hand over his face.

"The control of information in a murder investigation is a police matter," I said.

"I understand, but our residents are frightened, and fear does strange things to people. It's been particularly hard on me personally of course."

"How so?" Tyler asked.

"It's true that Mel and I had our differences, but it was never personal, at least not from my side. I didn't dislike Mel. On the contrary, I admired him for the strength of his convictions."

Tyler caught my eye, our thoughts in line. Usually Busy's lies were more discreet. The woman in white detested Mel, as did most people who spent more than five minutes in his company. Mel Dick evoked immediate loathing, the polar opposite of a devil like Jud Richt—now there was a man you had to know well in order to hate.

"I admire your attitude, Ms. Rhodes," I said. "Personally, I wouldn't be quite so forgiving if I were in your place."

"I don't understand."

"Mr. Dick's article in October's *Commentator* contained some pretty outrageous accusations about you."

Busy Rhodes's tanned face turned to stone. "Yes, I read the article, but I'm not a hater. Forgive and forget is my philosophy. It takes far too much energy to hate. Forgive and forget, I always say."

I shook my head. "You're a better woman than I. I could never forgive a man who attacked me like that. What did he call you in that article again?"

Busy Rhodes glared.

I slapped my forehead. "Stupid me, of course you've forgotten the slur—forgive and forget, right?" I produced the crumpled *Cove Commentator*. "Here it is. Mr. Dick calls you a 'modern-day Nazi who gleefully tramples the grapes of liberty,'" I read, adding air quotes. "He also compares the HCA to brownshirts that—"

Ms. Rhodes raised an imperial palm. "All of that is in the past."

"Since when?" I asked.

"Excuse me?"

"Since when did you forgive and forget Mr. Dick for his nasty comments. Was it before or after his death?"

A long stretch of silence. I could tell by Tyler's face that he thought I'd gone too far.

At last Busy said, "I don't appreciate your unprofessional attitude."

I ignored the comment. "If Mel Dick had insulted me like that, I would have run, not walked, to the *Commentator* office and had it out with him. What would you have done, Deputy Chief Andrews?"

"Same as you, Chief."

Tyler and I stared at the woman in white, the ball in her court.

Busy forced a smile. "This conversation is beginning to feel like an interrogation."

"I'm sorry you feel that way," I said.

Busy's eyes narrowed. My unapologetic apology hadn't slipped by unnoticed. "I don't have to, but I'd like to share something with you." She opened her hands in a gesture of supplication. "I have nothing to hide."

*Sure you do, Busy. We all have something to hide.*

"As a matter of fact I did speak to Mel about the article. I bumped into him at the Barnes and Noble in Founder's Centre shortly after the article came out. I was rather shocked to see Mel there—he's not much of a reader—but he'd come for Kristin Donald's book signing." Busy frowned. "She was there to promote her memoir *I Am Not a Witch*. That…that was the last time I saw Mel alive."

I pounced, smelling a lie, and decided to call Busy on it. "You were surprised to find Mel there, even though the *Cove Commentator* sponsored the event?" Eager for a big crowd, Mel had saturated Mystic Cove with news of Donald's upcoming appearance. Everyone in Mystic Cove knew that about the event and Mel's connection to it.

Busy took a swig of water. "I… I had simply forgotten that Kristin Donald's book signing was scheduled for that evening."

"Who is Kristin Donald anyway?" Tyler asked.

"Some politician," I said.

Busy smiled condescendingly and proceeded to enlighten Tyler and me. "Kristin Donald is a former prosecutor who unsuccessfully ran for the Senate a few years back—no one important, just one of Mel's political pets."

"Okay," I said, not sure what to make of that statement.

Busy wriggled in her uncomfortable chair. "As I started to say, it was happenstance that I ran into Mel that night. Somehow I managed to pry Mel from Miss Donald. I let him know that I thought his article dishonest and contemptible."

"Bet that got a rise out of him," Tyler said.

"Not really. He said politics wasn't for the faint of heart and if I couldn't take it, I should stay at home and bake cookies. After that he rushed back to Miss Donald's side. I left and that was the end of it."

That didn't sound like Mel, who never left a slight pass unchallenged. Either Busy was downplaying the exchange or Mel had become more reasonable.

"And now," Busy said, rising to leave, "if you'll excuse me…"

"Ms. Rhodes!" I said sharply. The woman in white's well-toned ass froze in midair. "Leaving so soon?"

"We're finished."

"But we haven't even discussed the golf cart crisis. Wasn't that the reason you requested the meeting?

"It can wait."

I gaped at Tyler, then at Busy. "But you said that you nearly canceled this meeting because of Mel Dick's death. I assumed your concern about the carts overrode any squeamishness over Mr. Dick's passing."

"I assumed the same thing," Tyler said, "but you know what they say about assumptions." Tyler and I laughed while Busy glared.

"I made a mistake in coming here."

"We all make mistakes, Ms. Rhodes. Have a good day."

When Tyler returned after escorting Busy to the door, he was bent over with laughter. "I could barely keep a straight face! You worked her over good. Better hope she doesn't complain to Richt."

"She won't go to Richt. She despises him almost as much as I do."

"I can't believe she thought we'd swallow that whopper about her and Dick being good buddies. Maybe she'll think twice about lying to us."

"I hope not."

Tyler shot a quizzical look my way.

"You learn a lot about people by the lies they tell. Sometimes you can learn more from a lie than from the truth."

"You mean a lie is as good as the truth."

"No, what I mean is that lies can be useful. If you can figure out why a person lies, you're that much closer to the truth."

"So why did Busy lie about admiring Mel Dick?"

"Maybe Busy is a conventional, old-fashioned sort who doesn't believe in speaking poorly of the dead."

"Busy isn't conventional."

"I'm not so sure," I said. "Busy Rhodes sees herself as unconventional, but that doesn't mean she is."

"So why did Busy lie? And don't tell me you don't know."

"It could be an ego thing. Busy has a need for moral superiority—I think that's part of the reason she always dresses in white. The vicious feud with Mel threatened that self-image somewhat, but with him gone, she can afford to take the high road."

"You mean, pretend to," Tyler said.

"Hard to say, there's a thin line between pretending and believing. People with healthy egos like Mel and Busy have a remarkable capacity for self-deception. It could be that Busy believes her own bull. Now that I think about it, Busy and Mel are a lot alike."

Tyler looked dubious.

"They're intelligent, ambitious, and proud to the point of arrogance. They only differ in style. Even so, Busy's little lies may not be relevant."

"Not relevant to what?" Tyler asked.

"Not relevant to the… I don't know." I stopped just in

time. I had been about to say *murder investigation*—a clear sign I was deeper in the mire.

"There is another explanation for Busy Rhodes's fib," Tyler said softly.

"I know." Maybe the cold war between Mel and Busy had turned hot, but hot enough for murder?

But it was past five and time to go. We were halfway out the door when the office phone rang.

"Let it go to voice mail, Addie," Tyler said.

"Go on ahead. I'll catch up with you at Eddie's."

It was Spooner. He wanted me at GCSO headquarters ASAP so that we could "finish our talk."

"I'm on my way, Sheriff." A long time ago I learned that anticipating unpleasantness could be a lot worse than the unpleasantness itself. Parents knew this—that was why they liked to warn their kids before punishing them. That way the kids' fear got a chance to fester, like a thorn beneath the skin.

I called Pop to let him know I'd be late.

"Adelajda," my father said in his old man's voice. I loved the way he spoke my name in all its archaic beauty: Ad-e-la-ya. American tongues got twisted over the Polish inflection and with Mom gone, he was the only who still called me by my given name. I was even Addie to my sisters nowadays.

"Does your being late have anything to do with Mel Dick's death?"

"How do you know about that?"

"The five o'clock news led with the story. Page Becket reporting live from Mystic Cove."

Tyler Andrews was right about Mel having been a player. His murder rated top billing on the local news program.

"It's no big deal," I said quickly. "Sheriff Spooner

asked me to stop by his office. I'll tell you all about it as soon as I can."

"Is it murder?"

"I'll fill you in when I get home."

"I'm dying to hear all your news, but please don't wait too long." He made a sound that in another place and time might have been laughter.

You see, my father was dying; it was sort of a joke between us.

WITH HIS DARK features and hook nose Bubba Spooner bore a remarkable resemblance to a hungry vulture as he hunched over his computer screen. Without diverting his gaze, he gestured for me to sit. I shoved some papers off of a chair. Finally Spooner closed whatever he had been working on and fixed his cool gaze on me.

"First thing," Spooner said in a soft voice that demanded attention, "I want you to describe the crime scene."

"I… I gave Berry my report. I don't know what I can add." I hated that I sounded petulant, but I was tired. My usual drive home to Lady-in-the-Hills took me in the opposite direction of rush-hour traffic, but today I'd driven down its throat.

"I'm not talking about your statement. Just describe the murder scene." Spooner's chair creaked as he leaned back. "Didn't you work homicide in Pittsburgh?"

"Baltimore."

"So take me through the murder scene."

I didn't know where this was headed, but I'd give Spooner what he wanted. I took a moment to recreate the scene. I have an excellent memory and the details came easily—the smell of fresh dirt and oleander, the dim light of early dawn, the dead body in the golf cart.

"At first I assumed it was a natural death." I looked pointedly at Spooner, but he didn't take the bait, just nodded and said it was a reasonable conclusion.

"Exactly," I said. "Old people tend to die and Mystic Cove is full of old people. And Mel did look awful peaceful in that stupid cart."

"The most peaceful I've ever seen him," Spooner agreed.

"Then I saw the head trauma. The shape of the wound and stippling indicated Mel had died from a close-range gunshot wound. Since Mel wasn't holding a gun, I figured it was murder, not suicide. There were no obvious defensive wounds, no signs of a struggle around the cart." The words were coming fast and hard now, and I kept glancing at Spooner for any confirmation, but his face told me nothing. "My best guess is that Mel was taken unawares. I also didn't see any casings near the body so the shooter either cleaned up after himself or I'm dead wrong about it being a close-range shot. Oh, and Mel was wearing someone else's clothes."

Spooner's head snapped. "I agree that Mel looked like a damn clown, but what makes you think they weren't his clothes?"

"The shirt was at least two sizes too small."

"That wasn't vanity? Dick has put on a little weight."

"Nah, and besides, a gaudy Hawaiian shirt and nylon shorts wasn't Mel's style." Like many of our male residents Mel lived in golf shirts and polyester pants. "And I know he wasn't dressed like that at the G and G."

"How can you be so sure?"

"Because…because Anita wouldn't have let him out of the house dressed like that, if only to keep him from freezing to death." Not the truth, but plausible enough. Spooner didn't need to know that Anita Dick wasn't the only witness I'd talked to today. I was pretty sure that if Mel had been dressed like a clown, José Barracas would have mentioned it, if only to dig at his adversary.

"Now tell me about your little chat with Anita."

"Sure, but first you need to know how I happened to find her." I related my lengthy conversation with Fairley Sable and the aborted one with Anita, stressing that I did not inform Anita about Mel's death. "She knew her husband was dead before I opened my mouth."

"I wish you hadn't talked to Anita Dick, but here we are."

*And where was that?*

"Everything you just told me," Spooner was saying, "fits with the statements we got from the merry widow and her girlfriend."

"You mean Anita and Fairley Sable?"

"When Berry interviewed them, he..."

"Berry?" I blurted. "Berry's the primary?"

"Yeah," Spooner drawled. "I can see Deputy Berry's made an impression on you. He does have that talent."

I wasn't sure if Spooner was playing with me, but his tone suggested Berry's memorability was not a good thing.

"How well do you know Anita Dick?"

"When I was a guard I saw her almost every day." In my early days with Mystic Cove security I'd often gotten stuck working the Admiral Street guardhouse. "We'd exchange pleasantries. She was pleasant, down-to-earth, although sometimes she seemed a little lost."

"In what way?" Spooner shifted in his chair.

I made a disgusted sound. "At the Cove she's a minnow in a tank of cichlids and parrot fish."

"Is she slow?"

"Not at all. If I had to guess I'd say she's of average or

above-average intelligence. But she's a shy, quiet woman, and in a country of shouters quiet people are often thought slow."

"I don't know about that, but she was confused as all get-out for the interview. It was like only half of her was there. For God's sake, you saw her. It was like she was miles away."

José had described Mel in almost the exact same words. What had been going on in the Dick household in the weeks before Mel's murder?

"Anita had a reason to be distracted, Sheriff. Her husband was just murdered."

"It was more than that, and I gotta consider if it's selective confusion. She told me that after Mel left her at the pub, she went home alone. Mel returned sometime around eleven or twelve—she's fuzzy on the time—and they get into a big argument. He left in his cart and that was the last she saw of him."

"Did she say what the argument was about?"

"Not at first, and when she did admit to knowing about the girlfriend, she was still pretty short on details. That woman is hiding something."

"How did she find out that Mel was dead?"

Spooner gave me a look. I feared I'd stepped over some invisible boundary, but then he leaned back in his chair. "It's quite a story, but I don't buy it for a second. Anita claimed that someone left a message on Mrs. Sable's voice mail this morning in which the caller referred to Mel's murder."

"And Anita overheard the message—sounds reasonable enough to me."

Spooner scowled. "Maybe, but Mrs. Dick didn't recognize the caller's voice, couldn't even say if the voice had been male or female. I had Berry check with Mrs. Sable and at first she told him there weren't any messages on her machine. Then a few hours later she called back and said she may have accidentally deleted her phone messages, so there could have been a message after all."

"That's a little twisted," I admitted, "but Anita's story could still be legit."

"Or Mrs. Sable wants to help a friend," Spooner said.

"Fairley doesn't impress me as the type who'd lie to the police, but who knows?" Fairley had made a point of telling me that she was loyal to her friends—had she been trying to tell me something? I felt the sheriff's eyes on me. I knew that look well enough. It was the way a prospective buyer might appraise a used car. It seemed like a good deal and was cheap enough, but what about the hidden costs? There were always hidden costs.

"I need your help," he said.

"Uh, Mystic Cove Security will assist GCSO in any way we can."

"No, I need *your* help, you personally. If I have the full measure of your boss, Jud Richt—and I believe I do— he's going to be a royal pain in my ass. He won't go as far as obstructing justice, but he'll push it as far as he can."

I had to smile. "Richt has already warned me not to be overly helpful with the GCSO."

"He strikes quick." Spooner said.

"But Richt isn't the reason you're asking for my help. At least not the only reason."

"No," Spooner admitted. "Last week Mel Dick called me to request a meeting. He refused to say what it was about but I agreed to meet with him. In my dealings with Dick, I've learned it's easier to give him what he wants, if at all possible. So we made an appointment for the next day, but he doesn't show. I just assumed he'd changed his mind and hadn't bothered to cancel."

"A reasonable assumption. Mel Dick wasn't exactly considerate."

"I forgot about it until yesterday morning when I came into work to find this voice mail waiting for me."

Spooner put his phone on speaker and pressed a button. A shiver rolled down my spine as Mel Dick's voice filled the office. It was definitely Mel, but he sounded different. He was slurring his words, as if his mouth were full of mashed potatoes. The message was brief—less than a minute—and much of it incomprehensible, though there was a patch near the end that was clear. I asked Spooner for a replay, and then I was sure.

"You heard it," Spooner said.

"It's…it's right before he hangs up. Mel Dick says, 'There's a murderer among us. There's a killer in the Cove.'"

## SIX

*Ignorance and Innocence Play Together*

I GRIMACED. COP coffee was even worse than I remembered, and what I remembered was pretty bad. Spooner pushed additional packets of creamer my way, but I pushed them back. I had already added a ton of creamer, and the stuff was still the color of dirt. Yet Spooner drank his black and, if not with pleasure, then at least tolerance. I did the same.

"So Mel was proven right. There is a murderer in the Cove. What does Berry make of it?"

Spooner laughed without mirth. "Oh, Berry doesn't see it that way. He's certain the murder was a botched robbery. Some meth monster snuck into the Cove with robbery on his mind. Berry's not a bad cop, but he does suffer from a serious lack of imagination."

"How does he account for Mel's message?"

"The neighborhood canvas revealed that our buddy Mel has been acting pretty strange lately—some folks even called it crazy."

"Jesse Potts mentioned that Mel had been acting… weird lately."

"Huh—that wasn't in his statement. But Berry thinks Mel's midnight message is more of the same. Delusional talk from a senile old man."

"Any evidence to support Berry's theory of the murder?"

"Nope," Spooner said. "Like you observed, there were

no defensive wounds or posturing, no signs of struggle. Cash and credit cards were still in Dick's wallet. 'Course Berry argues that the killer was interrupted before he could clean out the wallet."

"I guess it's possible."

Spooner gave me a look and we laughed. He pointed to my empty cup and I nodded. "The problem is Berry has decided the perp is an addled crackhead and nothing this side of hell is gonna change his mind."

"A common mistake."

"I got a bad feeling about this case, Addie." Spooner's chair squeaked as he shifted in it. "There's a lot against us, most of all Mel Dick himself."

"What do you mean?"

"Mel had a knack for shoving his nose into other people's business. He liked to think he was a real reporter but he was just a nasty little piggy who messed in people's business. I've read that newspaper of his and those nasty letters to the editor he's always sending to the *Newnansville Sun.* In a lot of ways he was a man begging to be murdered."

"You got Mel pegged. He always styled himself as a journalist. Say, do you think it's possible the old guy stumbled onto a real story?"

"Such as a murderer hiding out in the Cove?"

"It sounds ridiculous when you say it that way, but it's possible Mel uncovered a secret, a secret worthy of murder."

"It's possible," Spooner said, but his tone suggested it was more likely that monkeys would fly.

I wasn't sure I agreed with him. The sheriff saw Mel's irascible personality as an obstacle to solving his murder. It just might be the key that would unlock the mystery. Mel

Dick was just smart enough to dig up somebody's secret, but too arrogant to see the danger until it was too late.

"It's a lot to take in," I said. "A cryptic midnight message left by an intrepid amateur reporter who later turns up dead. Now I understand why you dropped by the G and G last night."

A little smile and Spooner said, "Oh, you know about that, do you?"

"We're not good at keeping secrets in the Cove."

"You're wrong there. Somebody in Mystic Cove is plenty good at keeping a secret."

"So how did you wind up at the G and G last night?"

"Like I said, yesterday morning I got Mel's message. Right away, I called the old man's house, but nobody answered. I left a message, but I still got that nagging feeling that something's wrong. You know the feeling?"

"Sure." It was a feeling every police knew and dared not ignore, if she wanted to stay alive, that was.

"I sent Deputy Berry to Dick's house, but nobody's home on Admiral Street. Next stop was Mel's office. Same story—nobody answered. At this point Berry checked in with me. I could tell he was sick of the wild-goose chase I sent him on so I told him to let it go."

"But you couldn't let it go."

"No, I couldn't let it go. On my way home I dropped by the Cove—I had to see Dick with my own eyes, just to be sure. You know," he said, giving me a nasty look, "I had to push your guard pretty hard to get him to let me inside Windbound Harbor. I kept telling him this was official business and not a social call. By the time I got to Dick's house I was either too late or too early. Nobody home.

"Next I decided to check Mel's office. I was on my way there when I spotted the cruisers in front of the

G and G. The OSCO deputy told me they had sent a cruiser to Dick's home. The deputy had found Anita at home, but no Mel. There was nothing more to be done. Barracas refused to press charges and there'd been no damages. I took a stab at talking to some witnesses, but your friend Tyler Andrews fixed that."

"Sorry."

"By then, I was done—put a fork in me. I had chased Mel Dick all day long with nothing to show for it. Then this morning I found out that Dick was dead. Sometime between him leaving the restaurant and you finding him in that clearing, somebody put a bullet in Mel Dick's head."

"And right now Anita's your prime suspect."

"At the top of the list. She wouldn't be the first wife to shoot her husband in a jealous rage."

"Nor the last, but don't forget about Gigi Tajani. Girlfriends are also prone to jealous rages." Since we were now partners of a sort I told Spooner about my conversation with José Barracas. "According to José, Gigi and Mel were on the outs."

"Don't worry, I'll keep an open mind about suspects." Spooner drank coffee and cupped his chin in his hand. "But you know, when I was in the Dick house today, I got a really bad feeling. Most homes reflect the people who live in it, but this place was different. Too cold and too quiet and too full of Dick, as if his ego was so big it left room for nothing else." He looked at me. "There was nothing of Anita in that house. Living like that would wear a person down."

"I can't see Anita putting a gun against her husband's head and pulling the trigger."

Spooner snorted. "She practically confessed."

"Like hell!"

"She denies shooting Mel and then admits that she wanted to—that's edging pretty close to an unqualified confession."

"Close, but no bull's-eye. All Anita said was that all wives think about murdering their husbands. What's the big deal?" Now Spooner looked at me as if I were covered in pink polka dots. "If you don't believe me, check with your wife."

"What do you know about it?" He pointed at my unadorned left hand.

"True, I'm not married. I'm also not a murderer, but I can think like one," I said, tapping my forehead. Spooner cracked a smile, and I did the same. "Say, have you got time of death yet?"

"I've got nada," Spooner said, his face darkening. This man was changeable as the Florida weather. "Coroner Blanding hasn't even started the autopsy, though he promised to get on it tonight. That's why I'm still here." The morgue was in the same sixties-era compound as the sheriff's office.

So the murder investigation was in limbo until Coroner Blanding got his ass in gear. The coroner had a piss-poor reputation among law enforcement. Some years earlier a body had been pulled from Okpulo Lake. Blanding determined cause of death as an accidental drowning, somehow missing the bullet hole in the man's neck. I mentioned the case to Spooner.

"That was our last murder in Grubber County, and unfortunately you got your facts right."

"Can't someone else perform the autopsy? Dolores Rio seems competent."

"She is and I suggested that to Blanding but he refused to assign the autopsy to Dr. Rio. He said a murder case requires his particular expertise, whatever that is. It's a shame. Dolores Rio is smart and a real pathologist."

"And Blanding isn't?" Maryland had medical examiners. My experience with coroners was limited to the crime novels I'd devoured as a kid.

"Blanding's an old-fashioned general practitioner." Spooner's twisted grin deepened—rictus sardonicus. "I suppose we should be grateful he's an M.D."

"You're kidding!"

Spooner's awful smile deepened. "Having a medical degree is not a job requirement for Grubber County coroner."

"So I could be coroner then."

"Sure, if you can charm enough people to vote for you. But given your personality, I think that's a long shot."

"No argument here."

"It's a bad system. Forensic pathology is a complex field, and Blanding was always more politician than doctor. For the life of me I can't figure why he wants this case. Rio performs ninety-nine percent of the autopsies. Blanding is a slippery bastard, but darned if I can figure what he's up to."

"You seriously think Blanding has an agenda in all this?"

"I don't know what I think. Like I said, I'm spooked. It's not even twenty-four hours since Dick's death and I already feel like I've run into a brick wall. You see why I need your help? You know these Cove people—I don't. I need you to keep your eyes and ears open. Keep me informed of anything out of the ordinary. Can you do that for me, Addie? Will you?"

There were a thousand reasons to say no. I was putting my crappy job at risk and I had my hands full with

Pop. It was easy to step into the muck but not so easy stepping out.

"We got a deal?" Spooner offered his hand.

I stared at his outstretched hand and wondered what this man really wanted of me. It was never as simple as their promises. Did Spooner want a partner, a patsy, or something else altogether? The whole thing felt suddenly unreal, almost a dream. But after the emptiness of the past few years, a dream didn't seem so bad.

I shook his hand.

Then I noticed the time. If I wanted to catch the guys at Eddie's I needed to haul ass.

Spooner gulped the dregs of his noxious brew and pushed back his chair. "I may as well hit the road too."

While we walked, Spooner vented about Blanding. I got his frustration, or thought I did. He longed to search Anita's house and hoped the autopsy would give him probable cause. Once outside, we paused, the cold shocking both of us. Suddenly vulnerable fingers buttoned and zipped and then jammed into pockets.

"We'll talk tomorrow then," I said, already shivering. It was another clear night, the stars scattered like cut glass in the darkened sky.

"I'll let you know when I get that search warrant," Spooner said.

"You're pretty confident."

"There is one piece of information I didn't mention earlier. Given his deep admiration for the second amendment, I wasn't surprised to discover that Mel Dick had a permit for a handgun, a thirty-eight special to be specific."

"A thirty-eight special, huh?" I was no expert by any stretch, but the hole in Mel's head was consistent with a Smith and Wesson thirty-eight special.

"Exactly," Spooner smiled, reading my face. "I'm pinning my hopes on the bullet buried in Mel Dick's brain. If it's not damaged too badly and the lab can identify it as being from a thirty-eight, I got my search warrant. And if we find the gun..."

He didn't need to finish. If the gun was found in her possession, it would go hard on Anita Dick.

LIKE ALWAYS THE crew was huddled in the shabby back room inexplicably called the banquet hall. I got a couple of pitchers and headed back. It was a small but promising group. There was Tyler of course, and Jesse Potts, but I was most excited to see Billy Blake and Oscar Wall, both of whom regularly worked Admiral Street.

"Just in time!" Billy said, taking control of the pitchers. Oscar gave Billy a sour look and shook his head. The two septuagenarians loathed one another.

We got the small talk out of the way and turned to the main event: murder.

"As far as I'm concerned," Billy said with an evil grin, "it was about time somebody killed Mel Dick."

"Stupid talk," Oscar muttered, the lilt of the Caribbean in his voice. I never could figure why Oscar came to these drinking sessions. He drank little and spoke even less.

"Why is it stupid?" Billy asked, taking the bait.

Oscar rolled his eyes. "It's stupid for a man to say he's happy a murdered man is dead."

"Are you saying I killed Mel Dick?" Billy's slight frame bristled.

Oscar shrugged and sipped his beer. "I'm just saying it's a stupid thing to say. It's obvious to any fool that one of Mel's friends killed him."

Billy slapped the table. "Mel Dick didn't have any friends."

"You're wrong there," Tyler said over raucous laughter.

"Busy Rhodes came to see the chief and me today and, according to Busy, her and Mel were bosom buddies."

"Friends with benefits?" Billy said. Another burst of laughter. Billy topped off everybody's glass, even though only his needed it.

"Come on, guys," I said. The meeting I'd had such hopes for was quickly deteriorating into a drunken bitch fest. "This is serious."

"None of this—" Billy pounded the table for emphasis, "—not a bit of it is any of our business." A rumble of assent.

"I gotta disagree." I used my big voice to smother their small ones and it worked. They all looked at me, curiosity and surprise on their faces. "Most of us used to be on the job. We protected people, kept them safe." I looked at each of them in turn. Heads bobbed and spines stiffened, just a little. "Now we're security for Mystic Cove. We still protect people and keep them safe, only in a different capacity. Last night one of our residents was murdered. How is it not our business?"

Jesse put down the coaster he'd been playing with. "But…but wouldn't we be stepping on some toes? This morning you said it was police business."

"I don't want to step on that sheriff's toes," Billy said with a belch.

"They're right, Addie." Tyler lightly touched my arm. "You step on Spooner's toes, and you're asking for trouble."

"Enough with the toes," I said loudly. "We're not going to step on any toes. I have reason to believe GCSO would appreciate our insights."

"Insights?" Tyler said. "You're starting to sound like Dr. Phil." A smattering of laughter that I extinguished with a cross look.

"But we don't know nothing about the murder or the murderer," Billy protested.

"Make no mistake," I said, raising a finger, "you do know this murderer." I couldn't be sure if this was true, but I suspected it was. And the solemn faces around the table told me that they believed it as well. "You all know this person. You've seen him, spoken to him, maybe even shaken his hand."

"You think the killer lives in the Cove," Oscar said, dark eyes dancing.

"I do."

"But…but how can we help?" Jesse sounded more confused than usual, and he was far too pale, a bleached ghost in the dim light.

"A murder investigation is like putting a jigsaw puzzle together. First thing you gotta do is gather all the pieces. That's where you can help. You guys who worked Admiral Street saw Mel Dick almost every day. You saw things no one else did."

"Nothing important," Billy groused, but he didn't sound so certain.

"This early in the game, we don't know what's important and what's not. For instance, had Mel changed his habits lately? What about his state of mind—had he been preoccupied or distracted? Was he angry with anyone?"

"More like angry with everybody," Billy said, pouring out the last of the beer.

"The old goat was awful forgetful lately," Oscar said. "He must have told me that story about Mr. Jinks growling at Ms. Busy in Barnes and Noble about fifty times."

"I heard that one too," Tyler said.

"I heard plenty more that I'd like to share." Billy waved his empty glass. "But my mouth is kinda dry."

I ordered another pitcher along with an order of nachos

and after that the dams burst. Everybody had a crazy Mel story. As I listened, I realized that the Mel Dick of recent weeks was very different from the man I had known. His natural suspicion had deepened into paranoia, his over-blown confidence transformed into megalomania. And there was a new wrinkle: Mel Dick's memory—formerly sharp as a tiger's tooth—had become a rusty sieve. Jesse's anecdote was typical.

One predawn morning Mel had caught the young man asleep in the guardhouse, although Jesse swore he was just resting his eyes. When Mel passed by an hour later, Jesse again apologized, but Mel had no memory of the incident.

"Then he got mad," Jesse said, "and told me to get with the program 'cause pretty soon the world would know who Mel Dick is."

"The prick always thought he was better than anybody else," Billy said through a mouthful of nachos, "but lately he's been ridiculous. He's been…"

Oscar fingered his mustache. "Grandiose?"

"I was gonna say stuck-up." Billy glowered at his old enemy.

Tyler snapped his fingers. "I got it—Dick was going senile."

Billy wagged his head. "There's maybe a ten percent chance at most that Mel Dick was senile." God, Billy was quoting percentages, a sure sign he'd had too much to drink.

"Dick must have been senile," Tyler repeated.

Billy's jaw tightened and he locked Tyler in his sights. "Listen to me, douchebag—Mel Dick hit the links two, maybe three times a week. The man was my age, only in his sixties and healthy as a horse, still a young man. You wipe that grin off your face, Andrews, or I'll do it for you! I'm telling you he was too young for Alzheimer's."

Jesse scooped up more nachos. "Aunt Charlotte Potts was touched when she was fifty or so. They called it early…early something."

"Early-onset Alzheimer's," I said.

"Mel didn't have Alzheimer's!" Billy thumped his chest, an aging silverback. "The trouble with you youngsters is that you assume all us old farts are senile. Well, we're not! Dementia is not a natural fact of getting old. It comes on gradual. Whatever scrambled Mel Dick's brain happened overnight. Even in his last days, there were times when he was the old Mel."

Tyler argued that this wasn't unusual. "Sometimes Alzheimer patients are clearer in the daytime and more confused at night."

"I know about sunsetting and this wasn't it." Billy's jaw was clenched so tight I thought it might break.

"You know," I said, "Mel's condition sounds more like delirium than dementia."

"Aren't they the same thing?" Tyler asked.

"The symptoms are similar—confusion, memory loss, disorientation—but dementia is a progressive disease while delirium appears suddenly and comes and goes."

"What causes it?" Tyler asked.

"Booze!" Billy guffawed.

"That's right," I said. "Also drugs, infection, even something as simple as dehydration can cause mental confusion." I'd had a scare last March when Pop got a urinary infection and bugged out, but once the infection cleared, Pop was sharp as ever.

"One thing for sure, it wasn't dehydration with Dick," Oscar said cryptically.

We all stared at Oscar until Jesse laughed. "Oscar's right. Mr. Dick was always drinking his sweet tea."

We agreed—even in cool weather Mel Dick carried a giant thermos of iced tea.

"Okay, so maybe it was delirium," Tyler admitted. "What does that mean?"

"I'm not sure," I said. "Delirium is certainly a medical emergency, a signal that something is terribly wrong. I'm wondering why the people close to Mel didn't get him to a doctor."

Tyler shrugged. "Maybe they didn't notice anything was wrong."

"If we noticed, they noticed," Oscar said through pursed lips.

Tyler frowned and pushed his plate of half-eaten nachos away. "Fair enough, but if Mel Dick didn't want to go to the doctor's, no one was gonna make him."

"So why didn't Mrs. Dick just call GCSO and Baker Act his butt?" Oscar asked. "At least then a doctor would have examined him."

"Anita Dick was a timid soul," I said, though Oscar had a point.

"Maybe so," Tyler said, "but if she had done the right thing, Mel would have been taken to a mental health facility for observation, and probably still be alive."

"Maybe she didn't want him alive," Billy said with an evil smile.

Oscar nodded at Billy. "For once you're right, old man."

"I'm only two years older than you, punk!" A sharp thwack when Billy set his mug down.

Oscar smirked. "If it was my investigation, I'd look at the wife."

"And what about Gigi," I said, "or the other people close to Mel? Who's to say one of them didn't have a stake in Mel's death?"

"I don't blame 'em for letting him die," Billy muttered,

staring into his glass. "Mel Dick never helped anybody else. It was all about what other people could do for him. Still and all, I'm with Oscar—look at the wife first."

"What about you, Billy?" Tyler asked with a sly smile. "You obviously had a grudge against Mel—can you account for your whereabouts on the night of the murder?" I kicked him under the table—why was Tyler provoking Billy?

Billy ran a hand through thinning hair. "Don't quit your day job, Andrews."

"It's wrong to talk about Mr. Dick like this," Jesse said, his voice pinched. "Can't we let him rest in peace?"

"No, we can't, not until his murderer is found." And maybe not even then, I added silently.

Jesse sighed. "All day everybody's been talking about Mr. Dick's murder, but I didn't see no tears. It's like nobody loved him."

Silence around the table. Was it shame?

"I don't know about now," I said, "but once Anita loved Mel Dick very much. I mean, when she married, she changed her name. Of her own free will she became Anita Dick. She must have loved him."

Jesse added, "And Mr. Jinks loved Mr. Dick."

"Mel Dick did love his god-awful dog." Oscar spoke for us all.

Billy cleared his throat. "So what if Mel loved his dog? So what? Hitler loved Blondie. The whole tri-county area is chockablock full of Mel Dick haters. If it were my investigation, I'd start with the people closest to Dick and work my way outward."

"Stupid man," Oscar said softly, his dark face shining. "You shouldn't look for people who hated Mel Dick, look for those who feared him."

Oscar had hit on something. People killed for lots of

reasons—money, lust, revenge. But fear was always a part of the equation, maybe the main part. So who feared Mel Dick? Based on my chat with José Barracas, I'd bet the owner of the G and G was one, but surely there were others.

"Addie?" Tyler's voice came from a thousand miles away. "You game for another pitcher?"

I glanced at my watch. It was past midnight and Pop had been alone all day, but I wasn't tired. I wanted to play the game a bit longer. Then I heard Grammy Ludwika's chiding voice, cracked with age, "Oh, Malutka, so many wishes for such a little girl. If wishes were fishes, there'd be no room for water." This time my conscience won out.

It didn't always.

After extracting a promise from Tyler to get Billy home safely, I said goodnight. To my surprise Oscar drained the beer he'd been nursing and fell in at my side. Outside cold rain pounded the desolate parking lot that sprouted potholes, thorny weeds and rust-bucket cars.

"See you tomorrow," I said, eager to get inside the Vic and crank the heat.

"I saw Mel Dick last night."

I wanted to tell him off for holding back, but that was Oscar. "We'll talk in my car."

"Good idea, it's cold as a witch's tit out here."

I switched the car heater to the max. A few years in the Florida sun and my blood had turned to rainwater.

Oscar stared out at the pattering rain. "Gonna be cold in Mystic Cove over the next few days—radio said it was Arctic air moving in." He turned to face me. "I liked what you said about us guards protecting people, but you were wrong."

"You said you saw Mel last night." I said, more sharply

than I'd intended, but I didn't have time for Oscar's game, whatever it was.

Oscar smiled, white teeth gleaming from his dark face. Strange, Oscar wasn't a man to take pleasure from many things, but he obviously enjoyed this. "As you know, I worked swing shift on Admiral Street last night. It happened around seven. Tyler was late in giving me my break so I was outside the guardhouse, watching for him."

I got the picture. When unhappy, Oscar prowled like a caged tiger.

"I heard the golf cart before I saw it, coming from Birnam Wood. Then it shot into Admiral Street like it was a comet—went by like that." Oscar pushed one arm in the air. "I acted fast. I stood in the middle of the street, waving my arms and yelling 'Stop!' but the cart kept coming. At the last second I realized it wasn't going to stop. I jumped into the swale, but not before I got a good look at the driver—it was Mel Dick, looking like the devil was on his ass."

"Did you tell the police?"

"Yeah, I talked to some guy. Berry. I also reported the incident to Andrews right after it happened, but I guess he didn't tell you about it. Am I right?"

Oscar took my silence for assent.

"It's a shame, ain't it, Chief? Nobody cares anymore. Adding insult to injury, right after I almost get run over by that maniac, I stuck my head out of the ditch just as a friggin' white Prius was sneaking by. The driver had to have seen me fall on my ass in the ditch, but he just drove on by. Didn't even check if I'm all right. It's a shame— nobody cares anymore."

"And do you care, Oscar? Do you?" I guess the imp of the perverse was on my shoulder that night.

He smiled broadly. "Of course I don't care, Chief. Why should I? Nobody else does."

That night Oscar's story nagged at me, vague disquiet nibbling like a minnow. I was missing something, but the source of my unease refused to be caught. Like when you tried to recall the name of a familiar song, the harder you tried, the more elusive the name became.

So I let it pass, trusting that the connection would reveal itself in its own good time.

# SEVEN

*Red Claw, Red Fang*

MY SLEEP WAS fractured by wild dreams I could not remember but disturbed me nonetheless. Yet when I woke in the predawn darkness, the question that had troubled me last night had risen to the surface. After getting off a couple of emails, I checked on Pop, who'd been asleep when I'd gotten home last night. I cracked his bedroom door and heard a soft moan.

*Does the pain follow you everywhere, Papa?*

As I dressed for work, I kept thinking how screwed up everything was. After moving to Florida, I'd sworn off the family business—not only was Pop a former cop but all four of my older sisters were in law enforcement—but the only job I could land was rent-a-cop at Mystic Cove, which turned out to be the worst of both worlds. I looked like a cop in my tan shirt and khakis and I could still put on a cop face, but I had no power, no responsibility. A scarecrow that couldn't scare a sparrow.

I heard noises. Pop was up and I had a full plate ahead of me.

"You should have woken me when you got home last night, Adelajda," Pop growled. Stanislaw Michal Gorsky could be tough as nails or soft as silk. This morning he sounded rusty as an old saw.

"I got in late."

"I wanted to speak with you." Pop gave me the hairy

eyeball. Then he smiled and said, "You're bright-eyed this morning."

"I don't know about that. Coffee or tea this morning?"

Pop arranged his bones in the worn recliner. "Maybe a little coffee."

A good sign, I told myself. Didn't Pop ask for coffee on his better days? I filled the chipped mug emblazoned with the Maryland state flag with equal parts coffee and cream and brought it to him, along with a plate of scrambled eggs and whole wheat toast.

"What's all this?" Pop asked.

"You need to eat." I set the coffee and food on the standing tray by the recliner and rolled it into place. Then I grabbed my plate from the kitchen counter and took my usual seat on the sofa.

"This looks good," my father said, eyeing the plate. "What time did you get in last night?" Most people didn't hear my father's accent, but I did. Unlike Mom, whose forebears left Krakow a century earlier, Pop's parents immigrated when he was five.

"Sometime past midnight." I mounded scrambled egg on a piece of toast, folded it in half, devoured it in two bites.

"A long day, like the old days." Pop was always bringing up the old days, carrying the past as if it were a backpack. Between bites I brought Pop up to speed, only smoothing over my ill-conceived conversation with Anita and Spooner's subsequent anger.

"This sheriff wants your help," Pop said.

"Yes, he does. It's an unusual arrangement, but I'm going to play along, at least for now. And I have to say that Spooner was appreciative."

Pop grunted. "Watch the faces of those who bow low,

daughter. And how does your boss feel about this arrangement?" Leave it to Stan Gorsky to cut to the bone.

"Mr. Richt doesn't know about it, but if he did I'm certain he would not approve."

"You and rules, like oil and vinegar."

I'd heard this before, more times than I could count. When I signed up for the police academy Pop hadn't approved. He had not voiced direct opposition—he wasn't that kind of father—but his doubts were written on his face. Not without cause he questioned my ability to follow the rules and procedures that went with the uniform. Parents never saw their children as complete adults, but as adult versions of the children they had been. Maybe there was truth in this vision, but there was blindness as well.

"Am I making a mistake?"

Pop sipped his coffee, lifting the mug with both hands. "Why risk your job? Why help Spooner?"

"And why do you always answer a question with a question?"

"Because that's where the answers are. But I'd like an answer."

I wasn't sure I had one. This wasn't about facts or logic, but something else altogether. At last I said, "Sometimes I dream about bubble boy—you know who I mean?"

Pop nodded slowly. "The boy with the immune disorder who lived in a germ-free bubble for all his years. The bubble gave him life."

"No, it gave him existence, not life. I guess I'm doing this because I don't want to dream about bubble boy anymore. Those eggs okay?"

Pop glanced at the untouched food, as if in surprise. He scooped a smidge of egg onto his fork and nibbled. "Delicious, but I've had enough for now."

I swallowed my anger and cleared the dishes—sometimes Pop didn't even try. When I returned to the living room, my father's eyes had closed. His breaths were so shallow his chest barely moved. Slowly, inexorably, my father was drifting away from me and there was nothing I could do to stop it.

Before taking off, I checked my email. Both Oscar Wall and Spooner had replied to my query. Oscar confirmed that Mr. Jinks had been at his master's side when Mel Dick blasted through the Admiral Street guardhouse, in a hurry to meet his death. The sheriff wrote, "Yesterday the Dick house was quiet as a tomb. There was no dog. Is this important?"

It might be, Sheriff, but only time would tell.

I emailed my guards, asking that they keep their eyes peeled for Mel's lost dog. I risked appearing foolish, but it was a risk I had to take.

I had to find Jinks, who'd very likely witnessed his master's murder.

A SUMMONS AWAITED me at the office: "Chief," Jud Richt's smarmy voice oozed from the phone, "I need to see you in my office at the Mansion ASAP."

I'd have to take the Vic as the large redbrick building that was home to Richt and the other Mystic Cove suits sat on the other side of Mystic Cove. It was officially named the Governor's Mansion, circa 1801 according to Richt's pseudo-history, but people in my circle called it the Outhouse, for obvious reasons.

Twenty minutes later the Barbie-doll receptionist herded me into Jud Richt's office. As I followed it struck me that Richt's receptionist was a ringer for one of those *Real Housewives* on TV, who all looked like one another: wavy blond hair, big breasts, big lips and small noses.

"Sit," Richt ordered, ensconced behind the huge desk.

I sat, a good dog for now, but I had teeth. As the minutes passed, my hopes for a quick reaming faded. Richt stared at his monitor, occasionally plunking a key or moving his mouse. My eyes traveled around the bright, expansive office. Everything about it spooked me, which was probably the point. Not for the first time I reflected that Richt had to be obsessed with big cats. Pictures of lions lazing in the savannah and jaguars bolting through the rainforest stared from the arctic-white walls while a menagerie of feline predators stalked his shelves and desk top.

A slow groan of leather as Richt shifted in his chair. "I thought I made my position clear yesterday, Addie."

"You did." I tried to meet his gaze but my eyes traveled instead to the ebony panther crouched on his desk. It was a primitive piece, crudely carved, which enhanced its brutality.

"Can you explain your bizarre interrogation of Ms. Rhodes?"

The harridan had complained to Richt after all. I must have blanched for Richt smiled. He always smiled when he drew blood.

"I'm also curious about your meeting with Spooner."

"I was the one who found Mr. Dick's body," I said. "The sheriff had some follow-up questions for me. How does that concern you?"

Richt's grin widened. "You're not here to ask questions, but to answer them. Does the sheriff have a suspect in mind?"

"He didn't say and I didn't ask." I looked Richt in the eye. "I was there to answer the sheriff's questions."

Richt's hands slapped the desktop. "I know you're investigating Dick's murder. You even tried to get your guards to act as your confederates!"

I managed not to flinch, but could not speak. Richt wasn't bluffing. One of my guards had ratted me out. Was it Billy? He'd sell his soul for a beer. Or maybe Richt had put the squeeze on naïve Jesse.

"I'm sorry it's come to this, Addie." Richt wagged his head like a disappointed headmaster.

"But…" I began, then stopped. Nothing I said or did could alter my fate.

"I warned you not to get involved, and yet you…" The office phone buzzed. Richt glared at it, as if willing it to silence, but it buzzed again.

"Lisa, I told you I didn't want to be interrupted and…"

Richt glanced at me, then swiveled his chair so his back was to me. The rest of the conversation was brief and all on the Barbie's side. When Richt disconnected he was different. The mask was back in place, but something new bubbled beneath the smooth façade.

"I'm sorry," he said, "but something's come up. We'll take this up some other time."

I wasn't sure if it was a full pardon or a temporary stay of execution, but I knew a break when I saw one. I sprinted for the elevator, in full flight mode. When the elevator doors split open, a stocky gray-haired man in a bowtie spilled out, nearly knocking me down. I was going to make a smartass comment—"Hey, I'm walking here!"—but I got a good whiff of boozy breath so I kept my mouth shut. Men in bowties were troublesome jerks; add alcohol to the equation and you've got a recipe for disaster.

But disturbing thoughts of bowties and booze vanished when the Outhouse receded in my rearview mirror. All I could think was how much happier I would be if I never had to return to this blasted place.

As I PARKED the Vic at the Admiral Street guardhouse, Jesse Potts stuck his head out the window. "I saw the BOLO for Mr. Jinks, but I ain't seen hide nor hair of him."

Nobody else had either. The only reply I'd received so far was a smartass email from Oscar that suggested the corpulent pug might have wound up as gator bait or a coyote snack.

"I just thought I'd have a look around for myself," I told Jesse. "Say, isn't this your day off?"

"I'm covering for Billy. He didn't feel too good this morning."

"I bet he didn't."

An hour later I had walked the length of Admiral Street several times. I sensed that my presence had created a quiet agitation within the shuttered McMansions. Faces peeked from window corners, and curtains twitched, but most stayed inside. Violent death had touched them and for most, fear trumped curiosity, though a few brave souls ventured outside, ostensibly to place letters in mailboxes or pick up a few stray twigs but really wanting to know what I was up to. I explained about Jinks, but no one had seen the old pug. To a person they promised to look, but I knew what their promises were worth.

I returned to the Dick house, standing in the shadow of the huge American flag. A shadow moved in the left dormer window. I shaded my eyes against the bright morning light, but when I looked again the shadow was gone. Seconds later the front door opened. Anita Dick beckoned me.

"What do you want?" Anita's voice was soft and indistinct, but there was a wariness behind the lidded eyes. I was halfway through explaining my doggy mission when she cut me off. "There's no need for you to search for the dog."

"It's no trouble, Mrs. Dick. I've already notified my guards to look for him."

"There's no need," Anita Dick repeated.

The door was closing; I stuck my foot in it. "I'll let you know if we locate your dog."

"Don't bother. If you find it, take...take it to the pound."

"But Mr. Jinks is an old fellow. Animal Control would have a hard time adopting him out and if they don't find a home for him..."

A wary smile and she said, "I know what they'll do."

After that I broke off my search. Driving to my office, I wondered if I had misjudged Anita. Yesterday I had seen her as a weak victim, but this morning she was a pitiless woman who would destroy an innocent dog. I had fallen prey to the either/or trap. People were not one thing or the other, but many things. A person could be both a victim and perpetrator. In fact, the two went hand in glove.

At the office I hit the phones. Anita Dick's heartless suggestion sparked an idea, something that should have occurred to me earlier. I called Animal Control to see if they'd picked up any morbidly obese male pugs. They hadn't but promised to contact me if any turned up. Next I called Sheila Green. She was working tonight, but agreed to meet me before her shift. She suggested a bar just outside Mystic Cove. I knew the place, and we agreed to meet at three.

"I APPRECIATE THIS," I said.

"Anything I can do to help." Sheila Green ran both hands through masses of thick red hair. She'd started early, an empty shot glass in front of her. We were at Fisherman's Pub, a favorite hangout of Mystic Cove employees because of its proximity to Founder's Centre. At night it was fairly busy but this afternoon she and I were the only patrons. The bartender slumped on a stool, watching *Sports Bloopers* with the glazed eyes of an addict.

I ordered coffee and another drink for Sheila, which turned out to be peppermint schnapps and a diet cola chaser.

"I'm not sure where to begin," Sheila said, eyeballing my notepad and pen.

"Be thorough. I want to see that night through your eyes."

Sheila thought about that for a long minute. Although she was in her twenties, I could see the older woman she would become. She disposed of the schnapps in one gulp, followed by a sip of soda. "The rain had cleared by the time I started my shift. It was the first cool day of the season, so I hoped for a good night. You know the cool weather brings 'em out."

Yes, it did, like worms after a storm. Mystic Covians and locals alike had wakened from their summer stupor, venturing from the air-conditioning to soak up the plastic ambience of Founder's Centre. I didn't get it. I'd rather be throwing back beers in an honest dive.

"As usual José's ass was glued to a barstool and his mouth to a scotch. He's not a bad guy and he used to be a decent boss. Some nights after closing we used to have a couple of beers, his treat, but not anymore. Do you know why he switched to scotch?" Sheila's voice was indignant, even angry.

"No idea."

"Some idiot told him that scotch doesn't give you a hangover, that it's purer or something, so he trades his rum for scotch. But from the look of him in the mornings, he was told wrong."

"When did Mel and Anita arrive?"

Sheila absently twirled the straw in her glass of soda. "It was around four, along with the other happy-hour regulars."

"So the Dicks were happy-hour regulars."

"Just him, not her. Used to be Mel would come with his friends, but lately it's just him by his lonesome."

"José mentioned that Mel's old friends were also there that night."

"The usual suspects." Sheila smirked, then frowned. "Fairley Sable was there around five, and Gigi a few minutes after her. I'm not sure when the Rands showed up."

"Why is that?" By now, I knew I'd struck gold with Sheila—as close to a competent, objective witness as I was likely to find.

"It was close to six when Marco groused that the deuce in the back needed refills—that's when I saw Mr. and Mrs. Rand for the first time. They must have ordered their first round from the bar and then sat themselves on the patio." Sheila shook her head and the red hair trembled. "People aren't supposed to do that, but they do."

I waved for a time-out. "You speak Spanish?" A headshake. "When I tried to interview Marco all I got was, '*No hablo ingles.*'"

Sheila's mouth dropped a mile and her face crinkled. "Marco played you. He speaks English real good, just like me, but when he doesn't want to talk with somebody he pulls that 'Me not speaka English' crap. He does it to customers all the time. He got you but good."

While Sheila was laughing her ass off, I got an idea. I was still having trouble visualizing the scene at the G and G so I turned to a fresh page in my notepad. I drew a big circle in the middle and wrote DICKS inside of it.

"The Dicks are here." I pointed to the circle. "Show me where the others sat in relation to them."

Sheila wiped her eyes with a napkin and studied my artwork. "No problem." A few quick scribbles and she pushed the paper back.

I almost laughed. If I connected the three points I'd have a nearly perfect equilateral triangle. As usual Mel had commandeered the best table for himself. He and Anita would have had a prime view of the glorified retention pond called Mystic Bay. His former friends sat to his back, not a great view of the bay, but an excellent view of Mel Dick.

"Things started percolating when Gigi Tajani made her grand entrance. She ordered a margarita and when I got back with it, she was at the Dicks' round-top, right next to lover boy."

"The old lady has balls."

"Tell me about it. Gigi was laughing and patting Mel's hand, chattering like a magpie. It was 'Oh, Mel, how are the margaritas tonight?' or 'Mel, are you going in costume to Harvest Fest?'"

"You heard her?"

"Gigi always talks real loud, like she's on stage or something, you know? But loud as she was, Mr. Dick ignored her. It was weird."

"What do you mean?"

Sheila slurped her cola dry. "It was almost as if he didn't know Gigi was there. Maybe he did it on purpose so she would leave—and it worked, she skedaddled back to Fairley pretty quick—but I don't think it was on purpose."

"Why not?"

Sheila put her elbows on the table and cradled her chin in her hands. "Mr. Dick was a big mouth. He wasn't scared of telling people what he thought of them, but that night he was all inside himself. Before José got him riled, Mr. Dick just sat there drinking and thinking and drinking some more, like he had a really bad problem that needed fixing. I don't know how to explain it any better."

"Was Mel drunk?" I imagined the old man tossing back drinks, marinating in his foul juices. Perhaps the mysterious cognitive decline my guards had noted in Mel was alcohol fueled.

"Oh, no, he only had two margaritas. When I say drinking, I mean water. I lost count of the times I filled his water pitcher, and it wasn't even hot out."

"Was this excessive thirst a recent thing?"

"Yeah, now that you mention it, it is." Sheila picked out a cube of ice from her glass and started crunching.

What caused Mel's greedy thirst? It could be diabetes or drugs, both legal and illegal. I had no idea what, if any, medications he was taking, but a lot of prescription drugs were notorious for causing dry mouth—Pop knew about that. Water, water, everywhere, nor any drop to drink—not quite Mel's situation but close enough.

"You said Mel didn't respond to Gigi. What about Anita?"

Sheila made a disgusted sound. "That mouse didn't squeak, but I could tell Anita was listening to every word Gigi was dropping, not like Mel. If it was me, I would have shut the old biddy up!"

"So you knew about Gigi and Mel's affair?"

Sheila shrugged. "They didn't make a secret of it."

"Did Anita know?"

"She had to have known about it. Like I said, Mel and Gigi didn't bother to hide it. I used to see them kissing on Long Pier all the time."

I quickly blocked out the unwanted image. "You said you used to see them kissing, does that mean the affair was over?"

"Sure looked like it, but who knows? The thing is, for

months Mel and Gigi flaunted their little love affair all over Mystic Cove—Mel didn't even care about his wife enough to be discreet, and Mrs. Dick just takes it and takes it. She's a woman who liked to suffer." Sheila wasn't as objective as I'd thought—she'd obviously taken a dislike to Anita Dick.

But then Sheila was young and the young were merciless. She had not yet learned that it was dangerous to try to gauge the truth of a marriage, which created its own particular truth. We were all on the outside looking in. Even so, Sheila's description fit with the Anita Dick I had met in Fairley Sable's backyard yesterday: a ventriloquist's dummy, minus the ventriloquist. But even the gentlest of souls had a limit. Had Mel finally pushed Anita too far?

I gestured to the bartender for a warm-up on my coffee and got Sheila another diet coke. All that ice eating was getting on my nerves.

"Did Alan or Tally Rand talk to Mel?" I asked. Sheila shook her head. "Fairley?" Another head shake. "Strange that Fairley didn't say hello to her good friend Anita."

"I didn't know they were good friends." Seeing my puzzled expression Sheila added, "But like I said, Anita didn't get out much."

I moved to another line of inquiry. "How did Fairley and Mel get along in general?"

"All right," Sheila said. "They used to come in for lunch or drinks and yap about that stupid newspaper."

"Fairley works at the *Commentator?*"

"Yeah, the way those two talked about it, you'd think it was a big-deal newspaper like the…the…" Sheila stammered, searching for an appropriate comparison.

"*New York Times?*" I offered.

"I guess." Sheila glanced at her watch and frowned. Not much time left.

"Let's fast-forward to the confrontation between José and Mel."

"I told José to let sleeping dogs lie, but he wouldn't listen—if men would listen to women, it'd be a better world. I was waiting at the bar for my drink order when it went down, so I saw it pretty good." Sheila eyes glistened. "After José had put down the check, Mel threw it back at him. Then Mel got to his feet, looking like he was going to punch José's lights out—like this." Sheila fell into a pretty tight boxing stance.

"Play nice, ladies," the bartender called from behind the bar.

Sheila gave him the finger. "It was sad, Addie. Everybody laughing and pointing. Just a big joke until Mr. Dick turned on his friends. That's when everybody got scared."

"Tell me about that," I said.

"It looked like Mel was gonna hit José until Gigi yelled for Mel in that big voice of hers. Mel looked at her like she was some kind of snake. Then he did the same to the others, glaring at them like they were snakes. He said he knew they'd been plotting against him. When he was done, Mr. Dick grabbed Mr. Jinks and ran away." Sheila's face screwed up. "Only…only he didn't really run. It was more like he hobbled away. That's when I called security."

"Describe Mel's affect."

"Huh?"

"What was his mood? His emotional state?" I already had a pretty good idea, but I needed every nugget out of this witness.

"That's easy—Mel Dick was scared out of his mind."

Oscar had smelled the same fear on Dick. "What did Mel's friends do then?"

"Everything was so crazy with the police and everything, I didn't see, but I guess they got the hell out of there. But I gotta go. It's already past four."

After she'd gone, I coaxed more coffee from the bartender and reviewed my notes. I now had a clearer picture of the events at the G and G, but it was like viewing the last act of a play without knowing what had come before. In murder, as in life, what's past is prologue. Something had driven these friends apart. Had that something also driven one of them to murder?

The obvious answer was that Gigi and Mel's reckless liaison had split the group, but I wasn't so sure. I had no idea how Alan and Tally Rand viewed the pathetic affair but Fairley Sable had certainly taken it in stride. And despite casting herself as Anita's good friend, Fairley Sable had no scruples in remaining on friendly terms with Gigi. Sheila, who was as close to an objective observer in this hot mess, believed the affair was in the past, an interpretation also encouraged by Mel Dick's harsh final words to his mistress: *Et tu,* Gigi?

But if the affair had ended, why had Anita chosen that particular time to confront her husband about his infidelity, especially given her penchant for burying her head in the sand.

But then the betrayed did not act rationally.

Mel's mental deterioration further complicated matters. Over the last weeks of his life Dick had swung between fearful paranoia and grandiosity. On the night of his murder Sheila and Oscar saw a frightened man, a man running for his life. But perhaps Mel had run from phantom demons, and the murderer he spoke of on Spooner's voice mail existed only in his diseased imagination. Dizzy with speculation, I slapped the notepad shut and headed back to the Cove. I was on Cove Road when I got the call.

"I've got the preliminary autopsy report," Spooner

crowed. "The bullet Blanding dug out of Dick's head was clean, and ballistics identified it as coming from a Smith and Wesson thirty-eight, a match to the gun registered to Mel Dick. I'm on my way to Admiral Street, search warrant in hand."

Things had gone from bad to worse for Anita Dick.

# EIGHT

*And Dog Will Have its Day*

USUALLY I PARKED the Crown Vic in the enclosed garage—
the Vic was Pop's pride and joy—but the parking lot next
to the Financial Building was nearly empty, not a Lexus
or Escalade in sight. Was it a holiday for the suits? Then
I remembered that the renovations of the upper floors had
begun today. During construction the financial advisors
had relocated to temporary quarters.

I punched the code to the rear entrance and hurried
for the stairwell in the back. Mystic Cove's armada of
golf carts sat in neat rows. Usually the vehicles evoked
childish memories of kiddie rides at Gwynn Oak Park,
but now they seemed almost sinister. I was hurrying to
the stairs when I heard something moving, coming from
somewhere in the nest of carts.

"Who's there?" Old instincts died hard, if at all—my
hand reached for the Glock that was gathering dust in my
closet. "I know you're there!"

A figure in Mystic Cove khaki stepped from the shadows. "Addie?"

"Jesus, Tyler, you scared the crap out of me!"

"Sorry, I was…uh…waiting for you. Got a minute?"

"Sure." I started for the stairs, but Tyler hung back.

"Thing is, I only got a couple minutes before I have
to relieve Oscar."

"Whatever—let's at least get out of the garage."

At the stairwell I punched another code. I sat on the bottom rung of the stairwell and signaled for Tyler to begin.

"It…it happened a couple weeks ago at the Cove Creamery." Tyler kept shifting his weight, like he had to pee or something. His face was unreadable in the muted light, but I supposed my little display of temper had put him ill at ease. Had Tyler grown a sensitive side since our breakup?

"Chocolate raspberry still your favorite?" I asked with a little laugh.

Tyler's shoulders unhunched and he sat next to me.

"Always and forever." He nudged my shoulder with his. "Thelma was scooping my cone when Mel sauntered inside. He had the dog in one arm and a drink in the other, neither of which was allowed inside the shop. Most people in Mystic Cove would have let Mel Dick slide, but not Thelma. You know Thelma?"

"I think so." Actually I was pretty sure I knew this hard-boiled Thelma, though not by name.

"Thelma told Mel that he needed to leave the drink and the dog outside. They argued a little bit, but old Mel blinked first. He was on his way outside when he bumped into Alan and Tally Rand, who were just coming in." Tyler slapped his knee. "You should have seen it. The two old guys sized each other up, sniffing around like a couple of pit bulls."

I clenched Tyler's arm. "You thought there was a potential for physical violence?"

"At the time I didn't think so, but now, I'm not so sure. What I do know is that something bad passed between Mel and Alan Rand."

"What happened next?"

"Rand backed down first."

"No surprise there."

"No, but he did get kinda rough with his wife."

"Really."

"He practically pushed Tally outside."

I was shocked. Alan Rand had always treated his wife with extreme consideration. "What did Mel do?"

"Just watched them go."

"When did this happen?"

"Couple weeks ago, more or less."

Back in my office I paced. More than anything I wanted to drive to Admiral Street to see how Spooner's search was progressing, but he'd made it clear he didn't want my presence. And why would he? I was an adjunct to the investigation, an optional accessory that might or might not be of use. I needed to accept that and stop thinking—and acting—as if I were the primary.

At five o'clock I didn't want to go home. I was too juiced. I called the Cove Creamery.

"This is Thelma Sky and who is this?"

My heart warmed at the nasal voice deepened by years of cigarette smoke and too many hard knocks. I identified myself and asked if I could drop by the Creamery for a few words.

"Sure thing," the old broad said, "I'll put on a fresh pot of joe for us—still cream and no sugar?"

So she did remember me.

We'd met shortly after I'd started at Mystic Cove. I'd wandered into the Cove Creamery for an afternoon coffee, but first needed the bathroom. I asked the tall wiry lady behind the counter where the bathroom was. Her jaw dropped a mile and a smile cracked the rutted face.

"The baffroom is down the hall and to the left, hon."

It was my turn to smile. "By any chance, are you from Balamer?" I asked, though I had my answer.

After that whenever I worked Founder's Centre, I stopped in the Creamery for a coffee. Since my promotion to chief I hadn't seen my old friend. Strange that we had never exchanged names, but then we hadn't needed them. To me she was the Arundal Lady, having confided that her first job had been at the Arundal Ice Cream Shop on Greenmount Avenue. "And here I am fifty years later still scooping ice cream." In between she had tended bar and waited tables and done what she had to, to keep bread on the table and the shadows off the door, but the end of life had circled back to the beginning. Whether that was cruel or kind, I could not say.

Fifteen minutes later I was shaking Thelma Sky's bony hand. Attached to the hand was an equally bony body. Her dyed brown hair was tightly pinned at the back, topped by a steely bouffant worthy of a Myrmidon or an honest-to-goodness Baltimore hon. Oh, there was no false softness about Thelma Sky and I loved her for it.

"Take a seat and I'll get our coffees." Thelma gestured at the small round table near the rear of the empty shop.

Settling into her chair, Thelma sighed with pleasure. "That feels good. If I could have a cigarette, this would be perfect."

"I appreciate this," I said.

"We Baltimorons gotta stick together. So what's shaking?"

"I need information about an incident that happened at the Creamery a few weeks ago." I related the particulars.

"Yeah, I remember—I thought Mel and Alan Rand were gonna have at it right inside the Creamery. Mel was always pissing people off, but he wasn't as bad as people thought. The mistake people made was in kowtowing to him."

"Not you."

"Nah, I never saw the point in kissing ass, even when I was young, and now that I'm old, there's even less point." She sipped her coffee. "Mel was a regular customer. Every other day he came in for his vanilla single-dip cone, and we'd dance our dance."

I smiled ruefully. "I wouldn't take Mel Dick for much of a dancer."

"We're all dancers, Addie." Thelma looked outside. It was twilight and the street was emptying of people. "Anyhow, on that day he came inside with Jinks and his jug of tea, like usual. I told him no service till he lost the dog and the outside drink. Also like usual. We squabbled back-and-forth until he backed down. So the dance was just about done and Mr. Dick was headed for the door when the Rands came in. When Alan saw Mel, he got a look like he had just crapped his pants. There was a Mexican standoff for a couple of seconds and then Rand ran off, dragging Tally along for the ride." She sipped her coffee. "That's what I like about this business. There's always something to see, if you're watching for it."

"What did Mel do?"

"Funny thing, I saw Mel's shoulders shaking and for a second I thought, oh geez, he's crying! Only he wasn't crying. He was laughing his ass off. Rand's discomfort amused him, which wasn't very nice." Thelma met my gaze. "Mel Dick wasn't as bad as people thought, but he was bad enough."

"Bad enough for someone to murder?"

Thelma's long face did a slow nod. "Now, the interesting part is what happened next. You see, Mel always had a couple of irons in the fire. I just figured Rand got burned and after a while things would return to normal between him and Mel, but that's not what happened."

I leaned close.

"The next time Mel came in for his vanilla cone, he was all right, but after that…he was different. Poor Mel." A shadow flickered over the lined face. I had seen shock and horror over Mel Dick's murder but not yet sorrow. Not until now.

"Different how?"

"Mel was never one to hide his light under a bushel but now he was the big butter-and-egg man. He owned the bragging rights in Mystic Cove."

"What did he brag about?"

"He didn't say exactly, which was a little unusual for him."

"Unusual?"

"Yeah, he'd always say things like, 'Did you read my letter to the editor?' or 'Last Tuesday I beat Rand in handball.' But now he said, 'Come November I'll be able to write my ticket.' That mean anything to you? Addie?"

The balls fell into their respective pockets. When Mel bragged to Jesse and the others that in a couple of weeks he would be a big shot, he was referring to the first of November when a fresh edition of the *Cove Commentator* was due. But what had he planned for November's *Commentator?* An announcement of some kind? A ball-busting editorial? Or was he working on a shocking exposé, the story that would finally bring him the fame that was his due?

"Tell me more about the changes in Mel."

"His memory was shot. Me and him didn't do our dance anymore 'cause he couldn't remember the steps. The last time he came in and ordered his cone, I handed it to him and he stared at it like it was crap on a stick. Then he turned those big peepers on me. I gotta say, for the first time in a long while I was scared."

"Scared of Mel?"

"Kind of, but mostly I was scared for him. He looked like he was doped up or something. And he was just as scared as me, maybe even more scared."

"Of what?" I asked in frustration.

"I don't know, Addie—I wish I did."

"Makes two of us." If I knew the cause of Mel's consuming fear, I'd be that much closer to an answer. "So what did Mel do next?"

"He threw the cone I'd just dipped onto the floor and accused me of trying to poison him. I tried to reason with him, but it was no good."

"He was beyond reason," I said.

"You got that right!" Thelma said with a finger pop. "That was the last time me and him talked, though I seen him a few times after that, shambling along the sidewalk with Jinks or buzzing along in his cart."

"Can you pinpoint when Mel's symptoms first appeared?"

"Geez Louise, I don't know."

I shrugged. It was a long shot.

"Hey, don't give up so quick," Thelma yelled, squeezing my arm. She disappeared into a back room, reappearing moments later with a supersized wall calendar, A Year of Adorable Puppies. She flipped back to September—a Chihuahua in a teacup, ugh—but quickly returned to October, which featured a couple of long-eared basset hound pups oozing adorability. As her crooked finger ran over October's days, I noticed nearly every square was filled with Thelma's chicken scratch.

"Here it is," she said, her bright eyes holding mine. "Mel started acting squirrelly around the middle of October. And I know this because on the day when Mel and Rand tangled, I was out of choc-razz and your boyfriend had to settle for rocky road."

"I'm not following."

"I ran out of choc-razz on October seventh. See—I wrote a note so I'd remember to reorder." A red talon pointed to the corresponding block. "I didn't get my restock until the twelfth. So that gives me a range for the tiff between Mel and Alan Rand. Since he started acting weird a few days after the tiff with Rand, Mel must have gone bonkers sometime around…"

"The middle of October," I finished.

"Give or take a few days," Thelma added.

"You're a born detective, Thelma!"

Thelma shrugged off the compliment. "I just like to keep an eye out. In this business there's always something to see." She placed her calloused hand over mine, her bright brown eyes burning with intensity. "Just get to the bottom of this mess, Addie. Mel Dick was an ass, but we're all asses at least part of the time. So find the person who did this—for all our sakes."

"All our sakes?"

"You know as well as me that sometimes murder can become a habit."

I gave Thelma Sky my personal number and asked that she call me if she heard or saw anything interesting.

"You bet, Addie." Her gaze fell onto the dark street. "You know, Mystic Cove is a strange place. These people who live here, they act like they're going to go on forever. These old people think they're never going to die. Don't they know the truth? Don't they know they're winter people?"

I WAS HALFWAY home when I got a call.

"We got your perp, Chief, or rather Mrs. Santiago's got him."

Gooseflesh erupted on my arms. It was a disturbingly

gleeful Oscar Wall. It wasn't like Oscar to joke around, unless it was at someone else's expense.

"I got Mel Dick's dog here in the office, along with Mrs. Santiago, the lady who found him."

"Are you sure it's Mr. Jinks?"

"Oh, it's him all right. But listen, I'm off the clock and I need to get going, so…"

"Stay put, Oscar! I'll be there in five."

But Oscar didn't stay put. At headquarters I found a middle-aged brown-skinned woman standing outside my office door. One hand held a plastic Publix bag and the other a slack leash. At the end of the leash sat a morbidly obese pug. I took in the gray muzzle and coat, glassy bug eyes, lolling tongue. Definitely Mr. Jinks, but the past twenty-four hours had been cruel to the old dog. He whined piteously and shook like a drunk with the DTs.

"Mrs. Santiago?" The small woman nodded and I realized she was as frightened as the dog. I introduced myself and hustled her and the dog inside my office.

Mrs. Santiago's English was on par with my Spanish, and so I only put the whole story together later. Irma Santiago worked as a domestic for a family in the Cove. Yesterday on her way home she spotted Mr. Jinks in the gloaming, limping along the side of the road. An animal lover, she lured the dog into her car with a stale cheese doodle. She brought Jinks home, planning to return tomorrow with the dog and search for its owner.

And that was what Mrs. Santiago and Jinks had been doing when Oscar Wall found them, after responding to resident reports of a "strange dark woman" lurking in the area. Oscar took firm and immediate action, whisking woman and dog back to security headquarters.

I mimed for Mrs. Santiago to take a seat and was making a similar offer of coffee when Jinks's constant whining took on sudden vigor. I crouched and offered the distraught animal my open palm, assuring him that he was a good boy. The cries lessened in intensity. The pug lifted his knobby head and sniffed my hand.

"You like dog," Mrs. Santiago said, looking down on us like a beneficent deity. "The man no like, but you like. You take him now." Just then a series of smelly farts—like toots from a spastic horn—sputtered from the dog's rear.

"He do that all night," Mrs. Santiago moaned. "I no sleep."

What had he done all night? Whine? Fart? Both?

I asked Mrs. Santiago where she had found Mr. Jinks. At first I thought I had connected by the way she smiled and nodded, but when I finished she said, "You take him now. You take. You like."

I accepted the inevitable.

"I feed him, but tomorrow you more food." Mrs. Santiago pulled several cans of Alpo from the plastic grocery bag. "I wash last night. Very dirty." Her face scrunched up. "Stink bad. The leash mine, but you keep. *Que mas?* Oh, he wear little *bufanda* when I find…*cómo se dice*… coat…jacket?" She gestured at her neck, frowned and retrieved a zipper baggie from the bag. Inside the baggie was a crush of faded blue fabric. I had partially unzipped the bag when Mrs. Santiago waved a finger. "No, no, smell bad—I no wash. Smell bad, like him."

I caught a foul whiff and lost interest in the *bufanda* or jacket or whatever. I zipped the bag and shoved it into a desk drawer.

"What about the collar, Mrs. Santiago? Is that yours?" I peered at the red leather collar that was curiously bereft of tags. Surely Mel Dick would have his beloved Mr. Jinks properly licensed and tagged.

"Yes, mine. Noche's old collar. This one no collar,

no tag. Only the *bufanda*. I go. I hope this dog bring good thing."

"As do I, Mrs. Santiago."

Mr. Jinks raised his gray face, snuffled loudly, and ripped a good one. Before hurrying away, Mrs. Santiago cast a long, pitying look in our direction.

JINKS AND POP got along surprisingly well. I had picked up a bag of chow on the way home and Pop insisted on feeding Mr. Jinks so that the elderly dog would feel at home. After eating, the old pug trotted over to Pop, circled three times, and curled into a tight little ball at the foot of Pop's recliner.

"It's good to have a dog around again," Pop said.

"I suppose," I said absently, wondering if Jinks was incontinent. I twisted the cap off my beer, poured a bit into a jelly glass and handed it to Pop, keeping the rest for myself. Pop had eaten a good bowlful of chicken soup and was now sharing a beer with me. A good day.

"We'll have to find other arrangements for Jinks next week though," I said.

"Why?" Pop asked.

"You start chemo next Monday."

My father wasn't new to the game—two earlier rounds of chemo had taught him what it did to the immune system. We could check with the doctor, but I didn't think he needed to be around a dog that might not even be potty trained. Pop had deflated like a pierced tire.

"Talk to me, Pop."

"I've canceled the chemotherapy. Enough is enough. I can't live and do the chemo. I had to choose. I choose to live."

"But without the chemo, you'll die." Somehow I managed to keep my voice level.

"That's unavoidable, for all of us," Pop said. "And remember our agreement."

I bit my tongue to keep the bitterness from spewing out. When I'd moved in I'd promised to accept Pop's treatment decisions. To the end, his life would be his own. But I loved my father. I wanted to shake him, ask him if his life meant so little that he would not fight for it. If he quit the chemo, the fight was over. But Pop knew this. Better than I.

"Are you sure?" A stupid question. A needless question. But a question I had to ask.

"Yes, Adelajda, it's time." He sipped his beer. Such a tiny sip, like a bird drinking from a puddle. "Don't be sad."

"It's hard." I hated that my voice broke. I liked to put on a tough front, especially to my father.

"Life is hard. Why should death be any different? Now, I want to hear about the investigation."

I told him everything and then some.

"A mess," he sighed. "Did the sheriff find the gun?"

"I don't know. Spooner hasn't gotten back to me. Though if I were a betting woman, I'd put money that he didn't find his thirty-eight."

Pop laughed and asked why.

"The sheriff would have called me if he'd found the murder weapon."

"Ah, you're psychic," Pop said.

"Nah, it's Psych 101, based on the fact that the sheriff is male and a cop. Spooner likes Anita Dick for the murder, and I don't. You better believe that if Bubba Spooner found the murder weapon in Anita's possession, he would have called by now, if only to crow that he'd been right. All men like to brag, Spooner more than most."

"You believe Anita Dick is innocent."

"I'm not arrogant enough to say that Anita is incapable of murder. On the contrary, I think the capacity to kill is in all of us."

"All of us? Even the saints?"

"Especially the saints, they're the fanatics," I said with a wicked grin. "But saints and sinners alike, we are a murderous species."

"We Poles know this well." Pop sipped another drop of beer. "So tell me why Mrs. Anita is innocent."

"First, she has an alibi, though it may be a little shaky. But I really, really have trouble with the method of Dick's murder. I saw the crater in Mel Dick's head. I smelled the gunpowder. I saw the soot, the circle of torn flesh. I cannot imagine that timid Anita Dick calmly aimed the muzzle of a gun at her husband's head and fired. That kind of killing takes exceptional coldness and viciousness, neither of which Anita Dick possesses."

"You know the woman well then."

"No, but I have to trust my instincts. If Anita committed this terrible act then she is not only a brutal murderer, but a consummate actress. That being said, I can't dismiss her as a suspect." I'd been down that road before, climbing the ladder of inference with disastrous results. "I just don't know enough yet. I'd love to get a look at that autopsy report."

My frustration provoked a rumble of laughter from Pop. "This sheriff may regret bringing you in on this case, Adelajda."

"What do you mean?"

"Like all police, the sheriff wants his murder solved, but you want something more. You want the truth."

"It's the same thing."

"Not quite. Not always. If Sheriff Spooner wanted easy answers, he's asked the wrong woman."

"I just want the truth, all of it," I said, getting a little hot. "Anything less than the whole truth is a lie."

"You've never accepted that most people, including many sheriffs, only want the truth that suits them. Remember your first homicide case, the pregnant girl with multiple gunshot wounds."

"Sabrina Edwards," I said. She had been all of sixteen years.

"Right—you had the murderer dead to rights, but you wouldn't let it go."

"The motive didn't fit. I wanted the whole story."

"Yes, and you pursued it until you had the answers, even though many people suffered because of your obsession."

"I strengthened the prosecution's case," I said. To his credit, Pop didn't call me out on my lie.

"All I'm saying is that you will have your truth, no matter the cost. So, if you want your autopsy results, go get them."

I drank off my beer in one gulp. "You know, I think I will."

I tried the sheriff's office line first, but it went to voice mail. Next I called his cell, which he answered on the first ring. As I surmised, the search at the Dick house had come up empty. Spooner was en route to his office and agreed to meet me there.

"Don't wait up for me, Pop. It's gonna be another late night." If the meeting with the sheriff didn't take too long, I planned a late-night visit to the Grub and Grog. Sheila Green had said Marco the busboy was working tonight. Come closing time I planned to be waiting for him in the parking lot. It was a long shot that he had much of anything for me, but the little prick had lied to me and I couldn't let that stand.

"Good hunting," Pop said, and something else as well, but I didn't hear the last, having already shut the door.

When I caught up with Bubba Spooner he was pissy. He wasn't a man who bore disappointment well and he was sorely disappointed. "Well, maybe I was wrong about Mrs. Dick, but she has such a sweet motive."

"Sometimes reality doesn't match up with our expectations." I brought Spooner up-to-date on what I had learned.

"Interesting," Spooner said, checking his wristwatch for the third time.

"Look, I know you're disappointed about Anita, but what about the girlfriend? Speculation is that Mel and Gigi recently broke up, probably at Mel's instigation. Did Gigi have an alibi?"

"Gigi told Berry that after leaving the restaurant, she went home and stayed there. The next-door neighbors noticed her return, but she could have snuck out later and shot Dick."

"And the Rands?"

"Same story, different characters. Mr. and Mrs. Rand went straight home after Mel's breakdown." Spooner shot another glance at his watch.

"Am I keeping you from something?"

"Dolores Rio asked to see me before I left for the night, something about Dick's autopsy." Spooner gestured at the blue binder in front of him. "I'm wondering what's keeping her."

"I thought Coroner Blanding performed Mel's autopsy."

"So he did." His tone told me to drop that line of questioning.

Several seconds ticked off and I said, "You know, we never had a chance to discuss the autopsy results."

"That's right. We haven't." Another look at his watch and he edged the blue binder toward me. "Tell you what, I'm going over to the morgue and see if I can find the deputy coroner. Entertain yourself till I get back."

"Take your time, Sheriff." My greedy hands were already reaching for the binder.

What do you know? Addie Gorsky had got herself an angel.

I had been at it awhile—Spooner had left not only the autopsy report but the entire murder book in my possession—when the sheriff buzzed my cell. It was already past ten.

"You may as well go on home." Spooner's voice was tired as dirt and tight as a cramped muscle, his day turned to crap. I asked what he wanted me to do with the package.

"Just put in the top desk drawer and close the door to my office. I'll lock up later."

I did as Spooner asked, but not right away.

Poor Bubba Spooner, I thought, as I sped to the Cove. I remembered the excitement in his voice when he'd called me earlier, just after he'd gotten his warrant. He'd been so certain he would find the murder weapon in Anita Dick's possession and that after that he would just play the table.

But the table had played him.

I could have told him, if he'd asked: only a fool praises the day before the sunset.

# NINE

*Blind as a Bat*

I PARKED IN the far corner of the Grub and Grog parking lot, hunched low in the driver's side of the Crown Vic. I had held my vigil for over an hour. The last person to exit had been Sheila Green, almost forty-five minutes earlier. I had expected Marco to be right behind her, but the minutes had stretched with no Marco.

By now the only cars left in the lot were Barracas's SUV; a couple of beaters, one of which I hoped belonged to Marco; and a silver Lexus parked in the handicapped space near the front entrance, gleaming dully beneath the penumbra of light of a black iron streetlamp. I was bothered that I couldn't account for the Lexus's presence. The customers were long gone, but perhaps its owner had imbibed too much and was unable to drive home. A reasonable theory, but it gave me no comfort.

I glanced up and down the empty street and felt a tingle crawl up and down my spine, a foraging spider. My instincts aroused, I saw menace in every dark, still corner of the night. And there were too many dark corners in Mystic Cove. On the drive in I had not passed a single car, nor seen a pedestrian. It was like being in a carnival haunted house after hours, when the real spooks came out. I'd give it ten more minutes, and if Marco didn't appear by then I would abort this fool's mission. The ten minutes were nearly done when José Barracas's angry shout cut through the night.

Two men spilled from the front door of the Grub and Grog. The first man, a tall, stoop-shouldered silhouette, hurried toward the Lexus, with José Barracas zigzagging at his heels, screaming incomprehensible obscenities. At the car door the thin man turned to face his pursuer, whether to implore or threaten, I do not know. Whatever the man hoped to achieve, it failed. The tall man's back was to me, but I saw José's angry face in the halo of light cast by the streetlamp. His face was a mask of rage, and his huge hands fisted mallets, ready to work. I had to act.

I opened the car door and yelled, "Security!"

José's head bobbled like a rag doll's—deaf, dumb and blind—but the stranger turned toward me. When I saw his face, illumined in the ghostly radiance, I gasped and stepped back into the shadows. The thin figure shrugged off the discombobulated José, fell inside the Lexus and sped away.

Wavering like a clump of pampas grass in the wind, José stared stupidly at the squealing car. His quarry escaped, José muttered a curse and shuffled inside the dark restaurant, too drunk or too angry to notice the woman in the shadows.

But Alan Rand had noticed, of that I was certain.

PULLING INTO MY parking space at the apartment, my heart did a triple somersault. Our apartment on the second floor blazed like a cathedral on Easter morning—every friggin' light was on! I took the stairs two at a time, imagining all sorts of horrors, but when I rushed inside all I found was Pop in his recliner, a pained expression on his face and a whining Mr. Jinks curled in his lap.

"He hasn't stopped crying since you left—not for one

second." On cue Jinks leaped to the floor and waddled to me, whimpering.

"You little bastard." I scooped up the circling dog and he stopped his racket. "Sorry, Pop."

"It's all right. I'll have plenty of time to sleep soon enough. Do we have any of that tea I like in the house?"

I checked. "We have chamomile and Earl Gray."

"Which is the one I like?"

"I don't know, Pop. You like them both as far as I know. How about chamomile? You don't need the caffeine this late anyway. I'll join you."

"You're having tea?" Pop said.

"I drink tea sometimes." I wasn't much of a tea drinker—such a tepid drink—but the night's chill had crept into my bones.

"How was your night?" Pop asked when I handed him his tea.

I told Pop about the drama I had witnessed outside the Grub and Grog.

"You must talk to this Alan Rand."

"I also need to talk with José again. Obviously he was less than forthcoming. He's a lot more involved than he let on."

"Did the autopsy clear anything up?"

"Mel Dick was in excellent health for a man of sixty-two years of age. The time of death was between ten and two o'clock on Tuesday morning, no surprise there. And there were no defensive wounds on the body."

"But there was a surprise in the report."

"Several," I said, taking a sip of tea. "Are you sure you want to hear this, Pop?"

"I can rest tomorrow. Tell me about the autopsy." Pop and I were alike that way—when it was a choice between what was good for us and what we wanted, desire almost always won the day.

Wordlessly I loped to the side table by the front door, scooped up the stack of papers, and dumped the packet in Pop's lap. I didn't answer the question in his eyes but waited for him to examine the papers. When he realized what he held in his hands, his face drained of whatever color it had.

"What have you done?" Pop waved the pilfered copy of Mel Dick's autopsy report under my nose. "Did the sheriff give this to you?"

"Not exactly."

"Never mind, I don't want to hear," Pop said, waving his hands. "Why do you always break the rules?"

"It's not that bad, Pop. Spooner gave me access to the report and I only copied a couple of pertinent pages. No big deal."

"I can't believe you were a police. I can't believe it."

"So do you want to talk about the case or not?"

Pop slid on his reading glasses.

I dumped my tea down the sink and grabbed a cold one from the fridge. "Mel Dick was shot twice. Gunshot wound A is the close-range penetrating gunshot wound to the right temple, as evidenced by the zone of soot around the entrance wound."

"The wound you saw," Pop said.

"Exactly. The bullet entered the right temple, turned left, went backward, and then down, lodging in the left ear canal," I said, my hands providing directions.

"A grievous wound."

"A mortal wound." I took a deep pull from my bottle. "Gunshot wound B entered the anterior left upper extremity and exited posteriorly, no fouling or stippling."

"Gunshot B was fired from some distance then."

"Blanding estimated the shooter was five feet from his target, give or take, but the resultant wound was relatively benign—no bone fractures, minimal hemorrhaging along the bullet's track—relatively minor damage." For reasons I couldn't articulate, gunshot wound B troubled me more than the fatal head wound.

"What they used to call a flesh wound in the old westerns," Pop said with a little laugh. Then he frowned. "But the wound would have bled. You said there was very little blood."

"That's right—I saw no blood other than the small amount from the head trauma."

"Was the bullet from gunshot B found?"

"It wasn't recovered from the body, nor were any casings or bullets found at the scene." I took another sip of beer. Now we were getting to the tricky part. "Blanding classified both wounds as perimortem."

"So both wounds occurred at or near the time of death," Pop said, a little puzzled at my intensity.

"Right, but Blanding wouldn't or couldn't determine the sequence of infliction, though he does conclude that both shots were fired in quick succession. But I don't see how that's possible."

When Pop asked why not, I dragged two dining room chairs into the living room and placed them side by side.

"Imagine these chairs are Mel Dick's golf cart. Mel sat here in the driver's seat when he was shot—hey, what are you doing?" I hurried to Pop, who was struggling out of the recliner.

"Let's do this properly," Pop said. "I'll be Mel Dick and you act out the killer's part." While Pop arranged his bones into the chair representing the driver's side, I scrounged for a suitable stand-in for the gun, settling for the TV remote.

"If Blanding is right about the two shots being fired in quick succession, there are two possibilities—either gunshot A came first or gunshot B."

"Of course, of course," Pop groused. "You don't need to state the obvious."

"I don't know about that. Nowadays the obvious is overlooked all the time. We'll act out both options."

Pop made a twirling his fingers in a hurry-up gesture.

"The killer approaches, gun in hand." I crept to the passenger's side of the cart.

"What does Mel do?" Pop asked.

"Nothing." Except die, I added silently. "Since Blanding found no evidence of defensive posturing on Mel's body, he was either unaware of the killer's approach or he knew his killer and didn't fear him."

"Murder between friends," Pop said softly. "So, fire away."

From the passenger's side I placed the remote inches from Pop's temple. "Bang," I said. Pop's head drooped to his left, anticipating the thrust of the gunshot. "That was gunshot A, the mortal wound. Now comes gunshot B and here's the rub. Gunshot B is fired from a distance of around five feet and hits the outer aspect of Mel's upper left arm."

"Of course," Pop said excitedly, "it would be difficult for the killer to make this shot from the passenger's side."

"It would have been impossible—watch." I backed away and positioned myself on the driver's side, about five feet away from my target. "Gunshot B would have had to come from this direction and around this distance." This time I pointed the remote at Pop's right arm.

"Wait, I have it," Pop said. "As the killer made his getaway Mel stirred. Realizing the job was not finished, the murderer returned and fired again."

"I doubt if Mel stirred after such a terrible wound."

"A moan then," Pop countered.

I had to give him a moan. "But that doesn't change anything."

"Of course it does. The killer was nervous and missed his shot."

"First of all, this isn't a nervous killer," I said. "Remember he had just fired a clean shot directly into Mel's brain. If he returned to finish Mel off, he would have taken his time and gotten off a good shot, the coup de grâce. Do you see my problem, Pop? It's almost as if there are two different shooters. One bold and the other tentative."

"Let's reverse the order of the gunshots then," Pop said. "The killer shoots, but the first shot goes awry, hitting Mel's arm. He comes closer and fires again, this time in the temple."

"Let's try it." I went through the motions, more quickly this time. Standing on the driver's side I extended my arm and fired the remote. "Bang-bang—Mel's shot in the arm."

Pop grabbed his left arm and groaned softly.

"Now for some inexplicable reason the killer moves to the passenger's side to fire his second shot."

"Maybe Mel was trying to escape that way," Pop offered.

"No forensic evidence of that." I placed the remote into position, inches from Pop's right temple. "Sit still— that's what Mel did. After being shot in the arm, he just sat there like a dummy while somebody plugged a bullet in his brain." For a moment I saw Mel's dead eyes staring out of my father's face.

"Bang-bang, and now you're dead!" Pop pushed the remote away. His hand was shaking. "This second scenario is even more unlikely," he whispered.

"It's impossible. All I can figure is that night the killer

had an accomplice or the gunshots weren't fired in quick succession."

"Is it certain that Birnam Wood was the murder scene?"

"Posterior livor mortis proves that Mel died sitting in his golf cart. But in my mind the coroner's history of incompetence casts doubt on all his findings. Maybe that's why it doesn't fit. Maybe that's why it's hot and cold."

"What was that?"

"I've always thought of murders as either primarily either hot or cold. I mean, the prototypical crime of passion is white-hot—a husband shooting a faithless wife, or vice-versa—but if a husband hires a hit man to get rid of a straying wife, then the killing is very, very cold. Mel's murder has elements of both. It doesn't fit easily into either category. The killer's method was cold-blooded, but there was deep rage behind it."

"This murder is a strange business, Adelajda."

After getting Pop to bed I took Jinks for a quick walk. A light rain fell, but I barely noticed. I was deep in darkness with no way out. Once inside I poured a short bourbon to shake off the cold. Jinks hopped into my lap. I scratched under his neck and drank.

A strange business, Pop had said. Stranger than he knew. I hadn't told Pop about the personal effects found on Dick's body. Most of objects were commonplace: a gold wedding band, keys, leather wallet, cell phone—the indispensable but mundane accessories of modern life. But thrust in the pocket of Mel Dick's shorts had been a dog collar festooned with an assortment of tags. There was the required rabies tag, a vanity medal declaring the wearer to be the *World's Best Dog,* and a heart-shaped medal that read in part, *Mr. Jinks, property of Melvin Dick.*

Some inner demon had provoked Mel to remove Jinks's

collar. Before Mel's murderer could be brought to light, I
first had to unravel the mystery of Mel's madness.

EARLY NEXT MORNING I was halfway out the door when a
piteous cry sounded from behind. I wheeled to face an
outraged Mr. Jinks.

"Shhh, you're gonna wake Pop!" I petted and begged,
but the wily pug refused to quiet. Every time I made a
move to leave, ear-shattering cries followed me down the
hall. I knew the dog would keep it up and Pop would get
no rest. What could I do?

As I hooked his leash, I swear the bastard grinned.

Once at the office I set Jinks up in the corner with the
nice blanket I'd brought from home. But when I tried to
leave, I got a repeat performance, only this one was Os-
car-worthy.

If Richt discovered that I was keeping a hysterical pug
in security headquarters, I'd be toast. I had no time to
make other arrangements so I wrapped Jinks in the blanket, dumped him into a wicker basket I'd found in the
storage closet, and drove to the G and G.

I didn't know about Jinks's training, but mine was
going quite well.

When we arrived at the Grub and Grog, I was relieved
when a hungover José Barracas finally answered the bell.
He was almost catatonic, sweating in yesterday's clothes.
Which was just as I wanted him. With the cobwebs from
last night's debauch still intact, I figured José would be
easy pickings.

I told José to freshen up while I made coffee. He
emerged several minutes later, his face and head sopping
wet and in a fresh polo shirt. Without a word he slumped
into a booth, cradling his head in his hands. When I set the
mug of coffee in front of him, he turned a queasy green.

"I...my stomach." José grimaced and clutched his stomach. "I don't know..."

"Try to drink the coffee. You'll feel better, but first take these." I shook out a couple of ibuprofen.

Barracas dry-swallowed the tablets, ignoring the glass of water I had brought.

"Where you keep the chili?"

"Chili?" José croaked.

"You'll thank me later—so where's the chili?"

I was nuking the chili in the microwave when I heard a soft cry in the dining room, followed by an angry yelp. I found José staring into the wicker basket, an ineffable expression of horror written on his pale face.

"I saw it move! It moved." José's bugged eyes met mine.

I pulled Jinks out of his makeshift carrier. "Don't be silly—it's only Jinks."

José licked his chapped lips. "But how? Why?" From the kitchen the microwave beeped.

"Chill out," I ordered, putting Jinks on the floor. "You have more important things to worry about."

I returned with the steaming bowl and a bottle of hot sauce. José's jaw dropped as I doused the chili with the sauce and slid the bowl over to him. "Eat as much of this as you can. It'll make you feel better."

"Why are you torturing me?"

"Just try a few spoonfuls—the hot spices will speed up your metabolism and burn off the hangover." I'd had more than my share of rotten hangovers in my day and swore by my chili remedy. And I needed José weak, not incoherent.

Mumbling that at this point he'd try anything, José shoved in a spoonful of the fiery stuff. I let him eat and drink coffee for a couple of minutes while the dust cleared.

José pushed away the empty bowl. "I do feel a little better." He looked me in the eye for the first time that morning. "I guess now I get to learn why you're playing Florence Nightingale."

"I just had an interesting conversation with Alan Rand."

José started, muttered something under his awful breath, a toxic cauldron of booze, desperation, and fear. What foul secrets bubbled inside?

"I know about your meeting with him last night."

José wiped his forehead with a napkin and drank his coffee, spilling some on the clean white shirt. "Has…has he gone to the police?"

"Not yet." I kept my face impassive.

Cornered, José went on the attack. "Rand has no right to say what he did. I don't care if he is a lawyer, I'm… I'm gonna sue him for libel."

I think he meant slander, but I let it pass.

"You didn't level with me before, but I'm giving you a chance to clear things up now. I urge you to take advantage of it." I hoped the vague statement would draw him out.

Malice hardened his features and he hissed, "How can you help, Chief? Who do you think you are?"

"Nobody," I admitted, "but I have friends who are somebodies. If you don't want to talk to me, I'll call the sheriff and let him handle it." That was a threat I meant to keep.

"No," José said, all the fight knocked out of him. "I'll talk to you. I gotta talk to somebody so why not you? And I didn't lie to you before, Addie. I just didn't tell you everything."

"Let's start with last night."

"Funny thing," he said mournfully, "last night was one

of the busiest nights in months. All day long people wandered in for a drink or a bite, but what they really wanted was dirt on Dick's death. I never thought murder would be good for business. Gosh, people are rotten."

I didn't disagree.

"Alan Rand showed up right before closing. He said he needed to talk to me in private. I tried to put him off, but he insisted. I told him I'd talk to him after closing." José wiped his face with a napkin. "So after everybody cleared out, I got myself a scotch and asked Rand what was up." He looked at me, anger flashing in his eyes. "I gotta say the old prick didn't pull any punches. He came right out with it!"

"With what, José?"

"Rand looked me straight in the eye and said he knew I murdered Mel Dick! In my own restaurant he accused me of murder. 'I know you did it. You have motive, means and opportunity. It had to be you.' I gotta tell you, I saw red."

"I can understand why that pissed you off."

"Right! So I told Rand to scram, but the old man didn't budge. He said he's going to get a confession, even if he has to beat it out of me!" José's eyes bulged with disbelief. "What is it with these old guys lately, Addie? All of 'em wanting to fight me."

"You deny that you killed Mel then."

"Well, sure I deny it…" He stopped short, stared at me with new eyes. "I get it now. You think Rand is right, that I killed Mel! Well, I didn't—there's your friggin' denial!" He stabbed the table with his finger.

"I don't think any of those things," I lied. I had a hunch. If I was wrong, the interview was over, but if I was right… "I don't know about means or opportunity but, according to Rand, you have one heck of a motive, José. Like I said before, this is your chance to explain things. To tell your side."

"All right," José said. "I'll come clean, but you got to believe me—I may be a pimp but I'm no murderer."

"CHIEF GORSKY!"

I turned. Fairley Sable's silver-blue eyes smiled up at me.

After hearing José's wild tale of crime and punishment, I had taken Jinks for a walk on Long Pier before heading for our next destination. I was at pier's end when Fairley waylaid us.

"I thought it was you. I've wanted to speak with you since the other day. And is this who I think it is?" Fairley sing-songed to Jinks, holding an open palm under the pug's quivering nose.

Not impressed, Mr. Jinks shrank from the hand, hunched and defecated.

"I'm sorry. He's an old dog."

Fairley backed well away while I scooped the mess into a plastic sandwich bag I'd brought for such an eventuality. After dropping the package into a nearby trash receptacle Mrs. Sable rummaged a hand wipe from her purse, offering it to me at arms' length.

"Can we talk a few minutes?" Fairley asked. Although anxious to confront Alan Rand ASAP, I might as well take advantage of the serendipitous meeting. I had some questions for Fairley Sable, particularly concerning the events at the G and G on Mel's final night. We sat on a concrete bench facing Mystic Bay, just past the entrance to Long Pier. Jinks hopped into my lap.

"I feel awful about what happened the other day at my house," Fairley said. "The sheriff was quite upset to find you talking to Anita, and I can't help feel responsible. You were only there because of me."

"Forget it." I asked how Mrs. Dick was coping.

"As well as can be expected," Fairley said. "I wish she would let me help her, but Anita is intensely private. Yesterday I stopped by with a chicken pot pie—she accepted the pie, but wouldn't let me inside."

"Mrs. Dick needs her friends—you just keep trying."

"Oh, I will. You know I believe you'd like to help Anita as well. Oh, have I said something out of turn?"

"Not at all," I said, irritated that she read me so well. "Mrs. Sable, could you clarify a few things for me?"

"Of course!" Fairley's face held an avaricious eagerness and I wondered what skin she had in this game.

"On the night of Mel's murder you and Gigi dined at the G and G. Tell me about that."

Her account jibed with what I already knew, but added little. I pressed for details about Mel and Gigi's affair, with even less success.

"I'm sorry," she said, holding up her hands, "but I don't know anything about the affair. I tried to ignore it, for Anita's sake. You must talk to Gigi. Gigi knows all of Mel's secrets."

I moved on. "What was Mel wearing at the G and G?"

The thin lips pursed and she looked at me with a disquieting avidity. "Excuse me?"

"It's a simple question."

"It's an odd question, but I'll answer. Mel wore navy blue slacks, a checkered shirt and that old blue jacket of his."

"Did his clothes fit?"

"Of course they fit." She laughed. "Mel wasn't overly vain about his appearance, but he dressed well enough. He didn't go about like a rag bag."

Except on the night he died. Sometime between leaving the pub and dying in that small clearing in Birnam Wood, Mel had exchanged his sensible clothes for fool's motley.

"Can you think of anyone who'd want Mel dead?"

"Only his friends," Fairley said with a smile. "Oh, I've shocked you. I tend to speak bluntly. It's just that Mel had a way of getting under people's skin. I was the newest member of his little group, you know. Perhaps I was more sensitive to his shortcomings. Mel has—had—the emotional maturity of a five-year-old. He demanded constant attention."

"Why did people put up with him?"

Fairley laughed. "Five-year-olds can be quite entertaining, but I think it was his power that kept the moths circling the flame. If knowledge is power, then he was the Mafia Don of Mystic Cove. We all kissed his ring." She looked around and leaned close, "Just between us, there are some in Mystic Cove who think Mel Dick got his just deserts in Birnam Wood."

"Is that what you think?"

"Absolutely not, Chief," Fairley said, voice resonating with real shock. "I put my trust in the rule of law." A frown creased the gamin face. "But I also believe in karma. For the most part people write their own endings."

Maybe, I thought, but sometimes others helped them along. "Who were some of the people who had a problem with Mel?"

"Well, Mel and Alan hadn't been on good terms recently, but I can't say for certain what started the disagreement." Fairley sighed and looked out on Mystic Bay. The sky was overcast, more rain coming.

"Take a guess."

"I suspect it had something to do with the *Commen-*

*tator.* Everyone forgets that the paper was originally Alan's baby."

"But that was some time ago, wasn't it?" I asked.

"Yes, but sometimes these things fester." Just then a few fat raindrops fell. Fairley glanced at the glowering sky and back at me.

"Thanks for your help," I told her.

"I hope Mr. Richt appreciates what a jewel he has in you." Her gloved hand moved toward my arm, but there was a low growl, and the hand retreated.

"I'm sure he does." Richt was good at determining the price of things.

As Fairley Sable toddled away I wondered if she bought into that karma bull. Did she really believe the world an honest place where each person was judged according to his or her true worth? She certainly didn't have the excuse of youth. She must have learned that fairness is a rarity and justice mostly an illusion.

But that was why we needed to work all the harder for it.

# TEN

*Red as a Beet*

NO ONE WAS home at the Rand residence—or at least no one answered—so I zipped four houses down to see what was shaking at the Dick house. Besides, I had the perfect pretext for a visit in the wicker basket, a small deceit that had the advantage of being true. I would tell Anita of Jinks's recovery and ask if she'd changed her mind about the dog. But as with the Rands, nobody was home.

Admiral Street was ominously quiet—silent houses with shuttered windows, like blind eyes. The eyes of the dead. A row of identical trash containers sat at curbs, awaiting pick-up, but where were the people who'd rolled them out? I debated whether to try my luck at Gigi Tajani's—she lived on Scylla Street, just one street south of Admiral—when Spooner rang my cell.

"I'm sorry I didn't get back earlier," he said, "but I got a situation here that demands my full attention. I'll give you the heads-up as soon as I'm able."

"Does it concern the autopsy?"

"Like I said, I got a situation."

"Can I run something by you, Sheriff? I talked with José Barracas and…"

"Gorsky, I got a…"

"Yeah, I know—a situation. Screw you!" I said after he'd ended the call. "I got a situation myself."

And I wasn't going to wait around for Spooner's permission to do something about it.

FIVE MINUTES LATER Jinks and I stood on Gigi Tajani's porch.

"Just a moment," a voice lilted from within. Jinks's ears perked at the sound, but then he must have been a regular visitor with Mel. The door opened, revealing Gigi Tajani in all her glory. She wore a purple caftan, with matching turban and sandals. The morning light revealed orange bands of pancake makeup that streaked her face like war paint. She glanced at Jinks on his lead—he refused to get back inside the wicker basket—but said nothing.

"What an unexpected surprise!" Gigi Tajani shrieked, speaking in exclamations as usual. She must be due for a collagen injection—her lips were almost normal sized, for once not resembling a couple of plump bratwurst about to burst.

She invited me inside for coffee on the "veranda." As she led me through her townhouse, I felt hundreds of eyes upon me. Although the old woman pursued the sweet bird of youth, she possessed an old lady's love of knickknacks. Herds of ceramic pigs, flocks of carved flamingos, creepy porcelain dolls with painted cheeks and rolling eyes—all these and more stared from shelves or tabletops. I thought of the great pyramids of the pharaohs, tombs crammed with the simulacra of life. Unwillingly, my eyes were drawn to an odd grouping of resin figurines, a drove of busty, big-assed old ladies.

Gigi stayed me with an imperious palm. "Do you like my collection?"

Before I could answer she grabbed one of the figures and thrust it in my hand. The buxom old lady was in full cowgirl mode—ten-gallon hat, denim hot pants, red-checkered midriff blouse, and curling whip in hand. The placard beneath read, *At my age I can still round up the boys!* Suppressing a shiver, I replaced it among its obscene fellows.

"Have a seat while I brew the coffee."

Once the old woman glided away I studied the so-called veranda, which was the standard Mystic Cove patio outfitted for intimate entertaining. Potted palms and flowering gingers provided plenty of privacy, the sole seating supplied by two large papasan chairs sitting side by side. A wicker sideboard was stocked with booze: several bottles of white wine, a couple of reds, along with an assortment of expensive booze including Courvoisier, Grand Marnier, Chambord. Must be nice—these days I could only afford the knockoff brands, if that. A small collection of barware gleamed on a tray, with two of everything.

I stuck my head through the French doors. "Can I help you with anything?" Gigi was taking her sweet time with the coffee. Was she stalling?

"No, no, no, just make yourself comfortable!"

I brushed Jinks out of the papasan chair and sat. Gigi Tajani's tastefully landscaped backyard was typical of the Cove, bursting with flowers, mostly oleander and purple ruellia. Beautiful but also dangerous—oleander was poisonous and ruellia an invasive exotic that if left alone would choke out all other plant life. But like Rappaccini's garden, Florida was full of beautiful and deadly things. The soft murmur of Spanish interrupted these dismal thoughts.

Across the swale a landscaping crew was hacking at the pinnate fronds of a tall, straight-backed palm in someone's backyard. Next door a bald man was examining rose blooms with the eye of a surgeon. A few houses down an American flag was fluttering in the cool breeze. A thrill of comprehension—without realizing it, I'd been looking at the backside of Admiral Street. Gigi's house was within spitting distance of her dead lover's, and if I squinted to my right I could see the Rand backyard. An almost incestuous closeness.

"Here we are!" Gigi shrieked in my ear. "Oh, did I startle you?"

Twenty minutes later I was drowning beneath a deluge of words, buried in irrelevant, endless chatter. To Gigi Tajani life was an endless movie and she the only character. Every time I tried to ask her about that fateful night at the G and G, she somehow steered the conversation back to her favorite topic, Gigi Tajani. Now she was recapping her yoga regimen, of all things. Time to pin this butterfly to the wall.

"Ms. Tajani!"

"Yes?" Blinking eyes in that strangely still face.

"I asked you about your relationship with Mr. Dick."

"I thought we had finished with that topic. As I said, Mel and I were friends."

"With benefits?"

A wag of a mummified finger. "You've been listening to the gossips, but it's true that we were lovers. And so what? We weren't hurting anyone. Just two lonely people finding solace in a cold world."

"What about Anita?"

"Anita? Anita," Gigi clucked, as if trying to place the name. "Anita was Anita. It had nothing to do with her."

"She was Mel's wife."

"Marrying Anita was the great tragedy of Mel's life. He deserved a strong woman." Her expression said that she saw herself as that strong woman.

"And yet your affair with Mel ended." I had no idea if this was so, but bet it would get a rise out of Gigi.

"That isn't so! We'd just reached a bump in the road." The tattooed brows shot up and anger flashed in those emerald eyes. "Who told you that anyway?"

"It's common knowledge that Mel hasn't exactly sought out your company recently, and that last night at the G and G he was positively hostile to you."

"He didn't mean those things he said. Mel was confused, that's all. In the end he knew he could come to me. He knew I was his friend. His true friend."

"How can you know this?" I asked.

"Because he…because a woman knows, that's why."

"Who are you kidding?" I said, raising my voice. "It was over between you and lover boy." I was pushing it, but I had to cut this woman to the bone.

"I don't know what you want from me!" Gigi pushed back. "It's painful for me to speak of that night and I've already told you everything I know. After the terrible scene at the pub I headed straight home where I read for a bit, had a cognac and went to bed."

"Was it a good book?"

The lips tightened. "It was a romance—*Passion in the Highlands*."

"And then you had a cognac on the veranda," I said.

"Yes, it was a pleasant night and I…" She blinked at me.

"Go on."

The eyes narrowed. "There's nothing more. I had a snifter of Courvoisier and went to bed."

"Did you hear anything unusual while you enjoyed your cognac?"

"I don't understand."

I moved my papasan closer. "It was a clear night and we both know the Cove is deadly quiet after dark. You sat right here, enjoying your cognac. The Dick house is just across the way." I pointed to the house with the flag. "Did you hear anything out of the ordinary?"

Gigi bared her teeth. "I don't like your insinuation, young woman." The metamorphosis was startling—the purring cat transformed into a snarling beast. Making it even more horrible, the woman's smooth face remained unruffled.

"I didn't mean to offend you, I..."

"If I had heard anything suspicious I would have reported it. How dare you accuse me! How dare you!"

By now Jinks was awake and yapping furiously, a cacophony of screaming old lady and angry dog.

"Ms. Tajani, please calm down."

"Get out now, the both of you—get out!"

She didn't need to tell me again. I grabbed Jinks and hot-tailed it out of that madhouse.

ALAN RAND WAS a man in trouble. He had dark smudges under his eyes, and his formerly leonine shock of silver hair hung like limp spaghetti around the gaunt face. But after the chaos of Gigi Tajani, Alan Rand's quiet despair was almost soothing.

"Thanks for seeing me, Mr. Rand."

Rand tried to smile. "I take my coffee black, but can I get you cream or sugar?"

"Just cream."

He returned with a blue-and-white Wedgwood jug filled with enough cream for a gallon of coffee. As he placed the jug on the dining room table, droplets of thick liquid spilled onto the linen tablecloth. Rand made a few half-hearted swabs at the spreading stain with a cloth napkin but soon gave up.

"I hope Mrs. Rand feels better soon."

"Tally's sick with the flu. I've had a bout as well."

Alan Rand crossed his legs, exposing mismatched socks. A slight blush. He unknotted his long legs, shoved them beneath the table. His long legs must have grazed Jinks, who huffed in irritation. Rand glanced at the dog, quickly looked away. When I'd arrived with Jinks in tow I'd been surprised that Rand hadn't questioned the dog's presence. Maybe Alan Rand had bigger things on his mind.

"I had a talk with José Barracas this morning," I said. Two spots of crimson lit up Alan Rand's cheeks. "He told me about the accusations you made against him."

Rand's spine stiffened momentarily but then released. "Accusations?"

"Mr. Barracas told me that you accused him of murdering Mel Dick." I said the words slowly, giving them plenty of time to sink in.

"That's...that is just..."

"That is just what, Mr. Rand?" My voice was hard as stone. Rand's passive demeanor had provoked my inner pit bull. I didn't like the way he avoided my gaze, hazel eyes darting as if the answer could be found in the elegant, cold room rather than in his own heart. "Did you accuse José Barracas of Mel Dick's murder?"

"I... I did."

"Why?"

"I had my reasons."

"What reasons?"

"You must take my word. Surely my word holds more weight than the words of a drunk." Rand tried on another of those ghastly smiles.

"I gotta say, I'm predisposed to accept Mr. Barracas's version."

"Why...why is that?"

"Barracas told me his story, that's why. If you'd level with me, it might change my mind."

Rand crumpled like the proverbial cheap suit. "It was Mel. It all started with Mel."

"What started with Mel?"

"Mel's story. That awful story."

"I don't understand, Mr. Rand—what story?"

Rand finger-combed his white hair from his face. "When Mel discovered that José Barracas was running prostitutes out of the Grub and Grog, he planned to expose Barracas in the *Commentator.* Barracas *must* have discovered Mel's plan and murdered him. He must have!"

Except for the murder part, this pretty much meshed with what I'd heard earlier from José. He admitted to playing pimp, but spun it as a simple favor rather than a lucrative crime operation. "I just gave the old guys a phone number so they can get their knobs polished, Chief. But I quit weeks ago after one of the guys told me Mel Dick was on to it. Is that a crime?"

Actually it was, but I hadn't argued the point. Even though I'd pressed hard, José swore that he'd had no knowledge of Mel's planned article until Rand had spilled the beans last night.

"I can understand why Barracas wants to keep this quiet," I told Rand, "but why didn't you go to the police?"

"I… I wanted to give Barracas a chance to defend himself."

I didn't buy that for a second. Rand had no reason to protect José. But Rand was right about one thing: José had a heck of a motive. If the prostitution story got out, then José and his restaurant were history at Mystic Cove— Jud Richt would make sure of it. I'd also bet that José's finances weren't too healthy. He was a man tottering on the edge—a little push and into the abyss. People have killed for less. A lot less.

"Tell me more about this conversation with Dick, the one where he told you his plans for Barracas."

"There's nothing to tell."

"Sure there is. For starters, when did the conversation take place? And where?"

"I'm trying to cooperate, but you're making it difficult."

"And I appreciate your cooperation, Mr. Rand." In fact I was astounded that Rand was talking to me at all. People like him let their lawyers deal with riffraff like me. And I hadn't exactly been polite. I was tempted to see how far Rand could be pushed. "So when did Mel tell you about the prostitution ring?"

Alan Rand stared at his lap. "I... I can't remember precisely."

"Try."

"Let me think. I believe it was September. Or was it October?"

"Was Mrs. Rand with you?"

"Of course not," Rand snapped. "Tally has absolutely nothing to do with this—nothing."

"Where did this conversation take place?"

"At Mel's office, or maybe it was the Grog and Grub."

"Which was it, Rand?" I slapped the table for emphasis. Rand startled violently, but I was sick of his equivocations and qualifiers. It was deniability worthy of a politician. "You keep saying *I believe* or *I think*. I wish to hell you'd tell me what you know."

"I don't appreciate your tone, Chief." A flash of anger at last.

"I need answers, Rand."

"This conversation is over and I want you out of my house."

"You're the boss," I said, pulling out my cell, "but first I have to notify Sheriff Spooner about the situation."

"Must you?" Rand's voice cracked. The last turn of the screw had done the trick: Rand was definitely hiding something.

I put away my cell. "Let's try again. Where and when did this conversation with Mel take place?"

"It was definitely September, sometime in September. I met Mel at the *Commentator* office. He was in a good mood. He insisted on drinks, though it was a bit early for me." The details were coming hard and fast now—amazing how a little threat can refresh the memory. "Mel kept showing off his latest acquisition, a book he'd just bought—Mel was so proud that the witch had autographed it for him.

"*I Am Not a Witch*—Mel's stupid book that he'd just bought. After Mel poured our drinks, he sprang his little surprise about Barracas, that he'd been running a call-girl operation from his restaurant for some time. Mel planned to publish an exposé in the *Commentator*. He wanted me to read the article, but I refused to look at it. It was all so…sordid."

"When did Mr. Dick plan to publish his article?"

"I had no idea, nor did I ask him, but if past history means anything, Mel never sat on his stories for too long. Really, Chief, we must wrap this up. I have to check on my wife. She's been ill."

"And you're certain this conversation took place in September."

Rand licked his lips. "Yes, definitely September."

"But the prostitution story wasn't in October's *Commentator*."

"I'm aware of that, but I was not privy to Mel's editorial

decisions. I know you don't believe me, but I'm doing the best I can. Why would I lie?" Rand spread his arms wide.

"I just want the truth, Mr. Rand."

"As do I."

*Do you, Mr. Rand?*

"Why did you disapprove of Mel's hooker exposé?"

"It was a bad idea for many reasons." Rand was on firmer footing here, his lawyer training coming to the forefront. "Firstly, there was the possibility of litigation on Barracas's part if Mel couldn't back up his accusations with evidence. Secondly, exposing such a terrible scandal would be the equivalent of setting off a bomb in Mystic Cove. It would destroy our peaceful life here. I tried to convince Mel to let go of it, but he had the bit between his teeth." Now Rand's attorney background seemed to desert him. His eyes brimmed and he twisted like a soul in torment.

"All Mel cared about was his story," Rand whispered. "That stupid newspaper story. If Mel had done as I asked, he'd still be alive."

I sensed Rand was telling the truth, but it still didn't feel right. His distress didn't fit the cause. Why was he so upset about the exposé? It wasn't Rand's fat in the fire, and he didn't give a plug nickel about Barracas. So what was it? "Why didn't Mel report the criminal activity to the police?"

Alan Rand laughed, a short, raucous bark. "Mel would bring the police into it only after the article was published. He didn't dare risk sharing the spotlight, not even with the police. I thought it reckless, but my opinion counted for nothing."

"When did you last see Mel?"

Rand took a sip of coffee. "Tally and I were at the Grub

and Grog the other night—Mel's last night. We both saw him then. For the last time."

"And before that?"

"I can't recall. Mel's insistence on going ahead with the prostitution story drove a wedge between us. In the last weeks of his life Tally and I avoided him."

"But you saw enough of him to see the change in your old friend."

Another appalling smile. "Mel stumbled about like a blind beggar in those last days, his mind going inch by inch."

"Dementia?"

"No, it was madness, a madness peculiar to Mel."

"What does that mean?"

A long pause. Rand glanced at the staircase and sighed. "I've answered your questions. If you'll excuse me, I must attend to my wife."

As I watched him leave, I wondered how to tease the truth from this pack of liars.

José had sworn he was leveling with me, but maybe more skeletons rattled around in that sodden brain. And Gigi's sudden anger suggested that she had a secret or two of her own to tell. As for Rand? I wasn't sure where the truth ended and the lie began.

I'd learned a lot, but not enough. Still more puzzle pieces to gather.

BACK AT MY OFFICE, I called Spooner, but when the call went to voice mail, I lost it. I didn't know why the sheriff had suddenly declared me *persona non grata*, but I wasn't going to play his game. I left a detailed message summarizing the dirt I'd dug up. If my information on José's extracurricular activities didn't earn a callback, nothing would.

A couple hours later I got a call, but not from Spooner.

"GCSO cruisers on Admiral Street, Chief," Billy Blake said, a little breathlessly. "They just passed the guardhouse."

When I arrived I found a second search of the Dick house seemingly in progress. I ran up to my old friend Deputy Berry, who was apparently guarding Anita Dick's garbage can, while uniforms swarmed around the house. "Berry?"

The deputy deliberately pulled off mirrored sunglasses and gave me the once-over. Then he frowned at Jinks, who was whimpering. Berry replaced the sunglasses. "Gorsky."

"I talked with Spooner earlier, but he didn't mention anything about another search."

A smile twitched on Berry's lips. "It just went down."

"What went down?"

Berry hitched his fingers in his belt. "I got the perp."

"Congratulations, Deputy." I managed a smile and stuck out my hand. After a beat Berry shook it. I asked the deputy how this came about.

"We didn't find jack in the first search, but my gut told me we'd missed something."

"I guess the...uh...gut knows best," I said.

"So today I came back for another go at Mrs. Dick. She wasn't home, but my gut told me something wasn't right. As I was leaving I noticed all the garbage cans on the curb." Berry's astute observation was correct. It was garbage day. The whole of Admiral Street was lined with cans. "You know what I did?"

I shook my head while my own gut took a tumble.

"I looked inside the can and right on top was a brown paper bag. I opened the bag and there it was—a Smith and Wesson thirty-eight. The murder weapon."

"Alleged murder weapon," I muttered as a uniform scrambled over.

"Still no sign of Anita Dick," the deputy told Berry.

"Calm down, son," Berry said, though the deputy was Berry's age and far from upset. "My gut tells me we'll have her in custody before the day is over."

"Good police work," I told Berry, who puffed like a bullfrog in heat. I gestured at the garbage truck that had just turned into Admiral Street. "I guess you were lucky pick-up was late today."

"This is a crime scene, Gorsky—authorized personnel only."

Jinks and I slunk back to security headquarters, tails tucked between our legs. It looked as if I was wrong again. I had not thought Anita capable of murdering her husband, but I couldn't deny the evidence. Perhaps my detective instincts had vanished after all, along with so much else.

I should be pleased that the case was about to be successfully concluded, but I wasn't. I had enjoyed the chase, the excitement of the puzzle, and now it was over. But the worst part was that I had been dead wrong about almost everything, especially Anita Dick. The thirty-eight in the trash can was damaging evidence. It was easy to imagine how it went down. Something had broken in Anita Dick that night at the Grub and Grog. As she had so many times before, Anita had returned to her lonely house to wait for her husband.

Only this time she'd waited with a gun.

AT THE OFFICE I found Tyler waiting for me.

"Don't tell me you already know about the gun."

"What gun? I just wanted to invite you to have a drink with me."

I told him about the thirty-eight Berry had found in Anita's garbage.

"Let's celebrate the successful conclusion of your investigation at Eddie's."

I stared at Tyler, trying to decide if he was being sarcastic. "No, thanks," I said at last, "and as far as I know, the case isn't officially closed."

"Once the cops find the old lady, it will be. Come on, Addie, let me buy you a drink."

"I'd be lousy company," I said. Tyler was on my last nerve. He had never learned when to leave me alone.

"How's Stan the Man doing these days?"

I took a deep breath. "Pop's okay."

"What's wrong, Addie? I know something is."

"Nothing's wrong," I said, turning my face away. "It's just that Pop's going into hospice care." Treasonous tears filled my eyes.

"That's…that's tough. I hope everything works out for your dad."

"That's highly unlikely." I flicked a tear from my cheek. "Sorry, I didn't mean to snipe. Thanks for your concern, and you're right—things will work out." They always did, only not in the way we wanted.

Tyler gave me a funny look and left. I should have followed, but I didn't want to go home. I didn't want to be around anyone right now—especially not Pop, who'd be bursting with questions about the case. I called home and Pop picked up on the first ring.

"I called Uncle Otto."

"Pop!" I saw where this was going.

"I was sure you wouldn't mind so I called Otto and got his opinion on the autopsy." Otto Rider was a former pathologist at Johns Hopkins and wasn't a real uncle but an eternal bachelor who became connected to my mother's family by dating Mom's sister Ethel. Even though the love affair didn't last, Otto Rider remained, eventually becoming enshrined as Uncle Otto.

"That's confidential information, and Uncle Otto must be a hundred by now."

"Don't be a smart-ass, Adelajda. He's only ten years older than me and sharp as a tack. Frankie faxed the papers to him in Baltimore."

"Frankie's involved?" Frankie Buchanan was our neighbor across the hall. He'd been on the job in Miami, and a couple times a week he and Pop got together to trade war stories.

"Frankie thinks it's a great idea. He thought the autopsy was fishy too."

"I wish you'd checked with me first. You could get us both in a lot of trouble." And by us, I meant me. Now I had two nosey former cops involved in this muddle.

"Don't worry, I blacked out Mel Dick's name and Frankie can keep his mouth shut."

"So what did Otto say?"

"Like us, Otto was confused over the two bullets. The first shot barely glanced the left arm, causing minimal damage, minimal bleeding. Otto says the second supposedly deadly bullet was positively the second gunshot."

"Positively?" I could hear Frankie putting in his two cents in the background.

"Blanding wrote that he observed no marked hemorrhage along the bullet track. If he's right, the head wound had to come second."

"Jeez," I said, feeling stupid not to have seen it earlier.

"That's right, Adelajda. Mel Dick was already dead when the second bullet was fired."

I was no forensics expert, but even I knew that dead men don't bleed.

# ELEVEN

*Betrayal Is the Only Truth*

AFTER POP'S BOMBSHELL I opened the bottle of bourbon I'd been saving for a rainy day and poured a healthy shot. When that was gone, I poured another. I guess I could have headed to Eddie's, but my mood was too foul to inflict on others. Tonight I would drink alone.

Now I understood Spooner's earlier disengagement. Mel Dick's death was no longer a murder. I wondered how hard GCSO was looking for Anita. It was a crime to shoot a dead man—desecration of a corpse?—but it wasn't murder. I refilled my glass. I supposed it was possible that Uncle Otto was wrong, but I thought not. The sheriff's sudden silence told me that something had gone desperately wrong at the coroner's office. But how could Blanding make such a glaring error? And if the bullet didn't kill Mel, what did?

I refilled my glass and stretched the desk chair all the way back. I patted my lap and Jinks hopped up. Since tripping across Mel's body, I had been burning it on both ends and was nearly out of wick. Outside the night fell, but it was always night in here. The wall clock ticked off the time, an ominous metronome, and my eyes fluttered shut. Every so often my hand would find the glass of bourbon. It was pleasant to let go, to drift in and out of twilight sleep, aware of my surroundings yet not part of them.

Images from the past days swirled around, like leaves

in a tornado. In a waking dream I saw Anita sitting on the concrete bench in Fairley Sable's backyard. A forlorn statue. And where was she now? An irony—they called Anita a dim bulb, a slow cow. But she had been smart enough to slip away, again and again.

Didn't she know this game of hide-and-seek was dangerous?

Again I saw Anita on that cold bench. If I'd only had more time I'd have pried her secret loose. She was ready to talk. A few more minutes would have done it. But fate had not given me those minutes.

Wait a second. Wasn't fate just another word for coincidence? And I didn't believe in coincidence. Something had conspired to keep me from Anita and it wasn't fate or coincidence. I pushed Jinks to the floor and grabbed my cell.

"Admiral Street Guardhouse," Billy answered.

"Is GCSO still out at the Dick house?"

"Yeah, they left a cruiser there in case Mrs. Dick returned. Why?"

I disconnected, my unease deepening. If I was right, Anita was in mortal danger. Even though Mel was dead when somebody plugged that extra hole in his head, the shooter didn't know this. In his mind he was a murderer. The game was still on and the danger as deep as ever. There was a murderer among us, and it wasn't Anita Dick.

I threw on my jacket, hooked Jinks's leash and set out into the night. It was already after six. I had wasted precious time crying in my bourbon when I should have been hitting the pavement. I wasn't surprised GCSO hadn't found Anita, since so much of Mystic Cove was inaccessible by car. But I knew the Cove as well as anyone. I would find her. I procured a golf cart and set off.

Outside the sky was a bruised purple. Night was falling fast and hard. My plan was simple. I would start out on the same path through Birnam Wood that I'd taken the morning I'd found Dick's body. After that I'd cover Windbound Harbor and then Founder's Centre. If Anita Dick was hiding in Mystic Cove, I would find her.

But in my heart of hearts, I didn't think she was hiding. Oh God, I didn't think that at all.

TWO HOURS LATER I sat on the bench I had shared with Fairley Sable earlier. Anita Dick was further from me than ever. There was no place left to look. I pulled my jacket tight. A breeze was picking up, rippling the waters of Mystic Bay. Jinks panted from our walk up and down the boardwalk, one of the few passageways in Mystic Cove that prohibited golf carts.

The lights from the parade of shops selling ice cream and useless fodder made in China bounced off the still face of Mystic Bay. Long Pier stretched into the fetid bay, its sides adorned with twinkly lights. To the right of the pier's terminus the stout lighthouse stood in its postage-stamp patch of dirt and concrete. The tower and dome were encircled with red lights, like the ribbons of a candy cane. Of course the fake lighthouse had no lens, dooming any wayward ships, and the lights twinkled prettily enough, but I preferred my fictions with more bite—give me the horrors of Innsmouth over this bland artifice. I noticed that the ground beneath the lighthouse undulated, like sand shifting in the wind.

I stood, rubbed my eyes, looked again. Another flutter of movement. Night birds? Foraging crabs? Or perhaps my inclination had come true and the deep ones of Innsmouth had risen from their silent depths. *Be careful what you wish for, Addie Gorsky.*

I went for a closer look, but Jinks kept putting on the

brakes. Tired of the game, I cradled him in my arms and walked briskly to the pier's end. I didn't have my flashlight with me but the ambient light was sufficient.

She lay face down at the base of the lighthouse. The lower half of her body was immersed in the rank water, but her torso had somehow landed on the scrap of dirt and concrete on which the lighthouse stood. The wind whipped her voluminous white tunic, thus accounting for the illusion of movement.

I had found Anita Dick.

ONCE MORE I stood at the scene of death, and as before, the circus came to town, but this was a different party altogether, as if Anita Dick's death was the coda to Mel Dick's murder. Even the sheriff wasn't immune.

"This might wrap it up," he said.

"Isn't that premature?"

Spooner sighed. "I'm just saying it might be suicide. You got to admit, it ties things up nicely."

"A little too nicely."

Spooner shrugged. "Wife shoots cheating husband. Consumed by guilt, she takes her own life."

"Consumed by guilt? For shooting a dead man?"

Spooner did a double take and said in a low voice, "So you know about that?"

"I wasn't absolutely certain, until now."

"It could have been a lot worse. If Dolores Rio hadn't caught the mistake when she did, we would have been up the creek without a paddle. Blanding's been hitting the sauce pretty heavy lately. When he took on Mel's autopsy I guess he cracked under the strain."

"That's a mother of a crackup," I said, and then, "Any word on a suicide note?"

Spooner shook his head. "We're still checking the house. She might have left it there."

Or maybe Anita figured her corpse would tell it all. I asked Spooner if Rio had a time of death yet.

Another head shake. "Dolores says the body hadn't been in the water too long, which is lucky. Christ, I hate drownings." Spooner rubbed his face, looked out on Mystic Bay. "By the way, I got your message about Barracas. Did you have any idea that he was serving up more than burgers and beer at the G and G?"

"Not a clue," I said, staring out at the water. The Mystic Cove I'd thought I'd known had never really existed.

"Berry's gonna talk to Barracas and Rand, but I doubt Barracas's illegal activities are relevant."

I startled, feeling Spooner's cold hand on mine.

"Go home and get some rest, Addie. It's all over."

Spooner was right. I wasn't needed here and hadn't been for some time. The detectives had finished with me an hour ago. Walking away, I felt the sheriff's eyes boring into my back. Did he see me as I saw myself? A failure.

Whatever little I'd learned, I'd learned too late. The full truth of this mystery had died with this woman. Anita might very well have murdered her husband, but that didn't absolve me. I had played my little game of detection, and now a woman was dead. I pulled out my cell. My hands shook so that it took me two tries to get through, but he answered on the second ring.

"Tyler, can I still take you up on that drink?"

JINKS AND I got home at just past two. I'd almost forgotten how nice it was to be with Tyler. As long as it didn't concern money or prestige, Tyler was a fun companion. When he saw Jinks was with me, he just shrugged and put out a bowl of water.

That night I slept better than I had in days—nothing like a good screw to get your head straight—and I dreamed.

In my dream I woke in darkness and a woman's voice called my name. "Adelajda." I recognized the voice and, in the way of dreams, found myself sitting next to Anita on the stone bench in Fairley Sable's backyard.

"How do you know my real name, Anita? I thought the dead know nothing."

Anita was a horror—covered in gooseflesh, her skin macerated, swollen and wrinkled as prickly pear, her sodden clothes dripping stinking water into the koi pond. Yet I wasn't afraid.

"You're right, Addie. The dead know nothing, but we remember."

I was sorry for that. Then I asked Anita what she wanted of me.

"You know."

When I woke I was bathed in sweat, the dream clinging to me. I was not superstitious, but the living ignore the dead at their peril.

In dreams comes responsibility. My responsibility. Anita was dead and beyond my help, but I would follow the trail a while longer. I would have my truth.

THE NEXT MORNING I overslept and had to hustle so I wouldn't be late. Pop didn't get my anxiety, but perhaps I had a presentiment of trouble. As it turned out I arrived at my office with five minutes to spare, but when I opened the door, Jinks charged inside, barking furiously at the tall man pouring coffee. I had thought there might be trouble and there it stood.

"Good morning, Mr. Richt," I said over Jinks's yapping. Involuntarily my eyes glided over the chaos of my office—the litter of papers on my desk, the open bottle of Jim Beam, the empty glass. I had intended to straighten up this morning, but you know what they say about good intentions. I took Jinks in my arms and he quieted, though he kept his glassy eyes peeled on Richt. How was it that dogs always knew?

"I can explain about the dog," I said.

"I already know about the dog, Addie. All of Mystic Cove is talking about you and Mel Dick's dog. I didn't come here about the dog of a dead man."

I shrugged out of my jacket and poured myself a cup, giving Richt my back. "I don't have anything on Anita Dick's death."

"I didn't come here about the old woman's death either. You're the sole reason for my visit and I'd like to have your full attention, Ms. Gorsky."

It clicked then. The reprieve was over and it was time to pay the ferryman. "Fine, we'll talk in my office."

I strode inside, Jinks trotting at my feet. I took my place behind the desk and gestured for Richt to take a seat. The moment was sullied somewhat when Jinks jumped into my lap and nudged me to scratch. What the heck—I scratched under Jinks's neck, the sweet spot.

"What can I do for you?"

Surprise flickered over Richt's features, but I was tired and more than a little hungover. I had come to the end of my rope and found courage there.

"You've disappointed me."

"I'm sorry about that, Mr. Richt. Say what you've come to say and let me go about my business."

Richt took a deep breath, his lips a thin line. "I took a chance on you when I promoted you to chief, even though I was cautioned that you might not be the right person for the job. Will you please stop fooling with that dog and give me your attention?"

"Sure," I said with a laugh.

"I know what you've been doing these past days. Playing detective at the Cove's expense—running here and there—did you really think I wouldn't find out?" As Richt counted off my transgressions, I wondered again who the spy had been, not that it mattered now. Richt might have bugged my office, but I doubted it. That wasn't his style—he appreciated technology as a means to an end, but his true appetite was in corrupting people.

"You've left me with little choice," Richt concluded, opening his hands in a gesture of false regret. This man must spend hours in front of a mirror practicing. His impression of a human being was really quite good.

"Get it over with, Richt."

Pleasure filled the reptilian eyes. "You're fired. I was going to give you two weeks' notice, but your adversarial attitude is intolerable. I want you out of here immediately. Tomorrow Payroll will have your final check cut—then you can clear out your desk."

"Was that as good for you as it was for me?"

Richt's smile turned into a snarl. "You impudent…"

"I'll clear out my desk right now, if you don't mind, and you can mail the check."

I had just put Jinks on the floor when the front door groaned open, followed by quick footsteps. I was about to ask who was there when I saw Richt's broad grin. Coldness filled my stomach.

"I'm in here," Richt called out.

"Coming, Mr. Richt. I got here soon as I could but…"

Our eyes briefly met, but Tyler Andrews quickly looked away. I didn't though. I wanted to remember this.

"Your timing is perfect," Richt said. "Ms. Gorsky prefers not to work her final two weeks after all, so you'll be assuming her duties immediately, per our discussion. Make sure she turns in her keys before she leaves."

"THERE'S NOTHING TO talk about, Tyler." After Richt left, I'd cleaned out my desk in a flurry, my earlier bravado a puddle on the floor. I looked around the office, thought I had everything. My belongings had easily fit into a shoebox, but then I wasn't one to fill my office with keepsakes and mementoes—I carried my mementoes inside, where they couldn't be lost or misplaced.

"I'm only acting chief of security anyways," Tyler grumbled, as if selling himself for twenty pieces of silver rather than the going rate of thirty made it better. "You're taking this the wrong way."

"Is there a right way to take it?" I laughed, almost feeling sorry for this man who was too cunning for his own good. "Did you know about this last night?"

"I…you…we…"

My God, the man had probably been on the phone with Richt seconds after I left his bed. "You don't even realize what you've done, do you, Tyler? You've bought yourself the dubious honor of being Jud Richt's dog at Kew. But maybe the kennel's the right place for you."

"Huh?"

I hooked up Jinks. "You made your choice. Don't expect me to make it easy for you. I'm not the easygoing type."

Tyler's face hardened. "You know, people say you're nuts and I'm beginning to think they're right. You are a sorry excuse for a woman."

"That may be, but you were dishonest with me. I can't fault you for working the angles—it's tough nowadays.

But you should have played straight with me. I would have understood."

"You've changed."

I smiled at that. "Yes, I have changed. We all change, Tyler, or we should. Only death stops the changing."

I closed the door with more force than I intended, sending a dull thud that echoed through the building.

IT RAINED ALL over Florida that October day, but it fell hardest on Mystic Cove. I could have waited for the storm to pass—Florida is an inconstant state, where not even the rain lasts all day—but I needed to escape. Jinks didn't like it but we braved our way through the slashing rain to the parking garage where the Vic waited. No more golf carts for me and Jinks.

Before quitting the Cove for good I drove to Admiral Street for one last look. Unaware of my changed status, Jesse Potts waved me through the gate, but it wouldn't be long before he got the memo. I was now an outsider, an interloper, one for whom the gates were meant to keep out. I pulled into the Dicks' driveway.

The rain had softened to a drizzle. The house had been forlorn after Mel's murder, but now had given up the ghost entirely. A couple of sodden newspapers lay on the thick lawn, and the infamous garbage can remained at the end of the curb, its lid yawned open. A real haunted house.

The front door burst open and a slim young woman stomped toward me, heedless of the rain. The puffy face and swollen eyes did not fully obscure her blonde prettiness, but something about the woman's angry stride was eerily familiar. Jinks started yapping and wagging his corkscrew tail.

I remembered Anita's mention of a daughter in Ohio. What was her name? Jessie? Judy?

"Julie," I said. The woman froze, her eyes wide with surprise. "I am so sorry for your loss."

ANITA'S KITCHEN WAS a feast for the eyes, gleaming with polished marble and dark woods, but its designer had never boiled water. Like so much else in Mystic Cove, it was built for show and not utility. The kitchen island at which Julie Breyer and I sipped coffee was way too big—more continent than island—and its marble top ridiculously vulnerable to everyday use.

"I can't believe they're both gone," Julie said. "I've woken to a nightmare." Should I tell her the nightmare had only just begun? No, some things—the important things—must be learned through experience.

Briefly I summarized my involvement in the tragic events.

"You found both bodies?" Julie's blue eyes darkened with incipient suspicion.

"It's not as unlikely as it seems. As security chief I am... I was always traveling around the Cove. And remember, I was actively looking for your mother last night."

"It makes as much sense as anything."

"If you want to talk, I'll listen."

A short nod and Julie told me how the nightmare had begun. Anita Dick had never made that call to tell Julie of her father's death. Now, there was no easy way to learn of death, but Julie's had been one of the cruelest. She often went online to see what her father was up to, and yesterday's search brought more than she'd bargained for. Brutal news delivered like tomorrow's weather. Unable to reach her mother, Julie called GCSO, eventually reaching Sheriff Spooner, who verified her worst fears.

"This morning I was on my way here from Newnansville Regional when Spooner called and…" Julie's eyes squeezed shut, denying the tears. "That's when I learned about Mom. How could this happen, and for the love of God why didn't Mom tell me about Dad's death?"

"If it's any consolation, the morning after your dad's death, Anita was wrestling with how to break the news to you. She intended to tell you."

"What good are intentions now?" Julie twisted on the stool. "Oh, Mom wasn't strong. She ignored unpleasantness if she could, but she would have never kept me in the dark about Dad's death! Mom would have called my husband or maybe Uncle Stu and have one of them tell me, but she would have made sure I knew. Why didn't she?"

I didn't know, but I wanted to. That morning in Fairley's backyard Anita had been confused, but not confused enough to forget to tell Julie her father had been murdered. No, something or someone had stopped Anita in her tracks.

"So what's your angle in all this, Addie Gorsky?"

"Angle?"

Julie's eyes were a laser focused on me. "I'm not stupid. You're way more involved in this than you're letting on. So what gives?"

I thought about it. Julie deserved the truth, or at least part of it. "Before I became security chief at the Cove, I was a homicide detective. Old habits die hard. I noticed certain…incongruities in your father's shooting and wanted answers."

Julie considered this. "So why did Richt fire you?" Her face came closer to mine. "Did it have anything to do with my parents' deaths?"

"There were lots of reasons, one of which was that, like you, my boss also noticed my interest in your father's death and didn't approve."

"Why are you interested in my personal tragedy?"

I took a sip of coffee. Julie's questions had taken on the flavor of an interrogation. "With all due respect, it's not just your personal tragedy."

Julie's mouth tightened, but I didn't back down.

"Someone shot your father in cold blood. He died." Maybe not in that order, but Julie could discover the facts of the autopsy from Spooner. "Then last night Anita died, under mysterious circumstances. These acts happened under my nose, metaphorically speaking." I paused to tamp down the anger. "I want to know what happened. It's a matter of justice."

Julie powered down and took a sip of coffee. "I get the feeling the cops think Mom murdered Dad and then killed herself. Is that what you think?"

I trod carefully. "It's possible. After Mel's death Anita was terrified, and terrified people do desperate things."

"You're wrong," she said flatly. "My mother was a devout Catholic. She would not take her own life."

Maybe not on her own, but what if somebody gave her a little push in that direction.

"There you go again," Julie said, but she was smiling. "You got that faraway look again, like you're thinking deep thoughts." Jinks waddled into the kitchen, his sharp claws clicking and clacking over the slick Italian tile. "Dad loved that stupid old dog, Mom not so much."

"Are you taking Jinks back to Ohio?"

"God, no! Don't you want him?"

I shrugged. I might as well get something out of this mess—why not Jinks?

"So are you going to answer my question, Addie? Do you believe my mother murdered my father?"

That was the question I'd struggled with for days, almost from the moment I stumbled over Mel's corpse, but the answer I gave Julie Breyer came straight from the heart, bypassing the mind entirely. "No, Anita is innocent."

Julie's hand shot across the counter, catching my hand in its grasp. Unlike many of my sex who touch—or, even worse, hug—at the slightest provocation, I reserved physical gestures for those I loved. But my heart went out to this lost daughter.

"Will you help me, Addie? I want you to investigate my parents' deaths. I'll pay—money's no problem. Will you help me?"

"Of course I'll help you."

It was time to walk the tightrope again.

# TWELVE

*What Is the End of Fear?*

"DON'T BE AFRAID, losing your job isn't the worst thing," Pop said.

"I'm not afraid." But that was a lie. My past was a graveyard of mistakes and the future yawned like a black hole. But I was also sick and tired of being a mouse. It occurred to me that fear was a funny thing—weird funny, not ha-ha funny. It was said that fear was the most primal emotion. True enough, but it was more than that. Fear was the natural condition of the human race and would consume us if we let it. Accept that and you accepted a lot. Accept that, and maybe then you could move on.

"There's half a chicken in the icebox if you're hungry."

"Maybe later," I said. "First thing I gotta do is get out of this god-awful uniform and shower, and then I need to talk to Uncle Otto. Can you get his number for me, Pop? I want to talk to him before I meet with Julie this afternoon."

When I returned to the living room, Pop had Uncle Otto waiting on the line. Otto and I talked for over an hour, with Pop throwing comments from the recliner, undeterred that he had but one side of the conversation. After disconnecting, my cell rang. It was José Barracas.

"Marco just showed up for his shift, on time for once. You still wanna talk with him?"

I did indeed. Five minutes later I was on my way to

the Cove, a route I'd traveled so many times before, but this time it would be different.

"WHAT'S WITH THE street clothes?" José snickered. "Going undercover?"

"Good one." I told Barracas about my change in employment and that I was now investigating Mel and Anita's deaths for their daughter. "So where's our boy?"

"Out back blowing leaves—follow the noise and you'll find him." José did an exaggerated double take at the pug sitting at my feet. "Hey, I see you got your partner with you."

"Everybody's a comedian." I found Marco in the rear parking lot, gleefully blowing leaves into the street. "Remember me, Marco?"

*"No hablo ingles. No entiendo, por favor..."*

"Don't pull that crap with me, Marco. I know you speak English." The profanity worked, shocking Marco into silence. "That was a pretty stupid trick you pulled the other day."

*"Que?"* Marco croaked.

"I hope you enjoyed your little joke because I don't think the police will."

"But you're no police," Marco said, trying a grin on for size.

"Maybe not, but I have friends at GCSO, and when they find out about your lies I don't think they'll be too happy with you. Cops tend to take a murder investigation seriously."

"Murder? I don't know nothing about a murder! I was just playing around, that's all."

"Tell me about that night."

"It was just Mel Dick being a dick." Marco chuckled at his wit.

"Fine, we'll do this the hard way. I'm coming back with the cops."

"No, no." Marco's voice had taken on an irritating whining quality. He sounded like my snotty nephew when he was trying to pull a fast one.

"Talk to me, Marco."

"Yeah, fine, but José can't find out. He'd fire me for sure, and I need this lousy job."

"Talk to me."

"I didn't do nothing wrong. Lots of people do it." Prattling all the while, Marco dug in his pocket, retrieved his cell phone and started punching. I was confused and told Marco there was nothing to gain by stalling.

"Gimme a sec. You're gonna like this a lot." He held the tiny screen in front of my face.

On the pocket screen, a red-faced old man stood in the middle of the crowded patio of the Grub and Grog, his wild yet solemn manner that of an old testament prophet delivering a jeremiad. I caught glimpses of the other players in his audience—Gigi and Fairley and the Rands, all of them squirming like worms on a hook.

Marco grinned at me, a student who'd just cheated his way to an A. The little bastard had recorded Mel Dick's breakdown at the Grub and Grog.

I GOT BACK to Admiral Street in time for my appointment with Julie and was surprised to find Spooner's cruiser parked in the driveway. Julie met me at the door.

"He turned up a few minutes ago," she said, hanging my jacket on a hook. "I stalled until you got here."

Sheriff Spooner was waiting for us in the living room, his long spare frame folded into a startlingly ugly blue-striped French Provincial wing chair—a chair that was so ugly it had to be expensive. Julie lighted on the more reasonable sofa and I sat beside her.

"Morning, Ms. Gorsky. Mrs. Breyer here says you're working for her now."

"That's right," I said, relieved that Julie had already explained how things stood. "I hope you don't have a problem with me sitting in."

"Not at all," Spooner said, turning to Julie. "First, I want to offer my condolences to you, Mrs. Breyer. I'm sorry for your loss."

"Empty words," Julie whispered, but Spooner's sharp ear caught the word.

"They are only words, but they're not empty. I am sorry for your loss and sorry that the sheriff's department inadvertently caused you additional pain."

"It was hurtful," Julie said.

"And I'm afraid what I have to tell you next is going to hurt you some more, ma'am."

Julie crouched slightly, prepared for the blow that Spooner landed as gently as possible.

"So my father wasn't murdered," Julie said when he'd finished.

"At this point Dr. Rio suspects heart failure."

"There was nothing wrong with Dad's heart!"

Spooner nodded, "Dr. Rio didn't find any signs of heart disease. That's partly why she hasn't settled definitively on a cause of death."

"This is absurd—it doesn't take an Einstein to figure out what killed Dad—a bullet in a brain!"

"The single certainty," Spooner said, "is that your father was already dead when he was shot in the head."

"Stop, stop, I've heard enough," Julie said, slapping both hands over her ears like the proverbial monkey.

The sheriff looked to me. I herded Julie into the kitchen

and laid it out for her. "If you're not feeling up to it, you can put this off."

"Or?" she asked, wiping her eyes.

"Or you can tough it out, get it over with. The bottom line is that Spooner has questions that need answers."

We retook our former places, and Julie waved for Spooner to continue. He asked many of the questions I had planned to ask. Mom and daughter talked on a regularly irregular basis, maybe every other week or so, with the conversation consisting of updates on the grandkids. Julie's contact with her father was mainly through her mom—a quick "Dad says hi" tacked on just before hanging up. There was the usual exchange of cards with the requisite Xs and Os on birthdays, Christmas, Mother's Day and any other holidays the greeting card companies could dream up. Sometimes Mel would email Julie, but never Anita. The sheriff perked at this, and I guess I perked a little as well.

"Tell me about these emails," he asked.

"A lot of times he didn't write anything at all, just sent a link to some article that he liked. Most of the articles were political. Dad is...was very active in politics. Sometimes he would mention some story was working on."

"For the *Commentator?*" I asked.

"Yes—is that important?"

"Did your father ever describe these articles?" I asked, ignoring Spooner's hard look.

"It depended. Dad was more closemouthed about what he called his investigative pieces." A small laugh. "Although he wasn't shy about telling everyone what masterpieces they were. I can't tell you how many times he said to Mom and me, 'After this story is published, I'll be bigger than Woodward and Bernstein.'"

"What did you say?" I asked, leaning toward Julie.

Julie's brow knitted, thrown off by my intensity. "It's just a family joke, that's all. Woodward and Bernstein were the reporters who broke the Watergate scandal. Dad liked to brag that he'd be bigger than them."

I had found Woody and Bernie. Mel had made the same boast to Jesse, who'd misheard the names. When Mel had bragged of his imminent celebrity to anyone and everyone who would listen, he referred to the first of November, when he would publish his story in the *Commentator*—the big story that would make bring him fame and fortune. Was it about hookers at the G and G or something else? Something bigger?

"Is it all right if I continue with my interview, Ms. Gorsky?" Spooner asked.

There were more questions and answers, but nothing of import. The sheriff was preparing to leave when Julie Breyer dropped her little bomb.

"Sheriff, when can I come to the morgue to see my parents?"

Spooner worked his hat in his hands. "You don't have to put yourself through that, ma'am."

"But don't you need me—" Julie swallowed, "—to identify the remains?"

A quick look passed between Spooner and me and he said, "No, ma'am. Your mother identified her husband, and last night Ms. Gorsky provided the official ID for Mrs. Dick."

"I… I still want to see them," Mel Dick's daughter repeated.

"Fine then," Spooner said, "I'll make arrangements and get back to you."

I followed Spooner outside—out of Julie's earshot—and ran my idea past him. He agreed, and I asked about Anita's autopsy.

"Dolores Rio says that Anita drowned though she hasn't gotten all the labs yet. The body was bruised, but postmortem injury is typical in drowning victims. A lot of time the body is buffeted by water currents."

"Mystic Bay is a drainage pond. There aren't any currents."

"There was some wind last night, and you did find Anita near the pier. Being whacked against those pilings could do some damage. There was one other thing. Some of the bruises were on Anita's upper and lower forearms, shoulders and back of her hands."

"All consistent with defensive posturing," I said excitedly.

"My thought as well, but Rio is certain the bruising occurred antemortem, a day or two before Anita's death."

"Oh, no."

"I knew you wouldn't like it."

I didn't. The defensive bruising—if that was what it was—occurred in the general time frame of Mel Dick's death. Maybe the quarrel between Mel and Anita on the night of Mel's death deteriorated into something physical. Sick and tired, Mel ran for the woods while Anita fumed. She got Mel's gun and went to search for her husband, eventually finding him in the clearing of Birnam Wood. She shot him in the temple, unaware he was already dead. A lot was still unaccounted for, but I had to consider the possibility that Anita Dick was the shooter after all.

"Is SOMETHING WRONG with the computer?" Julie asked from behind.

The second Spooner left, I'd pounced on Mel's computer, certain I would find the article he'd been working on at the time of his death.

"The monitor's not coming on," I said.

"Maybe it's not plugged in."

"That's not it." I pointed to the lighted buttons. I turned the computer tower around and asked Julie for a screwdriver so I could take a quick peek inside.

"Why don't you use my laptop?"

"I need to examine Mel's computer. I promise I won't break anything. Please, the screwdriver."

While Julie searched I rolled back the desk chair and stretched. I hoped Julie hadn't heard the irritation in my voice, but I responded poorly to micromanagement and she'd insisted on breathing down my neck while I scoured Mel's computer. I'd pleaded with her to get some rest, promising to call her if I found anything, but she wouldn't have it. Of course my motive was less than pure—in addition to searching for the article, I was itching to view Marco's video on the large monitor, preferably without Julie's help.

Five minutes later Julie returned with several screwdrivers. I picked one and got to work. The screws came out easily. I popped off the back, with Julie hovering behind.

"That doesn't look right," Julie muttered, peering inside the gutted tower.

"No, Julie, it isn't right. At least now we know why the computer doesn't work."

Someone had stolen the hard drive.

A QUICK INSPECTION of Mel's liquor cabinet revealed slim pickings: Bacardi, Smirnoff's and a bottle of no-name brandy that had probably been poured on last year's Christmas fruitcake. I called out the choices to Julie.

"Brandy seems appropriate," Julie said.

After our discovery of the missing hard drive Julie had collapsed into a broken heap. They said that what didn't kill you made you stronger, but people forgot that sometimes it did kill you. I poured the drinks, putting slightly more in Julie's snifter than mine. I also brought the bottle along. Just in case.

Julie slumped over the tan recliner like a sopping blanket. "Here," I said, placing her drink on the side table. I rolled the desk chair closer.

"What do you expect to find on the computer?" Julie asked.

"A motive for murder."

A harsh laugh. "Spooner said it wasn't murder."

I spoke slowly, carefully, as much for myself as for Julie. "That it isn't murder is a technicality. Whoever shot Mel meant to kill him. Furthermore, this person believes he was successful. So in his mind, he is a murderer. And that makes him dangerous."

Julie sipped her brandy, grimaced. "Do you think this murderer wannabe also took Dad's hard drive?"

"Oh, yes." When I saw the mutilated computer, I knew I was in the presence of an intelligent evil. "I believe that at the time of his death your dad was working on a pretty shocking story."

"Shocking?"

Without naming names, I outlined the prostitution angle. "I'd hoped to find something related to the story in the computer—notes, a rough draft, even the article itself. But someone beat me to it."

"So somebody shot Dad to keep him from publishing some hooker story in that rinky-dink newspaper of his? Sounds preposterous."

"Preposterous things happen all the time. More brandy? It's not half-bad."

"It's not half-good either," Julie said, "but fill 'er up." I refilled both snifters. "Even if you're right, we're too late."

"Don't give up. I'm betting Mel had backup files on

his office computer. I don't think I'll have any problem gaining access to it."

"Legally? The smile on your face is positively evil—you look like you're plotting something nefarious."

"I have a pretty good connection—I'm sure Fairley Sable will let me take a peek at Mel's office computer. All aboveboard."

Julie blinked in surprise. "Fairley Sable?"

"You know her?" Now I was the surprised one.

"I met her for the first time today, though I recognized the name when she introduced herself—Mom sometimes mentioned her. Fairley stopped by to offer condolences for Mom and Dad. She brought a big bouquet of flowers from her garden and a coffee cake."

"That was fast."

"I think she wanted me to invite her in for coffee and cake, but I just wasn't up to it. She seemed nice."

Since Julie seemed to be somewhat restored, I put my little idea on the table. "I'd like to have a second autopsy done on your father."

The eyebrows shot up and her mouth formed a little o. "Is that necessary?"

"I believe so."

But Julie Breyer wanted no part of it. She was going through her objections for the third time, when I made a hard decision. Julie said she wanted to be in the loop. I would take her at her word.

"In the days before his death your father underwent a startling change in mental status." I described the forgetfulness, the paranoia, the grandiosity. "I'm hoping a second autopsy will reveal the cause."

"No, no, no," Julie said. "I don't believe it—you make it sound like Dad was crazy! Who told you these lies about Dad?"

"They aren't lies, Julie. Several people, including my own security guards, witnessed Mel's aberrant behavior."

"Did you see it for yourself?"

I held her gaze and said, "Yes, and you can see it too."

It didn't take long to find Marco's masterpiece on Julie's laptop. I pressed Play.

A sharp intake of breath and Julie's harsh whisper. "Dad."

On the monitor José Barracas and Mel Dick were squared off like drunken prizefighters. José's back was to the camera, but Mel Dick's red face filled the screen, his features contorted by hate. My God, he was a volcano of hate. Mel's right arm reared back and then lurched forward, releasing a wad of paper that bounced off José's head. A shiver of cries roiled the crowd. José stumbled backward, nearly falling. The camera caught a glimpse of José's frightened face as he scampered off-camera. Mel launched into his rambling and mumbling *j'accuse,* almost incomprehensible. I assumed it was the poor audio, until Gigi Tajani's voice rang clear and true, "No, Mel, no!"

So the defect was Mel's.

After he'd expelled his venom, the old man lifted his frightened dog and cried, "This is my only friend!" As Mel lumbered from the patio, the video dissolved into kaleidoscopic chaos. When the picture resumed, Mel's Humvee was disappearing into the night, but then I saw something I hadn't noticed before—the hood of a white Prius, following in the wake of Mel's golf cart. Then the video ended.

A hollow pit opened in my stomach. Oscar Wall had mentioned a Prius. On the night of his death Mel had blazed past the Admiral Street guardhouse in his golf cart, and hard on the cart's ass was a Prius. I couldn't remember whether Oscar had said the car was white or purple or streaked with rainbows, but the way this case was unfolding, I'd guess it was white.

And who was the most famous—infamous?—owner of a white Prius in Mystic Cove? Why, the lady in white, of course—Busy Rhodes, who had sworn that she last saw Mel Dick at the Barnes and Noble, weeks before his death.

Now why would the lady lie?

AFTER SEVERAL ROUNDS of phone tag and multiple emails, Mel Dick's second autopsy was scheduled for seven that evening. It would be performed by Dr. Hackle, a forensic pathologist on staff at University Hospital in Newnansville and Uncle Otto's former protégée.

Next I called Fairley Sable, who agreed to meet me at the newspaper office within the hour. Driving past the Admiral Street guardhouse, I spotted Oscar Wall inside. A bit of luck—I could ask Oscar about the Prius. Smiling, I rolled down the car window, but my smile died when I saw Oscar's face. It was the mask of a dark Yoruba god up to mischief.

"Ms. Gorsky," Oscar said with a curt nod.

"Oscar, I wanted to ask you about the night of Dick's death. You said you saw a Prius—"

"Can I see your visitor's pass?" The voice of a stranger—I felt cold.

"Pass?" I didn't have a pass—Jesse Potts had waved me in, even though he'd known I was no longer chief. "What's all this ma'am crap, Oscar? It's me, Addie."

"What is your business in Mystic Cove, ma'am?" Oscar's eyes narrowed on Jinks, who, concerned at the delay, had bounded into my lap.

"I visited Julie Breyer at 1800 Admiral Street, but I want to ask you what color the Prius was."

"There's no one living in that house, ma'am."

"Goddamn it, Oscar." I gave him Julie's cell number. "And once Mrs. Breyer clears me, I want a week-long pass. I'm going to be seeing her on a regular basis."

Fifteen minutes later Oscar handed over the pass.

"But this is only good for today."

"New rules from the top," Oscar said with a vile grin. "Only daily passes from now on."

Then a sharp slap as the window snapped shut.

# THIRTEEN

*It Smells to Heaven*

FAIRLEY FLIPPED THE LIGHTS: "This is our reception area—isn't it nice? Mel believed the *Commentator* office should put forth the proper image."

To me the place had the charm of an upscale dentist's waiting room, with all the conventional accoutrements—a few potted palms, a stack of nondescript magazines, even an aquarium of angelfish. On sunny days, the large picture window would allow plenty of natural light, but on this rainy day the vertical blinds were shuttered. "I appreciate this," I said.

A shadow tempered Fairley's smile. "This is the first time I've been here since Mel's passing. It's so empty and sad. I hate to think what will happen to the *Commentator* with Mel gone."

"You never know, somebody might step up to the plate." I could care less about the *Commentator* and thought the best thing for all concerned would be for the paper to die a merciful death.

"But who? There's Alan of course, but I can't see him returning to the paper, what with Tally being ill."

"Is Mrs. Rand's illness serious?" I asked, remembering that Rand had guarded Tally like a Pekinese in the Forbidden City.

Fairley's hand flew to her throat. "I have no idea. I'm just repeating things I've heard." She laughed. "Didn't I warn you that I was a gossipy old lady? But let me give you the grand tour—that is, if your little partner promises not to leave any surprises." She wagged a playful finger at Jinks, who pressed against my leg.

"He'll be a good boy." Just in case I picked him up.

"This is our reception room. There's a small kitchen to the left. That's my little desk over there." Fairley pointed to an unassuming desk in the corner. "You can check my computer as well. I wouldn't mind."

"Not necessary, I just need Mel's." I followed Fairley down a short hallway at the end of which was a door marked with gold letters: Editor's Office. With a Vanna White flourish, Fairley opened the door and bade me enter.

Mel's office was worthy of the gilded age. It oozed masculine comfort, all gleaming hardwoods, buttery leather and shining metals. And yet it was too much, a jumble of costly trinkets that gave the impression of junk.

"Password?" I asked.

"Try *Commentator,* that's what I use for my computer."

A herd of folders filled the screen, one of which was conveniently named *morgue.*

"I've always hated that name," Fairley said, breathing down my neck. I wanted to tell her to give me some space, but was trying to play nice since I was here because of her.

"Morgue? It's just a name." The file for 2013 contained eleven folders, from January to November. At random I highlighted January, saw that it had last been opened on January 11.

"That's the wrong file."

I flinched at Fairley's shrill voice.

"I want to get a sense of how Mel organized his material," I said as my fingers tapped. "That way when I look at November, I'll be better able to gauge if something is…awry."

"You're so clever."

Another flinch as Fairley's hands squeezed my shoulders.

Mel's morgue was stuffed with information—finished articles, rough drafts, sources culled from the internet. As I skimmed the material, I realized that Mel's real talent was in plagiarism. Most of his purported articles were taken almost verbatim from other sources. The only original investigative piece I found was a breathless exposé on a small group of green-minded Cove dwellers who wanted to install clotheslines. Some journalist!

But it was time for the big event—I highlighted November. "That's strange."

"What?" Fairley whispered in my ear.

"This folder was last opened at 1:55 Friday morning."

"That's not unusual. Mel often came in at odd hours to work."

"At 1:55 Friday morning Mel Dick was lying in the morgue—the real one." I opened the folder.

It was empty.


"I DON'T KNOW why you had to call the police," Fairley said. "Anita and Mel are gone—why not let them rest in peace?"

"The police investigation is still open and, even if it weren't, Mrs. Breyer hired me to look into her parents' deaths. Who had keys to the *Commentator* office?"

"Only Mel, of course," she said.

"So how did you get in?"

"I only have a key because the other day I asked Anita for hers—I needed to water the plants and retrieve some things."

It was a good enough explanation, but I was troubled. I thought about the set of keys found in Mel's shorts, keys that as far as I knew were still sitting in a box in the evidence room. I expected that Mel would have kept his office keys with him, meaning Anita must have given Fairley a duplicate. In most cases this was no cause for alarm, but given Mel's deep-rooted suspicion of those around him—including his wife—I thought it odd that Anita had access to the duplicate key.

"Is there any way to recover the files?" Fairley asked.

"In theory," I said. GCSO lacked the resources to retrieve the data, especially with murder off the table. A loud rap told us that CSU had arrived to take the computer into evidence. While Fairley hurried to the door, I realized I hadn't checked the search history. When I did so I discovered that neither Mel nor the mysterious hacker had deleted the history. A clumsy oversight. I had just copied the last query in the short list when CSU investigators poured inside.

"What are you doing?" Deputy Berry groused.

"Waiting for you." I slipped the notepad into my jacket pocket.

As CSU techs swarmed the computer, Fairley Sable appeared at my side. "You found something on the computer, didn't you, Addie? You look as if you've just struck gold."

I only hoped it wasn't fool's gold.

SHERIFF BUBBA SPOONER waved me inside his office. Without preamble I told him about the keys.

"We now know that somebody tampered with both computers, and since neither the Dick house nor the office had been broken into, the perp must have had keys to both places. So, I'm wondering what keys were found on Mel's body."

"I get it. You think the shooter snagged the keys off of Mel's body." Spooner started scribbling. "I'll get Berry to check it out."

"The sooner the better. If Mel still had his office and house keys on him when he died, then I'm wrong and Mel's big story played no part in his murder. But if those keys are missing..."

Spooner held up a hand of surrender. "Berry will check out the key, and now, what else do you have?"

I did an exaggerated double take. "What makes you think there's something else?"

"You're an hour early for the autopsy and you could have called about the keys, but mostly it's the way you look—like a cat after a canary dinner. So what you got?"

"It would be quicker if I showed you. Can I use your computer?"

I WAS LATE in joining Spooner in the autopsy room. I lagged, obsessively checking my gear, afraid that I'd left some vulnerable part of my body exposed. In my homicide days, it'd been my least favorite part of the job.

"Dr. Hackle?" I said to the man bent over Mel Dick's corpse. "I'm Addie Gorsky. Both my client and I appreciate your help." Too late I saw the warning in Spooner's eyes.

The little man peering at Mel Dick's upper arm slowly straightened to his full height, which in shoes and socks might have measured a full five feet. Brown eyes above the mask met mine.

"Cut the crap, Miss Gorsky. I'm here as a favor to Otto Rider and nothing else."

"Of course," I said, backing away.

"He's a prickly son-of-a-gun," Spooner said, sotto voce. My communications with Hackle had been through Uncle

Otto and email while Spooner had had the pleasure of more direct interactions.

"Did I miss anything?" I asked Spooner.

Hackle peered at us over his glasses. "Why don't you two chatty Cathies come over here and make yourselves useful?" A worried glance between Spooner and myself, but we obeyed, albeit without much enthusiasm.

"It can be problematic to differentiate between ante-mortem and postmortem injuries, especially when those injuries are inflicted in the last few minutes of life. For example, if a person collapses, there might be lacerations to the head and scalp, which can be a bitch to interpret. But as there's no evidence of hemorrhage, I can say with certainly that the head trauma occurred postmortem."

"Dead men don't bleed," I said.

"As a general rule, if they do anything, they ooze," Hackle said.

"What about the arm wound?" Spooner asked.

"That is interesting!" Crinkles appeared around the lively eyes and Hackle pointed at Dick's upper left arm. "What do you see?"

"I see a small abrasion..." Spooner began.

"No shit, Sherlock. Look at the area around the wound. Now what do you see?"

I leaned close. Tiny white fibers clung to the area, forming a discrete band around the arm. I told Hackle what I thought I saw.

"Very good, Scarpetta—now what does that mean, boys and girls?"

Spooner laughed softly. "Somebody put a friggin' Band-Aid on the first gunshot wound."

BACK IN HIS OFFICE, Spooner produced a bottle of Jack. Both Hackle and I nodded and the sheriff poured. I preferred Jim Beam myself, but any port in a storm. We drank in silence for a few minutes. Somewhat restored by the whiskey, I opened it up. "So where do we stand?"

"Up the creek without a paddle," Spooner answered.

I disagreed. "Now that we know a not insignificant time elapsed between the two gunshots we can recreate the night of the murder more accurately. The gunshot wound to the arm happened elsewhere. After that, Mel cleaned his wound and changed clothes."

"Clothes that don't fit," Spooner said. He turned to Hackle. "Any chance the head wound also occurred elsewhere?"

"No way, lividity indicates Mel Dick died in that golf cart."

"After which he was shot in the head," I added.

"So Blanding was right about that," Spooner said.

"TOD is accurate as well," Hackle said. "Mel died between ten and two in the morning."

I said, "Mel was last seen alive a little after eleven, which narrows the TOD even more."

"We only have Anita's word on that, Addie," Spooner reminded me.

"I also agree with Blanding's assessment of general health," Hackle said. "Mel was slightly overweight but otherwise quite robust for a man of sixty-two. Apart from some slight scarring of the upper right lung, his organs were free of disease."

"So what was the cause of death?" I asked, exasperated.

"Most likely a heart attack," Hackle said.

"But you said he was healthy." This from the sheriff.

"The human body is not a car, Sheriff. You don't crack the hood and see the old parts. I said his organs appeared to be free of disease, including his heart. But it's not unheard of for seemingly healthy hearts to stop beating."

"Especially if they get a little help," I muttered.

"Is this murder?" Spooner asked, cutting to the chase.

"It's awfully suspicious, but I'm not sure if it's murder," Hackle said. "That's for you guys and the district attorney to decide."

"You're killing me," Spooner moaned, reaching for the bottle. After refilling his glass, he tipped the bottle to me and Hackle. I held out my glass but Hackle demurred.

"Dr. Hackle," I said, "might the first gunshot have precipitated the fatal heart attack?"

"Absolutely," Hackle said, rubbing his goateed chin, "but since we know so little of the circumstances of the initial wound, it's difficult to determine."

Spooner snorted. "Seems clear-cut to me. Dick was shot, the stress and loss of blood caused the heart attack—that's murder."

"First of all, there was insignificant blood loss, with no sign of hypovolemia. The bleeding was staunched immediately after the injury. And his stress level is unknown—he wasn't even concerned enough to get himself to the E.R. The arm wound was very minor. With minimal care it would have healed on its own. Now if Dick was restrained, and somehow prevented from obtaining medical care, then it's clearly murder." Hackle sighed and set his empty glass on Spooner's desk. "I've done my job, Sheriff. It's in your ballpark now. I only wish I had performed the first autopsy. I suspect there is a lot more Mel Dick had to tell me. These second autopsies are always problematic."

Spooner and I exchanged a quick look.

"You're right, Doc," Spooner said, fingers tapping over the keyboard. "Mel Dick does have something else to tell you. This video was recorded hours before Mr. Dick's death."

As Mel Dick's agony played out again, I focused on Hackle's reaction. The pathologist watched in mute concentration. When it was done he gestured for Spooner to play it again. In all Hackle watched the video a total of five times and with each viewing his brow grew more furrowed and his silence more impenetrable. What did he see?

"I've changed my mind, Sheriff," Hackle said at last. "I'll take you up on that other drink." A healthy slug of Jack and Hackle said, "I'll have to wait for toxicology results, but I'd bet that Mel Dick was suffering from anticholinergic syndrome."

"Is that the disease that killed him?" Spooner asked.

"Acute anticholinergic syndrome is not a disease, although it could certainly precipitate a fatal heart attack. The syndrome is usually caused by an overdose of an anticholinergic drug. In a patient of Mel Dick's age, I would expect the cause to be geriatric polypharmacy."

"You mean he took too much prescription medicine?" Spooner said.

"Many older folks are on multiple meds, Sheriff."

"Not Mel Dick." I explained that I'd scoured the Dick home searching for medications, hoping to find a clue to Mel's mental deterioration. "Apart from Anita's diabetic meds, all I found was Mel's Lipitor, which his daughter said he'd been taking for years. According to her, it was the only medication Mel was prescribed."

"The medication could have been prescribed for an acute condition of which the daughter was unaware." Hackle looked at Spooner. "Perhaps Mr. Dick carried the medication on his person."

"Sorry, Doc," Spooner said. "No medications were

found on the body or in the golf cart. Now, don't take this the wrong way, but how are you so all-fired sure that Dick had this syndrome?"

Hackle's lips made a straight line. "The parasympathetic nervous system regulates the so-called rest-and-digest activities. Peeing, pooping, salivating…"

"We get the picture," Spooner said.

"Anticholinergic medications inhibit the parasympathetic nervous system by blocking the neurotransmitter acetylcholine. This can cause a cluster of unpleasant side effects including dry mouth, increased thirst, flushing…"

Spooner slapped his desk. "You just painted a picture of Mel Dick on the night of his death."

I told Hackle about Mel's cognitive symptoms and asked if that fit with his tentative diagnosis.

"Yes," he said slowly, "but it might be helpful to think of Mel's condition as intoxication rather than disease. Paranoid delusions and grandiosity could be part of the picture while retrograde amnesia is typical. Of course I'm basing my diagnosis on a jittery video, but if you go through the video with a checklist of observable anticholinergic side effects, even a layperson can see it."

I was excited. Hackle might have discovered the cause of Dick's cognitive decline, that peculiar lunacy that waxed and waned like the moon. Faint bells rang. Playing devil's advocate, I asked, "But don't a lot of diseases have similar symptoms? For instance, increased thirst is a sign of diabetes."

"And folks turn red when they're pissed off," Spooner added.

Hackle raised his eyes to the heavens. "Since WebMD, everybody thinks they're doctors. You're both right, of course, and as I viewed the video, I asked myself the same questions. Let's go through the video again and this time I'll talk you through it."

Sheriff Spooner and I watched the video with new eyes. We hardly required Hackle's explication, it was all in front of us—the slurred speech, unsteady gait, flushed complexion.

"Pause it, Sheriff—this is rather interesting." It was near the end of the video. Mel Dick's red face filled the screen. He held Mr. Jinks to his chest, just after he'd declaimed the pooch as his only friend. "Look at his eyes," Hackle commanded.

"As big as saucers," Spooner said.

"When I saw those dilated pupils, I felt fairly certain this was anticholinergic toxicity."

"But what caused it?" I said. My head spun from all the jargon and we were no closer to the truth.

He knocked off his drink, stifled a yawn. "I don't know. As I said before, my best guess would be an accidental overdose of a prescribed med. Further muddying the waters, many other medications have anticholinergic properties—antipsychotics, antidepressants, antihistamines. The thing doesn't hang together." The frustration in Hackle's voice was almost palpable. "If Mel Dick was four or five decades younger, it'd make a hell of a lot more sense. Most clinical presentations of anticholinergic toxicity are hallucinating teenagers who stumble into the E.R. after ingesting *Datura stramonium* for a cheap high. The literature identifies rare cases of *Atropa belladonna* used for its hallucinogenic properties—now that's really playing with fire."

"Belladonna," I said. "Isn't that deadly nightshade?"

"That's poison," Spooner said.

"Yes," Hackle said, "an ancient poison especially beloved of the Romans. *Belladonna* means beautiful woman and *Atropa* refers to Atropos, one of the three Fates in Greek mythology."

"Aren't you a wealth of information," Spooner said.

"Atropos was the scary big sister." When Spooner and Hackle gave me the fish-eye, I explained that as a child I'd devoured Greek myth.

"I'll bite—what's so scary about big sister?" Spooner asked.

"She's the one with the scissors. When a person's allotted time is up, she cuts the life thread—a quick snip and oblivion." Hackle scissored the air with his fingers.

"What was that other plant you mentioned?" Spooner asked. "*Datura* something?"

"*Datura stramonium* has a long history of use as a hallucinogenic. It's a common plant. I've seen it growing in a lot of Florida backyards."

Spooner snapped his fingers. "You mean stinkweed?"

Hackle nodded. "That's one of its names, along with devil's grass, angel trumpet, jimsonweed."

Spooner threw back his drink. "A couple years back we picked up a boy walking naked down Center Street after eating stinkweed."

"As I said," Hackle said, "if Dick was a reckless teenager, I would guess datura poisoning secondary to self-medication."

"There's no way Mel would intentionally ingest such a dangerous substance," I said.

"I agree." Hackle stretched his back, followed by a loud pop. "It's far more likely to be an inadvertent overdose of a prescribed medication. That's what you should be looking for, Sheriff."

"Maybe Mel Dick didn't know he was ingesting the stuff," I suggested. "Maybe someone fed it to him."

"Poison?" Spooner asked, nearly falling from his chair.

"Highly unlikely," Hackle pronounced. "There are far more effective poisons available. Datura as a poison just doesn't make sense."

"There's a lot about this squirrelly case that doesn't make sense," Spooner said.

"That may be." Hackle pushed back his chair. "But right now I'm a tired old man who needs to get to bed."

With insectoid grace Spooner untangled his long legs. "I'll show you the way out. I'm ready to put this day to bed myself."

We walked in silence through the quiet house of the dead. At the exit Hackle paused, his face furrowed with the burden of age and memory. "Gorsky," he said gruffly, "if Mel's daughter is willing, I could autopsy Mrs. Dick as well." Before he had a chance for second thoughts, I accepted, certain Julie would agree.

"Good, good—I'm free tomorrow any time after two, just let me know."

Spooner and I tried to thank him, but Hackle waved us off and limped into the dark night, for the first time looking like the old man he was. I started to follow, but Spooner held my arm.

"Berry got back to me about the keys found on Mel's body. Mel Dick's house key was part of the set, but none of the keys fit his office."

# FOURTEEN

*Out Damned Spot*

"COME HERE OFTEN, Sheriff?"

"I prefer to do my drinking in Newnansville—my face is a little too familiar here." Bubba Spooner and I were the only customers at the bar, though a couple of Eddie's regulars were working the pool table, and sporadic whoops and laughter sounded from the banquet room.

"Are you from the area?" I asked.

"I've lived in Lady-in-the-Hills all my life, except for the years I was in the service."

I was starting to think that maybe this whole thing was a mistake. When Spooner offered to buy me a drink, I was too surprised to object and now found myself having a beer with a man whom until recently I had thought an enemy.

"I always felt that you and me got off on the wrong foot," Spooner said, reading my mind.

"It happens, Sheriff."

"I'm off-duty."

"Okay… Bubba." We both winced. The Southern nickname sounded downright peculiar when filtered through my Baltimore accent.

"My name is Brad."

"But I thought…"

Brad sighed. "Every Southern family has a Bubba. I just happened to draw the golden ticket." He laughed.

"I've tried to lose it, but things stick in small towns. And it does help come election time. Grubber County citizens love a good old boy named Bubba."

Brad smiled at the barmaid who'd just arrived with our beers, along with a bowl of stale popcorn. Immediately his large hand scooped up a handful of the stuff.

I stayed his hand. "I wouldn't advise that."

"But I'm hungry. I didn't eat dinner."

"Neither did I, but you don't want that." I explained that at the end of the night the staff married all the leftover snacks into a big plastic bag, to be served the next day and the day after that. I thought of the dirt-encrusted fingernails and greasy knuckles that had fondled the popcorn over the years. I liked dive bars, but you had to be smart.

Brad let the stale popcorn fall back into the bowl. Both of us started laughing. It was silly, but we'd been running on fumes for days and the beer had put us over the edge. It was also the nature of our business. In the face of human depravity—and what was more depraved than murder?—laughter could save your life.

"This is cozy," a voice slurred from behind. It was Tyler Andrews, decked out in Mystic Cove khaki and stinking drunk. At his side was Billy Blake, who would not meet my eyes.

"We're having a private conversation here, Andrews." In his slow way Brad eased off the bar stool, lean body coiled like a spring.

Tyler glared at the taller man. Billy edged away from the action, the scruffy guys at the pool table stopped their play, and the bartender looked up from the sink behind the bar. Bloodhounds all, scenting trouble.

"I see what it is, Spooner," Tyler said, "but it's okay. You can have my sloppy seconds." Brad took a step forward, a solid rock to Tyler Andrews's sputtering candle.

Blanching, Tyler stumbled away, waving his hand, like a magician at the climax of a magic trick.

I almost laughed—was he trying to make us disappear?

"Go to hell, the both of you. I'm leaving this dump."

When Billy tried to follow Tyler, Brad placed a hand on the old man's shoulder. "Don't let that fool get behind the wheel."

"I don't know what to say." I stared into my beer, too embarrassed to face him.

"Then don't say anything."

I shot a sideways glance at Brad Spooner, studied his profile as he drank his beer. It was a rocky sort of face but not unattractive. "Why'd you ask me here, Brad?"

"To watch you enjoy your beer." He laughed and added, "I thought we might kick around the case, if you were up to it." Was he kidding? It was after midnight, but I didn't feel tired. Sleep could wait and something told me that getting to the heart of Mel Dick's death couldn't. I needed answers, not sleep.

"The thing with the keys has me stumped," I said. "Why didn't the shooter take both keys off of Mel? If his purpose was to cleanse both computers of evidence, wouldn't he need the house key as well?"

"Anita didn't need a key to get into her own house," Brad said. A whoop from the pool table signaled somebody just got off a good shot.

"Not so fast," I said. "Fairley told me that Anita had her own key to Mel's office. Besides, I doubt Mel was writing an exposé on his own wife. No, one person tampered with both computers and I don't think it was Anita Dick."

"You could be wrong about that big story theory, and maybe Mel just misplaced his office key, but for the moment let's assume you're right. It's possible the perp only took the key he needed because he figured no one would notice it missing."

"Which is exactly what happened until I brought it to your attention," I reminded him. "Or the shooter didn't take the house key because he'd already stolen the hard drive from Mel's home computer."

"So after shooting Mel, he calmly goes through the keys and pulls off the one he needs, knowing exactly which key belonged to Mel's office. Pretty cool customer."

"And then at 1:55 Friday morning he snuck into the *Commentator* office and deleted the remaining file on Mel's computer." I glanced at the guys shooting pool— the loser was making a vociferous plea for another game.

"We just built a house of straw out of a lot of conjecture and very little fact." Brad glanced at the muted TV, which was showing highlights from last week's game. "Let's leave the keys for now, and review what we know for sure."

"Do we know anything for sure in this mess?" As I'd expected the pool players were setting up for another game. There was always another game.

"We know that Anita went right home after the disturbance at the restaurant. The OCSO deputy was at the Dick residence at six-thirty, where he found Mrs. Dick at home. She told the deputy she was alone, but she could have been lying."

"Six-thirty? Are you sure?"

"It could be off by a minute or two—why?"

"The timeline on the video had Mel leaving the Grub and Grog at six-twenty. How the heck did Anita get home so quickly? Somebody must have given her a ride."

"So what?" Brad asked.

"At the least, that person could clue us in on Anita's mood."

"I see that," Brad said, but from the look of him, he

didn't. "For now let's concentrate on what we know." He tapped the pitted bar for emphasis. "I think Anita's version of the murder night is accurate to a point. We have Fairley's statement for corroboration, and phone records show that somebody from the Dick house called the Sable house at 12:03 that morning." He paused while a young guy wearing a backward baseball cap ordered a pitcher.

"So we're pretty sure," Brad continued, "that Anita watched TV until sometime around eleven when the prodigal returned from God-knows-where. They argued over Gigi, and Mel took off. Things start to get murky when Anita gets to Fairley's."

"I wonder if Jinks was with Mel," I said, going off in my own direction as usual.

"Who?"

"Mel's dog. He might be our only witness."

"There might be some problems with him on the stand," Brad deadpanned. "But can we get back to the subject?"

"Sorry, my mind tends to jump around." I glanced at the pool players. From their body language the new game was going the way of the first—same winners, same losers.

Brad took a long pull on his beer. "As I was saying, things get murky at Fairley's house. Who's to say Anita didn't sneak out while Fairley was asleep and shoot Mel?"

I scowled. "I can't imagine anyone sneaking out on Fairley. I just can't." I tried to explain, but the words came hard. "She's...a very aware person, and yet there's something... I don't know...vague about her." I scanned Brad's face, but it was as confused as my words. "I guess it's just that Fairley is a bit of an odd duck," I said lamely.

"Mystic Cove is home to odd ducks."

We clinked bottles and laughed. Brad was right. They

were all a little off: drunken José, Alan Rand and his re-
clusive wife, Tally, Gigi, and of course Busy.

"But seriously," Brad said, "do you think Fairley's lying
about something?"

"I'm not sure, but from the beginning I've believed
that Fairley would stretch the truth to protect her friend."

"But Anita is dead. There's no longer a reason for Fairley to lie."

"True, but it'd still be hard for Fairley to admit she's
been less than honest with the police."

"Yeah, but Fairley Sable has gone out of her way to
be helpful. She's the one who reported that Anita was at
her house."

I nearly choked on my beer. "Are you kidding me?"

Brad shrugged. "Fairley called GCSO to say that Anita
Dick was sitting in her backyard. We were still canvassing
Admiral Street, so it only took us a minute to get there."

"That's what I mean about this woman, Brad—she's
really strange. First she begged me not to call the police
and then the first chance she got, she called you guys."

"The old lady got spooked, that's all."

"Or maybe she just wanted to make me look like an
ass—something I can do on my own."

"So I've observed." But before I could howl, Brad
laughed and signaled for another round.

"Are we done with Fairley?" he asked after the barmaid had left our beers. I gave a thumbs-up. "Good, because I want to talk about Mystic Cove's favorite pimp."
Brad explained that Deputy Berry had talked to José, who
admitted handing out a few phone numbers, but nothing
else. "And Berry didn't press. After Anita's death, the
case appeared solved." Brad took a long pull on his beer
and turned to me. "But now things have changed. What's
your take on Barracas?"

"He's pretty deep in the bottle and he does have a monstrous temper. He has motive and opportunity, but I don't like him for the murder. He's a sloppy drunk and this murder was anything but."

Brad agreed.

"And there's another angle to it. According to Rand, Mel finished his hooker exposé way back in September. That fact that Mel sat on his big story for over a month without publishing is pretty suspicious. Maybe Mel found a more profitable use for the information."

Brad raced ahead. "Blackmail?"

"Absolutely. Mel liked to think he was virtuous, but it was a convenient virtue. If he needed the money, he'd blackmail the pope. Maybe one of the johns got tired of paying."

He started scribbling in his notepad. "This is the first concrete lead we've had. Tomorrow we'll check Mel's finances for funny stuff and I'll have Berry drag the names of those johns out of Barracas."

"Good, I'm curious if a certain overprotective husband is on the client list."

His jaw dropped. "Not Alan Rand? Christ, you got a devious mind."

"Rand didn't play straight with me. I had to push hard to get any information out of him, especially about his September meeting with Mel. The man is hiding something and I want to know what it is."

Brad put his beer down and leaned closer. "You really think Rand was one of the johns and Mel was blackmailing his old friend?"

"Not really, but something caused a rift between them. If Rand was fooling around with hookers, it's more likely that he feared disclosure. That would end his marriage, and whatever his flaws, Rand loves his wife."

"Money and sex," Brad said softly. "It always comes down to that."

We kicked the can till last call. We kept going back to Mel's missing hours. The old man was MIA between six-twenty, when he left the Grub and Grog, to around midnight, when he turned up at home. A brief argument with Anita, and he disappeared again, until I found him in Birnam Wood. Where was he for those missing hours?

"Mel was disoriented," I said, "but behavior doesn't come from nothing. He was in the grip of a strong delusion, certain that his wife and his friends had turned on him. His only friend was his dog. Right or wrong, that was his reality."

"You're saying that crazy has a reason."

"I like that, Brad. Yes, crazy has a reason. Crazy finds a way. Mel must have gone to a place where he felt safe."

"He went to ground, and at some point in all that wandering he gets shot in the arm and changes his clothes."

I slapped the bar. "I think I know where Mel went after his fight with Anita. Gigi's!"

"But Mel and his girlfriend were on the outs."

"Yeah, but Mel Dick had run out of options. I'm betting that even in his deluded state he knew Gigi would welcome him open arms."

Before leaving, Brad promised to run background checks on the principle players—Alan and Tally Rand, Fairley Sable, Gigi Tajani, José Barracas.

"And Busy Rhodes," I added, pulling on my jacket.

Brad cocked an eyebrow. "Remind me who or what Busy Rhodes is."

I outlined the blood feud that was Mel and Busy's relationship.

"Why are you just mentioning this now?"

"It's a long shot." This would have been a good time to tell Brad about the white Prius in the video, which might or might not have been Busy's, but I wanted to hold on to that piece of information a little longer. Tomorrow I wanted to face the woman in white on my own terms. Now that I was no longer shackled to Mystic Cove security, I'd get the truth out of her, one way or another.

"Jesus Christ, Addie, don't let a man you love see you looking like that. That look on your face would turn his blood to ice. You're even scaring me a little."

I laughed it off. "Sometimes I scare myself, Brad. Sometimes I scare myself."

POP WAS SOUND asleep when I crept inside the dark apartment. Jinks, who had been sleeping at the foot of Dad's bed, let out a few squeaky barks and started running in circles. Once he'd settled down, I fired up the computer. I had a few more tasks to complete before I could put this long day to rest for good.

I started with a little quick and dirty research on *Datura stramonium*. My pulse quickened as I scanned the hits. Along with the expected botanical tracts and horticultural information, several sites dealt with the use of datura as a recreational drug, both pro and con. It was a showy plant that I was certain I'd seen before: trumpet flowers, some creamy white and others tinged with lavender, erupting from masses of large toothy leaves. I could understand its popularity in the flower garden, but this beauty had a dark side.

Datura's hallucinogenic properties were well documented, with perhaps the most famous occurrence at the Jamestown settlement. Nowadays most of datura's willing victims were stupid kids looking for a psychedelic experience on the cheap, unmindful of the plant's brutal nature. Seeking the release of dreams, they were trapped in nightmare. Next I turned to my main task.

From the pocket of my jacket, I fished out the scrap

of paper on which I had copied the search history from Dick's office computer. I frowned at the frantic chicken scratch. As a leftie, my handwriting has always been atrocious, but in my haste my writing resembled cuneiform. I thought I heard Sister Mary Margaret's laughter from beyond the grave. I never got past a D in penmanship at St. Andrews, despite the elderly nun's Cassandra-like warnings of the dire consequences.

Finally I deciphered the mess and other than a query on the weather, all of Mel's searches referenced the fugitive lists of various law enforcement agencies and crime-fighting organizations. I started with the FBI's Most Wanted and worked my way down. As I hopped around the websites, staring at the faces of anonymous fugitives from remote decades, their dead faces brought to mind the endless rows of glassy-eyed fish at the stalls in Lexington Market. I tried to pick out a thread of understanding, but it was useless. Without a context, I was lost in a pit of murderers and drug lords. Mel's search history was just another dead end. I was about to throw the scrap of paper into the wastebasket when I noticed my mistake. I had misread the first query as Weather, but it read Weatherman, or maybe Weathermen. Did it matter either way? Just a scrivener's error. I threw the paper away and shut down the computer.

The moment my head hit the pillow, I was asleep, wrapped in blissful ignorance. But the thing about ignorance was that while it might be blissful it was also often dangerous.

"WHAT A PLEASANT surprise!" Fairley Sable beamed as she ushered me inside her home. "I was just making a pot of tea. Would you like some?" Assuming acceptance, Fairley deposited me on her sofa and disappeared into the kitchen.

While I struggled not to sink—the sofa was far too soft and way too white, like sitting on a loaf of Wonder Bread—my eyes roamed over the living room, which I didn't like. The great white whale of a sofa and matching love seat faced off like opposing armies, separated by an enormous glass-topped coffee table, empty save for a neat stack of magazines. I sifted through the stack. The magazines might have been pilfered from a doctor's waiting room—*Senior Living, Herbal Digest, Modern Nursing.* If the inside of the Dick house was a showplace, Fairley's was an operating room. I started as the clack of dishware heralded my host's return.

"Another rainy day, I'm afraid." Fairley carefully set the tray down. "I hope it clears up for Harvest Fest. Oh!"

Fairley's gaze landed on the magazines on the opposite corner of the table. She abandoned the tea things and rushed over, straightening the stack with military crispness. Before resuming her tea duties, she sent a cross look my way.

"Where's your little friend today?"

It took me a second to realize that Fairley meant Jinks. I told her the dog was fine. And he was, sleeping in the Crown Vic in Fairley's driveway. Since she obviously wasn't a dog person, I thought it best that Jinks absent himself from this visit, which suited him just fine.

"Now, Mrs. Sable…"

"It's lucky for you, isn't it?"

"Lucky?" Was it me or was Fairley being deliberately obtuse? Or had she been taking lessons from Gigi Tajani.

"It's lucky you found a job so soon. Biscuit?" Fairley stuck a china plate stacked with assorted crackers and toast points in my face, not a real biscuit in sight. I declined.

Fairley measured a spoonful of sugar into her cup. "Julie's lucky she has you. I'm sure you'll find the answers, but I'm not sure what help I can be. I've already told you everything I know."

"I have a few follow-up questions."

Fairley stirred her tea, the metal spoon tinkling against the china cup. She tasted and looked at me. "It's painful, this digging into the past."

"The thing is, I've recently come into some new information and I need some clarification."

That caught her, as I'd hoped it would. She fixed her silver-blue eyes on me, like a sparrow eyeing a fat worm.

"Do you have any idea why Mel turned against his friends and wife?"

"Oh," she said, as if disappointed. "Actually, I've thought about that a lot. In a way it's all I've thought about since Mel died. There was discord in our little group because of Mel and Gigi's love affair. In truth, things hadn't been right for some time." She sipped her tea and sighed. "But I don't have any of the answers."

"Tell me about the recent hostility between Mel and Alan Rand." A quizzical look. "My information is that the two men had been going at one another pretty hard."

Fairley shrugged. "The antagonism between Mel and Alan was no more than usual and certainly no less. Those two men have always loathed one another, dear."

"That's not my understanding."

"Then your understanding is flawed," Fairley said bluntly. "The only change is that for some reason Mel and Alan recently discarded the pretence of friendship."

"So they did avoid one another." Rand had told me that after he learned of Mel's plans for José, he'd broken off the friendship.

"Socially, perhaps, but they kept up their professional association at the paper. In fact Alan stopped by the office not long before Mel's death, but there's nothing suspicious in that."

"When was this?"

"I can't remember the date. More tea? But you've hardly touched yours! I could make coffee, if you'd like."

"I'd like to return to that night at the G and G. Was Busy Rhodes there?"

"Do you think that b-i-t-c-h is involved in Mel's death? I'm sorry, but that woman is a terror! It wouldn't surprise me if she did have a hand in this. Is something wrong?"

"Please answer the question," I said, surprised at Fairley's antagonism toward the woman in white. Was this something she'd picked up from Mel, or was there another reason?

"I didn't see Busy at the G and G that night, but that doesn't mean she wasn't there. The pub was very busy, and there's a lot I don't see."

I almost challenged her on that. I was willing to bet that not much got past Fairley. "Describe Mel's physical appearance that night," I asked, curious if Fairley would tell the truth.

"He looked like a sick man, a very sick man," Fairley said softly. "I'd been telling Anita for weeks that she needed to get him to a doctor or at least take him to Walgreen's and check his blood pressure. He was positively red as a beet that last night."

"Why didn't you mention any of this earlier?"

Fairley fidgeted, folding and refolding her napkin. "Mel and I had our differences, but he was a friend. It would have grieved him to be remembered as he was in those terrible last days."

"And exactly how was he in those terrible last days?" Her eyes pleaded, but I didn't relent. "Tell me, Fairley."

"If you must know, he was mad as a hatter. I don't

know how else to say it. Mel was mad as a hatter! I can't take much more of this, Addie."

"Only one more question."

She wiped her eyes and nodded.

"After Mel abandoned Anita at the G and G, someone drove her home. Do you know who that was?"

Fairley's eyes widened and she said, "Why, I did of course."

"You? And you didn't think to tell me?"

"I… I didn't think it mattered. I'm sorry. I dropped Anita off and then went to my own home. It was perfectly natural, with us being neighbors and friends. Would you rather have coffee, dear? Your tea's gone stone cold."

# FIFTEEN

*A House Rests on the Woman*

AFTER SEEING FAIRLEY, I walked Jinks, more to clear my head than anything. She was a strange one; there were depths to her, maybe treacherous depths. But the thing was, I really, really didn't like her house.

But, more important, vague bells and whistles sounded in my head. Fairley said that Alan had continued to see Mel at his office, but that wasn't what Rand told me. Back at the Crown Vic I pulled out my notepad to double-check. Rand learned of Mel's plans for José sometime in September. After that Alan claimed to have avoided Mel.

I'd scrawled something to the side of the page. *I am a witch?* That's right—Alan said that the day of the meeting Mel was bursting with pride over his new book, *I Am Not a Witch.* I'd noted it because I'd heard the words before and had meant to connect the dots at a later time, which never came. I flipped back through the pages, scanning for any mention of witches and there it was, in Busy Rhodes's interview. The woman in white's purported final meeting with Dick had taken place at a book signing at Barnes and Noble. The guest author? Kristin Donald. The book? *I Am Not a Witch.* Busy had placed the date in early October.

But if Mel Dick possessed an autographed copy of Donald's memoir in hand when he spoke with Rand, the meeting had to have taken place after Donald's appearance at Barnes and Noble. A quick call to the bookstore confirmed that Kristin Donald's appearance had been on October second.

The hairs on my neck stood up. Rand had lied about the date of his conversation with Mel. Why? And what other lies had he spun? Oh, Alan Rand and I had a lot to talk about.

My cell buzzed. "Why did you take Jinks with you?" Pop yelled.

"Is that why you called?"

"No, but Jinks was fine last night. He only whined for an hour and didn't shake as bad."

"I don't have time for this so…"

"You know that show I like on the comedy station?" Pop said. "The one you hate, with the clips from the internet? When you told me about the busboy's video, it got me thinking. There are so many people taking videos, posting them, soon a person won't be able to take a dump without it showing up online."

"All true, but what's the point?"

"You said the restaurant was very crowded that night and…"

"Crap," I said, catching on at last. "There's a good chance Marco wasn't the only one who recorded the fracas. Okay, Pop," I said, my mind racing, "I need to follow up on this right away."

Pop was yelling at the other end. "But I've already found it, Adelajda—a second video."

"YOU SURE YOU don't want some, Addie?" Julie asked, pouring a tall glass of tea from a gallon container. "Dad made the best sweet tea."

"No thanks." I had already viewed the second video on my smartphone—Crazy Old Man 24—and now wanted to view it on Julie's laptop. "Are you sure you want to see this?"

Julie just moved her stool to the left so she could better see the monitor.

The video opened with José Barracas crab-walking away from a pugilistic Mel Dick. My pulse quickened. The quality of the video was superior to the first and offered a different perspective of the action. In fact, the camera had caught Marco off to the left, crouched behind a potted palm, cell phone aimed at the old man. Suddenly Julie's hand reached around and pressed pause.

"What the hell!"

"Why are you so jacked?" Julie demanded, hands on hips.

*Talk about micromanaging.* "I'm jacked because the video is shot from a different angle from the first. It's almost like a peek through the looking glass."

"You're fanciful for a detective," Julie said, her habitual scowl now aimed at me, but I didn't care—she called me a detective.

"Look, this video visualizes almost the entire patio. Now we can see all the players clearly." There Gigi and Fairley sat, Gigi's mouth wide as a big-mouthed bass and Fairley sitting ramrod straight, her expression inscrutable. And I could see the Rands trembling in their dark corner. The play of light and shadow suggested a web, but to my eye Alan and Tally were not spiders, but the prey of spiders. Panicked flies struggling against silken chains. I restarted the video.

Mel Dick tottered like a dying top as he shouted his jumbled jeremiad. His flushed face gleamed bloody in the light, and his eyes struggled to focus. A little collapse when the words were said—relief or something else? Mel disappeared beneath the table, reappearing with a scrap of fur clutched to his chest. The scrap moved and Jinks blinked at the world, only to quickly retreat, like a turtle retracting into its shell.

"My only friend," the old man cried. Then the flat-footed shamble to the Humvee. The picture twitched as the cameraman ran after his quarry, steadied again as the red cart sped away. A few excited onlookers—silhouettes in the deepening gloom—skipped after the racing cart for a few yards, like children after the ice-cream truck. There was an unintelligible shout from the cameraman as the people in the street jumped for the sidewalks. A Prius, gleaming like a polished pearl, glided by. The camera only caught the first three letters of the vanity plate, but it was enough: BZY.

I had my proof. The white Prius belonged to Busy Rhodes, the same woman who claimed to have last seen Mel Dick at the Barnes and Nobles weeks before his death. I'd said it before, but it was worth repeating: during a murder investigation people lied for all sorts of reasons.

I couldn't wait to learn Busy's.

DESPITE MY EAGERNESS, the face-off with Busy would have to wait. She wasn't available until late afternoon. No one answered at the Rand home, so Gigi Tajani drew the golden ticket. Hopefully she'd gotten over her anger. I was en route when Brad called.

Berry had got the client list out of José and was checking them out, but Rand's name wasn't on it. So far there were no red flags in Mel's finances, and the background checks were a bust. Some assorted traffic violations, a drunk and disorderly for José from last year as well as a misdemeanor drug possession from the nineties. Only one blip: as an adult Fairley Sable had accumulated not so much as a traffic ticket, but she had been in the juvenile justice system. Since DJJ files were sealed, I had no way of knowing the nature of the offense. A single blemish on a spotless record—maybe little Fairley had shoplifted a mood ring and her parents let her stew in juvenile hall for a couple of days. That was probably what happened, or something very like. On the plus side, Hackle's autopsy of Anita Dick was set for tonight.

"What's shaking on your end?" Brad asked.

I told him about Rand's inexplicable lie.

"Why would he lie about the date of his meeting with Mel?" Brad asked, as puzzled as I.

"If Rand wasn't a lawyer, I'd say it was just a stupid lie born out of nervousness."

"Well, Berry's gonna be having a chat with Rand later today. Anything else?"

"There's another video—can you believe my dad found it?"

"I'll take a look at it—oh, tell Mrs. Breyer if she still wants to go through with it, her parents' remains are available for viewing between two and four this afternoon."

"Darn it," I said. "I know Julie wants me to accompany her to the morgue, but I've made other plans."

"I can take her," Brad said.

"Are you sure?"

"You have no idea how charming I can be when I put a mind to it," Brad Spooner drawled, his accent thick as gallberry honey. "It might help make up for the awful way she learned about her parents' deaths. I can pick her up at two-thirty, if that's all right."

"Great!" Julie was stubborn, but so was I. I'd make certain she accepted Brad's offer, freeing me to fry more important fish.

"So what are you doing this afternoon?" he asked.

"Huh?"

"You just said you were too busy to be with your client when she viewed her parents' remains so I'm asking what you're gonna be busy with."

"Um… I want to research those plants Hackle spoke of last night." Silence on the other end. "And of course I want to look at the new video some more."

"Addie, stop," Brad said, his voice grating like metal on metal. "Just don't screw me over."

"I wouldn't do that," I promised and ended the call.

Don't screw me over, he said.

I wouldn't do that, she said.

Déjà vu, all over again.

THE DOOR YAWNED open to reveal a transformed Gigi Tajani. The bratwurst lips had deflated entirely, in fact her entire frame seemed to have shrunk several inches since our last meeting. Her open-toed slippers revealed chipped crimson toenails. The turban was still in place but lopsided, revealing a thin line of gray hair at the forehead. Even her silky rainbow-colored lounging pajamas seemed subdued and limp. Before I could speak she waved me inside.

I started to explain my purpose, but Gigi was way ahead of me.

"Yes, yes," she said impatiently, "Fairley said you were investigating Mel's death for his daughter. I suppose we must talk."

On the veranda Gigi topped off her wineglass from the open bottle of chardonnay. She offered me a glass, but I declined. After a deep drink she gestured for me to get started.

I thought I held a pretty good card and played it at once. "I know you saw Mel after he left the Grub and Grog on the night he was murdered, Ms. Tajani."

The old woman with the young face took another drink of wine. "I... I don't know what you're talking about."

"After the argument with Anita, Mel came to you."

"I've already told you what happened that night."

"Not all of it."

"What difference does it make?" Gigi asked in a flat voice. "Mel and Anita are dead."

"Do you know Julie Breyer?"

Gigi shifted in the papasan. "I've met her once or twice, and Mel often talked about her."

"She wants to know how her father died."

She hid her face with her hands, which were swollen and spotted with petechiae.

"Gigi?"

"Oh, I miss my friends," she said, wiping her eyes. "I miss them so much! We used to have such fun—Mel, Alan and Tally, Harry, even Anita in her mousy way. For years we were the best of friends and then everything changed and I don't know why. Why do things have to change? Why can't everything stay the same?"

"Because that's life," I said. "Now it's time to put things right. It's time to tell the truth."

"I wanted to tell the police about it, but I was afraid. I wasn't lying before. I just didn't tell it all. That night on my veranda I heard Mel shouting from across the way. He was so very angry. I tried to make out his words, but couldn't." A rueful smile and she said, "Not that it matters, he'd been talking such nonsense the past weeks."

"What time did you hear Mel's shouts?"

"I don't know—it was late, around midnight."

"Were there any other voices?"

"No, but Anita never raised her voice." Gigi poured the dregs of the chardonnay. "The yelling had gone on for maybe five minutes, and that's when I heard it." The green eyes grew wide, for a moment gleaming with their former brilliance.

I leaned close. "What did you hear?"

"The gunshot—only I thought it was a car backfiring! Dear God, people don't shoot guns in Mystic Cove— things like that only happen in the real world—not here!" Her frail body shuddered, momentarily racked by the violence of her sobs. "Shortly after I heard the…the pop, Mel appeared at my door. He was bleeding. I saw the blood on his shirt. I asked Mel what happened and all he said was, 'She shot me. I can't believe she shot me.'"

"Did he say Anita shot him?"

An angry snort. "No, but of course it was Anita. I begged him to let me take him to the E.R. but he refused. I should have called the police, I know, but Mel was the sort of man who insisted on having his way in everything. I got him out of that bloody shirt and pressed a towel against the wound." The shaking hand reached for her wineglass. I handed it to her; she drank it dry.

"I cleaned the wound, smeared on some Neosporin, put on a bandage. Not an easy thing to do—Mel kept squirming. Then I gave him some clean clothes to put on."

"A Hawaiian shirt and shorts," I said.

"Yes, they'd belonged to my late husband."

"And then?"

Gigi eyed the empty wine bottle and sighed. "Then I went to bed. I left Mel on the couch. I told him he could stay the night, but when I woke the next morning he was gone. Later I learned he was dead."

"What did you do with Mel's old clothes?"

A flurry of blinks. "At first I put them in the hamper, but when I heard that Mel had been murdered, I got scared and threw them away. That was wrong, I know, but I was frightened. And I know I should have called the police, even though Mel didn't want me to. But Mel was used to having his way and I was used to giving it to him. Maybe…maybe that wasn't such a good idea."

"What time did Mel leave your house?" I asked.

"I don't know, probably not long after I went to bed—he was in a fever to leave. I should have stayed up with him, but I was so tired. And nothing I could say would make him stay, once he had a mind to go."

"Why was he so desperate to leave?"

A manic grin split her face and the green eyes fixed on me. Her chest heaved, the smooth face contorted, and the wrinkled hands worked in her lap. She was in the grip of some strong emotion, but I needed answers.

"Talk to me, Gigi!"

Gigi popped to her feet like a jack-in-the-box and pointed at my feet. Jinks, who had been curled there, raised his head and stared at the accusing finger, ears pricked.

"You want to know why Mel left? I'll tell you." Gigi said, spittle flying. "During the fight with Anita, Jinks had run off, and so naturally Mel had to find him. He left me to look for that stupid friggin' dog!"

The stupid friggin' dog sprang to his feet, stout body taut, clouded eyes focused on Gigi.

I scooped him into my lap, held tight. "Gigi, there's no need to get excited." But she didn't hear me, and Jinks rumbled like a hot rod.

"If Mel hadn't left me that night, nothing bad would have happened."

A peal of frantic yaps and Jinks squirmed from my hands, lunging at the hysterical woman. "Jinks, settle." I reached for the collar, but too late.

"If it weren't for Mr. Jinks, Mel would be alive!"

And then a roiling scream as Jinks's sharp teeth sank into the soft flesh of Gigi Tajani's crimson-painted big toe.

THIRTY MINUTES LATER Gigi Tajani reclined on her lavender divan like Goya's Maja, propped with pillows and purring like a kitten on Valium. To complete the scene I placed a fresh bottle of chardonnay and remote control within reach. From within the bathroom Mr. Jinks kept up his yapping. Gigi glanced at the closed bathroom door and shivered delicately.

"If you change your mind and decide to see a doctor, let me know and I'll take care of the bill." I hoped Gigi would show some sense, or lacking that, compassion. The wound was no more than a scratch, but even scratches cost money, money I didn't have. Well, maybe I could bill Julie Breyer for it—the cost of the investigation and all that.

"I'll be all right," Gigi said, reaching for the chardonnay.

"Let me." I uncorked the wine and poured.

"Thank you—ahh." A little sip and Gigi eased back into the mass of silken pillows, her contentment palpable. As Jinks was momentarily silent—to catch his breath, no doubt—and Gigi the same, I dared pose a final question.

Earlier Gigi had said that for many years the group of friends had been happy with one another's company. Fairley had said the same. I wanted to know when the first fractures of dissent had appeared among them. Gigi considered the question, the emerald eyes focused inward for once.

To my surprise Gigi's answer was immediate and certain. "Everything changed after Harry died—that's when it began."

When Harry Sable died—was that when the snake had slithered into paradise?

AFTER JINKS'S MELTDOWN at Gigi's I couldn't take him to my meeting with Busy. My stomach growled, reminding me that these past days I had subsisted on coffee and alcohol. The Grub and Grog was just down the road, so why not kill two birds?

Five minutes later I found José Barracas sitting on the deserted patio of the Grub and Grog, staring at the rain. His ashen face sagged, and he looked more tired than a man had a right to be, but there was something different in his eyes.

"Take a load off," he said, gesturing to an empty chair at his table.

I sat and Jinks immediately collapsed at my feet, exhausted from his exertions. I did a quick three-sixty. "Open for lunch?" The restaurant's interior was as empty as the patio.

"Yeah, it's the crappy weather. These people think they'll melt in the rain." A half laugh and he gestured at Jinks. "I see you have your partner with you, so I guess this is official business."

"I just need a favor." I explained my need for a dogsitter.

"Sure, I'll watch the mutt for you, Addie." A shaky hand raised the coffee mug, which for once contained coffee. "Your buddies from GCSO were here earlier. I told 'em the truth, at least the truth I can remember. There's a lot I don't remember." He sipped his coffee, watched the rain. "Funny thing is, I don't mind the blackouts. It's the flashes of memory that scare me, with each one worse than the other. I don't know what's real anymore and what's not."

"Go easy on yourself," I said.

"It's just that my life is screwed and I don't know how it got that way. All this crap was going on around me and

I was clueless. But that's what my life has become—a jigsaw puzzle with missing pieces. Maybe if I hadn't been living in a bottle things would have been different."

"Things could always be different," I told him, "but that doesn't always mean better. It is what it is. Don't beat yourself up, José. We all make mistakes."

"I HOPE THIS isn't going to take long, Ms. Gorsky." Busy Rhodes said, peering through her white-framed glasses like a displeased school principal. She had herded me into a small office and sat me on the love seat against the wall while she took the chair behind a cluttered desk. Her slacks and cowl-neck sweater were a wintry white.

"This won't take long. I'm investigating Mel Dick's murder at the behest of his daughter."

Busy frowned at the notepad I'd just pulled out. "Yes, yes, I know all that, but I can't imagine how I can be of help, and I'm in the middle of something right now." She gestured at the jumble of papers and files on the desktop.

Taking her at her word, I said, "I know how to speed things. Could you Google something for me?"

Busy considered this, her lips forming a flat red line. "All right," she said at last, fingers poised over the keyboard. "What is it?"

"Crazy Old Man 24."

"DO YOU WANT to watch it again?" I asked Busy.

"No." I had to strain to hear.

"Maybe you don't think it was a big deal for you to deliberately mislead me, but I'm certain that when Sheriff Spooner learns of your little deception, he'll be interested."

"I know very, very little," Busy said, holding her thumb and index finger tight.

"So tell me."

"I followed Mel that night."

"I figured that much out already. Let's start with why you followed Mel."

"I was worried about him. He was obviously disoriented and a danger to himself and others. And I was curious—his behavior at the pub was so strange."

"Really?" My guess was that Busy followed Mel because she hoped to get something on him in his diminished state. Like Mel, the woman in white wasn't beyond a little discreet blackmail.

"Believe whatever you want," Busy said, giving me a look that would freeze beer. I shrugged and she continued. "I followed Mel to the *Commentator* office. I parked a half a block away, close enough to watch unobserved—not that Mel noticed much in his state. Around seven-thirty Mel left the office to walk the dog. After the animal had done its business—right on the bed of marigolds in front of the Dusky Shark Emporium—Mel returned to the office. I waited a few more minutes and when nothing happened, called it a night. That was the last time I saw Mel Dick. Dead or alive."

"Did you notice any unusual behavior on Dick's part?"

"Define *unusual*." Busy smiled. "Lately Mel's behavior had been nothing if not bizarre so I'm not sure what you mean."

"Come on, Busy."

"Well, Mel was fixated on the dog's bandana." Busy laughed at the memory. "Several times he bent over and tugged on the thing, as if checking if it were loose."

"Bandana?" Mrs. Santiago had told me that Jinks had been wearing something when she'd found him, but she called it something else. A *bufanda*.

"Yes, a bandana," Busy said through clenched teeth.

"An ugly scrap of fabric that was wrapped around the beast's neck. I call that a bandana."

I had shoved the foul-smelling bandana into my desk drawer and immediately forgotten it.

I tried to move to more fertile ground, but Busy was done answering my questions. Smart cookies like her didn't stay cowed for long. Still, I was pleased with the interview until on the way out Busy pulled a sucker punch that knocked me on my ass.

"Don't contact me again, Ms. Gorsky. Going forward you can speak to my attorney. Please pass the message on to your friend Sheriff Spooner."

I felt a sinking feeling in my gut—this would piss off the sheriff—but the feeling didn't last. I was far too pleased with myself. Thanks to Busy I could now account for more of Mel's movements on the last night of his life. After leaving the G and G, Mel Dick had scrambled to his office to dress his dog in a smelly bandana.

Fairley had called Mel mad as a hatter and who was I to argue?

# SIXTEEN

*Could this be Madness?*

When I returned to the Grub and Grog, the sun shone bright, draining off the rain puddles in quick order. The pub was working on a good crowd, and so took me a couple minutes to get José's attention. While he retrieved Jinks, I spotted two familiar faces at a corner table, their heads nearly touching and both pairs of eyes fixed on me.

"Hello, ladies," I said. Fairley Sable and Gigi Tajani giggled like a couple of schoolgirls.

"Why, it's our favorite detective," Fairley said.

"How's the toe?" I asked Gigi, who was obviously feeling no pain.

"Much better!" Gigi glowed with alcoholic goodwill. "My dear friend Fairley convinced me that…that I needed to get out of that dark house, and she was right."

Fairley gave me one of her helpless looks.

"I'm glad you're feeling better, Gigi."

José was heading our way, hauling Jinks as if he were a sack of potatoes. I made a face and gestured outside. José reversed direction and headed for the patio.

"Oh, it's your little partner Jinks," Fairley said. "Is he behaving himself? I heard he was a bad boy earlier."

Gigi twisted in her chair. "Jinks? Where?"

"José just took Jinks outside," Fairley said.

Gigi Tajani's goodwill burned off like cognac over

an open flame. "What is it with you and that damn animal anyway?"

Several necks craned and I heard clucks of distaste. The bartender glanced over, frowned.

"Language, Gigi," Fairley said, lightly touching her arm.

Gigi recoiled from her touch. "Don't chastise me, Fairley."

"You need to get her out of here and quickly," I whispered in Fairley's ear. I tried not to look at José's horrified face from the patio. Another storm brewing in the G and G.

"What? What did you say?" Gigi yelled at me. "You know, I'm not going to talk to you anymore. You talk to my lawyer from now on. I have to protect my interests."

"Let's go to the powder room, Gigi," Fairley said. The stubborn look peculiar to drunks came over Gigi's face and I thought Fairley had struck out, but then she added, "Your lipstick is smudged," and the other old lady powered down. Smudged lipstick was a horror that drove all else from her sodden mind. There was a scary moment when Gigi wobbled dangerously, but Fairley wrapped an arm around her friend's waist, preventing what would have otherwise been a nasty fall. Thank goodness Fairley always knew which buttons to push and when.

Before leaving, I warned José of Gigi's condition, and he promised to make sure she got home safely. I had just settled Jinks in the back seat of the Vic when my cell rang.

"Addie, you got to get over to Julie's right now," Brad said.

"On my way," I said. "What's up?"

"Things didn't go well at the morgue." He explained that Julie had completely broken down at the sight of her dead parents. Naturally he blamed me. "You should have warned me she was cracking. I would have never volunteered otherwise."

"I don't get it, Brad. Julie seemed okay to me." I had seen no fractures in Julie's tough resolve.

"Yeah, that's what I thought, but looks like we were both wrong. I finally got her to rest, but I don't feel right leaving her alone."

"I'm almost there." Fortunately Jesse was working the Admiral Street gatehouse and waved me through. As usual my route brought me past the Rand house. I tapped my brakes. Alan Rand's silver Lexus was parked in the driveway. I saw the slow rise of the garage door.

My frustration boiled over. Alan had been avoiding me—he and Tally were locked up like prisoners in that quiet house. This might be my only opportunity to speak with them. In a white heat, I made a sharp right into the driveway, pulling tight on the Lexus's ass. I caught the reflection of Alan Rand's frightened eyes in his rear-view mirror: I had him, a fox in a hole.

I bolted from the Vic and ran in front of Rand's Lexus, standing between the car and the garage door, which was now fully open. Our eyes locked.

"I just want to talk to you, Mr. Rand. Just a few minutes." For reply, the Lexus issued a throaty purr, its engine revved.

"Mr. Rand?" The engine roared and I saw the maniacal gleam in the old man's eye. He was really going to run me down! Still, I stood my ground, a suicidal deer in the headlights. A door slammed and a woman screamed. Alan and I turned our heads as one, the deadly spell broken.

"Alan?" Tally Rand was paler and much thinner than the last time I had seen her. She really had been ill. Tally saw me and her eyes widened with horror.

"Mrs. Rand," I said, leaping toward her, "I need to talk

with you." The door of the Lexus swung open. Alan Rand insinuated his body between me and my prey, his feeble hands grasping my shoulders.

"Tally, go inside," Alan ordered, but Tally did not move, her dazed eyes switching from me to her husband and back again.

"Just a few minutes of your time, Mrs. Rand."

"You!" Rand pointed a gnarled finger. "Get off of my property immediately!"

That roused Tally. She began sidling away, into the safety of her house where I could not reach her. Another moment and she would disappear, perhaps forever.

I started after Tally, but Rand blocked my way with his body. I veered to avoid the old man and continued after my quarry. From behind I heard a cry and a thud. I turned to see Rand sprawled on the ground.

"Are you all right?" I started toward the old man.

"Keep away." Rand sputtered, waving me off as if I were a spawn of Satan. He was back on his feet, slightly shaken but basically all right. By now Tally had disappeared inside the house, but the front door was wide open.

As Grammy Ludwika used to say, *In for an inch, in for a mile.*

I bolted into the Rand home. I looked around with wild eyes and froze.

Tally stared down at me from the top of the stairs. She trembled violently, both hands white knuckling the banister. "So you've come for me at last."

I gaped at the obviously ill woman—what the heck did she mean? But I didn't have time to wonder and got back on script, knowing my time was short.

"It's important that we talk, Mrs. Rand." I opened my hands in a gesture of supplication. "I'm investigating Mel's death and…" I stopped.

Tally's face was a vacant mask. She didn't hear me, and though she looked in my direction, I doubted she saw me. She was lost in a private dream. Or nightmare.

"She's inside," a gruff voice called from outside.

This had been a fool's errand and now I had to pay the price.

"This is Mystic Cove Security," another voice called, this one female. "Come out immediately—we have you surrounded."

*Surrounded? Next they'll be threatening to smoke me out.*

But I did as ordered. I even put my hands up and away from my body, just to be safe. Mystic Cove guards weren't supposed to be armed, but I knew a few of the old dogs carried.

Once I cleared the door, Oscar Wall and the female guard swarmed, each grabbing an arm. I took in the situation. Rand leaned against his Lexus, talking into his cell. He seemed okay, if overly excited, and I couldn't blame him. More important, no cops were at the scene. Just two Mystic Cove guards.

"So where do we go from here?" I asked, shaking off my handlers.

The two guards exchanged a nervous look. If the cops didn't show, maybe I could squirm my way out of this little snag. But then the roar of a car, traveling hard and fast, sounded through Admiral Street. Only cops and criminals rode their cars that hard. Or so I'd thought. I almost smiled as the car screeched to a halt. I knew this car. Had ridden in it many times.

Acting Chief Tyler Andrews had answered the call.

My two bodyguards ran to their new boss, and I followed. When guilty—as I was—the best defense was to act innocent. I planned to tell Tyler that I was leaving and if there was a problem, he knew how to get in touch with me. But my scheme was shattered when I saw a familiar figure striding Admiral Street like a gunfighter at high noon, with me in the crosshairs. I'd forgotten Brad had been babysitting Julie. Of course he'd heard Tyler's noisy arrival and was coming to investigate.

"What's going on?" Brad asked.

"Glad to see you, Sheriff." Tyler smiled, but his eyes were cold. "Mr. Rand claims that this woman—" he jerked his head at me, "—assaulted him, but he doesn't want the police involved."

"I did no such thing," I said quickly. "Sheriff, you need to talk some sense into Mr. Rand."

Rand had ended his call and now looked at us with an expression that could only be described as stark terror.

"What happened here, Mr. Rand?" Brad asked.

But Rand didn't even acknowledge Brad's presence. He only had eyes for Tyler. "I... I told you I didn't want the police involved," the old man sputtered, pointing a bony finger at the Acting Chief of Mystic Cove Security. "Mr. Richt won't like this one bit."

Tyler frowned. "I didn't call GCSO—tell him, Sheriff."

"I happened to be in the neighborhood. No one called me, but now that I'm here, you better tell me what happened."

Rand swallowed. "Nothing."

"Did you," Tyler said in a cracked voice, "or did you not just tell me that Addie Gorsky beat you up, Mr. Rand?"

"It was an accident. I fell," Rand said.

Tyler scowled at the feeble man. "That's not what you said a minute ago. You heard him, didn't you?" he asked his guards, but they were too engrossed in cloud-watching to answer.

"I was confused." Rand licked his lips, looked at the

house. "Now that I think about it, that woman didn't touch me."

"That's right," I said. "It was an accident."

"Was the forcible entry an accident too?" Tyler asked me. "Sheriff, when my guards arrived they found Gorsky inside the house, without Mr. Rand's permission—isn't that right, Mr. Rand?"

Rand didn't answer. He glanced again at his house.

"Mr. Rand!" Tyler's voice had more than a touch of hysteria. He had no idea what was going on, but I did.

"Mr. Rand wasn't inside the house," I said, "but Mrs. Rand was." Rand gave me a scathing look. "Ask her if she gave me permission or not. She can clear up any misunderstanding."

"Mr. Rand," Brad said, a voice of calm reason. "What do you want us to do?"

"I want all of you to leave me and my wife in peace."

"Then that's what we'll do," Brad said.

Tyler threw up his arms. "Do whatever you want. We're out of here."

After Mystic Cove Security quit the scene, Rand turned to Brad. Although Rand's words were for him, his eyes were on me. "I've just consulted with my lawyer, Sheriff. If Addie Gorsky comes near me or my wife, I will take out a restraining order."

"Ms. Gorsky understands." Brad and I started to head back to the Dick house, but Rand wasn't finished.

"To this point I've cooperated with your investigation into Mel's murder. I've been forthcoming with Deputy Berry. Going forward my lawyer will represent me at any future interviews."

WHEN WE GOT back to the Dick house, I told Brad that I was going to check on Julie. I wasn't particularly concerned about her—she was a tough cookie, like her dad—but I wanted to check on something. It also wouldn't hurt to give Brad a few minutes to get over being pissed.

I stuck my head in the guest bedroom. Julie was a lump in the bed. Next I slipped into Mel's office. Mel's library wasn't extensive and I found the book at once. Kristin Donald's memoir *I Am Not a Witch*. Since both Rand and Busy Rhodes had mentioned Mel's excitement over this latest acquisition to his library, it was worth a look.

Kristin Donald's bland face graced the cover. She was close to Mel in age. Was there a personal connection? But the inscription was formal. *To Mel Dick, Best Wishes, Kristin Donald.* I flipped to the inset of photos. Many of the pictures were from some trial in 1974. That was when Assistant District Attorney Kristin Donald had earned her bones by putting away some notorious sixties radical. I flipped back and forth through the photos, but they meant nothing. I closed the book. Just a tedious political memoir that would be in the discount bin next week.

I found Brad in the kitchen. The coffee smelled fresh so I poured two cups and pulled up a stool next to Brad.

"Julie slept through the excitement," I said. "Something to be thankful for." Brad didn't look thankful. "Look, I know that things could have gone better back there, but…"

"You think? Damn it, you could have been charged with trespassing, assault, forcible entry." He counted my crimes on his fingers.

"Not assault, Brad—I didn't touch Rand. In fact, I tried to help him when he fell, but he wouldn't let me near him."

"Can't blame the man."

"And maybe I was trespassing, but forcible entry? The front door was wide open, and Tally didn't ask me to leave."

Brad shook his head. I didn't know if he had kids, but

it was definitely a parental sort of headshake. "You're aw-fully lucky Rand isn't pressing charges."

"Lucky?" I opened the fridge, found a pack of bagels. "I'm not so sure. You saw the way Rand looked at me. He wanted my ass in jail."

Brad shook his head but there was just a ghost of a smile on his lips. "He surely did."

"Exactly," I said as I put a bagel in the toaster oven, "so why did Rand let me off the hook?"

"First, he did threaten you with a restraining order." I made a dismissive sound. "And Rand probably wants to keep the police out of it because he doesn't want to put his wife through the ordeal of a police investigation—you've said yourself that she hasn't been well."

"I guess."

"I just wish he and Tally hadn't lawyered-up—that makes my job a lot tougher."

"Uh-oh," I said, the words slipping out.

"What's that?"

"Earlier I spoke with Gigi Tajani and Busy Rhodes. I learned a lot of good stuff, but unfortunately they…"

"Let me guess—they lawyered-up."

"In a manner of speaking." The toaster oven rang, and I busied myself with smearing a little jelly on my bagel.

"So in one day's work you've managed to lawyer-up five witnesses." The fingers were out again.

"Only four, Brad—Fairley is still talking to me." As far as I knew, that was. "But after I tell you all I've learned, you'll agree it was worth it." First I told him about Busy tailing Mel.

"So Mel went to his office and dressed his dog in a sweater vest."

"Not a sweater vest—a bandana, or *bufanda*, depending on who you ask." I bit into my bagel and realized I was starving.

"What does it mean?"

"I don't get it either, but it was an odd thing for Mel to do." I reminded Brad that Jinks's collar had been found on Mel's body, in the pocket of his shorts. "So at his office Mel took off Jinks's regular collar and replaced it with that bandana. I wouldn't peg him for one to play dress-up with his dog."

Brad rubbed his temple. "Me neither, but so what? It's just more craziness from Mel."

"Busy said Mel kept worrying at Jinks's bandana."

"Let's move on, Addie."

If Brad was less than impressed, so be it. But the detail was important, even vital. In the last hours of his life Mel had fixated on his beloved dog. Crazy always had a reason. What was Mel's?

The sheriff showed more interest in my little talk with Gigi. "So if Gigi's account is accurate, then the first gunshot was fired in this very house, most likely by Anita Dick."

"I agree, but we don't know the circumstances. The gun might have accidentally discharged."

"Or Anita tried to kill Mel and was just a lousy shot." Brad pulled out his cell. "I'll get CSU out here. We need to find that bullet, compare it to the one we got out of Dick's brain."

"Tell CSU to start in the garage, that's probably where it went down. I figure Anita was waiting for Mel, and when she heard the garage door open she rushed to the garage to confront him."

"With the gun," Brad added.

"Probably," I said, "though it's certainly possible that Mel had the gun, at least initially. According to Gigi there was a brief argument, followed by the gunshot, during which Jinks ran off, probably through the open garage door."

"Then Mel took off to pay his girlfriend a visit," Brad added.

"What are you two plotting?"

Brad and I started like guilty children.

Julie Breyer was a sight, sweating in one of her mother's voluminous bathrobes. Brad and I watched in stunned silence as the unsteady ghost shambled to the sink, filled a glass with water, and drank. The glass dry, she slanted against the counter for support, a leaning tower of Julie.

"Have you eaten anything today?" I asked, going to her side. "I could fix you a bagel."

Julie shook her head. "Not hungry. The kids came down with the flu last week—I guess I didn't dodge the bullet after all." A weak laugh and she added, "Like father, like daughter."

"You should get back to bed."

"I heard what you said about Mom shooting Dad."

"I'm sorry for that," Brad said, "but you understand we got to check this out."

"Do what you have to do—you will anyway." She shrugged off my offer of help but asked if I would pour her a glass of sweet tea. I spotted orange juice in the fridge and suggested that might be a more appropriate beverage.

"No orange juice, I want Dad's sweet tea. In the summer Dad brewed a fresh batch every couple days. Mom can't drink it 'cause of the sugar." The smile faded. "But when the tea is gone, it's all gone. Dad won't be making any more."

"Sweet tea it is," I said.

As Julie stumbled away, clutching the glass of tea, she muttered, "Gone, gone, all gone."

CSU FOUND THE bullet wedged in the front leg of Mel's garage worktable, but the really good news was that the bullet was intact. Now there was an excellent chance that the lab could determine if the bullet matched the one recovered from Mel's brain.

"You were right about the garage," Brad said, joining me in the kitchen. "Addie?"

"What?" The past days had caught up with me, all at once. I was pleased about my hunch being right, but didn't have the energy to do a victory lap. Although I felt I had enough pieces of the puzzle to put at least some of it together, my sleep-deprived brain couldn't focus.

"You look like you're dead on your feet. Do yourself a favor and take the night off. Get a decent night's sleep for a change."

I shook my head. "Anita's autopsy is tonight."

"If by chance Hackle finds something that Rio missed, I'll call you. Go home, get some rest, say hi to your family."

"It's just Pop," I said through a deep yawn.

"Then go home and say hi to Pop."

Driving home, I keep seeing Alan Rand behind the wheel of the silver Lexus, the patrician face distorted by hate and fear, hands gripping the steering wheel, one foot hovering over the gas pedal, eager to pounce. But worst of all was that face, that awful, hateful face.

It was the face of a murderer.

I WOKE AS the day died. The rain pattered softly and the day's last light slanted through the window, painting strange shadows on the wall. From the living room I heard Judge Judy tearing some litigant a new one—Pop loved those idiotic court shows. My sleep had not been restful, shot through with dreams of these past days. But I have always been a dreamer.

"Hungry, Pop?"

"I can eat."

We had a late dinner. I found a couple of Portobello mushrooms only a little past their prime and a jar of Ragu. I even managed to coax out a couple of glasses of red wine from the box, hoping the wine would mellow my mood—it didn't.

Over dinner I caught Pop up on the day's major developments, leaving out the unimportant details, such as his daughter almost getting arrested.

"A clever mind is at work," Pop said, moving his pasta around the plate.

"An evil mind as well," I added.

"You still believe the murderer is one of Mel's friends."

"More than ever."

"Still, the bulk of evidence points to Anita," Pop said, taking a birdlike sip of merlot. "She shot her husband once, why not twice?"

"Anita and Mel were victims, Pop."

"Both murdered?" Pop asked, putting down his fork.

"I'm not sure about that. I do suspect that there's something more to learn from Anita's death. One thing I am sure of—Alan and Tally Rand are hiding something."

"It's all right, Adelajda. I know you will find your murderer."

"First of all, it's not my murderer and how can you be sure?" I shot back. "You didn't even think I'd make it as a cop, much less a detective."

"Why do you say that?" My father's shocked, hurt face should have stopped me, but I was on a roll.

"You didn't approve when I signed up for the police academy, and yet now you're so sure I'll solve this murder."

"You misunderstand, then and now. I had reservations about the academy. You're not like your sisters. You're different, more like me. You've never been good at following rules. You like to go your own way." He smiled sadly. "You see, a person doesn't wear a uniform, it's the other way around."

I stared at this man, my father. When I was a kid I had seen him as a knight, part of the blue line that kept the rest of us safe. I'd always thought it was his calling, but maybe the fit had not been as perfect as I'd imagined. Some of my anger left me and all I wanted now was for this conversation to be over.

"Maybe you were right about the academy, Pop, considering how it ended." One thing I've learned—it didn't matter how things began, it was the ending that counted. And my career at BCPD had ended badly.

"You've never talked about it."

"Nothing to talk about," I said.

Pop sighed. "But I know you'll succeed in finding the murderer. To hunt a killer requires a profane devotion, a single-minded ruthlessness, and you have these things."

I pushed my chair back even though I knew Pop wasn't finished. Wordlessly I cleared the dinner dishes, leaving them to soak in the sink. Seeing that I had sunk into one of my moods, Pop didn't waste his breath. He just padded into his bedroom, with Jinks right behind.

I stretched out on the couch to consider my next move, but couldn't focus. I shifted through several options, but nothing appealed. The long nap had left me restless, in mind and body. I walked out on the tiny balcony.

It was a beautiful night, cold and clear, the stars glittering like a carpet of shattered glass. Very like the night of Mel's murder. An idea formed in my brain. A mad idea, and I liked it.

A midnight stroll through Mystic Cove might be my way out of the labyrinth. Tonight I would follow Mel Dick's movements on the final night of his life. Walk in Mel's shoes, so to speak. Maybe then understanding would come.

There was just one thing—I needed to keep far, far away from Alan and Tally Rand.

BILLY BLAKE FIXED his clouded eyes on my visitor's permit, as if to commit the thing to memory.

"Come on, Billy." All I wanted was to get to the Dick residence, the starting point of my journey.

Billy tapped the paper and declared, "This permit is not valid."

"Of course it is."

"This here permit is for October twenty-eight."

"Which it is," I pointed out.

Billy showed off brown teeth and pointed to the clock on the guardhouse wall. Both hands pointed dead-straight at the twelve.

"You gotta be kidding me! You kept me waiting a good five minutes."

Billy didn't budge. I could have had him call Julie for a new permit, but she needed her rest. So I gave Billy a two-fingered salute, executed a three-point turn, and took off in the opposite direction, toward Founder's Centre.

I'd show Billy Blake that there was more than one way to skin a cat—or a security guard.

HOURS LATER I stood in the small clearing where Mel Dick had met his end, no wiser for all my effort. I danced the flashlight over the ground, searching for the past but finding nothing. I eased down and sat on the cold earth.

Billy's clumsy attempt to keep me out of Mystic Cove

had been easily circumvented. I'd driven directly to Founder's Centre, parked in the empty G and G parking lot, and begun my journey from there. After hopping over the low fence, I'd wandered around the Grub and Grog patio for a bit, seeing it as it had been last Monday night—Mel and Anita at the round table near the front, Alan and Tally in their dark corner, and Gigi and Fairley to the side, drinking and laughing. Where had Busy been? No doubt nearby, a silent witness.

It was strange, walking through those familiar streets and pathways. I weaved my way from here to there to back again, my path as inscrutable as an ant's. Next I passed the *Commentator* office. Pressing my face against the window, I imagined Mel in his plush office as he tied the ragged bandana around Jinks's neck. At this point in his journey he must have had possession of his office key, though he would lose it soon enough. I couldn't linger here. Though Founder's Centre was deserted, I felt exposed. When I turned into Birnam Wood, I let out a shaky breath, welcoming the darkness.

At Azimuth Circle the light was on in Fairley's living room. I thought I caught a glimpse of her moving behind the pillowy curtains. Fearful of Fairley's eagle eye, I didn't linger here either. Besides, my main business was on Admiral Street, ground zero.

I paused outside the Rand house, which was dark and ominous, no signs of life. I stayed here the longest. Maybe I was stupid, but I didn't fear Alan Rand's threats. Despite my trespasses, he had not called the law on me. Not because he was a nice guy—he wasn't—but because he was afraid. *Sleep tight, Alan. Before this is over, I'll know your secret too.*

The Dick home was lit up like the town drunk, light

pouring from every orifice. Perhaps the ghosts of Birnam Wood had come calling and Julie hoped to banish them with light. I considered checking in but didn't. Julie had to make her own peace. They were her ghosts after all.

I darted across the swale to Gigi's backyard, covering the short distance in less than a minute. Mel would have been quicker on his cart. Then it was back into Birnam Wood and the murder scene. The short distances among the houses of the principles in this dark drama gave me pause and a disturbing possibility came to mind. Suppose Mel had returned home a bit earlier than Anita claimed.

What if Anita had followed Mel to Gigi's house, taking the thirty-eight with her? The wronged wife hiding in the bushes while her rival tended to Mel. How Anita must have seethed—what woman wouldn't? People called her dull and slow, a cow. But even cows could be roused.

Anita's patience would have been rewarded when Mel left Gigi to search for his missing dog. *Now Anita trails her husband to the clearing where Mel parks his cart. She watches for a bit and, when Mel is seemingly fast asleep, she approaches. She aims the gun at Mel's temple and fires. The deed done, she returns home and calls Fairley, pretending that the argument with Mel has just taken place.* This might have accounted for Mel's shooting, but what about all the other stuff? The stolen hard drive, the deleted files, the missing office key, Jinks's *bufanda,* Mel's madness.

No, there was more to this—much more.

I sat cross-legged, breathed deep of the night air. The night-blooming jasmine was gone—the cold had killed it, at least until the spring. In the warmth the roots would send out shoots of green and it would grow again. But Mel and Anita were gone for good and I was no closer to an answer.

# SEVENTEEN

*The Wind in the Field*

THE NEXT MORNING—for the first time since leaving Baltimore—I went for a run. When I got back I was relieved to find Pop was still asleep. A quick shower and coffee and I sat down to review my notes. I looked busy, but I was just killing time until I could call Julie, not wanting to wake her too early from a sickbed. Finally nine o'clock rolled around. Julie answered on the fifth ring.

"Yes, I'm feeling much better."

"Good," I said, though I didn't buy Julie's return to health. She sounded dazed, like a prizefighter who'd taken one punch too many. "We should have news about the bullet match later today."

A long silence and Julie said, "What bullet?"

"The bullet CSU recovered from Mel's garage yesterday," I said.

"I have no idea what you're talking about."

So I told her.

"I sort of remember talking to Sheriff Spooner at the morgue, but not much else. I guess this flu knocked me on my butt."

"I'll be right over to fill in the holes," I said.

"No, no, give me a few hours—how about eleven?"

I wanted to drive right over, but she was Mel's daughter, so I agreed to wait.

"What's wrong, Adelajda?" I helped Pop into the recliner and offered to get him some coffee or breakfast, but he refused. All he wanted was an answer to his question. I sat back on the sofa. "I'm worried about Julie, Pop. She doesn't remember CSU being at the house yesterday. I guess she was a lot sicker than I thought." And my guess was she was still under the weather. On the phone she'd sounded lost, like a boat adrift.

My cell buzzed. "It's positive, Addie," Brad said. "The bullet recovered from Dick's garage also came from Mel's thirty-eight. Anita was probably responsible for both shots."

"Which is awfully convenient," I said, "because Anita can't protect herself."

"Come on, Addie."

"Later, Sheriff."

"Now what's wrong?" Pop asked.

"This thing is spiraling out of control. It's all smoke and mirrors and I can't figure it out." I laughed. "Maybe I'm not as ruthless as you think." I regretted the words, but they had been said.

"I hurt your feelings before. I'm sorry, but you didn't let me finish."

"I don't have time for this." I made a move to leave.

"Time is not my friend, daughter."

"Oh, Papa." I ran over to him. We embraced. We were not a physically demonstrative family, but we had our moments. This was one of them.

"I called you ruthless, Adelajda," he whispered in my ear, his frail arms around me. "And I stand by that, but you are also compassionate." He pushed me away, just a little, so that our eyes met. "That is a rare, powerful combination. That's all I wanted to say." Pop let go of me, folded his hands in his lap. I returned to the sofa.

"I'm going to miss you," I said.

"Don't be foolish. There's no need for you to miss me. I'll be with you, here and here," Pop said, pointing to his forehead and his heart.

"It's not the same, Papa."

"No, but it's the best we have." Pop smiled. "When you were a little girl you called me Papa."

I was twelve or thirteen when I abandoned the faintly European *Papa* for the good-old American *Pop*. "I've been thinking of those old days lately, the old days in Highlandtown," I said. "Remember how every Saturday you'd bring home a box of bear claws from Hoehn's?"

"I remember. These days I spend more and more time in the past. I can close my eyes to reality but not to my memories. But then the past is the province of the old and the dying."

And the province of those who would catch a killer. "There's comfort in the past," I said.

Pop's eyes clouded. "Yes, and other things as well."

So it was the same for my father. But maybe everyone's past was a minefield—take a wrong step and it blows up. Oh, there were the bittersweet memories of love and youth, but there was also regret, shame, ignominy. Since leaving Baltimore I'd tortured myself, obsessing over lost chances and wrong turns, the awful song of what could have been sticking in my mind like an unwanted jingle. I guess the past was a blessing and a curse, but without it we would not be human. I looked at Pop. Maybe the time had come to speak of the past.

Pop knew the prelude well enough. After a decade of false starts I decided to take up the family business and signed up for the academy. At first it went well. I graduated top of the class and was an exemplary police, my eyes always on the prize—the golden detective's badge I knew would be mine. Being a cop was a means to an end and as long as I worked toward that end, I could toe the line. Then I grabbed the brass ring—homicide!—but I couldn't hold it.

"That first day in Homicide was one of the best in my life, but it didn't take long for me to become…dissatisfied. It was the same old song, Pop. I felt constrained by the rules, and I didn't like the way too many investigations went. I thought I knew better. Soon I gained a reputation as a troublemaker and nobody wanted to partner with me. Remember how Grammy Ludwika used to call me an old goat?"

Pop laughed and shrugged. "You've always been stubborn, even as a child, but it's not always a bad thing."

"Ask Joey Spoletto about it."

"Your partner."

"My last partner. I was supposed to meet him that night, but like always I was off pursuing my own trail." I looked at Pop. "He caught that bullet because I wasn't there with him."

"You can't blame yourself. It was a trick of fate that the robbery happened when it did."

I faced Pop so he could see his daughter clearly. "I don't know about that, but I've never felt guilt over Joey's death, not really."

"No?"

"Well, maybe in the beginning, but that wasn't the reason I quit the job. I left because it wasn't working and it wasn't going to work."

"You had other choices besides quitting."

"Sure, I could have toed the departmental line, which would have made me miserable."

Pop smiled. "Easier for the scorpion to deny its sting."

"Or I could have continued on the road I was on, become a full-fledged loose cannon."

"A dangerous road, both for you and those around you."

"So I used Joey's murder as an excuse to quit."

"An excuse for who, Adelajda? Was this excuse for you or for others?"

I stared at Pop. "For both, I suppose—does it even matter? What matters is that my dream of being a detective was another failure. Another dead end."

"Then leave it in the past where it belongs. Leave it all behind!" He sounded almost angry.

"Pop."

"Focus on the job at hand, daughter. That's what matters now."

JULIE BREYER DIDN'T answer her door. The rational part of my mind said that Julie was just sleeping—undone by the virus that held her in its grip—but my reptile brain knew better. Danger was here and this time I was ready.

The front door was locked and I saw no obvious point of ingress. I sprinted to the back patio, my eyes darting like lasers. The patio door was flung wide, as were the French doors that opened into the dining room. But what I smelled scared me more—a distinctive burning odor. I pulled the Glock from my shoulder holster and went inside.

No smoke inside the empty dining room, but the burnt smell was much stronger. Moving quickly but quietly, I turned the dogleg into the kitchen and stopped short. Since yesterday a cyclone had struck the place—dirty dishes in the sink, a trail of crumbs around the toaster, the near-empty jug of Mel's sweet tea forgotten on the granite counter. I spotted the source of the odor, a coffee pot cooking on its burner.

The thick evil-looking sludge at the bottom of the pot testified to long hours on the heat, yet Julie Breyer had been oblivious, letting the noxious stew bubble and burn. With a potholder I grabbed the handle and placed the ruined carafe in the sink, where it hissed and cracked.

Where was Julie?

I cleared the downstairs first—living room, guest bedroom, Mel's office—every now and then calling for Julie. I was headed for the bathroom at the end of the hallway when I heard a familiar sound from above. Someone had just flushed the upstairs toilet. Whoever was in the house was in the master bedroom suite.

I hopped up the carpeted stairs and crept down the short hallway. The door to Mel and Anita's bedroom door was slightly ajar. I tapped it open. When I saw what had been done to Mel and Anita's bedroom, fear chocked my throat. A picture of madness, for only a madman could have done this. Tangled bedclothes formed a mound on the bed. Open drawers vomited Anita's huge bras and Mel's boxers. Several jewelry boxes were overturned, spilling knotted necklaces and old watches. But the thing that scared me most was the thin ribbon of light shining beneath the closed bathroom door.

"Julie? Are you there? It's Addie! Talk to me!"

No answer.

"This is Private Investigator Gorsky. Whoever is in the bathroom, I want you to slowly open the door." I held the Glock steady as the door groaned open. A figure in striped pajamas wavered in the doorway. *Mel?* I thought madly. Then the shadow laughed.

"Julie!" I cried, holstering my gun. Moving quickly, I helped the disoriented woman to the bed. She radiated heat but was bone dry, as if in the final stage of heatstroke.

"Addie?" Julie squinted at me, her pupils big as saucers. "I was trying to pee. Mom and Dad said you'd be by today.

I'm thirsty, so thirsty." She propped up on one elbow, reached for the glass of sweet tea on the bedside table.

*Mel's sweet tea.*

"No," I said, prying her fingers from the glass.

EMS arrived minutes later. When they asked me what had happened, I told them but there was doubt in their eyes. So I put on my steeliest cop face and dug my fingers into the paramedic's arm.

"I am a private investigator working a double homicide. There is a high likelihood—very high—that Julie Breyer was poisoned with a plant-based tropane alkaloid. They need to check for it."

I called Brad, who headed to the hospital while I waited at the Dick home for CSU. After the technicians bagged the evidence—the nearly empty gallon container of Mel Dick's sweet tea and Julie's half-filled tumbler—I raced to Dexter General, ready to run over anyone who got in my way.

WHEN I BURST into the E.R., Brad brought me up-to-date.

"Mrs. Breyer is stable, but still pretty confused. They'll keep her here until she clears, but the doc said it was definitely anticholinergic poisoning, probably due to ingestion of tropane alkaloids."

"Probably? Didn't the labs identify the type of poison?"

Brad grinned. "Funny thing—I had to press Dr. Killweather a little bit on that. He kept saying that a urinalysis was medically unnecessary, that he had made the diagnosis 'based on clinical observation alone.'" He supplied air quotes. "I had to push, but we came to a meeting of the minds." He shot a sly look my way and added in a low voice, "Personally, I think the doc was just pissed off about the instructions you sent along with Greg."

"Who the heck is Greg?"

"The paramedic you scared half to death," Brad said. "I happened to witness Killweather reading the poor guy the riot act after Greg had given him your little message. Doctors are territorial bastards."

"So are cops."

When we were done laughing, Brad poked my ribs with an elbow. "That's the peckerwood now." He pointed at a pock-faced man in green scrubs headed our way. "Hi, doc," Brad said, grinning and waving.

Killweather flinched. I don't think he liked Brad's casual form of address. Then the doctor threw a pointed look in my direction.

"It's all right," Brad said, "Private Investigator Gorsky is familiar with the case. Anything you say to me, you can say to her."

"Oh, you're Gorsky," Killweather said. "As I expected, the patient's urine is positive for atropine and hyoscyamine, both of which are indicative of tropane alkaloid poisoning."

"Did the urinalysis identify the specific source of the poison?" I asked. My earlier research had identified several plants sources of tropane alkaloids, though my money was on *Datura stramonium*.

"Of course not, and if you'll excuse me…"

"Hold on," Brad said, making his hand a stop sign. "You got any problem with me interviewing Ms. Breyer now?" His icy voice told the doc he'd better not have a problem.

To my surprise Dr. Killweather grinned. "There is no medical reason why you can't speak with her, though I doubt you'll learn anything."

"Why?" Brad and I asked in chorus.

"Amnesia," he said. "Mrs. Breyer was quite amazed to find herself in a hospital. She told me the last thing she remembered with any clarity was leaving the morgue with Sheriff Spooner. Oh, there's no need for concern, amnesia is common with this type of poisoning. And now, I have patients to attend to."

"I don't care what that bozo says, I'm still gonna talk to Ms. Breyer," Brad said after the doctor walked away. "Amnesia, that throws another wrinkle in things."

This case was like a runaway train. I asked if Forensics had begun their analysis of the sweet tea.

"Funny you should ask." Brad pulled a folded paper from his shirt pocket and stared at it. "Our crime lab tech says there are a couple of available tests. Either a thin-layer chromatography or a mass spectrometry can confirm the presence of atropine and scopolamine, both of which are found in jimsonweed."

"How long with the test take?"

"First off, our crime lab is not equipped to perform either of these tests so we're gonna have to send it out. It'll be at least a couple of weeks before we get the results."

I cursed under my breath. This was awful news, and yet Brad was cool as ice. "There's more," I said with a grin.

"The tech said that a distillation of jimsonweed plant material placed on an eyeball will cause the pupil to dilate. Of course, it will never hold up in court, but…"

"Oh God, he didn't put the tea in his eye!"

"No, but his twin brother raises rabbits and he brought one of the critters by the lab. Get this—when they put a couple of drops of Mel's tea in the rabbit's eye, it got big as a dinner plate. Like I said, it's not evidence, but…"

"It tells me everything I need to know."

"I'm gonna go talk with Ms. Breyer now. You wanna join me?"

"There's someone else I need to see first."

"Who?"

"Mel Dick."

THE TECHNICIAN LEFT, giving me privacy. I pulled back the sheet and considered Mel Dick's corpse. It had begun with the body in the woods, so I had returned to the beginning.

Death diminished us all, and Mel was no different. When I looked at the bag of bones and guts on the steel table, I could not reconcile it to the blustering man I'd known in life. The animating force was gone, extinguished in an unfathomable act of violence, pushed into eternity by an unseen hand. But whose hand?

At the very beginning I thought Mel's death had been quick and painless—wrong on both counts. Mel's end had been as slow and painful as any. First the poison tea to destroy the old man's credibility, and then the coup de grâce, a bullet into the dead brain, both done by one hand—I was certain.

At the very start Jesse and the other guards told me about Mel's boasts about his looming celebrity. Come November, Mel told them all, he would be a famous man. It took me a while—I was stubborn, not smart—but eventually I determined that Mel was working on a big story, the story he planned to publish in November's *Commentator*. But for the first and last time in his life Mel underestimated himself. His story was even bigger than he thought and it had nothing to do with hookers at the G and G. This was a story worth killing for.

Over the last days of his life, the mysterious story consumed Mel's life. A fatal obsession. But not exclusively—there was another.

That night at Eddie's with the guys, we all agreed Mel Dick loved his dog, but at the end of his life Mel's affection for Mr. Jinks became a mania. So in the days lead-ing to his death Mel's addled mind was in the grip of dual obsessions, his big story and his dog.

Were the two connected?

One by one, Mel turned against everyone—friends, wife, mistress—but not his dog. I saw him running from the G and G with Jinks cradled to his chest. Next stop on the Mel express, the *Commentator* office, where he removed Jinks's collar and replaced it with a smelly bandana. After that was the confrontation with Anita when Jinks pulled his disappearing act. The wounded Mel ran to Gigi, but only stayed long enough to have his wound bandaged. Then it was out in the night once more, compelled to search for his lost dog.

As if his life depended on finding Jinks, Gigi had said.

What if she had been right?

Mel Dick loved his dog, but he was also a self-centered bastard. Crazy or not, it was not simple affection alone that sent him out in the dead of night to hunt for his dog. Somehow, that fatal search was connected to Mel's story. I felt a prickling down my spine—I was so close.

Something else: Mel Dick wasn't the sort of man who dressed his dog in silly scarves just for kicks, even with a datura-pickled brain. Busy had said that when she spied Mel walking his dog, the old man keep kept worrying at the bandana. That smelly scrap of blue fabric. More craziness from Mel?

Sure, but crazy had a reason and now I knew it.

I was on my cell the second I was free of the building. I needed to get my hands on Jinks's bandana.

"ARE YOU SURE it's the right box, Pop?" I asked again.

Pop sighed. "Yes, it's the shoebox in the bottom of the hall closet, as you said. There's a coffee mug, a calendar, some pens and…"

It was the right one, all right. After getting canned, I'd flung my belongings into the cardboard box, my one and only thought to be gone. If the bandana wasn't there, then where was it? I seemed to remember shoving the reeking thing into a desk drawer.

It hit me like a skillet in the face: Jinks's bandana was locked away in what was now Tyler Andrews's office. Suppose Tyler had tossed it, now wouldn't that be a kick in the ass?

I disconnected and punched the number for Mystic Cove Security. While I waited for Tyler to pick up, I comforted myself that at least Pop wouldn't be alone tonight. His buddy Frankie was stopping by with a pizza and a six-pack.

Tyler Andrews's recorded voice said he was sorry to have missed my call and blah, blah-blah. I didn't bother with a message.

I started to call Brad to give him an update. For all the bumps in the road, he had done right by me, and there was nothing more to be done tonight. For once I'd do the smart thing and wait until tomorrow when Tyler would be in the office.

Right?

I opened my cell, but instead of calling Brad, sent him a text: *gone 2 cove MWBRL.*

When had I ever done the smart thing?

"WHAT THE HELL, ADDIE!" José Barracas barreled toward me, eyes wide and arms spinning like windmills.

I had just parked the Vic in the G and G lot and my hand instinctively touched the Glock beneath my jacket. "What's wrong?"

"Everybody says you went nuts. First you break into

the Rand house and beat up old Mr. Rand and now the Dick girl is in the hospital! What the hell!"

I didn't have time for this. "Listen, José, I just wanted to make sure it was all right if I parked my car here for a couple hours." A long pause, way too long. "José?"

"Sure, I guess."

"I don't know what that means."

"Suppose Mr. Richt says something about me letting you park your car here?"

"Has Richt spoken to you about me?"

José didn't need to answer—his face told me everything.

"Listen, Richt doesn't know my ride, and if he somehow figures it out, just tow it. I don't care."

"I need a drink," José said.

I wouldn't mind a drink myself. Then I wondered when wanting a drink became needing a drink and prayed to all the gods I'd never find out.

"It's all right, Addie. I won't tow your ride."

"Thanks." I hoisted the large purse on my shoulder. José was giving me the once-over. "What's wrong?" I said, checking my look. From José's stare I half expected to find my blouse unbuttoned or a trail of toilet paper hanging from my shoe, but everything was in order.

"You look different."

"You're used to seeing me in Mystic Cove khaki." I started away.

"No, that's not it."

I didn't turn around, just kept walking, only a little faster.

"I got it!" José crowed from behind. "It's that purse. You never carry a purse."

Just my luck—if José had been drinking he would have never noticed. I could only hope his newfound attentiveness wouldn't come back and bite me on the butt. José was right—I never carried a purse. I had purchased the carpetbag-sized pocketbook an hour earlier at the local megamart, along with a few tools that might come in handy later tonight.

You see, I was pretty sure I had a way inside the Financial Building, but might need a little help breaking into my old office.

TWENTY MINUTES LATER I was on the first floor, standing outside security headquarters. To this point my plan had come off without a hitch. I'd waited till eight o'clock when the building would be empty. And as I'd expected, Tyler Andrews hadn't bothered to change the security codes. All I'd had to do was stroll to the rear entrance, punch in the old code and waltz inside. I had a pang when I punched the code for the stairwell door and it hadn't opened, but on the second try, the lock released.

Now I faced the real obstacle. The door to security headquarters required a key, a key I didn't have.

I moved the knob back and forth. The quickest and surest method would be to take my brand-new hammer and give the knob a good whack. A good backup plan, but I was hoping for more discreet ingress. I extracted a credit card from my wallet. Earlier I'd gone through my cards, selecting the largest and most flexible. It had been a while since I'd done this but I figured it was like riding a bike. I slid the card into the door crack, held it at a slight angle, and pushed toward the lock. Then I pushed in the opposite direction, leaning hard against the door, and turned the knob. The lock popped and I fell inside security headquarters.

When I tried the door to my former office, I was surprised to find it locked, but my trusty credit card once again did the trick. As I passed my flashlight over the interior I felt a twinge of regret. True, I had not been happy here, but there had been happy moments. But I needed to be quick. I tiptoed to the desk and pulled a drawer. I pulled again and realized it was locked. I tried each of the drawers. All locked.

I cursed under my breath. It appeared that Tyler Andrews had something to hide. But I was prepared. I rummaged in the voluminous purse and pulled out a screwdriver. It was tedious work but I wouldn't be so unlucky as to have to unscrew every locked drawer. I started with the right bottom drawer, where I thought I'd stashed the baggie.

I pulled out a stack of DVDs bearing titles like *Donna Does It Doggy Style* and *Monster Jugs*. Now I knew why Tyler kept his desk locked, or so I thought. Buried beneath the porno horde was a manila folder containing a report on the soil conditions on the land that would become Captain's Castle, Mystic Cove's newest phase that was currently under construction. How did Tyler get hold of it and why was he interested in soil? The only dirt Tyler Andrews cared about was pay dirt. But Andrews's machinations were no longer a concern of mine.

I worked my way through the remaining drawers, finding a few scraps of additional porno and not much else. God help me, I had to face it—Tyler had found the baggie and either tossed it or put it somewhere else. Unable to accept the first possibility, I spent valuable time rifling the lost-and-found box and any other likely hiding places, but again came up empty. When I planned this adventure I'd counted on spending no more than five minutes inside the office. I'd been at it almost an hour and was pushing my luck. But I couldn't let go. Not yet.

I returned to the desk. This time I removed the right

bottom drawer, dumping its contents on the floor. I aimed my flashlight into the gaping hole, and there it was, resting on the carpet. The plastic bag must have wedged in the space between the drawer and desk and fallen onto the floor.

I sat at my old desk, prize in hand. It would have been smarter for me to leave, but I had worked so hard for this pearl of great price. I could not wait a moment longer to know its value. I took the blue fabric from the baggie and laid it flat on the desk. The flashlight insufficient, I flipped on the gooseneck desk lamp, directing its single eye at the faded blue fabric.

My immediate thought was that it was just a rag, an old man's sick fancy. It was neither a bandana nor a *bufanda,* just a cut piece of fabric, and poorly cut at that. Its maker had frantically hacked through the faded wool without concern for aesthetics—an image of a drooling Mel Dick mutilating one of Anita's shawls filled my mind.

On closer examination I saw that not all the edges were raw. One of the narrow ends was seamed, the stitching sloppy but extensive. There were three, maybe four lines of hand-sewn stitches. Pulse rising, I started patting the length of the wide seam, stopping on a hard rectangular object. I tore and bit at the stitching, but the seam resisted—Mel had taken pains to secure his treasure. Screwdriver in hand, I ripped the seam open. A flash drive fell into my sweating palm, the answer in my hand.

I turned the computer on—Tyler hadn't changed the password. Hoping my luck would hold, I inserted the flash drive. I was a little let down when I saw the drive contained a single file, but my disappointment disappeared when I opened the document and read the title, screaming across the monitor in caps and tabloid punctuation: THE MURDERER AMONG US!!!

I had found the story Mel Dick had been working on at the time of his murder. I printed it—a few short paragraphs along with a picture of a young dark-haired woman. While the printer hummed I cleaned my mess, throwing the spilled contents back into the drawer. When I came across the soil report on Captain's Castle, I thought, why not? It only took a few extra seconds to xerox a copy.

Heart singing and with the documents packed in my purse, I hurried down the hallway, toward the stairs that would take me to safety. My hand was almost on the doorknob when the stairwell door swung open.

A man stepped from the darkness and into the light, fear and amazement mingled on his face. "Addie Gorsky!"

# EIGHTEEN

*The Murderer among Us*

"ADDIE GORSKY?" JEREMY LOUIS said again.

I nodded a greeting, an unnatural smile plastered on my face. What in the world was a financial planner doing on Security's floor?

"I'm surprised to see you here," I managed at last.

"I might say the same about you."

We eyed one another, me grinning like an idiot and him looking like he'd just bumped into Jack the Ripper. It dawned on me that the residents of Mystic Cove probably believed their former chief had lost her mind.

"Jeremy, I… I don't suppose you saw Tyler on your way up?"

A head shake and the eyebrows furrowed.

"Tyler was nice enough to stay late so that I could pick up some personal property I'd left in the office."

"Oh?" Jeremy's shoulders relaxed, just a little.

"Yeah, I've been pretty busy with Mel Dick's murder case."

Jeremy Louis's eyes brightened and his ears pricked, just like a card-carrying German shepherd. "I heard you were investigating Mel's death for the daughter. Well, let's not stand around in this drafty hallway. We can talk in my office." He hustled me into a small room at the end of the hallway.

"Being low man on the totem pole—is all right to say

totem pole?—anyway, with me being the newest hire, they sent me here during the renovations." He gestured at the tiny space. "Of course, I can't meet clients here so I'm out and about all day. I stop by here before going home to catch up on paperwork. Please sit down."

I sat, a rat in a trap.

"I heard about the excitement at the Rand house."

"Just a little misunderstanding," I mumbled.

"And how is Mel Dick's daughter? I understand EMS was out there today."

Where was he getting his information? Maybe I should have been talking to this nosey parker all along. "Julie Breyer was overtaken with a sudden illness, nothing serious."

"Oh." He folded his arms and looked me in the eye. "I'm sorry, Addie. I never gave you a chance to explain what you were doing here after hours. Mr. Richt doesn't look kindly on trespassers."

Darn it—I should have thrown him some red meat.

"After I got my property from Tyler, I was halfway down the stairs when I realized I had... I had..." I stopped, run dry of lies. I took in a ragged breath. Jeremy leaned close, beady eyes wet. I buried my face in my hands, said a prayer to the god of liars, and as always, they answered. "It's just no good, Jeremy—I... I can't pretend that everything thing is all right when it isn't. Can I trust you with the truth?"

Jeremy nodded—good boy.

"Part of what I told you is the truth. I did pick up my property from Tyler." Jeremy's head tilted, eyes questioning. "It was only Jinks's little bandana, his *bufanda*—see!" I pulled the scrap from my purse, just for a second. Jeremy's nose wrinkled. I returned the *bufanda* and sealed the baggie.

"So it's true about you and the dog," Jeremy muttered, his worst suspicions confirmed.

"As I said Tyler gave me Jinks's bandana, but it didn't go well. We argued. I don't know if I should tell you this, but Tyler... Tyler and I were very close, Jeremy. Intimate, you might say."

"Intimate," Jeremy breathed.

"When Mr. Richt fired me and appointed Tyler chief, I felt betrayed. I told Tyler that. Do you blame me, Jeremy?"

"Not at all," Jeremy said, handing me a tissue. I wiped a dry eye.

"It was terrible—both of us saying awful things to one another. Finally I just ran off, but by the time I reached the ground floor, I had cooled down. I just couldn't leave those awful words hanging between us. I came back to apologize, but Tyler was gone. I was leaving when I bumped into you." I slumped in my chair.

"I knew the moment I saw you in the hallway that something was wrong. Poor Addie—you were smiling on the outside, but crying on the inside."

"You're an astute man."

"I've always had good instincts where people are concerned." He grinned. "You might say I'm a people person."

"Can you do something for me, Jeremy? Please keep all of this to yourself, for Tyler's sake as well as mine."

"This is between you and me." With that Jeremy Louis sealed his lips with a finger and pantomimed throwing away the key.

"I'm feeling much better now," I said. No lie there.

Before we parted Jeremy insisted that we hug. I bore it as well as I could and then made my getaway.

Of course I knew Jeremy Louis's promise to be worthless. Come tomorrow morning, midday at the latest, news of my nocturnal visit to security headquarters would be all over the Cove. This time tomorrow night I might be spending the night in the county jail.

If I was to act, I had to act now and quickly.

I WAS RELIEVED to find that José hadn't towed the Vic. It was parked where I'd left it, the last car in the lot. As good a place as any to read Mel Dick's final story.

THERE IS A murderer among us. Under cover of darkness, a viper slipped into our Eden of Mystic Cove. But this devil has the power to assume a pleasing face and so remained hidden for years, but not from me.

The danger begins in the past, as does my story. These are the main characters: Chris Silver, Jacob Bradley, Katherine Henderson. Infamous names from an infamous time, the sixties.

They were part of the Weather Underground, a group of radicals intent on the destruction of America. These traitors took the revolution to the streets of America, lighting up the decade with a series of bombings. One night in San Francisco a young policeman lost his life when one of the deadly bombs exploded. Again the same names were whispered: Chris Silver, Jacob Bradley, Katherine Henderson.

In the spring of 1972 the three fugitives were holed up in a Greenwich Village townhouse. Chris Silver and Jacob Bradley were assembling a nail bomb in the basement of a Greenwich Village townhouse when the bomb detonated, seriously injuring both men. Unfortunately Katherine Henderson had not been at home at the time of the blast. By the time the police sorted it out, she had vanished into infamy.

Still, there was a measure of justice. Silver died of his

injuries, and after a contentious trial Bradley was made
to pay for his heinous crimes. But since that spring day
in New York City when God caught up with the two traitors, no one has seen or heard of Katherine Henderson.

Until now!

Like the snake she is, Katherine Henderson shed her
former skin. She assumed an alias, married, and had children, reaping the benefits of living in this greatest of all
countries, America. Astonishingly, she chose to live out
her golden years in our paradise of Mystic Cove.

Study the photograph above and look into the face of
evil. It is Katherine Henderson, murderess, but you know
her as TALLY RAND!

I DID AS Mel bade and looked into the young woman's face.
It was the sort of picture you'd find in your grandmother's
photo album. At first I thought that was why it seemed so
familiar, but then it clicked. I had seen the same photo in
Kristin Donald's book, *I Am Not a Witch*, alongside mug
shots of Chris Silver and Jacob Bradley, whom Donald
had prosecuted. My assessment of Mel's journalistic talent had been accurate. He'd just gotten lucky. When he
came across the picture of Katherine Henderson in Kristin Donald's book, he'd recognized her as Tally Rand.
But was he right?

In the photo a young woman leaned against a picket
fence, laughing. White-capped mountains rose in the distance. I squinted at the lost girl. A helmet of thick brown
hair hung over her face, brown eyes peeked out from
behind tortoiseshell glasses, and her smile was so deep,
her cheeks puffed like two fat apples. The smiling young
woman in the photo was long gone. The face had aged
and thinned, but it looked like Tally's.

But I had to be sure, absolutely sure, before I called

Brad. More to the point, once the authorities were involved, my access to the Rands would be denied, or at
least dependent on the will of others. Now, I could care
less about Katherine or Tally, but if I was to get to the
bottom of Mel's murder, I needed to face the Rands alone,
without the police.

Patting the Glock in my shoulder holster, I glanced
around the vacant parking lot. No one in sight. As I hustled to the path that would bring me to Admiral Street, I
felt unseen eyes upon me, a sick fancy that passed only
when I was deep in Birnam Wood.

Fifteen minutes later I stood outside the Rand home.
Someone was home. A dim light shone from the living
room—either a table lamp or perhaps just the television.
I walked to the portico and rang the bell. It was a little
late for visitors, and the Rands would be wary, but somehow I knew they would answer. They tottered on the edge
of disaster and could not ignore the bell when it tolled.

The porch light lit and the door opened.

"Hello, Kathy," I said.

"You shouldn't have come," she said in a small voice.

I understood, or thought I did. Standing behind her in
the foyer, Alan Rand was pale and trembling, but the pistol he aimed at my heart was steady enough.

WE WERE IN the darkened living room. We had been there
for hours—Tally and I sitting side-by-side on the sofa
while Alan bounced around the room like a mouse in a
maze, twitching for a way out.

"Did you call the police?" Alan asked again.

"No, Alan. No one knows I'm here." I spoke in as calm
a voice as I could manage. Alan Rand was a man without
a plan and that made him dangerous. In my favor, the fool

hadn't even searched me. I felt the weight of the holstered Glock. *Please, Alan, don't make me use it.*

"Alan, dear," Tally said, rising to her feet.

"What are you doing?" Alan's head snapped round.

"I thought I'd make some tea."

"Tea?" For a moment I feared he would laugh. "No, no tea. Sit down. Please." Tally sat back down. It wasn't her first move to escape Alan's eyes—she was as much a prisoner as I.

"Alan, you must stop peeking out the window every two seconds. Addie is telling you the truth. If she had called the authorities they would have been here by now—it's been so long."

"Listen to her," I said. "The police don't know about Katherine."

"Don't say that name—that's not her name." Alan walked from the window and sat on the bottom step of the staircase. Every few seconds his gaze shifted from Tally and me on the sofa and back to the front window.

"You're wrong about everything!" Tally's voice broke, like a pipe under pressure. "Why won't you listen to me?" She turned to me. "All of this has been harder on Alan than me."

"All of what?" I asked.

"Quiet, you!" Alan warned.

"Alan hadn't known about Kathy Henderson until Mel told him. I had almost forgotten about her myself. It's all so strange, like a dream. It was so long ago and I was a different person. But I guess the past doesn't go away."

"Not for long anyway," I said.

"Quiet, both of you." Alan sat on the last rung of the staircase, looking like a lost little boy.

Tally cast a pitying look at her husband. "I knew I was doomed once Mel learned about my past, but poor

Alan kept trying to make things right. He thought he'd be able to convince Mel to change his mind, but Mel doesn't change his mind. Not ever."

I was in a peculiar position. Either Tally or Alan had shot Mel Dick—at the moment my money was on Alan— but technically neither was a murderer. I'd gone back and forth about sharing this information with the Rands, but Alan was too unstable to listen and Tally…well, I just wasn't sure about Tally.

"Mel wouldn't listen," Alan Rand said from the stairs. "He showed me that awful article."

"I wanted to turn myself in, but Alan wouldn't hear of it."

"Mel told me he was going to publish the article in the *Commentator*," Alan said, "but because I was a friend he was giving me a chance to 'do the right thing.' He actually expected me to turn against my wife—my wife! Mel Dick destroyed my life as carelessly as he would smash a mosquito." Alan started pacing again.

Tally half rose and murmured, "Oh, Alan!"

"Sit down, Tally!" Alan hissed. "It's never going to end, is it? I just want it to end!"

It was going south fast—Alan Rand was bouncing off the walls and talking a mile a minute, but his eyes were no longer on me. Carefully, so carefully, I eased the Glock from the holster and lay it on my right, tucked in the space between the sofa's arm and cushion.

"Mel said I could appear at the news conference after Tally was arrested. When I saw that our friendship meant nothing to him, I tried to bribe him." Alan's voice boomed through the house. "I offered him everything I had— money, political connections, my very soul, if he wanted it! All he had to do was forget about Kathy Henderson."

"Alan," Tally sobbed.

Alan's pigeon chest heaved, his breaths ragged. "I told Mel nobody cares about the Weathermen or this Henderson woman."

"Tally is tired," I told Alan. "She needs to rest now. Let me take her to bed."

"I didn't know what to do," he said, "but I couldn't let the police take you away."

"I'm tired, Alan, so very tired."

"I'm tired too, Tally, but we have to stay together. I'll never let you go."

"But she just wants to rest for a little while," I said. "Let me take her upstairs."

"You!" Alan cried. "What do you care? You're not Tally's friend. You're not my friend. You're here to find Mel's murderer. Nobody cares who killed that piece of crap! What's that?"

Blue lights danced over the walls, casting ominous shadows. Alan Rand rushed to the window, peeked out. An anguished moan like that of a wounded animal.

"It's the police!" Alan shouted, brandishing his gun. "You lied! You lied!" He sobbed and fell silent.

I was on my feet, knees locked, both hands gripping my weapon. From somewhere far away Tally screamed and someone pounded the door. But Alan Rand and I stood like two gunfighters in an old-timey Saturday matinee.

"Drop the gun, Alan. It's over." And it was—I caught Brad in the corner of my eye. He stood in the hallway, weapon drawn and aimed at Alan Rand.

Still, the old man did not move, the raised pistol shaking in his frail hands. And then something broke inside. Alan sobbed and took a deep breath. "I shot Mel Dick. I blew his brains out with his own gun."

"No, Alan!" Tally screamed. "You're wrong!"

"I killed the bastard. I shot him dead." Smiling, Alan

lowered his arm and let the gun fall from his grasp. In a flash, Brad was on him, slapping cuffs on bony wrists.

"You're hurting him!" Tally cried.

I grabbed her, held her tight. "Alan's all right." Only who was I kidding? Alan Rand was about as far from all right as a man could be, lying on the floor like a sack of flour or a puppet with broken strings.

Outside the frantic yelp of a GCSO cruiser announced that backup had arrived. While GCSO took control of the scene, Brad looked to me for an explanation.

I gestured at Tally Rand. "Sheriff, say hello to Katherine Henderson."

AFTER HEATING UP my coffee, Brad took his seat. He looked tired; I didn't want to think what I looked like. The hours since Alan Rand's confession to a false murder had passed in a haze, but slowly the haze was clearing.

"Brad, you never did explain how you showed at the Rands when you did."

"After I got your text saying you were headed to the Cove, I called you back, but you didn't pick up. I even called your home phone and talked to your dad. At first I wasn't concerned and figured you would call when you were good and ready, but when the night dragged on and there was still no news, I got worried." Brad drank his coffee, shrugged. "I figured it wouldn't hurt to drive to the Cove and have a look-see. At Founder's Centre, I spotted the Crown Vic in the Grub and Grog parking lot. So naturally I made a bullet for the Rand house."

"Why naturally?"

He gave me a level look. "Because that was the one place you weren't supposed to go."

"Oh."

"All's well that ends well."

"Has it ended well?"

"At this point I'm happy with any ending to this screwup." Brad tapped the yellow legal pad on his desk. "I gotta say, this is as pretty a murder confession as I've ever seen. Too bad there's no murder to go along with it."

"So you think Alan is telling the truth."

"I do," he said, sliding the pad over, "but go ahead and read it for yourself."

I smiled my thanks.

I ACTED ALONE. The murder, from inception to execution, was mine. My wife had no knowledge of and took no part in this crime.

It began the day after Mel's birthday dinner. Mel called and asked that I drop by the newspaper office. I assumed he wanted to discuss November's *Cove Commentator*. It turned out that my assumption was correct, though hardly in the way I imagined.

We had drinks, my first clue that Mel was in a celebratory mood. Then he showed me the reason for his cheer, an article he planned to publish in next month's *Commentator*. In a matter of minutes I read the words that would destroy my life. Incredibly, the article claimed that my wife was this fugitive Katherine Henderson. "Is this a joke?" I asked Mel.

He smiled and said, "It's not a joke, but it is sort of funny." I'll never forget that smile, that smug grin. Maybe that's when I decided to kill him.

At first I didn't believe any of it, but the photo of Katherine Henderson was my Tally. When I asked Mel why he told me of his plan, he seemed surprised and said, "Because you're my friend." He wanted to give me the chance to distance myself from my wife; he even offered to let me attend the press conference he intended to hold after the story was broken.

Over the next weeks I begged Mel to suppress the article for the sake of our long friendship. He refused. I appealed to logic—no one cared about this Katherine Henderson person!—but he wouldn't listen. I even tried bribery, but I had nothing Mel wanted. I pleaded, but Mel wouldn't relent. I grew more desperate, the first of November hovering like an executioner's axe. Then came my chance, that night at the Grub and Grog.

Tally and I had gone to the pub for drinks. We saw Mel and Anita there, but said nothing to them. Mel was dazed. Of course his strange behavior was the talk of Mystic Cove. Busy Rhodes said Mel had Alzheimer's, and even Mel's girlfriend Gigi Tajani whispered that Mel's memory was Swiss cheese. Fairley Sable called him hot as a hare and dry as a bone. Initially I thought they exaggerated Mel's decline, but when I saw him at the G and G that night I knew they'd understated the depth and breadth of his madness.

After Mel verbally attacked us, his former friends, at the pub, Tally and I returned home, having no wish to be present when the police arrived. Tally went to sleep, but I couldn't rest. There were mere days left before the fatal blow would fall. I had to make Mel see reason! I decided to make one last effort.

I had just left my house when I saw Mel's golf cart bolt onto Admiral Street, obviously coming from Gigi Tajani's townhouse. I watched it turn into Birnam Wood and followed.

Mel hadn't gone far. I found him parked in a small clearing, a place he often went to. I walked up to the cart, not sure what I was going to do, but when I reached it I saw, lying on the passenger's seat, a gun. I grabbed the weapon, aimed at Mel's right temple, and fired.

When I returned home. I locked the murder weapon inside my safe and waited for the night. I knew that for Tally to be safe I must destroy all evidence of Tally's true identity.

While Tally slept I went to Mel's office, using a key I'd retained from when I was editor of the *Commentator*. I erased all traces of Katherine Henderson from Mel's computer. Now there was only the gun to be disposed of.

That evening I rolled our trash receptacle to the curb for morning pickup. I looked up and down—a row of garbage cans lined Admiral Street. In the dead of night I retrieved the weapon from my safe, slipped outside and dropped it into the Dicks' trash can.

I never meant for suspicion to fall on Anita Dick. My only thought was to be rid of the gun. I am sorry about Anita.

"QUITE A PIECE of writing," I said.

"It is what it is, Addie, but it fits with the facts."

"Not perfectly."

"Rand knows details about the murder that weren't released to the public—that Dick was shot in the right temple, for one."

"But Rand doesn't mention stealing the hard drive from Mel's home computer. And what about the missing office key? If Rand didn't take the office key off of Mel's body, who did?"

"Maybe Mel lost it in his travels. Maybe he left it in the office."

"And the poisoned tea?"

Brad rubbed his tired face. "Rand vehemently denies any knowledge of that, and I believe him. Why admit to shooting Mel and not cop to tampering with the tea?" He gave me an astute look. "You know who poisoned Mel's tea, Addie."

"I do?"

"You may not like it, but the jimsonweed tea was Anita getting her jollies off." He smiled in that self-satisfied way men have. "In a way I was right—Anita was responsible for her husband's death, though I don't think she meant for him to die. The jimsonweed tea and the shock and stress from the initial gunshot wound precipitated Mel's fatal heart attack, which was unlucky for Mel, but incredibly lucky for Rand. Case closed."

"But if Rand shot Mel, why did he accuse José of the crime? Wouldn't it have been smarter to just lay low?"

"Maybe he was fishing for a fall guy."

"Not the smartest move," I countered.

"And since when are murderers smart?"

"This one is."

"But now that I think about it," Brad continued, "the deal with Barracas might have been a slick move on Rand's part. Don't forget that Alan Rand is a lawyer—he can't help but think like one. He knew that Mel planned to expose Barracas as a pimp. Maybe Rand was trying to establish reasonable doubt by bringing another suspect to light."

"I suppose it's possible. Before the shit hit the fan, I'm sure Mel told Alan about the prostitution story. Of course, once Mel ran across Tally's picture in Donald's book, all bets were off. He forgot about José's transgression and went after the bigger story." I stifled a yawn and added, "But your theory is still pretty farfetched."

"So only your farfetched ideas deserve consideration?"

I had to laugh. "Look, I don't know what part of Rand's statement is true, and what is false, but he's not being completely honest with us. I mean, he says that Tally was in the dark about Mel's plans—that's total bullcrap! She knew everything. He's lying to protect Tally."

"I don't buy that, and I'll tell you why," Brad said. "Alan Rand now knows that Mel was deceased when he was shot, yet he stands by every word in this statement, even though murder charges are off the table. What's he protecting his wife from now?"

"I don't know." I shoved Rand's confession back to Brad. I waited until we'd both stopped bristling, then said, "Say, are Anita's labs in yet?"

"Nope, but I don't know what you're hoping for. Both Rio and Hackle agree that Anita drowned. It's over. Pat yourself on the back for a job well done and move on."

"First I have to go to Dexter Memorial and tell Julie Breyer that her mother killed her father after all. At least her husband will be here soon." I glanced at the clock. Breyer's plane was due in at three-thirty, an hour from now. Soon, but not soon enough—Julie needed all the support she could get.

"You can soften the blow."

"You don't know Julie Breyer," I said, pulling on my jacket. "She doesn't like soft-serve."

There was a rattle of knocks on the door, but before Brad could say anything, the door peeped open and a gray-haired man stuck his head inside. His voice was a Southern purr as he asked if he might have a word with the sheriff.

After the door closed, I gaped at Brad. "What's drunk bow-tie guy doing here?"

"You know him?"

I told him about my brief encounter with bow-tie guy at Jud Richt's Outhouse. "He was in such a hurry to get to Jud Richt's office the old drunk nearly knocked me down."

Brad chuckled, but his face was dark granite. "Bow-tie guy, huh? Around here we know him as Coroner Titus Blanding."

# NINETEEN

*The Mask of the Beast*

THE NURSE WAS going over Julie's discharge instructions when I slipped into the room. The afternoon sun slanted through the blinds, casting zebra stripes over the room. I closed my eyes. It was one week to the day since I'd found the body in Birnam Wood, but the ordeal was almost over.

"Addie?"

I startled awake. I hadn't heard the nurse leave. I mumbled sorry and dragged my chair to the side of the bed. So far all Julie knew was that someone named Alan Rand had confessed to murdering her father, but little else.

"I'm all done here, but I told the nurse to give us a few minutes. I need to know the truth. Did Alan Rand shoot my father?"

"He's confessed to it," I said carefully.

As I'd feared, Julie demanded the details of Rand's confession. I took a breath and told her. When I was done Julie leaned back into her pillow. She took so long that I actually hoped she'd let it go for once. But she proved true to her blood. "Did this Rand also poison the tea?"

"Alan Rand denies tampering with the tea."

"So the police think Mom did it," Julie said. "And you?"

"It's possible."

"So Mom killed Dad after all." A choked laugh. "And she almost killed me as well."

"Don't think of it that way. We don't know the circumstances of the initial gunshot—it might have been an accidental misfiring, for all we know. And even if Anita did put the jimsonweed in Mel's tea, her intent was to punish, not to kill."

"And Mom's death?"

"There's nothing new."

"But the cops think it's suicide, right? That fits with their theory. Mom was guilty about Dad and drowned herself."

"Julie, maybe it's not a good idea for you to go back to Admiral Street. I could take you to the Seascape Motel in Lady-in-the-Hills—it's very nice." Actually it was a dump, but it beat that lonely house on Admiral Street.

A heavy sigh. "Dwight's on his way. I told him to drive straight to Admiral Street, where I'll be waiting."

"Plans can be changed. Wouldn't you rest better somewhere else?"

"No, no, no," she said, shaking her head slowly, punctuating each no. "My place is at Admiral Street. I need to do my duty to Mom and Dad. I need to go through their things, decide what to keep, what to sell, and what to throw away.

"And then I need to bury my dead."

I DROVE JULIE Breyer to the empty house on Admiral Street, waited with her until Dwight arrived, and then left them to their sorrow. But there was one last stop before I could take my rest.

"Thanks for coming," Tyler Andrews indicated a seat.

"Did I have a choice?" I asked, checking the shadows of my former office for a lurking Jud Richt.

"We're alone," Tyler said as he shut the office door. When he'd called and said he had to see me right away,

I figured it was about my unlawful visit to his office last night—some deduction, right? But the only thing I didn't get was why I was still walking around and not sitting in jail.

"I guess congratulations are in order, Addie. I heard about Rand's arrest."

Not the tone I'd expected, but I was in no mood for pleasantries. "You didn't ask me here to congratulate me, Tyler, and I'm too tired to play games."

"All right then, I spoke with Jeremy Louis and I know you broke into my office last night. I don't know why it couldn't have waited until today, but I wanted to give you a chance to explain."

"Frankly, after the scene at Eddie's I didn't expect you to help me," I said. Tyler had the grace to blush. "But the bottom line was that it couldn't wait for the morning. I had to get my hands on the dog's bandana last night." Then I spewed out some bullcrap about lives being at stake and to my surprise Tyler lapped it up like cream.

He whistled and said, "Poison tea, huh? I can understand your urgency."

Really? Tyler acted as if I held the whip and not he. Either way, it worked out in my favor. I said something vaguely conciliatory and prepared to leave.

"Not yet, Addie," Tyler said, his hand grasping my arm. I sat back down. "I also know you were in my desk last night."

"Well, yes, that's where I found the flash drive."

"That's not all you found."

I stared at Tyler. Was this about the porno? Then I remembered the report on Captain's Castle that I'd found in his desk. My pilfered copy was sitting in the glove compartment of the Crown Vic, where I'd shoved it last night. ASAP I needed to take a closer look.

"I'm sorry I had to break into your desk, Tyler," I said, playing dumb.

"I know you saw the report. You notice things. You have to promise me that you won't tell Mr. Richt about what you saw in there." Tyler's hand clenched tighter. "Promise me."

"I'm not interested in your business."

"Promise," he said, his hand crushing my arm.

"Sure, I promise."

Tyler examined my face. When he was satisfied, he released my arm. "Still friends, Addie?"

"No, Tyler, we're far from being friends."

I turned and left.

I PICKED UP Chinese takeout on the way home—two bags full, enough for me, Pop, and Frankie Buchanan. Good old Frankie had spent the night on the sofa, watching over Pop like a mother hen. Well, a mother hen with the vocabulary of a sailor and the disposition of a bull gator. But we were all a bit raucous at the dining table, drinking beer and slurping noodles.

"No need to thank me, Addie. I couldn't leave the old man in the state he was in—nervous as a friggin' whore in church." Frankie grinned, chomping on a rib.

"What are you talking about?" Pop reached for another egg roll. "I was the one holding your hand. I told you my girl would figure it out."

Frankie tipped his bottle of Bud my way. "It was a good piece of work, Addie."

Pop grabbed his beer. "To Addie Gorsky, private investigator."

"Hey, I like the sound of that," I said, and I did. "But there are a few loose ends."

Frankie belched into his hand. "From what Stan says, the case sounds pretty tight."

"My daughter doesn't like the truth she found, but the truth doesn't care."

"Geez, Stan, the way you talk."

My cell buzzed; it was Hackle. I excused myself to take the call. Anita's labs were in. As Hackle went through the results, I found my mind wandering, but was jolted to attention when he said, "The vitreous humor analysis was interesting."

"Remind me what vitreous humor is again." I asked, not that I'd ever known.

"It's a clear gelatinous mass between the eye lens and the retinal lining. Got it?" As usual, Hackle didn't wait for an answer. "Anita Dick's vitreous humor not only revealed a dangerously high glucose level, but was positive for ketones."

"Meaning what?"

"As you know, Mrs. Dick was a type one diabetic, dependent on insulin."

Actually I hadn't known that at all. When Julie told me her mother was diabetic, I assumed it was good old type two, like half the overweight people in Mystic Cove.

Hackle continued, "And there was evidence of cerebral edema, but of course that could have been due to blunt trauma from the drowning. However, the presence of ketones suggests diabetic ketoacidosis might have been the cause. Without treatment and, of course, if she hadn't fallen into Mystic Bay, Anita Dick would have slipped into a coma and died, sooner rather than later."

"So she was depressed after Mel's murder and didn't keep up with her insulin," I said, not getting Hackle's excitement.

"But if the cerebral edema was caused by DKA, then

Anita Dick was a very sick woman before she fell or jumped into Mystic Bay."

"Just how sick, Doctor?" I asked, feeling a quickening in my gut.

"There would have been extreme mental confusion, labored breathing, emesis, decreased reflexes, tachycardia."

"But how could someone so ill elude the police for several hours and then get herself to the pier?"

"I doubt she could have, although people set on taking a life—be it their own or another's—are often highly motivated, so I can't discount it entirely."

"Does Spooner know all this?"

"Of course, Gorsky," Hackle huffed. "I'm calling you as a…a courtesy."

Or maybe the sheriff was not exactly enthusiastic and Hackle knew I'd be more receptive. I turned the conversation back to Anita. "I just need to be clear on this one point. If you're right about the ketoacidosis, would Anita have been ambulatory?"

Hackle sighed. "I think someone as sick as Anita Dick would have been hard-pressed to answer her telephone or go to the bathroom without assistance."

"Someone helped her off that pier," I said, and Hackle did not disagree.

AFTER SENDING FRANKIE on his way, Pop insisted I get some rest. He noticed how quiet I got after Hackle's call and knew some new wrinkle had popped up, a wrinkle I had to iron out before laying the case to rest. But Pop was right. A little nap and I'd be a new woman. I pulled the shade tight and collapsed on my bed.

I don't know if it was sunshine peeking through the curtains or the smell of brewing coffee or the scratchy tongue on my cheek that woke me. "Bad Jinks," I said, pushing the pug off the bed. I propped up on one elbow, disoriented by the bright sun. Crap, I had slept through the night and into the next morning.

"You should have woken me," I groused to Pop.

"But I did—I sent the dog in to wake you."

"You should have woken me last night. Oh, and you shouldn't let Jinks on the furniture. He just jumped on my bed like it was nothing."

"Here, drink your coffee." Pop set the steaming mug in front of me. "You're always grouchy before your coffee—just like your mother."

"Dammit, I am not grouchy."

A few minutes later, Pop caught me up on my messages. People were clamoring to see me, or so it seemed. Julie had called to remind me about today's memorial service for her parents at Mystic Cove, Brad had called but left no message, and some madwoman named Page Becket had phoned, requesting an interview with Mr. Jinks.

"Page Becket at Channel Twelve, the local news leader," Pop said, outraged over my ignorance. "It's not just Jinks, Adelajda. I'm sure she wants to speak with you as well."

"Jesus," I muttered.

"Here are Page's numbers—including her personal cell and—"

"Pop, please." Pushing the paper away, I swiped my cell.

"Sleeping Beauty awakens at last," Brad drawled.

"I'm sorry, Brad. My father should have woken me when you called."

"I told him to let you sleep. I wanted to give you a heads-up. The press caught wind of your involvement in the case and will probably be knocking on your door. Katherine Henderson's arrest has become a national story."

"Too late," I said. "Some reporter named Page Becket is leaving messages."

Brad whistled. "Page Becket? She's a journalistic institution in these parts."

"You're as bad as Pop. And FYI, this journalistic institution wants to interview Mr. Jinks. I'm an afterthought." Then I asked if he'd gotten things straightened out with Titus Blanding.

"Titus Blanding and I came to an understanding, more or less. You'll hear about it next week when he resigns so he can spend more time with his family."

"How'd you manage that?"

"I'd misjudged Coroner Blanding. I knew Richt was a contributor to Blanding's last campaign, but I didn't fully appreciate the closeness of the relationship. Evidently Blanding doesn't wipe his ass before checking with Richt. The drunk fool actually thought he was doing Richt a favor by delaying Mel's autopsy. When Richt disabused him of that belief, our soon-to-be former coroner went into an alcoholic tailspin."

"And that's a good thing?" I'd never heard an alcoholic tailspin described in such glowing terms.

"Yeah, Dolores Rio is taking over as coroner."

"By the way, I spoke with Hackle."

"I'll give you that the lab findings are suspicious," Brad said, anticipating my train of thought.

"You add a bunch of possibilities together, and pretty soon you're talking about probability and after that…"

"Addie, unless you have something other than conjecture, I don't wanna hear it. You got any evidence?"

I admitted I had nothing. At least not yet.

THE MEMORIAL SERVICE for Mel and Anita Dick was just long enough to be respectable, though it was a good turnout. Mel Dick had a long list of acquaintances and co-conspirators who showed up to pay their respects. But when the pastor asked if anyone wished to speak, only a few responded, and those few spoke only of Mel. Even in death, Anita was a postscript.

When it was done, the mourners, myself included, were unwilling to move on. We milled around Mystic Bay Chapel like foraging ants. I knew what I sought, but wondered what kept the others here, murmuring in small groups. It didn't take me long to figure it out.

"Over here, Addie!" José Barracas flapped his arms like he was trying to take flight, his face split by an incongruous grin. "Pretty exciting stuff, huh?"

"The memorial service?" I said, playing dumb.

"You know what I mean." José gave my arm a light punch. "Say, I heard they put Rand on a suicide watch." Two older gentlemen—Mystic Covians by the look of them—edged closer, obviously eavesdropping.

"Addie," another voice cried. I cringed as Jeremy Louis trotted over.

And so it went. People who I'd barely known greeted me like an old friend, full of questions.

*Is it true they put Mr. Rand on suicide watch?*

*I heard that Tally was the real mastermind.*

*How's Mr. Jinks holding up?*

The scene was repeated ad nauseam as the good citizens pumped their former chief, all seeking grist for the grinding mill. I was about to quit the scene when I spotted the faces for which I had been searching. I found them together, congregating by the little Shakespeare garden adjacent to the chapel—Busy Rhodes, Gigi Tajani and Fairley Sable. I pasted a smile on my face and greeted the weird sisters.

"I suppose congratulations are in order," Busy said,

though her face told another tale. "According to the papers you successfully cracked the case." A self-deprecating smile and she added, "Listen to me—I sound like a detective in one of those television shows."

"I'm just glad it's over and things can get back to normal." Gigi's restless gaze passed over the crowd.

Fairley touched my arm. "I'm still confused on one point, Addie. The newspaper said you found something in Jinks's scarf. A flashcard or something—that doesn't make sense."

"No, Fairley." Busy patted the shorter woman's shoulder. "I told you—it was a flash drive, for a computer."

"Oh, I give up," Fairley said. "When it comes to all this technology, I'm at a loss."

"So what are you three ladies plotting?" I asked.

"Fairley and Busy were talking about the *Commentator,* of all things," Gigi said. "With Mel gone, I can't see the paper carrying on."

"I agree," Busy said. "With Mel dead and Alan…gone, the paper should go the way of the dinosaurs."

"You're probably both right, but it seems a terrible waste. The paper is well established. If the right person took control—" Fairley glanced at Busy, "—the *Commentator* could be reborn in a new form."

"Like the Phoenix." Busy stroked her chin. "Perhaps I have been hasty. With a little work the *Commentator* could be refashioned into something glorious."

"I wonder if nice Mr. Lee needs a date for the Harvest Fest tonight." Gigi's eyes settled on a short balding man standing by a stone angel.

Fairley flashed a knowing smile my way but spoke to Gigi. "I think Mr. Lee will most likely attend Harvest Fest with his wife Millie." Then she frowned. "I'm still not sure that we should go out gallivanting so soon after the tragedy."

"Of course we should go," Busy said. "Life must go on."

"I'm going as Cleopatra," Gigi gushed. "What about you, Busy?"

"Miss Havisham."

Gigi turned to Fairley. "And your costume?"

"An angel."

"If you'll excuse us, Addie, we were just heading for the Grub and Grog." Busy herded her new friends across the street. Peculiar, the way Mel Dick's death had brought those three women together, but maybe murder, like politics, made for strange bedfellows.

But Pop was waiting at the apartment. His appointment with the hospice doctor in Newnansville was at three. I had to hurry if we were to make it on time.

Without a backward glance I left Mystic Cove for what I thought was the last time.

POP AND DR. Hazel Addison hit it off right away. She was a trim, attractive woman with kind brown eyes, but her most beautiful asset was her voice, a rich mezzo with golden tones. As she went over the differences between medical and palliative care, I slowly realized that hospice didn't mean that the doctors and nurses had given up on Pop, which had been my greatest fear. Now the focus would be on Pop's quality of life rather than the extension of days. I felt a sense of deep relief. The journey would continue, albeit with a change of itinerary. Dying wasn't the same as dead.

The consultation wound down and Pop and I were about to leave when, apropos of nothing, Pop mentioned the Mel Dick/Katherine Henderson case.

"I read about it in this morning's *Sun*," Dr. Addison said. "You must be very clever, Ms. Gorsky."

Before I could answer, Pop said, "That she is—it runs in the family."

"Dr. Addison isn't interested in this, Pop."

My father was undeterred. "This was a very interesting case, with many twists and turns—betrayal, fugitives, madness, a mysterious poison—what was the poison, Adelajda?"

*"Datura stramonium."* Seeing Addison's puzzled face I added, "The victim suffered a fatal heart attack from untreated anticholinergic toxicity."

"Anticholinergic syndrome is not my area of expertise, though I still recall the mnemonic I learned as a young med student. Hot as a hare, red as a beet, dry as a bone, blind as a bat, mad as a hatter. It's an easy way to recall the signs and symptoms. Are you all right, Ms. Gorsky?"

"Could you repeat the mnemonic? Please, just repeat it."

She did so, slowly this time. A train of similes constructed as a memory tool, odd images that would stick in the mind.

When Fairley Sable whispered them in Alan Rand's ear, describing Mel Dick's deterioration, the words had stuck in his mind so well that he unwittingly repeated them in his confession. His false confession. And she had brazenly repeated part of the mnemonic to me when she'd called Mel mad as a hatter. A true murder after all.

From the beginning she had inserted herself into the matter of Mel's death, a bottom-swimming stingray stirring up mud. I counted our meetings over the course of the investigation, her insidious helpfulness and her uncanny habit of popping up at every turn, like a freaking whack-a-mole.

Then I thought maybe it wasn't coincidence. Maybe Fairley Sable had had me in her sights all along.

# TWENTY

*Hot as a Hare*

I MADE THE calls while Pop was inside Walgreens, waiting for his prescriptions to be filled. He gave me a funny look when I told him I'd wait in the car, but my father knew when to ask questions and when to keep quiet.

I called Brad first. "I need to see Tally Rand, Brad. Alan's confession is cut from whole cloth. Someone else murdered Mel."

"Murder?"

"Oh yes, it's murder. I know who she is and a good idea of how she did it. What I don't have is motive. Tally can help me with that." I told him about the GPS tracker I'd found on the Crown Vic, attached to the inside right fender of my car like a leech. A true hunter, she'd tracked me from the beginning. Brad wanted me to bring the car in so the lab could check for prints.

"A waste of time," I said. "I'm sure the GPS tracker is clean—she wouldn't be so careless—and any prints we found would have no probative value. She's ridden in my car."

Brad had heard enough. He said he would do what he could to get me in to see Tally, but warned that it wasn't his call. "And there is something you should know about Tally. Turns out she wasn't going to take Mel's threats lying down—she had plane reservations for Morocco, which coincidentally doesn't have an extradition treaty with the U.S."

"So she and Alan had a backup plan. They were going to fly the coop if Mel didn't back down."

"Not exactly," Brad said. "The reservation was for one."

"So while Alan was running after Mel, Tally had been making plans of her own." This put a wrench in my plans. I could only move Tally by exploiting her love for her husband, and now I wasn't sure if their happy marriage wasn't just another Mystic Cove mirage. "Brad, there's was one more thing I had to know—Does Tally know that Mel was dead when he was shot?"

"A good question, but not one I can answer."

Next I called my sister Angelina. Angie had been on the fast track at the FBI until she married an Irishman named Michael O'Shaughnessy and started producing carrot-headed kids with names like Sean and Seamus at a prodigious rate. Nowadays she stuck to private work, usually when she needed the bucks—when the twins' teeth came in crooked she kept pretty busy for quite awhile—but sometimes Angie helped somebody free of charge, just because they needed the help. I fit in the latter category.

Angie picked up on the second ring. "O'Shaughnessy."

"Hey, O'Shaughnessy, what's up?"

"Addie!" Angie shouted and then, "Hey, kids, it's Aunt Addie on the phone." High-pitched squeals in the background—by all the screaming going on, it sounded as if she and Michael had added a few more to the brood.

"Have I interrupted a party?"

Angie laughed. "It's Halloween, we got half the neighborhood at our house. From what I've seen on the boob tube, you've got your own party going down there." Since the Katherine Henderson story broke, cable news had been hot and heavy over it.

I explained my involvement and told her what I needed. "And I need it ASAP—time's not on my side." Dead silence, so I added, "Get it to me when you can."

"It's not that, Addie. It sounds like you're swimming with the sharks down there. Stay safe."

"It's Florida, after all," I said with a show of bravado. "But I'll be careful. Just get the goods on Fairley Sable."

THE VISITING AREA was empty except for me, the guard and the woman on the other side of the glass. She was outwardly calm, sitting in the caged cubicle with her arms neatly folded on the narrow counter. The fluorescent light and orange jumpsuit gave her skin a jaundiced tinge, but her eyes had lost that clouded look. I took a deep breath and picked up the phone.

"Hello…" I paused.

"Call me Tally." Her voice sounded hollow. "I've been Tally for so long. I can't remember being anyone else."

"Thanks for seeing me."

Tally did a slow survey of the steel gray room. "Don't thank me. I have no intention of answering your questions. That's why you're here, isn't it, Addie Gorsky? To ask your questions."

I felt as if I had walked in on the wrong movie. I was prepared for Tally Rand, not this steely-eyed woman. Or was this Katherine Henderson?

"In fact, I have a question for you," she snarled. "Are you pleased with the results of your idiotic investigation? Are you pleased that you've destroyed two lives?"

"Tally, let me…"

"I wanted to tell you to your face that my husband is absolutely innocent."

"Innocent?" A spasm of anger fired in my gut. Though I agreed Alan was innocent of shooting Mel, he was far from innocent. "Your innocent husband almost got both of us killed."

"You pushed him to it," Tally said.

"Like hell," I shot back. Then the guard caught my eye. I got his message loud and clear—the interview was dangerously close to being terminated before it even got started. I took a moment to tamp down my anger before it blazed into full-blown rage. I had to get this woman to talk to me. "You're a smart lady, Tally," I said in a low voice. "You know I didn't put that gun in Alan's hand. The gun that was pointed at my heart."

Once more I saw Alan Rand's mad face and the shaking pistol in his hand. By the look on Tally's face she saw it as well.

"If you and Alan had leveled with me in the beginning, it might not have come to this. I was never interested in Katherine Henderson. I was only trying to get at the truth of Mel's death—I still am."

"My...my husband's confession is a pack of lies. He didn't murder Mel. I've been trying to tell that to the police, but no one will listen."

She said *murder*, so I was still in the game—Tally didn't know her husband had confessed to shooting a corpse.

"How can you be certain that Alan didn't kill Mel?"

A sharp laugh bounded off the concrete walls. "I know what you're thinking. I see it in your eyes. I didn't kill Mel and neither did my husband. I now know he's incapable of killing."

"But you didn't always know that, did you? You suspected Alan of murdering Mel."

Tally examined the scarred counter, which bore carved mementoes from previous occupants. "Only for a moment."

"Damnation only takes a moment, Tally."

She looked up. "But I never believed it in my heart. I know my husband is not a murderer."

"Too bad he doesn't return the favor."

For a beat I'd thought I'd blown it. The woman leaned close to the glass partition, her face a lethal mixture of hate and respect. "You know then."

I nodded.

"Then you must go the police, tell them that Alan is innocent…"

I held up a hand. "I need proof to bring to the cops, Tally."

"What good are you then?"

"I may not be much but I'm all you got right now. I know that Alan confessed to a crime he didn't commit to protect you from being charged with murder. And just to be clear, I'm not talking about the dead policeman from the sixties."

Tally tried to glower, but then exhaled and slumped into the hard chair. "Alan is convinced I shot Mel," she said in a tired voice. "Nothing I say or do can persuade him otherwise. He's sacrificing himself for nothing." She shaded her eyes with her hands; her nails were bitten to the quick. "Oh, if only I'd gone to bed that night!"

"What do you mean?"

She started, as if she'd forgotten I was there. She was putting on a good front, but inside she was crumbling. "The night of Mel's murder I took a Xanax as usual. Since this nightmare began that was the only way I could rest. But that night I fell asleep on the couch instead of going up to our bedroom. If I had, Alan would know I couldn't have murdered Mel."

"Why is that?"

"My husband's a light sleeper. I could have never snuck out of our bed without waking him. The sad thing was neither of us could alibi the other."

My suspicion was right. Tally and Alan had each believed the other guilty of Mel's murder. The Rand home had been a compost pile of deceit, a perfect environment for Fairley's treachery. Poor Alan and Tally never had a chance.

"When I woke the next morning on the couch, I found Alan standing over me, a queer expression on his face, as if he were stuck somewhere between heaven and hell. That's when he told me I was safe, that Mel was dead. That's when I thought he…" Tally shook her head, shaking off the memory. "Why can't the police see through Alan's lies?" she hissed, anger bubbling up. "Or is it simple expediency? They have their confessed murderer, no matter that he's innocent."

"As it turns out," I said in what I hoped was a soothing voice, "much of Alan's confession fits with the facts of the murder."

"I don't believe that!"

"I've read Alan's confession. He knows certain details that only the murderer could know."

"So you lied before. You do believe Alan is the murderer!" Her face was as hard as the glass that separated us.

"I want to help you and Alan, if you'll let me."

"Liar! You don't care about Alan or me!" The guard had unlocked his arms—eyes and ears open wide.

"You're right, okay? I don't give a damn about you or Alan. I want the truth and you can help me find it."

"Why should I?" She started to put the phone in its cradle.

"Don't hang up! I believe that the truth, in this case at

least, will set Alan free. If you *really* love your husband, you'll talk to me."

I feared I'd gone too far, but when she put the receiver against her ear, the anger had left her eyes. She was mine now, hooked and landed.

"There is another explanation for Alan's knowledge of the murder. Someone could have fed him details."

"But that would have to be…"

"The murderer."

"You know who the real murderer is," Tally said.

"I have a pretty good idea, but I need your help to know for sure. Will you help me?"

"What do you want to know?"

"Tell me about the first time you met Fairley Sable."

Surprise flickered in her eyes but was replaced by weary compliance. She took several deep breaths and cast her mind back to the past. "It was April. The weather was still nice. We were at our regular table on the patio, having mimosas. We were all curious about Harry's new bride, who we were about to meet for the first time."

"Who was there?"

"Mel and Anita, Alan of course, and Gigi. For a change, Gigi was alone. She had just broken up with Paul Bergman and was casting about for her next victim." Tally frowned. "I don't think any of us dreamed that her next conquest would be Mel."

"They did make an odd couple."

"I used to think so, but now I'm not sure. Maybe it was just a matter of time before they…found one another."

Tally had a point. Maybe it was fate that Mystic Cove's ageless coquette and its most famous Lothario had wound up together.

"Harry didn't waste any time in remarrying," I said.

"Personally I wasn't all that shocked that Harry remarried." Tally frowned at a fingernail, bit off a cuticle. "I told Anita at Ellen's memorial that it wouldn't be long before Harry started looking for a replacement. Harry was the kind of man who required a wife. It wasn't a sexual thing, but Harry needed someone to keep his life in order, a role most cheaply and efficiently filled by a wife. It was his haste that was disturbing."

"Let's move on to Fairley."

"The first time I saw them, they were holding hands, something Harry and Ellen never did. But it looked very sweet."

"What was your first impression of Fairley?"

"Not much. I saw an attractive petite woman with white hair that was hacked in an unattractive bob. I remember thinking that a short crop would be much more attractive and vowed to get her into the salon as soon as possible, which I did. Gigi called Fairley a creep mouse and that's as good a description as any."

"A creep mouse? What did Gigi mean?"

"I took it to mean a frightened creature that kept out of everyone's way, which seemed to describe Fairley. An old-fashioned kind of woman who listened much and spoke little."

"Like Anita?"

"In the beginning Fairley was careful not to tread on toes or speak out of turn. A bland little woman who would fill her new role as water fills a glass. Mel said Fairley was the kind who goes along to get along. Later I wondered what Fairley got out of all that going and getting along, but not at first. The doubt came later."

"Doubt?"

Tally grimaced. "*Doubt* might be too strong a word. It's just that after a time I noticed certain oddities in our new friend. The excessive cleanliness that bordered on OCD for one, and then I caught her lying to me—not once, but several times. Stupid, meaningless lies that served no purpose that I could see. But I wasn't concerned, not really."

"No?" I didn't bother to hide my skepticism.

"We all do stupid things that can't always be easily explained. I thought Fairley's lies and quirks were harmless eccentricities. But after Harry died I changed my mind about her." A short laugh. "In fact, after Harry was gone, everything changed."

"Including Fairley?"

"On the day of Harry's funeral Mel had too much to drink. He was angry over the way Fairley handled Harry's remains, along with the funeral arrangements. I agreed with Mel on this point. Fairley didn't do right by Harry."

"In what way?"

"She cremated him, for one."

"Maybe Harry wanted cremation."

Tally shook her head. "Harry had a perfectly good plot in Lady-in-the-Hills Cemetery, next to Ellen, his wife of forty-seven years."

"That sucks." I felt bad for the first Mrs. Sable, condemned to an eternity of lonely nights by the villainous Fairley.

"In Mel's mind Fairley's crime was compounded when she cremated Harry before a proper viewing of the body could take place. He whined to everyone who would listen, 'I wanted to say goodbye to Harry.' Fairley grew so agitated that she pointed to the cheap urn on the mantle and said, 'Harry's right there, Mel. Go say your goodbyes.'"

"So the creep mouse found a voice," I said.

"It was astonishing!" Tally actually smiled at the memory. "At the time I was heartened that Fairley defied Mel, not an easy thing to do. But after that one courageous act, Fairley slipped back into her familiar role of going and getting along. She even volunteered to help Mel at his newspaper."

"Why?" I found it difficult to believe that anyone would volunteer to spend time in Mel's company, at least not without an ulterior motive.

"I'm not sure." I could tell this wasn't the first time Tally had wondered about this. "At the time I thought it was because she enjoyed the work, though why anyone would enjoy such drudgery is beyond me. Most of the time she answered the phone or made coffee." Tally shifted in the hard chair. "Still, Fairley did have a busy sort of mind. Not deep, but very busy. Working on the paper would have kept her occupied." Tally frowned and her eyes lost focus. "And to be honest, life in the Cove can be deadly dull. After Harry died, we all settled into familiar ruts. Other than the distraction of Gigi and Mel's tawdry affair, everything seemed the same as before. We ate and drank together and talked about the things we had talked about forever."

"But it wasn't the same."

"No it wasn't. As with all friends, there had always been tensions in our little group, but when Harry was alive these irritations simmered below the surface and could be forgotten or at least minimized by a margarita or a joke. But now all the ugliness bubbled to the top, like a pot of stew turned to high. We were mean to one another. Not like friends anymore."

"If you were so unhappy why didn't you break off with Mel and the others?"

"I wanted to. I told Alan that we should consider quitting the group. But for once in his life Alan was firm. He told me, 'They are our friends. We can't turn against our friends.' Friends!" Tally spat the word as if it were a curse.

"Too bad Mel didn't feel the same way."

"I put all my hopes on October when Alan and I would take our annual trip to New Hampshire. I was a New England girl, you know."

I remembered the picture of the smiling dark-haired girl and the endless snowcapped mountains.

"At last it was October and there was one final celebration before Alan and I would leave for New England, Mel's birthday dinner at the Grub and Grog, inside the restaurant proper rather than on the patio. The night started badly. There was a mix-up with the reservations so we had to squeeze into a table smaller than Mel liked. Mel had been drinking. He was puffed up on pride and Absolut, bragging nonstop."

"Isn't that Mel's natural state, with or without martinis?"

"Yes, but it was worse than usual, and there was a sharpness to his words that put us all on edge. He kept boasting that he was about to publish the story of the century in next month's *Commentator*." She looked at me pointedly. "He actually called it the story of the century—can you believe it? I teased him mercilessly. I'd had my fill of Mel Dick's ego." Tally's voice was razor sharp.

"What form did this teasing take?"

"Oh, I called him delusional, accused him of exaggerating, even dared him to let us in on the secret—those sorts of things. All the while I assumed he was talking about that ridiculous prostitution story."

"So you know about the hookers at the G and G."

Tally's shoulders straightened. "Alan tells me everything."

"And vice versa?"

Tally glanced at the guard, rubbed the side of her nose. "Alan and I have no secrets."

I nearly bit my tongue off that time. I wanted to ask Tally about that plane reservation for one—had Alan known of Tally's escape clause? I didn't think so, and yet despite the deception I believed she loved her husband. And to be fair, there was plenty Alan had kept to himself. It was a sad truth, but when disaster threatened, the Rands had spun off in separate directions—their love was no protection against Fairley Sable.

"Even Gigi begged Mel to tell us his secret story," Tally continued. "Mel told her that like everybody else she'd have to wait until November to read his scoop. I said something like, 'How big of a story can it be, Mel? This is Mystic Cove—nothing ever happens here.' Well, he recoiled as if I'd struck him, glaring at me—you know how Mel could be."

I nodded. Mel Dick held tight to his anger. "What happened then?"

"He smiled, and I knew from his smile that I'd gone too far." Tally shivered. "That death grin would have turned Mystic Bay into a skating rink. Even Fairley saw the horror of that smile. She was sitting next to me. Her body tensed, and she gripped the edge of the table for dear life. I was so confused. Why was Mel so angry?"

"Couldn't you guess the cause?"

"Maybe," she whispered, "I felt a flicker of fear, like a worm crawling out of the earth. But I pushed it away, back in the dirt. How could Mel know about my past? I had been safe for so many years." She twisted in her chair. "I was a blind fool."

"We see what we want to see."

"When Sheila returned with Mel's fresh martini he greeted it like an old friend, drinking deep, not spilling a drop. I can't forgive that steady hand. An executioner's hand. Then Mel spoke those words that would change everything forever."

I bent forward, as close to the glass as possible.

"He stared into me and said, 'I know who you are and what you did. You won't escape justice this time.' There was nervous laughter, but I didn't laugh, and neither did Fairley."

"And the next day the other shoe dropped," I said.

"Mel summoned Alan to his office and told him about Katherine. When Alan returned from the meeting he told me we'd have to postpone our trip north, managing a lame excuse."

"But you knew something was wrong," I said.

"I didn't press. Maybe it was a presentiment of doom. I didn't want to know the truth."

"Most people don't, when it's an unpleasant one."

"Even so, my husband is not a keeper of secrets, and not long after his conversation with Mel, he told me everything. That's when the future died for me."

"How did Alan deal with it?"

"Foolishly," she said shortly. "Alan ran in circles, trying to find a way out. He was sure he'd be able to convince Mel to forget about Katherine, but I knew it was pointless. Even when Fairley told me about Mel's mental deterioration, I knew it was hopeless."

"You saw a lot of Fairley during this period?"

"Yes, we saw quite a bit of Fairley after Mel let her go from the *Commentator*."

"Mel fired Fairley? When?"

Tally yanked the receiver from her ear and the guard glared—me and my big voice.

"A few days before Mel's birthday dinner—either October fourth or fifth—Fairley dropped by the house, upset that Mel had just fired her from the paper. She wanted to know if we had any idea why Mel had let her go. We didn't of course."

My, but October had been a busy time in the secret life of Mystic Cove. On October second Mel bought his autographed copy of *I Am Not a Witch*. At that time, or shortly after, he discovered Katherine Henderson's photo and put two and two together. Paranoid and secretive on his best days, Mel had probably given Fairley the boot so he could work on his big story in privacy. Somehow that thoughtless action had provoked a murderous reaction in Fairley.

"You said Fairley became a frequent visitor—tell me about these visits."

"Those awful days are jumbled together. But I suppose Fairley saw that Alan and I were going through a rough patch and wanted to cheer us. She often brought us news of Mel's increasingly bizarre behavior, even made fun of Mel's madness, which cheered me." Tally almost smiled. "It cheered Alan as well, though for different reasons."

"How so?"

"Alan hoped that in his madness Mel would forget about Katherine Henderson, but I knew Mel would never forget, never forgive. If anyone deserved madness, it was Mel Dick."

"You said Fairley made fun of Mel. Do you remember what she said? Her exact words?"

"Yes, I do—they were so strange. Fairley had fallen into the habit of calling Mel the Mad Hatter and she'd say things like, 'The Hatter was blind as a bat at lunch, he spilled half of his salad in his lap' or 'He was hot as a hare last night.'"

"Dry as a bone and red as a beet," I murmured.

Tally stared long and hard. "Yes, Fairley said that as well."

"Let's move to that last night at the G and G."

"The last act," Tally said, her jaw clenched. "It was Alan's idea to go to the G and G that night to see Mel. To beg him to see reason."

"How did Alan know Mel would be there?"

Tally blinked. "Why, I don't know. I hadn't thought of it."

I had a pretty good idea who had blabbed to Alan of Mel's whereabouts.

"Alan said that Mel would listen to the both of us," Tally said, "but when we saw him even Alan had to accept that it was no use. As we hurried home, he kept saying that Mel was raving mad, beyond reason, though he didn't care much for my response."

"How's that?"

She met my gaze, her eyes hard. "I told Alan that he was right—one can't reason with a madman. A madman must be stopped."

"And someone did stop mad Mel that night."

"But it wasn't Alan and it wasn't me. You know the rest of the story. I took a Xanax and fell asleep on the sofa. The next thing I know, Alan wakes me with the news that I was safe. Mel was dead, murdered. He couldn't hurt us anymore. That night Alan went to the *Commentator* office and deleted the file on Katherine Henderson."

"How did he get inside?"

"With a key he had from the time he was editor," Tally said, backing up Alan's story.

"Did anyone else have keys?" I asked.

"Absolutely not," Tally answered.

"Not even Fairley?"

"Not even Fairley. For the last weeks of his life Mel was locked up alone in that office. If he had known that Alan still had those old keys, Mel would have changed the lock."

"And the incriminating files on Mel's home computer?"

Tally's brow furrowed. "I don't know about that. All I know is that when Alan returned from the newspaper office, he held me in his arms and told me that I was out of harm's way. The nightmare was over."

"But it wasn't over."

She shook her head. "After that, it was different between Alan and me. Mel Dick's ghost stood between us and he wasn't going anywhere. It wasn't long before we could barely look at one another for fear of what we would see—a murderer."

## TWENTY-ONE

*The Devil Sends a Woman*

"AND WHEN YOU appeared on our doorstep the other night," Tally said, "I knew it was over."

"When I showed up, it was almost as if Alan knew I was coming. Is it possible someone warned Alan about me?"

"A little before you arrived, the phone did ring, and Alan answered."

"Does Alan always answer the phone?"

"Recently he has. Even…even before all this I would let Alan answer. There was nothing sinister or unusual about Alan taking the call."

I wouldn't bet on it. "Tell me about this phone conversation. Did he take it in front of you?"

Tally's brow furrowed. "We'd been in the living room, watching TV. After Alan took the call, he walked into the kitchen. But Alan is thoughtful that way—he didn't want to disturb my television viewing."

"How long was the call, Tally?"

"A minute at most."

"And what did Alan do after?"

"He went upstairs. I heard him moving around. I even muted the television and listened for a moment. I almost asked him what he was about. Oh no—he was getting his gun!"

"Any idea who called Alan?"

"Alan didn't use a name and as I said the conversation was brief. You think it was the murderer on the phone, don't you? The real murderer."

"Did you hear the voice on the other end of the call? Was it female?"

"You think the murderer is a woman?"

"Why not? Women kill for the same reasons men kill, though we may go about it differently. I thought you understood that." I stopped myself just in time. I had almost called her Katherine. I steered Tally back to her story.

"After several minutes Alan rejoined me on the sofa, but he was restless. He kept jumping up and looking out the window. Believe me, if I'd known he had the gun I would have called the police myself."

I kept my trap shut for once. Over the past weeks she'd had plenty of opportunity to call the police and hadn't. All this death and mayhem might have been avoided if she had. "How much time elapsed between the phone call and my arrival?"

"Fifteen minutes, twenty at most."

About the time it took to walk from the Grub and Grog's parking lot to Admiral Street.

The killer's eyes had been on me from the start and that night was no different. Alerted by the GPS device she'd planted on my car, she'd known I was back in Founder's Cove. When she saw me slip into Birnam Wood, she knew where I was headed. A quick call to Alan to warn him that Addie Gorsky was coming his way, bringing doom and destruction to his door.

The trap was baited and set, only foiled because Brad Spooner had been worried about me. Poor Alan Rand— Fairley Sable had played him the way Paganini played the fiddle, convincing him of Tally's guilt, feeding him lies and half-truths as she had fed Mel Dick jimsonweed.

"Oh, Alan," she might have said, "I saw Tally follow Mel into the woods and she had a gun! What does this mean?" Alan would believe her; Fairley had no reason to lie. From that moment Alan's life would have been in her hands.

"You know who the killer is," Tally said. "Who is this stranger who's ruined my life?"

"Not a stranger, Tally, but a friend."

AFTER THE INTERVIEW, I touched base with Angie. As I learned of Fairley Sable's true identity, I formulated a rough theory. At last count Fairley was three times a widow, with each husband dying unexpectedly and all quickly cremated. I'd assumed Harry Sable's sudden death was natural. But nothing about Fairley was natural.

"You've got to talk to Pete Santos," Angie said. "He's retired from Phoenix Police Department, but he worked a case back in the eighties involving Fairley. Talk to Santos."

Pete Santos picked up on the first ring, as if he'd been waiting for the call—and maybe he had. His voice was hoarse and cracked with age, but the years had not dimmed his memories of Fairley Nixon. "Fairley was working as a home health aide for Mrs. Blair, an elderly widow. A couple weeks after changing her will in Fairley's favor, the old gal passed away in her sleep."

"A lot of money involved?" I asked.

Santos chuckled. "Depends on who you ask. From a detective's salary it was a quite piece of change, but not a fortune. The medical examiner found high amounts of calcium oxalate crystals in body tissue, but that wasn't enough for a finding of murder. Fact is, I only put it together later, when I learned about the others."

"Fairley poisoned Mrs. Blair."

"I believe Fairley fed Mrs. Blair a cocktail of lemon-lime soda and antifreeze, though I could never prove it."

We talked for over an hour—or rather he talked and I listened. Fairley Nixon was Pete Santos's case, the one he couldn't forget. After retiring, he'd taken the case files home, still searching for the thread that would bring Fairley Sable to justice.

I started to call Brad, but what did I have to bring him? If Fairley was a black widow, with Harry her latest victim, how did Mel get ensnared in her web?

Mel's birthday dinner had provided the spark. Fairley must have been in a strange mood, her defenses aroused after Mel inexplicably threw her out of the *Commentator* office a few days earlier. She must have brooded on it, searching for the reason.

When Tally described Mel's threat she'd said that Fairley was extremely nervous. Fairley nervous? The woman was ice and steel, not flesh and blood. What had Mel said? *I know who you are and what you did. You won't escape justice this time.*

Mel had been talking to Tally, but what if Fairley thought his words were meant for her?

It was possible—Fairley had been sitting next to Tally.

*I know who you are and what you did. You won't escape justice this time.*

To my mind, there was only one interpretation a vicious creature like Fairley could put to those terrible words. She must have assumed that Mel had learned of her murderous past. If I was right, Mel's murder was a mistake, a miscalculation made by a guilty mind.

Not a bad theory, but it hung on a tissue of innuendo and guesswork, and I had nothing close to probable cause to bring to Brad. I needed evidence. I had to get inside the murderer's lair.

Tonight Founder's Centre would be crowded with revelers for Harvest Fest, including a mummified Queen of the Nile, a deranged old woman who could not leave well enough alone, and an angel of death.

Fairley Sable's home would be empty and I knew where she hid her key.

I PARKED ON a dead-end street on the outer edge of Founder's Centre, foregoing my usual space at the Grub and Grog. It added to my walk but was a small sacrifice. Harvest Fest was underway and I could not chance running into familiar faces. Tonight I would pass unnoticed through the paths and byways of Mystic Cove; tonight I was the ghost of Birnam Wood.

I was suitably dressed in dark jeans, black leather gloves and boots, black satin blouse and charcoal tailored jacket, accessorized with shoulder holster and Glock loaded for bear. Red lipstick and mascara completed the picture of a Harvest Fest reveler who had taken a wrong turn into Birnam Wood. But more important, if Fairley monitored the GPS tracking device she'd attached to the Crown Vic, she would rest easy. The Vic was safely parked in Lady-in-the-Hills.

"Your dad's junker finally crap out?" Frankie had said when I'd asked to borrow his beater.

"The Vic's got plenty of life in her," Pop groused.

"The Vic's fine. I just need another ride for tonight."

Frankie's eyes popped and he looked at Pop, who gave a what-the-heck shrug. Without a word he dropped the keys in my hand.

"One last thing," I'd said, pulling on my jacket, "if you need to drive the Vic, go ahead—just stay away from Mystic Cove."

And now it was showtime. I touched up my lipstick,

stuffed the small flashlight into a jean pocket, and stepped into the cool night.

It was just past seven and Harvest Fest was in full swing. The *thump-thump-thump* of old disco tunes drifted over Mystic Cove like an invading fog. I walked fast, my mind a beehive. Mystic Cove festivals started early and ended earlier. Although the festival would limp on until its official closing time of eleven, by nine o'clock, nine-thirty at the latest, most Mystic Cove residents would be tucked in tight, perhaps enjoying a final nightcap before taking to their beds. No matter what, I needed to be out of Fairley's house by eight-thirty. With no complications, I would have an hour to complete my search. Would that be enough time?

It would have to be.

I wasn't sure what I hoped to find in Fairley's lair. A bag of bones, crystal jars marked with skull-and-cross-bones, a manifesto written in the blood of husbands? I slowed my pace, having reached a poorly lit patch of trail, but then these trails were made for daylight traveling, not midnight strolls. I thought I heard a rustling to my right. I danced my flashlight over the shrubbery—nothing. I shivered. It felt colder than the predicted forty degrees, and there was a lull in the far-off music. Only the sound of Mystic Cove breathing.

I shook off my anxiety and continued, but for some reason my legs wanted to break into a run. If I didn't get control of my fear, I would be a basket case by the time I got to Azimuth Circle. Just then a rapid crunch and crackle sounded from the undergrowth, again from my right and rapidly approaching. A form emerged.

We stared at one another in the darkness. I was about to get into character—*Can you tell me the way to Found-*

*er's Centre?*—when my flashlight caught brown khaki. It just kept getting better. *Please, don't be Tyler Andrews.*

"Who's there?" I asked.

The shadow relaxed. "Chief?"

"Jesse," I said, passing my flashlight over Jesse Potts's smiling face. "What are you doing in the middle of Birnam Wood?"

"I'm working the Admiral Street guardhouse. Oscar was late in giving me my break and I just couldn't wait any longer to go. I'm sorry."

I shook a finger at my former guard. "You need to stop drinking those Big Gulps, Jesse. If you get caught taking nature breaks in the woods, you're gonna get fired. And you don't need to apologize to me about anything. I'm not your chief anymore."

"So where you headed?"

"I was at Harvest Fest and thought I'd drop by and check on Julie Breyer."

"No sense you walking. My cart's hid in the clearing. I didn't want nobody seeing me. Come on. Nobody will mind my giving you a lift, seeing as you're a local celebrity and all."

A local celebrity soon to be uncovered as a local criminal nut-job, I thought as I fell in beside Jesse. I had lied myself into a corner and now had no choice but to go with the flow.

When we reached the cart, I stopped short. "Jesse, is this…?"

"Yup, the same place you found Mr. Dick. I walk out here a lot, thinking about Mr. Dick. Do you think we'll ever know the truth?"

While we drew closer to Admiral Street, I searched for a way out of this. It was hard to concentrate with Jesse babbling nonstop, like a kid on Santa's lap. I might loiter on the Dick porch until Jesse moved on or, if he lingered, as I suspected he would, I could ring Julie's bell and go inside. A quick visit, and then I'd make my excuses and head for Azimuth Circle. But these thoughts and all others flew from my head when Jesse let out a whoop and slammed the brakes.

"I forgot! Mr. and Mrs. Breyer left for dinner not fifteen minutes ago."

Someone else, someone smarter than I, would have packed it in then and there. It took brains and a certain kind of wisdom to know when to surrender. I had neither. "I'll just wait for them," I said, hopping from the cart. We were on Admiral Street, less than a block from the Dick residence.

"But they just left. They won't be home for hours."

"Thanks for the ride, Jesse," I said, already walking away.

I exhaled when I heard the receding whine of the golf cart. I was in the clear.

If Jesse hadn't shown, the path through Birnam Wood would have dropped me directly onto Azimuth Circle. Now I could either travel to Fairley's den via the streets or take a shortcut through several backyards, which would undoubtedly trigger motion lights and maybe even house alarms. I could risk no further encounters, and so chose the streets, though I didn't stray from the shadows. At last I stood in Fairley's verdant backyard.

I looked about wildly. The bronze urn of impatiens under which the house key lay was gone. Had all this been for nothing? Then I realized my mistake. The planter was there, but the impatiens had turned to mush in the recent cold, not a single bloom spared. I nudged the planter and scooped up the key when my gaze fell on Fairley's garden.

The bright moonlight illumined the fairy landscape.

My eyes were first drawn to the bench where Anita and I had talked, only a few days ago. A lifetime ago. The recent cold had been cruel to many of the plants. Brown splotches mixed with green but the large white trumpet flowers were still triumphant, drooping from the arbor like hanged men.

I tore off one of the lovely blooms. Instinctively I sniffed. My head drew back, repelled by the rank odor. Too late I recalled that *Datura stramonium* was sometimes called stinkweed. It had earned that name, as it had earned all its names—mad apple, devil's weed, angel's trumpet. I thought of Fairley at Harvest Fest, an angel in white chiffon and plastic wings swathed in gauze. I stuffed the deadly flowers into a pocket and made for the house.

The kitchen was distressingly normal, the cabinets stocked with pasta and cans of tomato paste. For a second I thought I'd found the mother lode in Fairley's herb cupboard, which included several small jars of dried leaves and seeds, all unlabeled. I opened one of the jars and sniffed. Oregano. The other containers were also innocuous: dill, basil, rosemary. At first glance the refrigerator was another disappointment—skim milk, orange juice, mustard—until I pulled out the produce tray. Beneath the onions and potatoes lay a bag of syringes, a nest of sleeping vipers.

The first bedroom was unoccupied, holding only a double bed and a stack of cardboard boxes. I stomped to the other side of the house, time nipping at my heels like hounds. I started down the short hallway but wheeled around after seeing what appeared to be a small purse hanging on a hook by the front door. Low-hanging fruit too easy to resist.

It wasn't a purse, but some sort of pouch or carrier. I fumbled with Velcro and straps, a task made more difficult by the dim light. The thing finally opened, I directed my flashlight inside. It was a monocular of some sort. I pulled it free, turned it in my hands. A reading aid? Many Cove residents had vision deficits and often carried personal aids such as electric magnifiers or lights, but Fairley's eyes were eagle sharp. I read the body of the device and gasped: it was a night-vision monocular, small enough to fit in a pocket. I repacked the device and hurried to Fairley's bedroom.

The door was shut. I hesitated—what if Fairley was on the other side, waiting with a syringe full of poison? I threw off my fear and went inside. The air was saturated with gardenia and jasmine—L'air du Temps, Fairley's scent. I passed my flashlight over the bare walls, pockmarked with rectangles of faded lilac paint where pictures had recently hung.

Like the rest of the house, Fairley's bedroom was a study in Spartan necessity. Bed, dresser, one bedside table, a small desk. The dresser top was an expanse of shining wood that smelled of lemon Pledge, the bedside table held a lamp and nothing else, but the desk carried a pretty sweet computer setup—pretty impressive for a woman supposedly cowed by technology. I longed to crack the computer's secrets, and briefly considered stealing the laptop, but the risk outweighed the gain. I left the computer and stepped into the master bathroom.

Naturally it sparkled, not a whiff of murder or a trace of soap scum. Next was a walk-in closet almost as large as my current bedroom. Pin-neat clothes on wooden hangers, sensible shoes ready to slip into, and lots of neatly folded scarves. I muttered a curse under my breath. Murders begin in the past, but how could I unearth Fairley's past in this empty tomb?

A quick rummage through the dresser drawers yielded

nothing but lingerie, although one drawer was dedicated to housekeeping detritus, things like electric bills, receipts, old income tax forms. I looked under the bed. The space underneath my bed is chock-a-block with flat storage boxes filled with those accumulations I'm not yet ready to discard. Perhaps Fairley did the same. I pulled back the snow-white quilt—nothing, not even a spider's web.

I was giving the room a final examination, about to cut my losses when I saw something lying on Fairley's bedside table. It was an old black-and-white snapshot of a morbidly obese teenage girl and stern older man—father and daughter? I didn't notice a resemblance, but there was a similarity in the way the two stared into the camera. There was something unsettling in those dead stares. I saw her, peeking out beneath the rolls of adipose tissue—the fat girl was Fairley Sable.

No, that wasn't quite right. The girl in the photograph was not Fairley Sable, at least not yet. But more important, who was the man? But now was not the time to ponder. I aimed my cell and captured the image. Perhaps Angie could unlock the picture's meaning.

I shut the bedroom door and hurried down the short hallway. I was almost in the living room when I heard a sharp thump. I watched in horror as the front door creaked open.

Fairley Sable was home.

AN ETERNITY PASSED as that door groaned open. There had been no warning, no engine noise or clatter of the garage door opening. Fairley must have walked to Harvest Fest. So I had not been the only shadow slinking through Birnam Wood that evening.

I had two choices, both bad. I could retrace my steps and hide in Fairley's lair, trusting that later I'd be able to escape. Or I could just make a run for the back door and hope for the best. I decided to run—the time for hiding was over. I'd taken a deep breath and was about to begin my mad sprint when a male voice called for Mrs. Sable. I stepped back into the shadows. Fairley's mysterious visitor was making enough noise to wake the dead. A dangerous trick on All Hallows' Eve.

"What are you doing, Jesse?" Fairley Sable cried out. Then a sharp thud as the front door slammed shut.

Jesse Potts?

More voices—Jesse's hearty bellow and Fairley's hiss—but I wasn't going to stick around to listen. Jesse had given me an out and I grabbed it.

I sprinted for the back. I unlatched the French door and bolted onto the patio. Then out in the cold, running over the manicured lawns of Mystic Cove like a rabbit with a coyote on its ass. Motion lights popped left and right, but I didn't stop until I reached the sheltering darkness of Birnam Wood.

I had escaped, but not entirely. Whatever knowledge my prowling had gained was offset by several unpleasant and dangerous facts. Fairley would see the unlocked doors and notice the faint but unmistakable signs of trespass. She would intuit both the intruder's purpose and identity.

Fairley Sable now knew that I knew. I had lifted the mask and found a murderer. A shiver traveled along my spine. Someone walking on my grave, Grammy would have said.

But the one thing I didn't know was this: what did Fairley plan to do about it?

## TWENTY-TWO

*Mad as a Hatter*

"How do you know all this?" Brad asked. We sat in a counter at a doughnut shop, a box of doughnuts between us. Outside a red dawn was breaking, but the highway already thrummed with traffic. I had just told Brad almost everything, but he still didn't buy Fairley as a serial killer.

"I've known for some time," I said, dunking my doughnut. "I just didn't know that I knew, but once I talked to Tally and Pete Santos, I had the motive. It all came together."

"You got any evidence that Fairley was stalking Mel?"

An awkward question. I could have told him about the night-vision monocle I'd found in Fairley's house, but then I'd have to tell Brad about breaking into Fairley's home—that had been a close call. Sometimes it was better to be lucky than good and last night I'd been very lucky.

Last night when I'd returned home, I'd called Jesse to get the story. I hadn't fooled him with my bullcrap about visiting Julie. Instead of returning to the guardhouse, Jesse had stashed the cart and followed me. From the shadows, he watched me commit my clumsy break-in, serving as sentinel while I was inside her lair. Then when Fairley had returned, he distracted her long enough so I could escape. "She's a hunter, Brad. She tracked Mel and shot him down."

Brad sighed and rubbed his temples. "You're putting

me in a tight spot here, but I do agree that Rand did not shoot Mel Dick's corpse."

"What changed your mind?"

"I asked Rand if he was the one who deleted the files on Mel's home computer. First he looked at me funny. Then he said he deleted the files on Mel's home computer, same as he did to Mel's office computer."

"A bald-faced lie, the person who tampered with Mel's home computer took the entire hard drive."

"I confronted Rand with that fact, but he's sticking to his story."

"But why? Like you said, Mel was dead when he was shot. Murder's off the table—Tally doesn't need his protection. You sure you don't want one?" I asked, reaching for another doughnut.

"I'm fine with this." Brad pointed to his coffee. "I may have been wrong about that. Alan's still protecting Tally. He knows that it will go a lot harder on Tally if it's believed she attempted murder."

"Or maybe he's told so many lies he doesn't know which way is up."

"Eventually he'll come clean, Addie."

"Not good enough." I thumped the table, sending shivers through our coffees. "We need him to talk now. Rand can verify that Fairley warned him of my coming the night he held me hostage. I also believe she was instrumental in convincing him that Tally murdered Mel. He needs to talk and soon." I was a little punchy. I hadn't slept much last night. In my dreams Fairley's true face kept appearing, the murderer's face she hid from the rest of the world.

"I still think your purported motive is pretty weak."

"I disagree. Mel Dick's murder was a big mistake, a miscommunication. At his last birthday dinner Mel drank too much. Tally teased him, but Mel wasn't in the mood.

He knew who and what she was and he couldn't keep quiet any longer. So he spouted his reckless threat, but Fairley, who was sitting next to Tally, was the one who heard it."

"Why would a smart guy like Mel clue Tally he's on to her?"

"Mel's lips were loosened by vodka, but it wasn't just that. Keeping a secret is hard, even for people like Mel Dick. Secrets leak. They want to come out. When Tally teased Mel, he couldn't keep silent any longer. Mel was human after all, and it cost him his life."

Brad set down his coffee and folded his arms on the table. "Can you explain why Fairley believed Mel was talking to her when he was really threatening Tally? I got a problem with it, Addie."

This was my chance to seal the deal. If I could get Brad to buy motive, everything else would follow. "Unlike Tally, Fairley's suspicions were already aroused before Mel's birthday dinner."

"You mean when Mel fired her from the paper."

"She couldn't figure why Mel had dumped her and it was driving her crazy. Given her OCD tendencies, she probably thought of little else. So she was primed and ready. When Mel said those reckless words at his birthday party, she put it together. Only she put it together wrong."

The shop was busy now. Sleep-eyed people trying to wake up with sugar and caffeine.

I ate the last of my doughnut and sipped my coffee. "Tally buries her crimes deep inside, so deep that she believes herself innocent. Sure she was disturbed by Mel's words, but she was able to rationalize them away, at least for a while. But Fairley keeps her murders close, just beneath the surface so she can play with them. And like so many killers, she's a narcissist. Of course Fairley Sable thought Mel's threat was directed at her. Who else could it be for?"

Brad didn't answer. I couldn't tell if he was buying my theory, and I was nearly out of ammo. I slurped coffee, preparing for another round, when Brad leaned over the table.

"All right then," he said, "tell me how Fairley killed Mel."

"The day after the fateful dinner party Fairley put her newly hatched plan to work. She assumed she had until November when Mel would expose her crime in the *Commentator*. The first order of business was to slap a GPS tracker on Mel's golf cart so she could keep tabs on him. Then she started feeding Mel datura."

"How'd she accomplish that?"

"Easily," I said. "She and Anita were friends. While having coffee in Anita's kitchen, it would be a simple thing to slip a little datura into Mel's tea jug when Anita wasn't looking."

"What if Anita drank the tea? That would put a fly in the ointment."

"You forget—Anita was diabetic, which Fairley knew. What Fairley didn't count on was Julie drinking the tea. That was a break for us, Brad."

"So why didn't Fairley just kill Mel and be done with it?"

"First Fairley wanted to destroy Mel's credibility. Her most pressing task was to get rid of any evidence. She had to gain access to his computers. She expected the datura would get Mel out of the office so she could examine the computer and destroy the evidence—then and only then would she would kill him."

"What about Mel's computer at home?"

"Once Mel was gone it'd be a piece of cake to get to

Mel's home computer. Fairley feeds Anita some BS, and she's in. But initially Fairley's focused on Mel's office computer."

"Unfortunately for Mel Dick the plan backfired." Brad glanced at the group of students who'd just invaded the shop.

"It was a comedy of errors, Brad. If Fairley had succeeded in hacking Mel's office computer she would have realized her mistake immediately, and Mel and Anita would still be alive." I looked outside. The traffic was touch and go, but the sky held promise of another day in paradise. "Another thing, Fairley also didn't anticipate the datura's effect on Mel—it made him more suspicious, more paranoid. He guarded his secret more closely than ever. That must have angered her deeply. Maybe it became personal after that."

"And it wasn't before?" Brad asked.

"Not at all. Fairley was just protecting herself, and Mel set it up perfectly for her. At the G and G he brought all the buried conflicts of the group to light, creating a slew of potential suspects—the shadow fight with José Barracas, his public indictment of his friends, including his wife, the messy affair with Gigi, which Fairley made sure Anita knew about. In a way, Mel was an accomplice to his own murder." I laughed softly. "From the outside looking in, the only person who lacked a motive to kill Mel was Fairley Sable."

"She had me snookered," Brad said, his mouth tight.

"After Mel's breakdown at the Grub and Grog, Fairley took Anita home. She might have spent a few minutes with Anita, but not much longer. She needed to be home so she could track Mel's movements, which she did until Anita called. Fairley spirited her distraught friend to her house and put her to bed, but not before giving her something to make sure she would sleep soundly. When I talked to Anita that morning, I should have seen that she'd been drugged." I remembered the zombie I'd met in Fairley's garden. At the time I'd attributed Anita's disorientation to shock or illness, but now I knew it had been Fairley's poison.

"Addie?" Brad leaned across the table.

I rubbed my eyes. "Sorry, didn't get much sleep last night." I took a breath. "Next Fairley located Mel's golf cart on the GPS. He was in the clearing in Birnam Wood. She'd been trailing Mel for several weeks and knew the spot. She found him there, presumably asleep. And that was when she made her big mistake. She shot him, or rather shot his corpse."

"How did she get Mel's gun?"

I grimaced. "I don't know yet, and I also don't know how Alan Rand wound up with the murder weapon. Everything that happened after Fairley shot Mel is hazy, though I'm pretty sure that's when she got her murderous hands on the hard drive from Mel's home computer."

Brad poked my arm. "But before you said Fairley was more concerned with hacking the office computer."

"Yes, and I stand by that, but after she shot Mel, everything changed. Now there was going to be a murder investigation, something Fairley had avoided until now."

"I get that. She couldn't take the chance that the police would examine Mel's home computer. But how'd she get inside the Dicks' house? Mel's house key was found on his body."

"She either squirreled Anita's key out of her purse, or left a door unlocked when she picked up Anita."

"The only hard piece of evidence is the GPS tracker on your car, and that was free of prints."

"That's why we need to talk to Rand. If we can get him to talk, the other pieces would fall into place."

"All right," Brad said, reaching for the phone, "but forget about this 'we' crap. I'm talking to Rand—alone."

I WATCHED FROM behind the curtain, along with a red-faced prosecutor named Jimmy Crippins. The prosecutor tried to hide it, but he was as nervous as me—a couple of turkeys come the third week of November. Brad waited in the interview room his long legs stretched and crossed at the ankles, doodling squiggles and curlicues on the legal pad in his lap. At last the door cracked open. Alan Rand shuffled in, butter-smooth attorney at his side.

Before Brad could get a few words out, the buttery lawyer butts in and it looked like the interview was going nowhere, with Alan just sitting there like he was in a dream. And maybe he was.

"We'll try it this way then," Brad said. "I'll talk and your client listens. You can listen, can't you, Mr. Rand?" No response. Maybe Brad was wrong; maybe Rand was beyond listening.

Brad went over Rand's confession with a fine-tooth comb, challenging Rand on several points, but the old man didn't take the bait. "Let's move on to the night you were arrested, Mr. Rand."

The lawyer issued another warning while his client stared at the concrete floor.

"Your wife told us that you received a phone call just before Ms. Gorsky's arrival. Is that true?"

Alan Rand lifted his chin slightly, but then let it fall to his chest.

"I thought we were just listening here," the lawyer piped.

"Am I to assume that your wife lied about the call?" Brad asked.

That got Rand's attention. "My wife does not lie."

I laughed—good thing Rand didn't have a sense of irony.

"After the phone call Mrs. Rand said you became very nervous," Brad said.

"I don't see…" the lawyer said.

"Look, Mr. Rachet, you really, really want your client to listen to this." The lawyer melted a little under Brad's stare.

"I think this caller told you that a visitor was coming your way." An almost imperceptible nod from Alan. "I have an idea who this person was, but I'd appreciate it if you'd just go ahead and tell me the name."

A small sigh and Rand said, "It was Fairley Sable, a friend of ours. She was out for her evening walk and had seen the Gorsky woman snooping around Founder's Centre. Fairley knew that Addie Gorsky had been harassing us and just wanted to make sure we were all right."

"Did you and Fairley ever discuss Mel Dick's murder?"

"Yes, but I don't understand why you're asking about this." Rand looked to his lawyer, who patted his hand and whispered in his ear.

"Tell me about these conversations."

"There were so many. Fairley was interested in the murder. We often talked about it." Rand paused while his lawyer whispered more sweet nothings. When they finished, Rand said, "I meant to say Fairley was interested in Mel's death—there was no murder."

"Whatever you say—please go on, Mr. Rand." Brad's Southern accent was getting more syrupy by the minute.

"Fairley's the sort of person who likes to be on top of things and she kept abreast of the mur—death investigation. She said Gorsky often confided in her, told her all sorts of things."

"Liar," I muttered, ignoring the dirty look Jimmy Crippins sent my way.

"What sort of things did Fairley tell you? Be specific, Mr. Rand."

"Well," Rand said, stroking his chin, "she told me when the police found the gun in Anita Dick's trash can, the gun I put there." Rand waved off his lawyer.

"Anything else?"

"I… I can't remember exactly. There were several conversations."

"Why all this conversing between you and Fairley?"

"What does it matter? I didn't kill Mel—he was already dead—so what does it matter? I want to go back to my cell now."

Alan Rand was done, at least for now. But I caught the doubt and puzzle in his eyes as he was led away. Was he awakening to the truth at last, that he was just a pawn in Fairley's murderous game?

"WHY THE LONG FACE, Addie?" Brad asked. "Things are breaking the way you wanted them to."

Brad was right. Fairley Sable said she was more than happy to help the police, and would be at GCSO headquarters at four o'clock sharp, if that was convenient.

There was no point in hanging around the sheriff's office all day, so I picked up a bag of tacos from Mexico Loco and headed home, my stomach growling like a pit bull on steroids. I hadn't had supper last night and breakfast had been toast and coffee. Meals and sleep had been catch-as-catch-can since this started. The game was nearly done, though I did not know the manner of its ending.

The second I opened the door, I sensed something was wrong, all wrong. The apartment smelled like a funeral parlor, the cloying scent filling my nostrils. I spotted the flowers on the coffee table, a chaotic bouquet of yellow carnations, purple lobelia and—oh God, no!—white angel trumpet.

"We're in here, Adelajda."

I followed Pop's voice into the dining nook where he sat with Fairley Sable, a pot of tea between them.

"What did you call your daughter, Stan? A-del-ee-a?"

"It's hard for American tongues," Pop said, laughing. "That's why everyone calls her Addie. That's a good American name."

I walked up to Fairley, glared down at the petite woman. "What are you doing here?"

Pop gaped—even I am not normally so rude—but Fairley calmly sipped her tea.

"You have no right!"

Fairley Sable met my gaze. "I was so sorry to have missed you last night, Addie. If I'd known you were going to visit, I would have stayed home. As I told Stan, I was in Lady-in-the-Hills shopping and thought I'd stop by. I am one to return the favor, you see."

"Get the hell out." I snatched the cup from her hand, threw it to the floor, smashed it to bits.

"Adelajda!"

"That's all right, Stan. I'll leave." Fairley pushed away from the table. "Please, enjoy the tea, both of you. It's my special blend."

"Get out now!" Instinctively my left hand moved toward the Glock. Pop noticed for I heard him gasp. I kept my eyes peeled on the treacherous old witch until she cleared the door. I locked it and ran back to Pop. "Did you drink the tea?"

"Yes, we both did."

"You're…you're all right then."

A slow nod. Pop looked okay, and now that I was calming down, I could see it didn't make any sense for Fairley to poison Pop. No, her intent was to terrorize, and she had succeeded.

A reversal of fortune—now I was the hunted.

After dumping Fairley's tea down the drain, I called Angie, hoping against hope that she had come up with something more I could use against Fairley. She did have something, but was it enough? My next call was to Frankie, who came right over. I made him promise that if Fairley Sable showed, he was to call me or Brad Spooner.

"Don't let her in the apartment, Frankie. Don't let her near you or Pop!"

"We'll be fine, Addie," Frankie said.

I paused at the door, stared back at the two old men. I wanted to say more, but the weight of time was on my shoulders. Was this how Pop felt?

I flew down the stairwell. It would be a throw of the dice, but I had no choice. Pop was in danger and it was either Fairley Sable or me. There was much, much to do before four o'clock came round.

"THANKS FOR COMING IN, Mrs. Sable."

A brief handshake and Brad guided Fairley Sable into the interview room. After a fake apology about the interview room being the only room available and the usual offer of coffee, which Fairley wisely refused, Brad got down to business. As before, I sat on the other side of the glass with Jimmy Crippins for company. The prosecutor was even more nervous now. I hadn't been present when Brad talked to Crippins, but I could tell he had more than his share of doubt. Truth be told, so did I.

"I have a few questions for you, Mrs. Sable, a couple loose threads that need to be tied off."

"Any way I can be of help," Fairley said, returning the sheriff's smile. That had been her mantra since showing up thirty minutes early for the appointment: "Anything I can do to help, any way to be of service to the police."

"GCSO is grateful for your cooperation." Spooner opened a portfolio and shuffled papers.

Fairley's blue eyes crinkled. "It is rather ironic that you called, Sheriff. All morning I've been debating whether or not to call you myself."

Brad dropped his papers and looked at her. "Call me?"

"Well, not you personally, but the sheriff's department. You see, I was burgled last night."

The portfolio closed with a snap and Brad slanted his body toward Fairley.

"Someone broke into my house while I was at the Harvest Fest." Fairley's voice carried the right note of puzzlement—bring on the Oscars. "Only they didn't break in exactly. There were no broken locks or windows. That's why I hesitated to call the police. Our new security chief Tyler Andrews thinks it may have been some sort of Halloween prank. Unfortunately one of his guards—Jesse something or other—was involved. Chief Andrews fired him, so I consider the matter closed."

"But you're certain someone broke into your house."

"Yes. I'm rather a bad girl. I keep an extra house key underneath a planter in my backyard. Our former chief, Addie Gorsky, used to warn me that it wasn't safe to hide it there. She said that's one of first places thieves look, but I didn't listen. I can be a hardheaded old woman, Sheriff." Fairley's blue eyes cast downward.

I ignored Crippins's stare and wiped off the beads of cold sweat that had broken out on my brow. My stomach clenched when I saw that Brad's face had drained of blood.

"Was anything stolen, ma'am?"

"Nothing," Fairley said. "That's what makes it all so puzzling. I could tell someone had been through my things—a woman always knows when her things have been touched—but nothing was taken."

"Later you may discover that something was taken," Brad said. "When we're done here, Deputy Berry will take your report."

"If you think it best—after all, you're the expert. Now, how can I help you?"

"On the night Alan Rand was arrested, he said that you called him."

Fairley bobbed her head. "Indeed I did. I was on my evening walk and happened to see Addie Gorsky. She was sitting in her car in the Grub and Grog's parking lot. I was going to come over to say hello, but before I could speak to her, she left the car and ran into Birnam Wood."

Crippins made a disgusted sound. I started to give him the finger, but retracted just in time.

"Did you follow Ms. Gorsky into Birnam Wood?"

"Of course not—why would I do such a thing?"

Brad smiled and shook his head. "People do all kind of things, ma'am. What did you do after Ms. Gorsky left the Grub and Grog parking lot?"

Fairley fidgeted. "I was worried that Addie was going to see Alan and Tally, even though Addie's initial visit was nothing short of a disaster. Like me, Addie is a determined woman. It's not a bad quality but it can get us into trouble now and again." A self-deprecating smile. "So I called Alan to tell him that Addie Gorsky might be paying him a visit."

"Why'd you do that?"

"I thought I'd made it clear. Addie's earlier visit to the Rands ended with Alan sprawled on the ground and Tally frightened to death. I was afraid there'd be further violence. I called Alan to let him know that Addie was in the neighborhood." Fairley leaned toward Brad. "Of course at the time I had no inkling about Tally being this Katherine Henderson person. I was simply looking out for my friends. You...you believe me, don't you?"

"Why didn't you tell the police about this phone call?"

"Maybe I should have, but I didn't think it was important. In all this, I've only wanted to be helpful! That's all!"

"Calm down, Mrs. Sable. There's no call to get upset. Can I get you a glass of water?"

"No, I'll be all right if you'll just let me explain."

"I'm listening."

Fairley smiled her thanks, then took in an exaggerated breath and let it out. "In my defense, I intended to tell Addie about the phone call during one of our bull sessions, but I never got the chance. Alan confessed and the murder investigation was done. I thought it was over."

Brad's brows knotted and his jaw tightened. "Back up a second—what do you mean by bull sessions with Addie Gorsky?"

"Conversations, that's all," Fairley said. "Addie and I often talked about the murder investigation. She took pity on a lonely old woman and kept me up-to-date."

Brad's jaw tightened another notch. "How often did you and Ms. Gorsky have these...bull sessions?"

"Quite often," Fairley said. "I liked to think that we were partners, though I'm really just a foolish old woman who's read too many mystery novels."

"This is your murderer?" Jimmy Crippins hissed at me. All prosecutors had a bit of bully in them, but Crippins had more than his fair share and now he smelled blood in the water—my blood.

"Still," Fairley continued, "I think our conversations helped Addie. She carries a lot of guilt from when she was with the Baltimore City Police. She told me herself that she felt responsible for her partner getting shot. He died, you know—that was hard for Addie." Her silver-blue gaze held the sheriff's for a long moment.

"How did she…? I never," I whispered, overwhelmed by her capacity for deception.

"Addie has been carrying around a heavy burden for several years," Fairley said. "I believe that sharing the investigation with me helped her with that burden."

"What sorts of things did Addie Gorsky share with you?"

I inadvertently winced when Brad said my name, an accusation.

"Oh, lots and lots of things," Fairley said, finger tapping her chin. "I remember being struck by one oddity though. From the beginning Addie was certain Anita had nothing to do with Mel's death. I remember she was quite upset when she told me your men had found the gun in Anita's trash."

I heard Crippins curse under his breath. Despite my warnings of Fairley's capacity for deceit, did he believe her lies? Even Brad was cold and still, as pitiless as a moai.

"And there was that business about José's illegal business enterprise, and everything about the autopsy just went right over my head. I was quite lost with all those medical terms."

Still Fairley poured it on. Her lies rained down like physical blows, much worse than an ass-kicking. Had she planned this from the beginning, that first morning when she came into my office, asking for my help?

"Tell me, Mrs. Sable," Brad said, "did you repeat any of this to anyone?"

Fairley looked away, readjusted her skinny ass in the hard seat. "Addie warned me not to speak of it, but I may have mentioned it to my friends. That was wrong, wasn't it?"

Brad demanded details—who did Fairley talk to about the murder—what was said and when.

"I can't remember precisely. Alan and I talked about Mel's murder a few times, and Tally a little bit—she's been ill, you know. Gigi Tajani and I had spoken of it, but briefly." Fairley smiled. "Gigi is a creature of sweetness and light and prefers not to dwell on unpleasantness."

Brad pressed, but that was the best Fairley could come up with, and the ruinous interview wound down. Crippins threw an angry look my way and stormed from the observation room.

It hit me then, right in the face. To the world at large my reputation was a thing of shreds and patches, irreparably destroyed, if I could not catch this vicious killer.

But it was showtime. I took a deep breath and rushed into the hallway to find Brad. The hallway was crowded but I caught Brad's gaze.

"None of it was true. She lied, Brad!"

Cold eyes met mine. "It's Sheriff Spooner, ma'am."

"Sheriff Spooner," I said. "You don't believe her, do you? Tell me you don't."

"This isn't the time or place."

"Fairley Sable lied!" I yelled.

The place was deadly quiet. Brad's chest heaved dangerously. Instinctively I took a step backward. Brad showed his teeth and pointed a finger right at me, as if I were a piece of crap that needed to be picked up.

"Your part in this is over, Ms. Gorsky. You have contaminated this investigation, probably beyond repair. You are not to speak with anyone involved, especially Mrs. Sable—you've bothered that lady enough. In fact, I want you to keep away from Mystic Cove, GCSO, and me. Deputy Berry, please escort Ms. Gorsky from the building."

Berry grabbed my arm. I tried to wrench free but he held me fast. As I was led away, I tried to keep my eyes focused straight ahead. Even so, I saw her, feigning distress but inwardly rejoicing—Fairley Sable.

Who was this woman? A demon out of history, an implacable Adicia bringing chaos to the world? No, that gave her too much credit. All in all, she was a murderer, and murderers could be caught.

There was one chance left, if I had the guts and wits to pull it off.

# TWENTY-THREE

*All Cats Are Black in the Dark*

"I THOUGHT YOU might show up at my door, but not quite this soon."

"I couldn't leave it as it was, Fairley." Dizzy, my hands shaking, I struggled to keep my emotions in check. I wanted to split this monster open and see what foul things poured out.

She cracked the door. "Is that gun of yours hiding beneath that ugly jacket? I wouldn't want any accidents."

I opened my jacket for inspection. I had left the Glock behind—the temptation to shoot Fairley Sable in cold blood might be one I couldn't resist.

"Good," Fairley said, "I dislike guns."

"They have their uses, though," I said. "We need to talk."

"You're wrong. I don't need anything—you're the one who needs."

"Then just listen," I said, pushing inside.

"I was in the middle of preparing dinner, but if you insist."

I followed her to the kitchen but hovered at the entryway. She hadn't been BS'ing about dinner. It was waiting for her, neatly arranged on a wooden tray: an open bottle of cabernet sauvignon, a composed salad of micro greens and orange slices, a healthy wedge of blue-veined cheese beside a crusty baguette, still fragrant from the oven.

"I deserve some answers," I said.

"You deserve nothing, and what makes you think I have any answers to give?" Fairley opened the oven, releasing the smell of chocolate. A quick peek inside and the door snapped shut. Then she faced me. "Really, Addie, you didn't expect me to break down and confess. I'm not Alan Rand." Her silverfish eyes fixed on mine. She was an ice sculpture, serene, cold, heartless. How could I break through the barrier of ice and pierce the heart of her? Did monsters like her even have hearts?

"I want the truth of the murders, Fairley."

"Murders?" she said with a laugh. "Who else have I done away with, other than Mel Dick? Anita, I suppose! Goodness, why don't you go home, Addie? The game is over and I've won."

"Murder is a game with you, isn't it? A diversion."

"Call it what you please, but I'm the winner. That's all that matters."

"I'm certain you killed Mel Dick and pretty sure you murdered Anita as well."

"Belief is one thing, proof another. I did not murder Mel. I had no reason to harm him."

"That's the first true statement that's come out of your mouth. You had no reason to hurt Mel—all this bloodletting, all this havoc, was unnecessary." I crossed my arms and leaned against the clean white wall. "When did you learn that Mel hadn't known of your murderous ways? Oh, you may have won your game of murder, but it was your stupidity that caused the whole bloody mess."

"I didn't take you for a sore loser."

"I admit that I was a poor enough adversary, but at least I own up to my mistakes. You bury yours."

"Mistakes?" Fairley scoffed.

I forced a laugh. "This case unraveled like a pilled wool

sweater. A competent investigator would have pierced this mystery in a heartbeat! Although now that I've come to know you, I understand how your guilty conscience was working on you the night of Mel Dick's birthday dinner at the Grub and Grog. Naturally you assumed Dick's threats were directed at you."

"I don't have a guilty conscience," Fairley said.

Another truth. People like her weren't burdened by conscience.

She slapped her forehand and scowled. "You made me forget about my cookies—they better not be burned."

I was speechless. This woman who crowed of winning had brought chaos down upon us all—Mel and Anita's deaths, Alan Rand's imprisonment, Tally's exposure, and, last and most certainly least, the loss of my paltry reputation. It had been just so much collateral damage for Fairley. The cost of doing business.

Fairley calmly scraped the fat chocolate chip cookies off the tray and placed them on a cooling rack. She shot a cross look in my direction. "They're more done than I like—hard and crunchy rather than soft and chewy, but they'll still taste good. I'm about to sit down to dinner. Why are you still here?" She turned on the faucet, squirted some soap into her hands, scrubbed her hands in the steaming water.

"The thing I don't get is the jimsonweed tea. It was a clumsy move. I mean, it's a pretty ineffective way to poison someone."

"Maybe it was harmless fun, a little foreplay before the main event. Maybe the poisoner wanted to expose Mel as a fool, let the world see the great man as he truly was."

"I guess I can see that." I shrugged. "You destroyed Mel's credibility the way you destroyed mine."

"I said maybe, Addie. It's all hypothetical." After turning off the faucet with an elbow, Fairley tore a sheet of paper toweling with her fingertips and dried her hands.

"But I don't get why you left the poisoned tea in the Dicks' refrigerator."

She paused, her face clouded, then resumed drying.

"Why didn't you pour it down the drain when you had the chance? You had plenty of opportunity—you could have dumped it when you stole the hard drive or later, when you visited the grieving widow. For me, that was the real break in the case, when Julie became intoxicated after drinking her dad's iced tea."

"What fool would drink days-old iced tea?" Fairley muttered, the mask slipping.

"Julie drank the tea because she missed her dad. It was a way of being close to him. But you don't get that, do you?" No answer, but I could tell she was listening. "After I found the jimsonweed tea, I knew that the murderer had access to the house. That's when I starting thinking about you, Fairley. While visiting Anita it would be a simple thing to dump a little datura in Mel's tea. Then I found you were spending time with the Rands, spreading more poison. What tripped me up was motive. Once I had that, I had you."

"You have nothing," Fairley said, wheeling on me, "but I'm curious, what was my motive?"

"You thought Mel found out that you murdered Harry."

Surprise filled Fairley's wide blue eyes, but then the eyes grew glacial-cold. "As I said, you know nothing."

I knew this wouldn't go much longer. Soon she'd throw me out. But before that happened, I had to get the truth out of her. So far she had deflected my clumsy jabs and accusations with ease. I suspected that we could go back and forth like this all day. I needed to attack from another direction. "I saw the picture of you and your first husband, Asa. Did your daddy make you marry that old fat prick or did you figure that was the best you could do?"

"That's none of your business." One of my darts had hit home at last. Who knew? Even angels of death looked homeward.

"What's wrong, Fairley? You did your homework on me and I did likewise." I smiled. "I'm also one to return the favor. Tell me—was your first husband your first?"

"How dare you!"

I forced a laugh. "No, you misunderstand. I don't care who you screwed or when."

"You vulgar trash!"

"I'm just wondering if Asa was your first murder victim."

Fairley slid a balloon glass from the wine rack above. As she filled the glass with dark red wine, her hand was rock-steady. In mid-pour I grabbed the bottle from her grasp, raining crimson droplets over the spotless countertop. While Fairley scrambled for the paper towels I turned the bottle in my hands.

"Black cherry and berry notes with a hint of ginger. Pretty fancy stuff for a hick out of Alva, Georgia."

"Get out of my house."

"It must have been hard on you, being the preacher's daughter in a town where everybody knew everybody else."

"It was a small town like any other."

"I'm not so sure. Some of those old Southern towns have a quaint charm that shines through the decay, but Alva's butt-ugly, just like you."

"Shut up!"

"Just a salad and cheese for dinner? Not much of a meal by my count, but I can see why you watch your calories. You were a fat little porker. You must have weighed at least two hundred pounds, and you're so tiny—five foot at a stretch. Better not eat too many cookies or you'll be tipping the scale again."

"You are no one, Addie Gorsky!" Fairley shouted. "I saw to that. Your friend Sheriff Spooner despises you. When I'm through with you, you'll be lucky to find a job washing dishes at the Dixie Diner."

"Children can be so cruel. I bet they teased you terribly—'*Fatty, Fatty, two by four, couldn't get through the bathroom door, so she did it on the floor, licked it up and did some more*.'"

"Why are you doing this? You don't like these people any more than I. So what if I killed a few of them. They don't matter." Fairley Sable took a step toward me, filled with some secret emotion. The mask was ripped off and the murderer stood before me. Somehow I stood my ground, though how I longed to run.

"Tell me about Mel, please. For my own sake, I have to know the truth."

For the longest time she studied me with her awful eyes. Whatever she saw convinced her that I was no threat. Then her eyes turned inward to some secret place, and she smiled.

"It was complicated with my first husband." Fairley poured out a glass of cab and sipped. "Asa was diabetic, like Anita, only Asa was type two. If he had eaten better and exercised, he would have never gotten sick, and I would have never had to give him insulin injections in the first place. I was curious about how much insulin the human body could safely absorb. Let's just say I satisfied my curiosity." Another sip of wine.

"And Mel?"

"You're right about guns being effective. Mel had been drinking the tea for weeks, with mixed results. His credibility was damaged and I'd been tracking his movements almost constantly via GPS, but I still hadn't gotten my hands on either of his computers. The fool had the constitution of an ox and the mentality of a flea. Ultimately I concluded that I needed him incapacitated, either permanently or temporarily. Only then would I be able to search his computers and purge any incriminating material."

"And opportunity knocked," I said.

"And I answered." Fairley opened her arms wide, as if embracing the world. "That night when I saw Mel at the Grog and Grub, I knew I was looking at a dead man. After he raced away in his golf cart, I took Anita home. She wanted me to stay with her, but I had business elsewhere."

"I can guess the next part," I said. It was strange, but we had fallen into our familiar routine. A discourse on murder.

"Yes, that part of the night happened pretty much as I told you. Anita called me after she shot Mel. The fool actually wanted to call the police, but I convinced her otherwise. At my house I made her a nice cup of chamomile tea, which calmed her right down." The grinning Santa Muerte added, "Of course the several milligrams of flunitrazepam I slipped into the tea aided the process."

"You gave her roofies!"

Fairley shrugged. "And why not? It's an effective sedative with the added benefit of producing anterograde amnesia. With Anita out for the night, I checked the GPS tracker. Mel was parked in one of his favorite spots in Birnam Wood. I had wasted enough time on this man and was prepared to end it then and there." She frowned. "If I'd stuck to my original plan, things might have gone a bit smoother—I prefer injections or discreet medications to firearms—but it turned out well enough, I suppose." She smiled brightly at me, letting me in on the joke. "It

was certainly a lot more fun than Harry's dull death—
don't you agree?"

"I don't know if *fun* is the right word."

"Anyway, when I reached the clearing I found Mel
asleep, or so I thought. Were the papers correct in that
Mel was dead when he was shot?"

"Oh yes."

"A shame," Fairley said. "I saw the gun resting on the
passenger's seat just as that pissant dog of Mel's started
yapping. I grabbed the animal by the scruff of its neck and
hurled it into the bushes. Then I took the gun and fired. I
pocketed his office key but left the gun on the passenger's
seat. I can't tell you how pleased I was when it turned up
in Anita's trash can."

"I bet you were."

"Next I let myself into the Dicks' house with Anita's
key. I didn't have Mel's password. I tried Commentator
and a few other obvious options, but nothing worked."
She frowned, shook her head. "If I'd had more time I
could have gotten in, but I had to get to the *Commentator* office. So I took the hard drive." She poured herself
more wine. "You can imagine my shock when I opened
November's file and found nothing about me! It was all
about Tally being this Henderson person."

"Oops!"

"Exactly," Fairley laughed, taking a sip of wine. "I
don't mind saying I felt more than a little foolish. I had
made a mistake, a small one. I thought it best to leave November's file intact. Then if anyone happened to discover
it, the suspicion would fall on Alan and Tally."

"So Alan did delete the files," I said.

Fairley looked at me as if I were a bag of dirt. "Obviously. But I was quite pleased when you discovered the
deleted file."

"I got to give the devil her due—you played me good, Fairley. In fact, you played us all."

She nodded at the compliment. "The morning after Mel's death, one look at Alan's insipid face told me all I needed to know. He must have stumbled across Mel's body after I'd shot him, and assumed Tally had done the deed, an assumption I encouraged."

"And Anita?"

For the first time Fairley's face clouded. "Anita Dick wasn't as stupid as people thought. You should always watch out for the quiet ones, Addie—they're the dangerous ones."

"Anita was on to you?"

"I didn't let it get that far. After Mel's death I didn't like the way she looked at me when she thought I didn't see. But the fact is Anita should have been more careful with her insulin regimen."

"So it was like Asa."

"Not at all," Fairley said. "Asa's problem was too much insulin, while Anita's was too little."

I wanted to strike her, to wipe that self-satisfied smile off of her lips, but Fairley Sable's smile died of its own accord when she saw my own grin. "I've enjoyed this bull session, Fairley, but I think we've heard enough."

"What? What's that?"

"Did you get all of that, Sheriff?" I said.

It was a stupid thing to say, but I had to see that look on Fairley's face when she knew the game was over for her. That was my payment, the due she owed me.

Fairley's eyes flashed with rage and her face turned the color of puke, realizing what she had just done. Unlike the rattler, she gave no warning. Her right hand struck with lightening speed, grabbing a butcher's knife from the block on the counter and plunging it into my gut.

An explosion of pain as I collapsed on the floor. Fairley glowered over me, knife in hand, face contorted with rage. Her arm reared back, prepared for another strike.

As darkness took me, I was aware of two things. Brad Spooner was going to be pissed and those chocolate chip cookies smelled delicious.

BUT DARKNESS DID not last forever, at least not on that day. When I opened my eyes, two balloons floated in the warm ether above. Oddly, the balloons had faces.

"Papa?" I said.

"I'm here, Adelajda."

"How's our girl?" the other balloon asked.

"Brad?"

"Don't try to talk," the Brad balloon said. "The doc says you're gonna be fine."

I tried to move, but the pain stopped me. "Fairley?"

"Fairley Sable has been charged with two counts of homicide. Feeding Mel the poison tea directly contributed to his fatal heart attack. A bottle of insulin with Fairley's prints all over it was recovered from the Dicks' refrigerator. The insulin had been replaced with distilled water. The little lady ought to consider herself lucky it's only two counts."

"You found the whole kielbasa," Pop said, kissing my cheek. "I'm going to tell the nurse you're awake."

After Pop glided from the room, an icy hand covered mine. I flinched a little and mouthed, "Cold."

"And you're too damn hot," Brad said, squeezing lightly. Still, neither hand stirred. Why had I thought the sheriff looked like a vulture? No, he was an ibis or a crane.

"It's over," I said.

"Fairley Sable's gonna fight it and she's got the resources to put up a good fight, but the confession you got out of her is ironclad." Brad added that Rand had finally come clean. As Fairley surmised, he had found Dick's body in the early morning and assumed Tally was the killer. To protect his wife Rand grabbed the murder weapon. Later he deleted the files from Mel's office computer and dropped the handgun in Anita's trash can.

"I can't believe you fooled Fairley into confessing," Brad said.

I could. With the background Angie had dug up I knew I could rattle her, but first she had to believe I was no danger to her. The little play the sheriff and I had acted out for her benefit had convinced her. I had bet on her need to turn the knife in my back—bad choice of words. I must have winced for Brad asked if I was all right.

"I am."

"Well, I hope you learned not to taunt the perp, at least not until she's in cuffs—you could have died back there."

"I'm a scorpion—can't help it."

Brad gave me a funny look, then sighed. "You feel like eating something? Not this hospital slop—I'll run out and get you whatever you like."

"Some chocolate chip cookies would be great."

A FEW DAYS later I was back home with Pop. Somehow the knife hadn't struck any vital organs—a few centimeters to the left and it would have been a different story. I had been lucky. I had crossed Fairley Sable's path and survived. How many others could make that claim?

I had been home a week when Brad called. He had something he wanted to discuss, only not on the phone. I told him to stop by anytime. Crazy Jinks greeted my friend with the unbounded joy of a puppy, dancing around Brad as if he were a maypole. How was it dogs always knew?

"Have a seat on the sofa. You want something to drink? I got beer." I wasn't quite sure why I was babbling like a teenybopper on a date with Justin Bieber, but there it was.

"Just sit your ass down. You shouldn't be jumping around like that."

I joined Brad on the sofa. "I'm not an invalid."

Brad looked around the small apartment. "Where's your dad?"

"Visiting a neighbor." After I told Pop about Brad's visit, Pop had decided he wanted to visit Frankie.

"According to the papers, the case against Fairley Sable is pretty tight," I said, assuming Brad wanted to discuss some aspect of the case. Media coverage of Fairley's arrest had been intense, bouncing Katherine Henderson off the news cycle. Until yesterday that was, when yet another Mystic Cove scandal had blasted on the scene, pushing murderous Fairley to the back pages.

"I'm not here about the case. I'm here about you."

"Me?" Habit had me wondering what I'd done wrong now. Since being on medical house arrest my ability to cause trouble had been curtailed but not entirely extinguished.

"What are your career plans, Addie?"

"I've...uh...been kicking around a few ideas. Why?"

"Why not apply to GCSO? We could use you."

"I'm speechless," I said.

"I hear a *but* coming," Brad said.

"But I'll have to say no."

"Think it over for a couple days and get back to me."

"There's no point, I've made up my mind. I've made my share of mistakes in my life, but not the same one twice. The uniform isn't for me. It never has been."

"That's too bad," Brad said. "It'd be a criminal waste of talent for you to work some dead-end security job."

"I'm not going to do that either. I've applied for my private investigator's license. Initially I'll start with an online presence but I hope to have a brick-and-mortar office someday."

"You sound pretty sure about all this."

"I am. I have the skills to do the job, and as a PI I'll have the freedom to do it my way."

"I can see how that setup would suit your…particular personality," Brad said, giving me the once-over.

"And it's not just that. I just…"

"You don't have to explain if you don't want to."

"I know, but I want to." I took a deep breath and felt the familiar twinge in my side. "I'll never forget the look on Julie Breyer's face when I was able to tell her the truth of her parents' deaths. I'm not pretending that she doesn't hurt any less, but she was grateful for the truth. Maybe now she can pick up the pieces of her life. It'll never be the same, but now she can go on."

"Gonna set up shop in Grubber County?" Brad asked.

"Sure," I said, "it's where I live."

Brad groaned. "Why do I get the feeling that my life just got a lot more complicated?"

"Let's celebrate with a beer—it's okay, I'm off my meds."

Brad insisted on getting the beers, and I told him to grab a treat for Jinks while he was at it. Brad and I clinked bottlenecks and drank.

"I heard from Jesse Potts this morning," Brad said. "The Cove's new security chief offered our boy his old job back."

"Good."

"You don't seem so surprised."

"I'm not. It's smart damage control. Jud Richt understands public relations and, once it got out that Jesse had unfairly lost his job because of Fairley Sable's machinations, it made sense that Richt would bring him back into the fold. Besides, Jesse is a good employee."

"You got a point, and I guess in the immediate future Richt will be busy keeping his own ass covered."

"So you read this morning's *Ledger*," I said.

"I missed the *Ledger* article, but the story's everywhere. *Eyewitness News,* the *Newnansville Sun*, even the alternative paper with the funny name is covering it."

Just a partial list of the news organizations to which I'd anonymously forwarded copies of the soil report I'd found in Tyler's office.

My first order of business after getting sprung from Dexter General had been digging out the purloined soil report. A little research and I discovered it was a five-year-old geologic survey that documented sinkhole conditions on the land slated to become Captain's Castle. Construction was well underway on the property, in direct violation of Florida law. I didn't know why or how Tyler had gotten possession of the report—my best guess was that he had been blackmailing Richt, though it was also possible that Andrews and Richt were working on some nefarious scheme together.

"What are you grinning about?" Brad asked.

"Maybe I'm just happy—it has been a while."

Brad drank his beer. "You know, it is kind of strange how all those different news organizations got their hands on that report."

"Obviously it was the work of a whistleblower, probably a disgruntled Mystic Cove employee who came across the report and did the right thing. There's no lack of disgruntled employees at the Cove."

"Or disgruntled former employees," Brad added. "There's speculation that Tyler Andrews is the culprit.

The thinking is that Richt fired Andrews after he spilled the beans to the press."

"I can see that." In fact Tyler Andrews had complained of this very misperception when he'd called me right after the story exploded. I'd told him—once he'd calmed down enough to listen—that I didn't care how he handled things, but that he better leave me out of it. Tyler even had the nerve to cry foul, whining that I'd broken my promise to him to keep the report secret. I reminded him that I'd only promised not to tell Richt of the report. Telling anybody else was fair game.

But my final words to Tyler had been hard and unequivocal—if he dared mention my name in any of this, he'd be sorry. I meant it too. I'd had enough of Mystic Cove to last a lifetime. I didn't know if Tyler would keep his mouth shut about me or not, but I didn't care. I had my full share of regrets, but making that survey public was not one of them. It was the right thing to do and as a bonus I got a little of my own back.

"However the story came out," Brad said, "Jud Richt is in a pile of trouble if it can be proven that he knew about the sinkhole conditions. It burns me that Richt put people in danger like that. There was a sinkhole in Okpulo County last year that ate a whole house with a man in it."

Suddenly my first beer in days didn't taste so good. "Richt will weasel out of it. People like him don't get punished."

"Fairley thought she was above the law," Brad said, his voice low but intense, "but she's in jail facing murder charges, thanks to you. Maybe someday it'll be Richt's turn to pay the piper. Sometimes justice happens."

"Not often enough."

"We have to take it when it comes."

We talked for some more and finished our beers. Before Brad left, he took my hand in his and said, "You did good work, Addie—enjoy it."

"We did good work," I said.

"Maybe we can do it again sometime."

"Count on it."

I should have fetched Pop, but I needed to be alone with my thoughts. I called Jinks—we could both use a walk.

I stepped into the clear, cold night. Above the stars glittered, a flying carpet of glass. I took a deep breath and felt the pang in my side, but it was a shadow of what it had been. I was on the mend, and soon the pain would be a memory, though the scar would remain.

I kept thinking about what Brad had said about Richt and Fairley and justice. Fairley was a murderous force of nature and now she would spend the rest of life in prison. And Richt? He was the poster boy for the well-fed and satisfied, people so full of themselves that they had time for nothing else—as if they weren't flesh, blood and bone like the rest of us. But I had not hurt Richt, merely inconvenienced him. A spark of anger clenched my guts—more proof that the enmity between us was personal. It would always be personal.

But Brad had a point. No one knew the future. I wasn't going anywhere and neither was Jud Richt. Maybe someday I could bring him to justice. Maybe someday I'd extract my full pound of flesh.

Stranger things had happened, just ask Fairley Sable.

"Come on, Jinks, let's go home."

\* \* \* \* \*

# REQUEST YOUR
# FREE BOOKS!

## 2 FREE NOVELS
## FROM THE SUSPENSE COLLECTION
## PLUS 2 FREE GIFTS!

**YES!** Please send me 2 FREE novels from the Suspense Collection and my 2 FREE gifts (gifts are worth about $10). After receiving them, if I don't wish to receive any more books, I can return the shipping statement marked "cancel." If I don't cancel, I will receive 4 brand-new novels every month and be billed just $6.49 per book in the U.S. or $6.99 per book in Canada. That's a savings of at least 19% off the cover price. It's quite a bargain! Shipping and handling is just 50¢ per book in the U.S. and 75¢ per book in Canada.* I understand that accepting the 2 free books and gifts places me under no obligation to buy anything. I can always return a shipment and cancel at any time. Even if I never buy another book, the two free books and gifts are mine to keep forever.

191/391 MDN GH4Z

| | |
|---|---|
| Name | (PLEASE PRINT) |

| | |
|---|---|
| Address | Apt. # |

| | | |
|---|---|---|
| City | State/Prov. | Zip/Postal Code |

Signature (if under 18, a parent or guardian must sign)

### Mail to the **Reader Service:**
**IN U.S.A.:** P.O. Box 1867, Buffalo, NY 14240-1867
**IN CANADA:** P.O. Box 609, Fort Erie, Ontario L2A 5X3

**Want to try two free books from another line?**
**Call 1-800-873-8635 or visit www.ReaderService.com.**

* Terms and prices subject to change without notice. Prices do not include applicable taxes. Sales tax applicable in N.Y. Canadian residents will be charged applicable taxes. Offer not valid in Quebec. This offer is limited to one order per household. Not valid for current subscribers to the Suspense Collection or the Romance/Suspense Collection. All orders subject to credit approval. Credit or debit balances in a customer's account(s) may be offset by any other outstanding balance owed by or to the customer. Please allow 4 to 6 weeks for delivery. Offer available while quantities last.

**Your Privacy**—The Reader Service is committed to protecting your privacy. Our Privacy Policy is available online at www.ReaderService.com or upon request from the Reader Service.

We make a portion of our mailing list available to reputable third parties that offer products we believe may interest you. If you prefer that we not exchange your name with third parties, or if you wish to clarify or modify your communication preferences, please visit us at www.ReaderService.com/consumerchoice or write to us at Reader Service Preference Service, P.O. Box 9062, Buffalo, NY 14240-9062. Include your complete name and address.

SUS15

# REQUEST YOUR FREE BOOKS!

## 2 FREE NOVELS PLUS 2 FREE GIFTS!

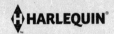 **HARLEQUIN**®

## ROMANTIC suspense

### *Sparked by danger, fueled by passion*

**YES!** Please send me 2 FREE Harlequin® Romantic Suspense novels and my 2 FREE gifts (gifts are worth about $10). After receiving them, if I don't wish to receive any more books, I can return the shipping statement marked "cancel." If I don't cancel, I will receive 4 brand-new novels every month and be billed just $4.74 per book in the U.S. or $5.49 per book in Canada. That's a savings of at least 12% off the cover price! It's quite a bargain! Shipping and handling is just 50¢ per book in the U.S. and 75¢ per book in Canada.* I understand that accepting the 2 free books and gifts places me under no obligation to buy anything. I can always return a shipment and cancel at any time. Even if I never buy another book, the two free books and gifts are mine to keep forever.

240/340 HDN GH3P

| Name | (PLEASE PRINT) | |
|---|---|---|

| Address | | Apt. # |
|---|---|---|

| City | State/Prov. | Zip/Postal Code |
|---|---|---|

Signature (if under 18, a parent or guardian must sign)

### Mail to the **Reader Service:**
**IN U.S.A.:** P.O. Box 1867, Buffalo, NY 14240-1867
**IN CANADA:** P.O. Box 609, Fort Erie, Ontario L2A 5X3

**Want to try two free books from another line?**
**Call 1-800-873-8635 or visit www.ReaderService.com.**

\* Terms and prices subject to change without notice. Prices do not include applicable taxes. Sales tax applicable in N.Y. Canadian residents will be charged applicable taxes. Offer not valid in Quebec. This offer is limited to one order per household. Not valid for current subscribers to Harlequin Romantic Suspense books. All orders subject to credit approval. Credit or debit balances in a customer's account(s) may be offset by any other outstanding balance owed by or to the customer. Please allow 4 to 6 weeks for delivery. Offer available while quantities last.

**Your Privacy**—The Reader Service is committed to protecting your privacy. Our Privacy Policy is available online at www.ReaderService.com or upon request from the Reader Service.

We make a portion of our mailing list available to reputable third parties that offer products we believe may interest you. If you prefer that we not exchange your name with third parties, or if you wish to clarify or modify your communication preferences, please visit us at www.ReaderService.com/consumerschoice or write to us at Reader Service Preference Service, P.O. Box 9062, Buffalo, NY 14240-9062. Include your complete name and address.

HRS15